THE NOBLEMAN AND OTHER ROMANCES

ISABELLE DE CHARRIÈRE, née Isabella Agneta van Tuyll van Serooskerken in 1740, was a Dutch aristocrat who adopted the French language as her own. She was also known as Belle de Zuylen, after the family castle near Utrecht, where she grew up. Handsome, clever, and rich, the oldest of seven children, she caused a splash in society with her unconventional ways, publishing *The Nobleman*, a satire of her class and its obsession with pedigree, when she was only twenty-two. She published nothing else until 1784, but thereafter maintained a steady output of novels, pamphlets, plays, and opera (both music and libretti) until her death in 1805. She had suitors from all over Europe, including Samuel Johnson's biographer, James Boswell; the Marquis de Bellegarde; Baron Christian von Brömbsen; and an English rake, Lord Wemyss. While considering their respective virtues, she conducted a clandestine correspondence with a Swiss general, Constant d'Hermenches, whom she had met at a ball in 1760, and their extraordinary letters foreshadow in many ways the fiction that would follow. She would later meet his nephew, Benjamin Constant, and enjoy a similarly intimate epistolary relationship. In 1771, to general disapproval, she married her brother's ex-tutor, Charles-Emmanuel de Charrière, and went to live in his native Switzerland. It was there that she wrote most of her work.

CAROLINE WARMAN is a lecturer in French at the University of Oxford and a fellow of Jesus College. She is the author of *Sade: from Materialism to Pornography* and has written on the history of ideas in the eighteenth and nineteenth centuries, with topics ranging from vitalism or physiognomy to Stendhal's relationship with the science of crystallization. She has collaborated with Kate Tunstall on an edited translation of Marian Hobson's essays, *Diderot and Rousseau: Networks of Enlightenment*, and is currently working on Diderot's late text, *Éléments de physiologie*. The Charrière project grew from translating *Letters from Neuchâtel* for her aunt, Joyce, as a birthday present.

ISABELLE DE
CHARRIÈRE

The Nobleman and
Other Romances

Translated with an Introduction and Notes by
CAROLINE WARMAN

PENGUIN BOOKS

PENGUIN BOOKS

Published by the Penguin Group
Penguin Group (USA) Inc., 375 Hudson Street,
New York, New York 10014, U.S.A.
Penguin Group (Canada), 90 Eglinton Avenue East, Suite 700, Toronto,
Ontario, Canada M4P 2Y3 (a division of Pearson Penguin Canada Inc.)
Penguin Books Ltd, 80 Strand, London WC2R 0RL, England
Penguin Ireland, 25 St Stephen's Green, Dublin 2,
Ireland (a division of Penguin Books Ltd)
Penguin Group (Australia), 250 Camberwell Road,
Camberwell, Victoria 3124, Australia
(a division of Pearson Australia Group Pty Ltd)
Penguin Books India Pvt Ltd, 11 Community Centre,
Panchsheel Park, New Delhi - 110 017, India
Penguin Group (NZ), 67 Apollo Drive, Rosedale, Auckland 0632,
New Zealand (a division of Pearson New Zealand Ltd)
Penguin Books (South Africa) (Pty) Ltd, 24 Sturdee Avenue,
Rosebank, Johannesburg 2196, South Africa

Penguin Books Ltd, Registered Offices:
80 Strand, London WC2R 0RL, England

This translation first published in Penguin Books 2012

1   3   5   7   9   10   8   6   4   2

Translation, introduction and notes copyright © Caroline Warman, 2012
All rights reserved

LIBRARY OF CONGRESS CATALOGING IN PUBLICATION DATA
Charrière, Isabelle de, 1740-1805.
[Selections. English.]
The nobleman and other romances / Isabelle de Charrière ; translated with
an Introduction and notes by Caroline Warman.
p. cm. — (Penguin classics)
Includes bibliographical references.
ISBN 978-0-14-310660-9 (pbk.)
I. Warman, Caroline.   II. Title.
PQ1963.C55A2 2012
848'.509—dc23   2011045323

Printed in the United States of America
Set in Sabon

Contents

Acknowledgments

I have been looking forward to writing these acknowledgments for months, and have kept complicated records with thirteen separate categories and cross references to enable me to get them right. However, in case I make a mess of them, can I just first and foremost declare my undying thanks to all those who have helped me complete this project and who feel, like me, that committed readers of literature absolutely need to make the acquaintance of the works of Isabelle de Charrière because until they do, their life will be incomplete.

I would like first of all to thank Robin Banerji and Ruth Maclennan for introducing me to Stephen Morrison of Penguin Books, to Stephen himself for his intelligent interest, and to his colleagues Elda Rotor and Lorie Napolitano for the endlessly enthusiastic welcome that they have extended to Charrière, and to my copy editor, Kym Surridge, for taking such care over the final text. The editors of Charrière's *Œuvres complètes*, Jean-Daniel Candaux, C. P. Courtney, Pierre H. Dubois, Simone Dubois-De Bruyn, Patrice Thompson, Jeroom Vercruysse, and Dennis M. Wood, as well as its committed publisher, G. A. van Oorschot, are also owed thanks: without their crucial critical edition, this translation would have been impossible, while reading any Charrière text at all would be quite hard. For advice, encouragement, and examples of various sorts, I would like to thank Davide Antilli, Simon Birks, C. P. Courtney, Jacqui Johnson, Chris Miller, Sarah Perry, Angela Scholar, Michael Sheringham, Eleanor Sunley, and Suzan van Dijk. Many thanks to Judith Still, whose course on eighteenth-century French women writers I taught at the University of Nottingham in 2002–2003, and thereby first came into contact with the *Lettres neuchâ-teloises*; typically generously, in late 2010 Judith also sent me the relevant chapters of her then unpublished work *Aspects of Enlightenment Hospitality*, which were particularly useful in understanding Charrière's exotic novella, *Constance*. Interested readers will find this volume in the Suggested Reading section. Thank you to Alexandra Franklin of the Bodleian Libraries' Centre for the Study of the Book, who invited me to speak about Charrière at the conference she and Robert McNamee of the Electronic Enlightenment Project organized about Enlightenment Correspondence in November 2010. It was a crucial first outing for my nascent introduction, and I am very grateful to Alex for the opportunity she gave me.

I recruited my second-year students, just off on their year abroad, for translation correction services, and their contributions and opinions were invaluable, as well as not uniformly complimentary. I would like to thank them all very much indeed, and look forward to getting my own back in next year's classes: they are Ben Brock, Natasha Clark, Paul Isaacs, Charlotte Martin, Yosola Olorunshola, and Hannah Wood. Emily Danby also kindly read one of the stories, despite being busy preparing for her finals. I was sorry Rishi Patel didn't volunteer to read any, as I know he would have enjoyed a mention.

I also called on a band of close family and friends past and present to read one or more of the translations, and I am very grateful to them for their careful reading, and for their various suggestions or views. They are Kate Clanchy, Sarah Gracie, Ann Maher, Matthew Reynolds, Catherine Rolfe, Joanna Walsh, Christopher Warman, Elizabeth Warman, Eric Willcocks, and Dan Zeff. Sarah Gracie wrote me a particularly beautiful letter about her response on encountering Charrière's work for the first time that I truly treasure. Mary Warman and Joyce Willcocks read every single story as I finished it, and I religiously refused to revise anything until I'd digested their comments. Christopher Warman should be thanked for setting high standards of writing in the Warman household, but not in any way held responsible for the actual standard achieved.

My dear colleagues Gillian Dow, Catriona Seth, and Kate

Tunstall read the entire revised manuscript prior to submission. I thank and salute them. Gillian also sent me her unpublished work on Charrière's reception whose importance is attested to by the number of references to it in the introduction. They all answered numerous knobbly footnote queries. Catriona was very supportive of the project from its inception. I had a great time with Kate cotranslating a volume of Marian Hobson's essays, *Diderot and Rousseau: Networks of Enlightenment*, during this same period, and that experience of academic translation was an important limbering-up exercise before turning to Charrière: I am grateful to Kate and to our editors Jonathan Mallinson and Lyn Roberts, of SVEC and the Voltaire Foundation in Oxford, for the patience they all had to exercise as I veered between projects, and overran every deadline. I am also very grateful to Brycchan Carey, Hugh Doherty, Perry Gauci, Matthew Grenby, Richard Scholar, Alain Viala, and Neil Younger for generously contributing their expert opinions along the way. I hope I have duly acknowledged their help in the appropriate places.

Finn Fordham operated as a sort of troubleshooter and consultant when I got particularly into a twist. The title of the collection as a whole was his idea, as was the translation of the title of the fairy story addressed to Marie Antoinette, "Aiglonette et Insinuante." Thank you to him and also to Max and Taddy Fordham and to Ann Maher, all of whom made it possible for me to work on the translations even when we were supposed to be on holiday. Thanks to Ann, again, and to Cato, Milo, Leo, and Viola Fordham for cycling with me to Slot Zuylen in April 2011 to visit Charrière's family castle. Joanna Walsh used the photos I took there to create her marvelous cover picture: thanks to her for the imagination and wit she brought to that commission. My mother, Mary Warman, comes in a particularly garlanded and indefinable category all of her own: special thanks are owed to her for the immeasurable amount of general support that she gives me and Finn and our children, Leo and Viola. Without her I don't really know how we'd get through the week, let alone complete enormous tasks such as this translation.

Thanks to my employers, Jesus College and the Faculty of

Modern Languages at the University of Oxford, whose crucial sabbatical provision and general support of academic values made it possible for me to undertake this project. Academic freedom, let alone the opportunity to study a wide range of subjects at university, each of which feeds into the others, combining to create a dynamic cultural and intellectual life, is much imperiled at the moment. The funding shortfalls caused by greedy and blinkered banking systems have provided an opportunity for governments to start slashing at subjects and at universities, and the United Kingdom is a severe and distressing case of this: I hope that Charrière's work provides a compelling example of why it is important to not lose contact with other languages, cultures, or periods. And that contact doesn't just happen, even in a capitalist world of choice where we assume everything is available somehow. You have to be able to read French to read Charrière, and if you're not French already, you have to learn it. In order to learn it, you have to have some form of system that will teach you, and people who can do the teaching. Or, to look at it from the other end, you have to have an institution that will make it possible for someone who can read French to translate it into English. And it's not just about building bridges across language divides, it's also about knowing literature and history, and having someone whose work brings her into contact with Charrière wanting you to hear about her, too. It's all about time and money, and about trusting academics and their values to produce work of relevance and importance to us all. So thank you Jesus College and Oxford University. And thank you Katrin Kohl, my close colleague in Modern Languages at Jesus, for her example, her persistence, and her support.

I would like to end by starting at the beginning, as it were. In 2008, with no idea of publication, I translated the *Lettres neuchâteloises* for Joyce Willcocks's birthday, just because I thought she'd like it. Joyce is my aunt and godmother. It is to her that I would like to dedicate this volume, with love and thanks.

CAROLINE WARMAN

Jesus College, Oxford, July 2011

Introduction

Isabelle de Charrière (1740–1805), née Isabella Agneta Elisabeth van Tuyll van Serooskerken, and also known as Belle de Zuylen, after the castle where she was born, is the French, Swiss, and Dutch Jane Austen all rolled into one. French because she wrote in that language and embraced that culture with immense enthusiasm; Swiss because she married a Swiss gentleman, lived in Switzerland for more than half her life, and set many of her novels there; and Dutch because she was born Dutch, noble, and free-spirited, and never forgot it, although, as she wrote to her intimate friend, the Swiss officer Constant d'Hermenches, in 1764, "it is in truth an extraordinary thing that I am Dutch and my name is Tuyll."[1] And Jane Austen? Simply because, despite all possible differences, for liveliness and wit, for the ability to capture the different tracks and layers of feeling in a room among a number of people as they observe each other, and for the riveting portrayal of growing love, she is equaled only by her more famous (and younger) contemporary. As the critic Jean Starobinski has observed, it is not surprising that there should be similarities, both œuvres having emerged from the same moral and social context.[2]

Yet, where Austen kept to her famous "square inch of ivory" and to "three or four families in a country village," Charrière ranged well beyond: origin, experience, and political turmoil compelled her to do so. We meet clear-minded women trying to see their way to happiness, beset by social taboo and malice, and we watch them at balls, on walks, on visits, trying to establish lines of communication to the people they wish to be with, and from whom convention cruelly tries to divide them. They are women of rigorous intelligence and inventive self-control who sometimes, but not always, manage to find happiness. Allied to them are imperfect men who perhaps recognize their own imperfection, or whose very delicacy exposes them to manipulation. In tone, Charrière's writings range from the witty energy of *The Nobleman* to the finely controlled *Letters from Neuchâtel*, the seriousness of *Cécile*, the political daring of *Eaglonette and Suggestina*, the anxious excitement of the *Émigré Letters*, and the melancholy of the only-just-averted disaster in *Saint Anne*. Alongside these are the real tragedies: the claustrophobic marriage in *Letters from Mistress Henley* and the catastrophic tale of the unjustly betrayed slave girl we hear about in *Constance's Story*. If Austen refused to go beyond what she knew, or to say everything she suspected, Charrière partly knew more, and partly dared more. She was an avowed intellectual, and also directly caught up in the debates of the Enlightenment: she met the editor of the famous *Encyclopédie*, Diderot; she espoused the theories of Rousseau; she visited Voltaire; and she refused to visit Germaine de Staël despite that lady's repeated requests. She wrote stories, caused scandals, was courted by men from Holland, Switzerland, Germany, France, and Britain: Boswell was one of them. She lived through the French Revolution, was passionately excited by its possibilities, and immediately used fiction to explore the new sorts of futures being revealed. She debated it in a series of now celebrated letters exchanged with Constant's nephew, Benjamin, the soon-to-be-famous author of *Adolphe*, and raged against the crimes committed in its name during the Terror. Her late works reflect the melancholy of Romantic literature, but the disappointment they express is tightly related to the outcome of the Revolution. Her themes are woman, injustice, happiness, nature, and society, and the arenas in which she plays them out range from the small village or town with the few families to Paris, London, the Rhineland encampments of the émigré armies, and the West Indies. As much as Jane Austen, then, George Eliot and George Sand also provide meaningful parallels.

For a writer of real stature, she is very little known beyond a small but fervent band of enthusiasts. There are reasons for this, of which the fact that she was a woman is probably one—a woman, moreover, who emphatically did not confine herself to the limits of the marriage plot, and happily interspersed her novels with such things as constitutional reform and criticism of slavery. She also offended every possible target audience of her time: aristocratic readers, those who liked their fiction decorous, and even potential suitors might have been horrified by *The Nobleman* (1763), whose forthright heroine uses antique family portraits as stepping-stones across a muddy moat and thinks longingly and explicitly of her lover's embraces. *Might have been horrified*, we are obliged to say, given that her parents were *actually* horrified, and bought up almost every copy to restrict the readership and notoriety of the aristocratic young author as much as they possibly could. She published nothing else for twenty-two years, until well after her marriage in 1771 to her brother's former tutor, Charles-Emmanuel de Charrière. When *Letters from Neuchâtel* came out in 1784, they so offended the inhabitants of that town that she felt obliged to publish a self-justificatory poem in the second edition; readers and (the single) reviewer seem to have failed to notice the story almost entirely. Her *Letters Written from Lausanne*, which we have called *Cécile*, after its heroine, drew similarly indignant responses from the Lausannois. Her Swiss readership, in high dudgeon, defiantly rejected her.

Her Dutch readership was limited by two things—first, the only piece she ever published in Holland was withdrawn rather rapidly from circulation, and second, of course, she wrote in French, her language of predilection, and set her novels in France, Switzerland, and England, but never in Holland. Despite *Observations et conjectures politiques* (1788), which attests to her very real engagement with Dutch and Swiss politics, the Dutch have had difficulty claiming her as one of their major writers, as demonstrated by the fact that although her *Œuvres complètes* were published in ten volumes between 1979 and 1981 by the committed Dutch publisher G. A. van Oorschot, there is no complete translation into that language, and the individual novels are only sporadically available.

Nor is Charrière fully embraced by French literature: historically, her works were little noticed in France, and only the second part of *Letters Written from Lausanne, Caliste*, was published in Paris (by Prault, who also brought it out in Geneva), as well as her brief *Eloge de Jean-Jacques Rousseau, qui a concouru pour le prix de l'Académie française* (in praise of Jean-Jacques Rousseau, an essay submitted for the Académie française prize, 1791). In fact, in France, her reputation owes more to the two vivid epistolary relationships she conducted with Constant d'Hermenches and his nephew, Benjamin Constant: the French critic Sainte-Beuve drew attention to her crucial influence on the latter and his work in *Literary Portraits* (1844); this essay was published as the introduction to her novel *Caliste* in 1845, which has ever since been viewed as a pre-Adolphe *Adolphe*. To complicate matters further, some of her later works first appeared in German, translated by her friends Thérèse and Ludwig Huber. Her important novel, *Trois femmes* (Three Women), is one such, coming out as *Drei Weiber* in 1795, four years before publication in French, although even then, it was actually published in German-speaking Leipzig, and not much reviewed in either language. Nor would translation in general save her from oblivion; nothing but *Caliste* was ever translated into English during her lifetime, or for that matter, until 1925, when Lady Sybil Scott, wife of Charrière's Bloomsbury biographer, Geoffrey, published a lively rendering of *Four Tales*, which included *The Nobleman, Mistress Henley, Letters Written from Lausanne*, and *Caliste*.

In sum, her publication history has been scattered geographically and chronologically, and no nation or language has ever firmly laid claim to her—moreover, Sainte-Beuve's compliment that she wrote "excellent French" sounds more like a school report than the serious appreciation of a first-rate writer. Add to this the problem of her name, which suffers more than most premodern women's names from a marital identity crisis, and the confusion becomes dangerously complete: she is habitually known as either "Belle de Zuylen," with "Belle" being the pet name her family used and "Zuylen" the name of her moated home, or "Isabelle de Charrière," her married, gallicized name. The *Œuvres complètes* give both these names, as does the journal dedicated to her work, *Cahiers Isabelle de Charrière/Belle de Zuylen Papers*, while Cecil Courtney's unsurpassed biography carries the title *Isabelle de Charrière (Belle de Zuylen)*. She is also known by her own jokey pseudonym, Zélide, and indeed, Geoffrey Scott's 1924 biography used this name; Richard Holmes's recent edition of this classic work is entitled *Scott on Zélide* (2004), and there is nothing on the cover matter that links her either to Belle de Zuylen or to Isabelle de Charrière. In France, she is most commonly called Madame de Charrière, as in Madame de Sévigné, and so on, a name that, although polite in premodern terms, firmly pigeonholes her among that worthy subgenre of writers in general, *women* writers.

In this volume, we call her Isabelle de Charrière, and Charrière for short: her writing identity was French, and all the pieces in this volume, apart from *The Nobleman*, were written once she had become Isabelle de Charrière. She needs no feminization, pet names, or borrowed masculine authority to be interesting, and while her identity may be multilingual and multifaceted, it is ultimately unhelpful to replicate this multiplicity with multiple names, as it causes her and her oeuvre to fragment and lose coherence. She is one writer of immense talent and range, and she should have one name, armed with which she can join her anglophone novelist cousins, Richardson, Fielding, Johnson, Burney, Wollstonecraft, Godwin, Inchbald, Austen, Thackeray, Dickens, and Eliot, and her francophone siblings, Marivaux, Prévost, Voltaire, Diderot, Rousseau, Staël, Constant, Balzac, Sand, and Stendhal. All, like her, can be situated on a spectrum from satire to realism, and all, like her, refract their social commentary through the picaresque fate of a young hero or heroine in search of fulfillment—that is, they ask what it is like for an individual to live in a given society, and use the novel to present his or her likely experience, choices, impressions, reactions, and constraints.

This volume contains nine out of her twenty-three surviving

pieces of prose fiction. It leaves aside entirely her other compositions, which include drama, poetry, opera, political theory,
polemical pamphlets, and open letters. Her oeuvre in fact runs
to 212 separate items, finished and unfinished, published and
unpublished, not including the voluminous correspondence.
All of these have now been made available in the crucial
Œuvres complètes (Complete Works): her letters fill the first
six volumes, with volume 7 devoted to her twenty-six plays and
volumes 8 and 9 to her fiction; essays, verse, and music are to
be found in the final volume. Almost all of this work was produced in the fifteen intense years of her maturity, from the mid-
1780s to the end of the 1790s, a period defined by the French
Revolution and its aftermath, which provided much of the dramatic material for her later works.

The nine pieces included here are, in chronological order,
The Nobleman (1763), *Letters from Neuchâtel* (1784), *Letters
from Mistress Henley* (1784), *Cécile, or Letters Written from
Lausanne*, part 1 (1785), *Eaglonette and Suggestina, or, On
Pliancy* (1791), *Émigré Letters* (1793), *Fragments of Two Novels Written in English* (1796), *Constance's Story* (1798), and
Saint Anne (1799). It has been both a straightforward and a
difficult task to decide which particular works to include: constraints of space and time made it inconceivable to offer all her
prose fiction, and some parts are better known than others;
this therefore felt like an opportunity to introduce the reading
public to a wider selection. The aim has been to include as
much of her best work as possible, as well as to give a wide
range of her styles and subjects. The two principle omissions
are *Three Women* and *Caliste*, and they have been omitted
mainly because they are better known and are also, or will
soon be, available in good translations—*Three Women* in the
MLA Texts and Translations series, edited and translated by
Emma Rooksby (2007), and *Caliste* in a pairing with Marie-
Jeanne Riccoboni's *Histoire de Monsieur le marquis de Cressy*
(1772), to be translated by Angela Scholar with the Other
Voice. Leaving aside these relatively lengthy pieces, painful
though it has been, means, however, that there is room to
include some unfamiliar and in some cases unpublished works,

along with old favorites, such as the extraordinary *Mistress Henley*, a powerful precursor to Charlotte Perkins Gilman's *The Yellow Wallpaper* (a fine edition of this text does already exist in the MLA series). Four tales—*Eaglonette*, *Émigré Letters*, *Constance*, and *Saint-Anne*—have never before been translated. Two very short pieces, joined under the title *Fragments of Two Novels Written in English*, were in fact, as the title indicates, written in English in the first place; they remained unpublished until the *Œuvres complètes* came out in 1979–1981. They are given here for the sheer exuberance of Charrière's idiosyncratic but expressive English, and to provide an entertaining contrast to the freshly translated texts.

Charrière uses a variety of fictional forms. *The Nobleman* is a short story, and bears allegiance to the Voltairean philosophical tale as well as to the romantic fairy tale; *Eaglonette and Suggestina* is a political and moral fairy tale that Charrière sent, as if it had been a letter, to Marie Antoinette. *Constance's Story* and *Saint Anne* both follow the late eighteenth-century trend away from the epistolary form to a single sustained narrative: *Constance* is a third-person narrative framed in a first-person narrative, while *Saint Anne* has an omniscient narrator. However, the dominant form, certainly in the first two-thirds of her writing career, is epistolary. There is no single model: *Mistress Henley* and *Cécile* present their story by means of a single correspondent writing to an absent friend; in *Letters from Neuchâtel* three separate voices write (for the most part) to three absent correspondents; one of the *Fragments* presents two friends writing to each other; *Émigré Letters* is formally more ambitious and interconnecting, with multiple principals who write to more than just one other correspondent, all of whom reply; they also send each other copies of previous letters, and comment on them.

Readers of fiction are less used to epistolary novels than they once were; if many novels of the eighteenth century used that form, most since have eschewed it. We find it disruptive, artificial, and self-conscious; we want more context and background; we want something altogether more filmic, something we can lose ourselves in. But Charrière's characters are trying to find themselves, not the opposite: what other form could render the individual voices of the three main actors of the *Letters from Neuchâtel* as they each struggle to find a place in society, or the effect that it has when one of them falls silent? The letter condenses individual perspective to its purest form. Written by one person to one other, an intimate friend or close relation of the former, it avoids generalizing ventriloquism; writer and addressee are always known, intimate, and in Charrière's versions, sincere, although sometimes self-deluded or self-deceiving. It is always the marriage of self and written word. When the letters disappear, their writer also vanishes. This is no coincidence: Charrière was herself a consummate letter writer, and the twenty years of seeming literary inactivity between 1763 and 1784 were in fact overflowing with letters, written in bed, by the fireside, first thing in the morning, over weeks, for public consumption or utterly secret, hidden and denied.

Constant d'Hermenches closes one letter to Charrière with the following passionate declaration: "Here I am, ecstatic as ever, loving you with every part of my soul, my heart, and my mind. Surely this grants me the right to kiss your hand, and even gives me permission to aspire to your cheek . . . blush to withhold that permission, as I blush to think of taking advantage of it." And she replies, "There is no one, man or woman, to whom I write as I do to you, with whom my letters so naturally follow my mood; I know that you will always understand me, and that you love me too much ever to despise me, whatever I may say." Letters, writing, mood, self, and addressee all fuse. In the same letter, she exhorts him to "love my letters then, praise them—it always flatters me—but don't ever be unjust, don't ever do it at the expense of a man I love; you are disrespectful towards me when you speak ill of your own letters, your own thoughts, your own reflections."[3] She and her letters can be equally, interchangeably loved and praised, as can he and his letters. The substitution of self for letter amounts to more than a euphemistic way of facilitating passionate declarations of love between two people who cannot marry because Hermenches already has a wife; the identity they develop through their letters is inseparably written, intimate, and immediate, held in the moment of communicating with another. Moreover, its being in the present means that it is always slightly vulnerable, awaiting a reply that has not yet arrived (perhaps none will be written) and that is subject to the vagaries of the post (perhaps it will be lost). Their relationship is plaited together by letters; the letters are the plait that, without the next letter, will fall apart. This precariousness is amplified by the topic they often discuss, which is whether a marriage can be brought about between Hermenches's friend, the Marquis de Bellegarde, and Charrière; they discuss it for years, and never manage to bring it to pass: one letter makes it seem possible, even imminent; another dashes it away; the next brings it back again.

This uncertainty about the future is a quality that Charrière transfers to her epistolary novels, where it becomes a mainspring of narrative tension and drama. Often, readers are denied a clear resolution; it is withheld, or remains suspended at the climax. We may think, fear, or hope that events will tend a certain way, but we cannot be sure. This can be a painful experience—Germaine de Staël, romantic novelist, early interpreter of Kant, moderate republican, adversary of Napoleon, political refugee, and neighbour of Charrière in Switzerland, wrote to tell her that she had been touched to the quick by *Letters from Neuchâtel,* but that "I know of nothing more excruciating than your way of starting without finishing; you separate us from our friends, and the cessation of all correspondence with them makes me feel almost as cross with you as I do with the Paris post office" (August 27, 1793). As Staël's words betray, this crossness, this experience of the cessation of communication as painful, is not about a weakness in Charrière's writing; rather, it is a testimony to the power and immediacy of the letters, to the implicit fragility and anxious incompleteness of the letter form, consummately applied to literary ends.

Charrière, it seems, increasingly chooses to exploit the art of the cliff-hanger, and if *Mistress Henley* and *Letters from Neuchâtel* elect not to cross the *t*'s and dot the *i*'s, *Letters*

Written from Lausanne, with its part 1, *Cécile*, and part 2, *Caliste*, twists uncertainty to a new pitch, as "will he, won't he" becomes the central motif of both. While *Caliste*, as a framed narrative, is resolved, the framing narrative, the story of Cécile, is left open. Even more intriguingly, Charrière returned to her tale on various occasions to sketch out diverging new paths. Henceforth, all her stories, whether exploiting the letter form or not, generated sequels or responses of one sort or another, incomplete and unpublished in some cases. Where this applies to stories in this volume, we give them. We provide these sequels for two reasons: first, so that the reader can have the pleasure of knowing what happens next, and second, because the uncertainty of an ending can also be the uncertainty of a beginning, and therefore, by definition, have multiple possibilities, multiple versions. Like Charrière's stop-start epistolary relationships with the Constant family, a story is never decisively terminated. In the case of *Émigré Letters*, history itself intervened, in the guise of the Terror, to block certain sorts of plot development; it is perhaps the most dramatic example of the sort of cliff-hanger that a letter novel, set in the present and drawing on it with great immediacy, can produce.

It would not have been possible to choose to emphasize this formal aspect of Charrière's work had the editors and publisher of the *Œuvres complètes* not bravely included all fragments and sequels as part of their decision to make all her writing, published and unpublished, from the private letter to the published discourse, available on an equal footing. Their choice has been crucial in terms of revealing her range, especially given the difficulty, constraints, and delay that Charrière experienced with publishers during her lifetime. The unpublished *Constance*, a daring exposé of the economic exploitation of woman refracted through the explicitly exploitative medium of slavery, is not polite or decorous in late eighteenth-century terms, but it is a probing treatment of its subject, and is gaining in recognition: the critic Judith Still has brought it into view in her study, *Aspects of Enlightenment Hospitality: Cannibals, Harems, and Adoption* (2011). Of course, it was not uncommon in the eighteenth century for writers to be unable to publish their work, or to choose not to for one reason or another; Diderot, for example, never published the works that he is arguably now most famous for, *D'Alembert's Dream* (written in 1769) and *Rameau's Nephew* (probably commenced in 1761). *D'Alembert's Dream* circulated to some limited extent in manuscript form but was not published until 1830, while *Rameau's Nephew* led an even quieter existence until its first appearance in Goethe's 1805 translation. So questions of publication, and the status associated with it, were not the same in the eighteenth century, and cannot be taken for granted. Genetic criticism, which looks at compositions as they come into being, rather than in their static, finalized, finished form, also has something to teach us with respect to Charrière and her open-ended, always recommended writing, as we have begun to suggest in our brief sketch of the way she uses the immediacy of the letter to imperil as well as to renew her dramatic narratives.

That these narratives are dramatic is because they are so immediate, so caught inside the surprise, anxiety, and suspense of lived moments. What will you make of what happens when, in *Letters from Neuchâtel*, Henri, out for a walk with a friend and caught out by treacherously icy conditions, meets Marianne and her friends, also out for a walk and similarly caught out, and, while helping them home, comes across Julianne being attacked by snowballs? Or of when Marianne asks Count Max to sit in between her and Henri at a dance so that she can discuss intimate matters while seeming to behave in perfectly conventional and sedate fashion? Or of what happens in *Cécile*, when the unhappily married officer cousin cuts his finger and needs it bandaged? Or of how her mother makes sure Cécile sits with her back to the window so that her expression and pallor are partially camouflaged? Or of what happens when Mr. Henley criticizes the fact that his wife allows her cat to sit on some family heirlooms? These moments, always recounted by one of the participants themselves, are not glamorizing or heroic. They might even sound comical or commonplace. But I defy any reader not to be gripped by each drama as it unfolds.

This immediacy also shapes her style, which is extremely direct and has a certain racy rapidity and informality that modern readers can hardly believe is faithful to the original. "Too modern and colloquial," read my mother's annotation of a sentence from *The Nobleman*. "Harmonize!" she ordered. But that pretension-popping, democratically disrespectful style, which we call modern, is precisely what Charrière aims to achieve. For example, the noble baron, in the middle of an idiotic and pompous speech about the importance of aristocratic ancestors, is interrupted by his daughter, "*Nous en avons depuis le grenier jusqu'à la cave,*" literally, "We have them [ancestors] from attic to cellar," which, in its plain and rude claim to having or owning these ancestors and to their being all over the house, and in its contrast to the baron's elaborately reverent attitude, seems best rendered by the following expression: "We are stuffed with ancestors from attic to cellar."[4] *Stuffed* and its synonym *crammed* are both to be found in Jane Austen, and have been in use in the English language since the sixteenth century, the *Oxford English Dictionary* tells us. This translation tries to avoid both archaism and anachronism, and to retain Charrière's sometimes startlingly direct tone.

The supporting information provided in the footnotes has to range surprisingly widely; we hope that while the reader who is footnote-averse will feel free to pass over them, they will nonetheless provide clear, concise information for the curious. Charrière assumes a great deal of information, and she likes to be precise. Thus, we know which books Cécile's mother takes on holiday, which chess manual Cécile uses, which illnesses are common to that part of Switzerland, and how much income they have. There are also passing comparisons to, for example, the free navigation of the River Scheldt. All this requires explanation for the text to be properly meaningful. The four pieces that Charrière sets in a French Revolutionary context, *Eaglonette*, *Émigré Letters*, *Constance*, and *Saint Anne*, each require detailed historical elucidation. References to models from antiquity are frequent; Charrière playfully evokes specific literary inter-texts, and so on, and so forth. The extraordinary thing is to observe the range of her culture, and the quality of her engagement with it. To accept that Charrière's work needs extensive footnotes is to acknowledge its complexity, and the complexity and seriousness of fiction in general. It does not exist in a solipsistic world of emotional immersion and entertainment; it is active and reactive; it gains from being seen in context.

Contemporaneous reactions to her work, as already suggested, were generally negative, no doubt because they were themselves mired in a reviewing convention that insisted on moral evaluation first and foremost; they provide a salutary reminder of why we should ensure our own readings are not exclusively determined by any given context, however carefully footnoted, and why we should permit the texts to have their own independence. As Gillian Dow has remarked in an as yet unpublished analysis of Charrière's reception, reviews of Charrière provide a "clear example of how even one of the most talented eighteenth-century women writers could be subjected to peculiarly biased and negative reviewing."[5] She concludes that in the British reviews, in particular, the "importance of 'good morals' is stressed to the exclusion of other criteria," and indeed this remark could easily be extended to characterize reviewing style in general at the time.[6] *The Nobleman* seems to have provoked a lively response in the Hague, Netherlands, as its reprinting in a second, corrected edition goes to show, but there are no extant reviews in the press.

Letters from Neuchâtel received one twelve-page review in the *Nouveau Journal de littérature et de politique de l'Europe, surtout de la Suisse* (New Journal of the Literature and Politics of Europe, Especially Switzerland) on June 15, 1784. This was the erstwhile *Journal de Neuchâtel*, that is, Charrière's local paper. Its author, Henri-David Chaillet, was a friend of hers, and he concentrated principally on the reactions of other unpublished critics—indeed, as Dow remarks, it is "an intriguing example of a bridge between the public and private reception of a work."[7] He lambasts those inhabitants of Neuchâtel who want a key to the characters, subtly hints at who the author might be, and satirizes the sort of critical remarks made about it, one such being, "Ah! It's not really quite as good as Richardson's novels," dubbing this an "absurd way of judging it"; we do not disagree![8]

Letters from Mistress Henley received wider attention, not least because it was reprinted in a Parisian edition, along with the novel it was a response to, Samuel Constant's *The Sentimental Husband*, and a defense of Mr. Henley by a different author altogether.[9] The *Année littéraire* reviewed them together, as if written by the same person, in 1785, providing a plot summary of the first two, suggesting that for a dying woman, Mistress Henley certainly talks a great deal, and concluding that the aim of "the author" is to remind wives not to abuse their power, and husbands to indulge their wives' feelings.[10] The *Mercure de France* of April 22, 1786, again confuses the authorship of all three works, but it does single out *Mistress Henley*, stating that this work by "Mme de C . . . de Z." (Madame de Charrière de Zuylen—a further variant on her name) "is worthy of great respect both for the background and for the details," although it has reservations about the dénouement, which, it declares, "is not skilfully enough woven." It does, however, enthuse about the "extreme pleasure this work gave" its reviewer. A month later, the *Journal de Paris* carried a statement by Charrière to the effect that *Mistress Henley* was a separate piece, written by a separate author, and that no permission had been given to publish it with *The Sentimental Husband* or with Mr. Henley's justification.

Letters Written from Lausanne was first reviewed in the *Nouvelles de la République des lettres et des arts* in 1786; the review takes the form of a letter from a "Swiss correspondent," which says that perhaps it would have been better not to include the name of the town in the title, seeing as Lausanne's customs are not analyzed; the reviewer nonetheless finds it well written and original, and remarks that he looks forward to seeing the sequel to *Letters from Neuchâtel*. The review in the *Journal général de France* of September 16, 1786, is four lines long and, as Dow puts it, "short, and dismissive, but not entirely unfavourable": It singles out the "little circumstances" and the "gossip" but also mentions the judiciousness of the views the novel expresses.[11] *Lausanne* was also reviewed in the *Journal encyclopédique*, which loftily commends its "verisimilitude," so difficult to maintain in "this sort of literary lie" (October 15, 1786), and the *Mercure de France* does not review it until February 1788, when it examines parts 1 and 2 together, saying that both works are "truly distinguished" and remarking that Charrière, whose identity it clearly knows, wrote them in a language that was not her own, for which she deserves extra credit; it also considers that her being a woman makes the works more interesting. *Letters Written from Lausanne* also has the merit of having been the only work by Charrière that was much noticed in England; the second part, *Caliste*, which is mostly set there, was published in translation in 1799, under the title *Letters Written from Lausanne*; it did not include *Cécile*. It was found to be a moving tale, but as it is not part of the present volume, we shall not give details of its reviews.

Eaglonette and Suggestina, or, On Pliancy, is a short fairy story that Charrière wrote to and for Marie Antoinette. She refers to her maneuverings to get it seen by the royal eye in a letter of June 10, 1791, but there was no response, and we shall probably never know whether Marie Antoinette read it or not. It was published simultaneously, and reissued in Paris the same year in a collection of different authors. There are no extant reviews.[12]

Émigré Letters fared slightly better, its German translation being enthusiastically received by the German *Gazette d'Iena* (*Allgemeine Literatur-Zeitung*) of November 1794, which praises its "high simplicity and naivety," its "energy" and "free flourishes of the mind."[13] There seem to be no other reviews. The *Fragments of Two Novels Written in English*, as well as *Constance*, were not reviewed, not having been published. The last work in this volume, *Saint-Anne*, was published as part of a collection of novellas, *L'Abbé de la Tour* (1799); *Three Women* was also part of it. It opens with a startling exclamation, "She doesn't know how to read!" and depicts a young woman, Mademoiselle d'Estival, who has great strength and freshness of character, despite, or perhaps because of, not knowing how to read. It was not reviewed in French, but Charrière records in a letter of July 24, 1799, that her nephew Willem René was shocked by its fierce criticism of convention and education, as were her Neuchâtel readers; she mentions them sending her "very pretty little notes in praise of it," without having understood it at all, in her view: they seem all to prefer the counterpoint heroine, Mademoiselle de Rhédon.[14] It was translated into German in 1800 under the title *Babet von Etibal* and met with some warm comments: the narrative was thought to flow well, and it was full of "good reflections" (*Oberdeutsche allgemeine Litteraturzeitung*, January 27, 1801), while another praised its simple but interesting point of view, and although stating that it does not rank as high art, finds its knowledge of human character pleasing (*Allgemeine Literatur-Zeitung*, April 19, 1802). However the tidy ending, which we will not give away, was just too tidy for the reviewer in the *Gazette d'Erlangen* (*Litteratur-Zeitung*, June 4, 1802), who does not refrain from sarcastic remarks. Poor Charrière! She can't win: her endings are either too open or too tidy. There were no other reviews, and as her biographer, C. P. Courtney, remarks, "the work seems to have enjoyed little success."[15] Perhaps its moment has come. It is for you, reader, to decide.

CAROLINE WARMAN

Suggestions for Further Reading

EDITIONS (IN FRENCH)

Isabelle de Charrière, *Œuvres complètes*, ed. Jean-Daniel Candaux, C. P. Courtney, Pierre H. Dubois, Simone Dubois-De Bruyn, Patrice Thompson, Jeroom Vercruysse, and Dennis Wood, 10 vols. (Amsterdam, Netherlands: G. A. van Oorschot, 1979–1984).

Isabelle de Charrière, *Une aristocrate révolutionnaire: Ecrits 1788–1794*, ed. Isabelle Vissière and Jean-Louis Vissière (Paris: Des Femmes, 1988).

Isabelle de Charrière, *Une Liaison dangereuse: Correspondance avec Constant d'Hermenches 1760–1776*, ed. Isabelle Vissière and Jean-Louis Vissière (Paris: Editions de la différence, 1988).

Isabelle de Charrière, *Lettres neuchâteloises*, ed. Isabelle Vissière and Jean-Louis Vissière, preface by Christophe Calame (Paris: Editions de la différence, 1991).

Isabelle de Charrière, *Lettres de Mistriss Henley publiées par son amie*, ed. Joan Hinde Stewart and Philip Stewart (New York: Modern Languages Association of America Texts and Translations, 1993).

Isabelle de Charrière, *Lettres trouvées dans des portefeuilles d'émigrés* (1793), preface by Colette Piau-Gillot (Paris: Côté femmes, 1993).

Isabelle de Charrière, *Sainte Anne*, ed. Yvette Went-Daoust (Amsterdam, Netherlands, and Atlanta: Rodopi, 1998).

Isabelle de Charrière, *Sir Walter Finch et son fils William, suivi d'une Lettre à Willem-René van Tuyll van Serooskerken*, ed. Valérie Cossy (Paris: Desjonquères, 2000).

Romans de femmes du XVIIIe siècle, ed. Raymond Trousson (Paris: Laffont, 1996). This contains *Lettres neuchâteloises, Lettres de*

Mistress Henley, and *Lettres écrites de Lausanne*. For those who read French, Trousson's general introduction, as well as specific introductions, are excellent and thorough.

ENGLISH TRANSLATIONS

Isabelle de Charrière, *Letters of Mistress Henley Published by Her Friend*, trans. Philip Stewart and Jean Vaché, with an introduction by Joan Hinde Stewart and Philip Stewart (New York: Modern Languages Association of America Texts and Translations, 1993); the partner volume to the edition of the same text.

Isabelle de Charrière, *There Are No Letters Like Yours: The Correspondence of Isabelle de Charrière and Constant d'Hermenches*, translated with an introduction and annotations by Janet Whatley and Malcolm Whatley (Lincoln, NE, and London: University of Nebraska Press, 2000).

Isabelle de Charrière, *Three Women, a Novel by the Abbé de la Tour*, trans. Emma Rooksby (New York: Modern Languages Association of America Texts and Translations, 2007).

Madame de Charrière, *Four Tales by Zélide*, translated by Lady Sybil Scott (New York: Charles Scribner's Sons, 1925); containing slightly abridged versions of *The Nobleman*, *Mistress Henley*, *Letters from Lausanne*, and *Letters from Lausanne—Caliste*.

Madame de Charrière, *Letters from Switzerland*, edited and translated with a biography by James Chesterman (Cambridge, England: Carole Green Publishing, 2001); containing *Letters from Neuchâtel*, *Mistress Henley*, *Letters from Lausanne (I)*, and *Letters from Lausanne (II—Caliste)*.

BIOGRAPHIES

C. P. Courtney, *Isabelle de Charrière (Belle de Zuylen)* (Oxford, England: Voltaire Foundation, 1993).

Philippe Godet, *Madame de Charrière et ses amis, 1740–1805* (Geneva: A. Julien, 1905).

Geoffrey Scott, *The Portrait of Zélide* (London: Constable, 1925); reprinted with the title *Scott on Zélide: the Portrait of Zélide*, ed. Richard Holmes (London: Harper Perennial, 2004).

Raymond Trousson, *Isabelle de Charrière* (Paris: Hachette, 1994).

CRITICAL STUDIES

Jenene J. Allison, *Revealing Difference: The Fiction of Isabelle de Charrière* (Newark, DE, and London: University of Delaware Press, 1995).

Katherine Astbury, *Adapting the Revolution: Therese Huber and Isabelle de Charrière's* Lettres trouvées dans des porte-feuilles d'émigrés, in *Translators, Interpreters, Mediators: Women Writers 1700–1900*, ed. Gillian Dow (Oxford, England: Peter Lang, 2007), pp. 99–110.

Jean Bloch, *Rousseauism and Education in Eighteenth-Century France* (Oxford, England: Voltaire Foundation, 1995).

Cahiers Isabelle de Charrière/Belle de Zuylen Papers, 2006–.

Valérie Cossy, "*Nature and Art* d'Elizabeth Inchbald dans la bibliothèque britannique et dans l'œuvre d'Isabelle de Charrière (1796–1797)," *Annales Benjamin Constant* 18–19 (1996): 73–78.

C. P. Courtney, "Constant d'Hermenches: Correspondent of Voltaire and Belle de Zuylen," *Voltaire and the 1760s: Essays for John Renwick*, ed. Nicholas Cronk, *SVEC* 2008:10: 89–100.

———. "Isabelle de Charrière and Voltaire. *Trois femmes and Candide,*" *De Achttiende Eeuw* 38 (2006) 1: 77–92

Joan DeJean, *Tender Geographies: Women and the Origins of the Novel in France* (New York: Columbia University Press, 1991).

Elizabeth C. Goldsmith and Dena Goodman, eds., *Going Public: Women and Publishing in Early Modern France* (Ithaca, NY, and London: Cornell University Press, 1995).

Carla Hesse, *The Other Enlightenment: How French Women Became Modern* (Princeton, NJ, and Oxford, England: Princeton University Press, 2001).

Lynn Hunt, *The Family Romance of the French Revolution* (Berkeley: University of California Press, 1992).

Kathleen M. Jaeger, *Male and Female Roles in the Eighteenth Century: The Challenge to Replacement and Displacement in the Novels of Isabelle de Charrière* (New York: Peter Lang, 1994).

Doris Jakubec, Jean-Daniel Candaux, and Anne-Lise Delacrétaz, eds., *Une Européenne: Isabelle de Charrière en son siècle* (Neuchâtel: Editions Gilles Attinger, Hauterive, 1994).

Medha Nirody Karmarkar, *Madame de Charrière et la révolution des idées* (New York: Peter Lang, 1996).

Linda S. Kauffman, *Discourses of Desire, Gender, Genre, and Epistolary Fictions* (Ithaca, NY, and London: Cornell University Press, 1986).

Joan B. Landes, *Women and the Public Sphere in the Age of the French Revolution* (Ithaca, NY: Cornell University Press, 1988).

Jacqueline Letzter, *Intellectual Tacking: Questions of Education in the Works of Isabelle de Charrière* (Amsterdam, Netherlands, and Atlanta: Rodopi, 1998).

Sigyn Minier, *Madame de Charrière: les premiers romans* (Paris and Geneva: Champion, Slatkine, 1987).

Paul Pelckmans, *Isabelle de Charrière: Une correspondance au seuil du monde moderne* (Amsterdam, Netherlands, and Atlanta: Rodopi, 1995).

Giovanni Riccioli, *L' "esprit" di Madame de Charrière* (Bari, Italy: Adriatica Editrice, 1967).

Samia Spencer, ed., *French Women and the Age of Enlightenment* (Bloomington: Indiana University Press, 1984).

Jean Starobinski, "Les *Lettres écrites de Lausanne* de Madame de Charrière: inhibition psychique et interdit social," in *Roman et lumières au XVIIIe siècle*, ed. Werner Krauss (Paris: Éditions sociales, 1970), pp. 130–152.

Sonya Stephens, ed., *A History of Women's Writing in France* (Cambridge, England: Cambridge University Press, 2000).

Joan Hinde Stewart, *Gynographs: French Novels by Women of the Late Eighteenth Century* (Lincoln: University of Nebraska Press, 1993).

———. *The Enlightenment of Age: Women, Letters and Growing Old in Eighteenth-Century France*, foreword by Joan Dejean, SVEC 2010:09 (Oxford, England: Voltaire Foundation, 2010).

Judith Still, *Aspects of Enlightenment Hospitality: Adoption, Cannibals, and Harems*, SVEC 2011:03 (Oxford, England: Voltaire Foundation, 2011).

Mary Trouille, *Sexual Politics in the Enlightenment: Women Writers Read Rousseau* (New York: State University of New York Press, 1997).

Suzan van Dijk, Valérie Cossy, Monique Moser-Verrey, and Madeleine van Strien-Chardonneau, eds., *Belle de Zuylen/Isabelle de Charrière: Education, Creation, Reception* (Amsterdam, Netherlands, and Atlanta: Rodopi, 2006).

Laurence Vanoflen, "Sortir du monde ancien: Isabelle de Charrière et les vertus de l'émigration," in *Destins romanesques de l'émigration*, ed. Claire Jaquier, Florence Lotterie, and Catriona Seth (Paris: Desjonquèrcs, 2007), pp. 129–142.

Kees van Strien, "The Publication History of *Le Noble*," *Cahiers Isabelle de Charrière/Belle de Zuylen Papers* 5 (2010): 27–34.

Yvette Went-Daoust, ed., *Isabelle de Charrière (Belle de Zuylen): de la correspondance au roman épistolaire* (Amsterdam, Netherlands, and Atlanta: Rodopi, 1995).

LINKS

http://www.belle-van-zuylen.eu/site-charriere/ (a bilingual Dutch/French site that also has many articlcs in English)

A Note on the Translation

All texts come from the *Œuvres complètes*, edited by Jean-Daniel Candaux et al. Apart from the fact that they're in English and not French, the only way in which our texts diverge from their sources is that we have introduced shorter paragraphs and indented dialogue in line with modern practice. We have used the magnificent *Harrap's New Standard French and English Dictionary*, by J. E. Mansion, revised and edited by R. P. L. Ledésert and Margaret Ledésert, 4 vols. (London: Harrap, 1972–1980), backed up by a bilingual dictionary much used in the eighteenth century, Abel Boyer's *Royal Dictionary Abridged*, by J. C. Prieur (London: printed for E. Bathurst, R. Dodesley, P. Valliant, T. Osburne, W. Goldsmith, J. Murray, R. Brotherton, P. Nourse, E. Dilly, and J. Bew, 1797). We have also freely used the *Oxford English Dictionary* online to verify historical usage, and plundered *Collins Thesaurus A–Z* for suppleness of vocabulary. The irritatingly advert-ridden online-literature.com nonetheless provided us with an extremely effective search tool to check our selections against Jane Austen's lexis.

The Nobleman and
Other Romances

The Nobleman

A Moral Tale

(AMSTERDAM, 1763)[1]

On ne suit pas toujours ses Aïeux, ni son Père.[2]
We do not always follow in our ancestors' footsteps, nor in
our fathers'.

LA FONTAINE

This delightful story having been read with much pleasure in
the *Foreign Review in Association with the Literary Year,* in the
month of August 1762, it was our view that we ought to repub-
lish it separately so as to extend the readership still further.[3] We
have taken great care to refer to the manuscript and correct certain printed passages that did not accurately reflect the original
conceptions of the author. Should any further similar produc-
tion reach us from the same pen, we shall certainly share it with
the public.

In one of the provinces of France, there stands a very ancient castle, inhabited by an old offshoot of an even more ancient family. The Baron d'Arnonville was always alive to the merit of this antiquity, and he was right to be, for he lacked much else in the way of merit, and his castle would have been in a better state had it been a little more modern. One of the towers had subsided into part of the moat, and in the rest there was nothing other than a little muddy water, with frogs instead of fish. The family ate frugally, but the antlers of stags his forefathers had killed in times past still reigned over the dining room. The baron never forgot the meat days when he had the right to hunt, nor the fast days when he had the right to fish, and, content with these rights, he ungrudgingly allowed lowly financiers to eat pheasant and carp without ever feeling a tinge of envy. He spent his modest revenue on pursuing a case that concerned his right to hang people on his lands. It never occurred to him that there might be better uses to which he could put his wealth, nor that he might leave his children something better than high and low jurisdiction.[4] Any remaining money he spent on renewing the coats of arms that bordered all the ceilings and on restoring the portraits of his ancestors.[5]

The Baroness d'Arnonville had died long before, and had left him one son and a daughter, whose name was Julie.[6] The young lord had every right to feel aggrieved at the portion nature and education had bestowed on him, and yet he did not complain. Content with the name of d'Arnonville, and with the knowledge of his family tree, he did without talents or knowledge. He went hunting sometimes, and ate his game with the girls from the local inn; he drank a good deal, and gambled every evening with his servant. He was disagreeable to look at, and good eyes would have been needed to detect in his face those features that according to some people are the infallible mark of illustrious birth. Julie, on the other hand, had beauty, grace and wit. Her father had made her read some treatises about heraldry that were not at all to her taste, and she had read some novels that she liked much more. She had been to stay with a lady related to her in the capital of the province, and had acquired some knowledge of the world: not much is needed to give polish to someone with a penetrating mind and a good heart.

An artist who was giving a new layer of paint to her ancestors and their coats of arms taught her to draw; she painted landscapes and embroidered flowers; she worked with skill, sang with taste, and as her face and figure needed neither art nor improvement, she always looked very well dressed.[7] She was exceedingly lively and cheerful, although affectionate too, and every so often jokes about the nobility did slip out; but the respect and fondness she had for her father always kept them in check. Her father loved her too, but he would have preferred her to embroider coats of arms rather than flowers, and to study the crumbling scrolls of parchment that recorded the family titles instead of *Télémaque* and *Gil Blas*.[8] He was angry to see that in her bedroom the modern prints were close to the window, while the old portraits were relegated to a dark corner; and he had often chastized her for preferring a young and amiable bourgeoise from nearby to some young lady as ugly and sullen as she was noble, who happened to be staying in the neighborhood. He would have preferred her never to yield precedence to anything other than good proof of ancient titles, but Julie never did consult the documents of entitlement; she always yielded to age, and would have preferred to be mistaken for a common woman than supposed arrogant. Out of sheer absentmindedness, she would have assumed precedence over a princess; out of indifference and politeness, she would have let the whole world go ahead of her.[9] Whenever the Baron d'Arnonville wanted to dissuade his children from doing something he disapproved of, he would say, "This is not appropriate for a person of your rank; it does not befit your noble birth." He never deigned to use anything so low as an argument to make them do anything at all, not thinking that anything other than perfect uselessness was worthy of high birth nor that it was beneath them to be good for nothing.

Julie didn't want to be too clever, and that was what was so appealing about the cleverness she did have. She didn't know much, but it was clear that this was only because of the absence of any opportunity to learn; her ignorance didn't seem like stupidity. Her lively, sweet, and laughing physiognomy attracted everyone who saw her, and her gracious manner confirmed the initial bias in her favor that her physiognomy had created. If she had affected an air of grandeur and reserve, people would have taken as many steps backward as her manner in fact encouraged them to take forward. We wish primarily to please the person who pleases us: if that person does not greet us with warmth, we are mortified; we turn against them and call them disdainful, when perhaps it was merely a bad habit on their part.[10] And yet, often, they will have lost us forever.

Julie had greatly pleased a lady from Paris who had seen her at the home of the relation I have already mentioned, and this lady invited her to come and spend some time in the country. Julie obtained permission from her father; he advised her to remember what she was, and she departed. This lady was very rich; she had an only son who was nonetheless very agreeable and well brought up. He was very good-looking; Julie was beautiful: they pleased each other at first sight, and to begin with they didn't think either to mention it or to hide it. Bit by bit they came to an understanding, and they found each other even more agreeable once they knew that each was liked by the other—in company, at table, on walks, Valaincourt would often whisper riddles and sweet nothings to Julie; but once they were alone, and he could have said everything, he said not a word.[11] She was surprised, but happy nonetheless; she had read or she had divined that love is timid and tender where it

burns strongest; although no speeches gave her such pleasure
as those of her lover, she loved his silence even better. Valaincourt had, apart from the reasons that Julie sensed, a motive
to keep quiet that she did not know about. She had seen that
he had big eyes, fair hair, beautiful teeth; she found that he
had much sweetness, wit, and generosity; she had noticed
order, decency, and wealth in his house; but she had forgotten
to ask which of his ancestors had been ennobled. Unfortunately it was his father who, after meritorious service and
great virtue, had earned this distinction. Wise men opine that
when nobility is acquired in this way, the newest creations are
the best; that the first noble in a family deserves the greatest
glory for the title that he has founded; that the second is better
than the twentieth, and that it was more likely that Valaincourt resembled his father, than Julie her ancestor of thirty
generations back. But the wise are not competent judges of the
work of prejudice. Valaincourt was aware of the prejudice and
he knew how far Julie's father carried it. The time for her
departure approached; both were distressed, and were the
fonder for it. As each retired to bed they found themselves
alone in an unlit corridor. Valaincourt took Julie's hand, and
kissed it more fervently than he had ever done before; for he
had kissed it before, and for some days already Julie had been
removing her gloves whenever she thought she was going to
need to give her hand to Valaincourt. On the following day
Julie made sure she was in the corridor; there was light, and
Valaincourt extinguished it and gave her a tender kiss, and
then another. Julie wanted to return them . . . fortunately it
was the last evening . . . the next day Julie left.

All the while she had been with Valaincourt she had never
thought of anything other than the pleasure of seeing and
hearing him. When she could no longer see him, she felt the
pain of being separated from him; she thought of ways to see
him again, and to keep on seeing him forever. I don't know
what else she felt and thought about, but happily the young
man for his part was thinking the same things.

One day when she was alone at home, busy with her embroidery, he came in. She remembered the corridor, and blushed;

Valaincourt seemed not to remember it, so respectful was his manner of approaching her. With a woman one respects, and who has a modest air, a man almost doubts the favors he has received from her. Valaincourt could not believe that his lips had dared touch the face of this divinity. After the first compliments had been exchanged, he fell back, silent. Julie never supposed it was her manner that was responsible for keeping him at a distance; she thought that he had seen enough of her not to be quite so timid anymore, and thinking he must perceive a part of what she was feeling, grew vexed at his silence. "In his place," said she to herself, "I do believe that I would speak." At the same time she rose to ring the bell and, as the footman was coming into the room, said to Valaincourt, "How polite you are, sir, to come so far, seeing as you have nothing to say to me. Bring the coffee, and if my father is at home, please ask him to come and have some."

"Oh! Mademoiselle," replied Valaincourt, "how difficult it is to speak when one thinks that all your happiness or our misery depends on what one is about to say . . . what if I set about it the wrong way . . . Oh! Good God! What if I fail to utter the right words . . . ! Julie, adorable Julie, tell me . . . what must I say? What speeches, what reasons, what assurances could ever convince you to give yourself to me?"

"Ah! Valaincourt . . . !" said Julie with a look and a sigh that promised everything, that replied yes to everything he would have liked to say.

Valaincourt, who understood that look and sigh, asked for nothing more; beside himself, he takes her hands and ecstatically kisses them; he even dares—he dares in broad daylight—to press his mouth on hers. The father might have come in right then, but they weren't thinking about that; what could they have foreseen, what could they have feared in their delirium? It didn't last long, however; Julie became alarmed at the ardor of her lover, and at her own willingness.

"Let go, let me go," she said. "Valaincourt, we forget ourselves."

At that moment they heard a noise, and hurried to sit back down. Julie bowed her head over her work to conceal her confusion; the young man went up to Monsieur d'Arnonville with an air of submission that seemed to predispose him in his favor.[12]

"I have taken, monsieur, the liberty of coming to see mademoiselle, your daughter, to whom my good fortune has introduced me."

"Had you never seen my château?"

"No, monsieur; I had never had any pretext to dare to come and pay you my respects."

"It is very worthy of being seen," said the old lord. "A Baron d'Arnonville whose great great great grandfather had been knighted under Clovis had it built in 624.[13] We should not wonder at his having had it built as large as it now is; in that time the nobility was respected as it should be; it was rich and powerful; it was also much purer and much less prevalent than nowadays. At present it is an ordinary recompense; nothing is more common, and I set little store by those little nobles without ancestors—"

"We are stuffed with ancestors from attic to cellar," said Julie.

"And most of the ancient families," continued the baron, "have polluted themselves through misalliance. There are very few families, I dare assert, which have maintained themselves in all their purity; and I therefore hope that my children—"

"It is doubtless," interrupted the young man, able to contain himself no longer, "it is doubtless a satisfaction and an extra reason to be virtuous when one finds examples of virtue and love of one's country in one's ancestors. When one joins a great name to great merit, and instead of vanity—"

"As you have never seen the château, you have never seen the portraits. I must show them to you; it could only be useful for your study of history. Sir, would you like to follow me?"

"Will mademoiselle be coming with us?" said Valaincourt unhappily.

"No," replied Julie, laughing. "I have lived long enough with my grandfathers, and I know them well."

Julie stayed at her work, or rather at her daydreaming. Lord! How agreeable it was. Never had a moment of solitude been more delicious for her. But how wretched Valaincourt was!

The baron, well-disposed toward him, spared him not one portrait, not one coat of arms, not one anecdote, and each portrait,
each coat of arms confronted him with thoughts that pierced
poor Valaincourt's heart. It is not that he was mortified by such
a ridiculous display; he would not have had his nobility conferred by King Ninus himself if he'd had to be as vain and as
mad as the Baron d'Arnonville—but Julie![14] Finally they arrived
at her bedchamber, and he trembled.

While the father was getting tangled up in the history of the
first ancestor to be transmitted to posterity on the end of a
paintbrush, Valaincourt's eyes wandered over the creations of
the daughter's taste. On a table he saw one landscape she had
finished, one she had started, and among the brushes and
paints he saw a little Catechism, Segrais, Racine, and Gil Blas.[15]
He saw the beautiful prints she preferred over old portraits,
he saw the flowers . . . but he stopped saying anything once he
had espied the portrait of Julie. It was drawn in miniature; it
looked like her. Valaincourt no longer thought about anything
other than getting the father to look somewhere else.

"Who is that respectable man," he said, "who is there, sir,
behind you?"

The baron turned round. "That's the one I was telling you
so much about; didn't you hear me?"

"Ah! Sir, I apologize; I do remember it."

Valaincourt had the portrait, and desired nothing more; but
seeing that the father was starting again, he also took the
pretty landscape he liked. Finally they left the bedchamber. "It
is there," said Valaincourt under his breath, "it is there that
live, that repose so many charms!"

"It is there," said the baron, "that my most ancient portraits
are kept; we are finishing our tour with what is most curious—
I kept it for last as a special treat."

"How right you are, sir," said Valaincourt, who smiled
despite his distress. "There is nothing more precious than the
pictures in that room." And although he thanked him with
every sign of the liveliest gratitude, despair was in his heart.

"Is it not true," said Julie when they rejoined her, "that I am
rich in grandfathers? My grandmothers are not beautiful, but

they are ancient. I count on having myself painted many times; beautiful or ugly, in three hundred years my portrait will be worth its weight in gold."

"Ah! Mademoiselle," said Valaincourt, "your portrait will never be as dear, as precious as it is today. Then, vanity may venerate it, but today love adores it."

"Have you seen it, monsieur?"

"Yes, mademoiselle, you will see that I have seen it as I should see it; I also saw your books, and your landscapes—"

"Were you not vastly entertained to see my ancestors?"

"No, mademoiselle; I only looked at what related to you."

All this was said in hushed tones. Julie smiled, and Valaincourt was relieved to see that the daughter did not have the same respect for antiquity as her father. It was late; Valaincourt said his good-byes and left.

"Is that young man your lover?" the baron asked his daughter.

"I believe so, Father."

"Is he thinking of marrying you?"

"Yes, Father."

"Is he a gentleman?"

Julie had no idea, but supposed so, and again said yes.

"Of an old family?"

"Yes, Father."

"Where does their nobility derive from?"

"From Renaud de Montauban," replied Julie, more out of playfulness than for politics.[16]

"What? Daughter, from Renaud de Montauban! My God, how lucky you would be! What joy for me to see you married so well!"

And so saying, he embraced her with such tenderness that she was disconcerted. She was sorry that she had deceived him over something that seemed so important to him, and was fearful what the consequences of her joking might be, should it come to light. She was also exasperated by the extent of her father's folly, and all these feelings together agitated her so much that she was obliged to withdraw. She sat down in her bedchamber, arms leaning on her dressing table, head bowed in her hands.

"My father does not ask," said she, "whether he is virtuous, wise, or whether he has a good heart; he asks whether his family is ancient . . . on that assurance, he gives me to him. . . . Ah! If Valaincourt turned out not to be so noble, he would not give me his permission! He would be even more rigid because of my deceit. Good God, how imprudent! Good God, how wrong I was!"

She pondered this sadness for a while longer; then, getting up and pacing round the room, she wanted to look at the landscape that Valaincourt had been talking about to distract herself. Unable to find it anywhere, she turned to her portrait; then she understood what Valaincourt had wanted to tell her. The theft diverted as much as it moved her; she imagined her father on one side saying, "This is Jean-François-Alexandre d'Arnonville," while Valaincourt was thinking, "Here is Julie d'Arnonville; I must carry her off." When a young girl sees that she is tenderly loved by her lover, her griefs are easily softened; deep joy easily lifts the heart. Julie thought that if Valaincourt was not descended from Renaud, he was probably descended from someone; that she would be able to make her trick look like a mistake; that moreover it wasn't impossible that some use could still be made of it; that she should warn Valaincourt, and work on his genealogy with him.

"If reasonable motives don't touch my Father," she thought, "am I not allowed to trick him a bit? Should we be the victims of such ridiculous prejudice?"

This rather relaxed morality suited her, and she looked no further. It occurred to her to write to Valaincourt to warn him. She took her inkstand, pens, and paper; she imagined how she would get the letter to him; and I would swear to it that she would have written something if only she could have been happy with her style and spelling, but Julie quickly passed over her true motives for not writing; she persuaded herself that the whole panoply of prudence, reserve, modesty, and respect for decorum was what was stopping her, and she congratulated herself on virtues that she did not possess. Julie was called down to supper. Her father had already imparted her hopes to the young baron; they could barely contain themselves in front of

the servants. Hardly had these been dismissed before they
were drinking to the health of Renaud's descendant; but Julie,
unable to bear the sight of their joy, withdrew once more,
equally ashamed of her mistake and of their foolishness. Alone
in her room, she started to cry. Love, repentance, fear, and
hope mingled in her heart and oppressed it. When a young person is agitated by different feelings that she can no longer disentangle, her way out will be to cry. By the time Julie stopped
crying, the chaos that had seemed so overwhelming had almost
dissipated; soon there was nothing left but the idea of her lover.
She saw him as she had seen him when they met for the very first
time. She remembered his marks of tenderness; she reproached
herself for responding to them too much for decency and not
enough for love; she remembered kisses, and who knows if she
did not wish to receive them again? Finally, she got into her
bed, and on doing so, she reflected that a very long time had
passed since she'd last seen it. "Was it only this morning," said
she, "that I got up? Was it only this afternoon that Valaincourt
came?" No day had ever seemed longer to her, because no day
of hers had ever been so filled with such different and interesting sensations. She could not comprehend how it was possible
for her to have felt and thought so many things, of having had
such joy and such grief in such a short amount of time. Julie is
not the only one to whom time seems much longer in the rapid
succession of varied impressions than in the languor of inaction. Julie fell asleep in spite of her tender feelings; her dreams
held no disturbing omens. The following day no presentiments
came to trouble her; she spent the morning painting in her room.
Her father was dining at the neighboring château, her brother
was hunting, and so she was alone. Many times did she wish
that Valaincourt would come and interrupt her solitude, and
take advantage of moments that were slipping away for nothing!
Having started to read on a bench in the avenue, she finally
saw him approaching, but he was with her father. He had spent
half the night looking at the portrait of his mistress, and half
the day too, but he wanted to see his mistress herself again; he
first set out after dinner, and met Monsieur d'Arnonville on

his way home. The baron wasted no time before speaking of
the thing that alone occupied his heart.

"I have learnt, monsieur," he said, after having bowed to
him many times, "I have learnt that you have fallen in love
with my daughter, and that you were hoping to marry her."

Valaincourt was stunned by this opening and his only reply
was a deep bow. Surprise and anxiety were painted on his
face, and kept him silent. "My fate will be decided," he said to
himself. "Good God, what will he say?" This eagerness to discuss his love announced either happiness or extraordinary
unhappiness. He hardly dared listen.

"I have long been decided, monsieur," continued the baron
with a gracious air, "only to give my daughter to a man of
illustrious birth: the d'Arnonvilles would dishonor no family;
they can aspire to anything. My ancestors—"

"Ah! Monsieur," cried Valaincourt, imprudent and in love,
"I know how superior to me you are. I know that I am not
worthy to be allied to you, but if the most tender, respectful
love, the keenest desire to make your daughter happy could
stand in lieu of an older line; if honor, probity, my devotion to
you . . ."

By this time Julie had reached them, she had heard what
Valaincourt was saying, and her confusion explained all this
mystery. Valaincourt was looking in the opposite direction
and hadn't yet seen Julie, but the father was not listening to
Valaincourt anymore. He threw her a look that made her
crumple at his feet. Valaincourt, interrupted by these actions,
watched the daughter and the father without being able to
understand what was causing this touching scene; he didn't
know what to think or what to say. Julie, eyes bowed to the
ground, allowed her tears to flow, and said nothing. The furious father was unable to speak. Finally he recovered it:

"Daughter unworthy of me and of my forefathers," said he,
"have you been trying to deceive your father; is everything you
said about the birth of your lover nothing other than a fiction?"

"Oh, Father!" Julie replied. "I am guilty, but . . . but I was
in love with Valaincourt."

"What, Julie, have I betrayed you?" Valaincourt cried. "I should have guessed, I should have kept quiet. . . . Oh! It is for my sake that you have done this, and I'm the one who is betraying you! Monsieur," he continued, falling to his knees next to Julie. "Monsieur, forgive an error that love made her commit, and which we therefore share. Allow me to love your daughter; her graces, her wit, the beauty of her soul as well as her birth raise her high above me. She deserves a throne . . . but no king could be more ardent; she would never find more love in his heart than in mine; never will her perfections be more adored. . . . Again, allow me to love her and see her, and see you, and let your own judgment decide my fate."

"Renaud de Montauban!" said the father, without seeming to have heard him. "How long has your family been titled?"

Valaincourt did not reply.

"Tell him," said Julie. "Be more honest and open than I was."

"Thirty-five years."

"Thirty-five years! And you want me to give you my daughter! Go, mademoiselle; go and weep for your shame, and do not reappear before me. And you, monsieur, let us see you here no longer. Remove yourself from my sight this instant," he told Julie, who was still on her knees and weeping, "I can hardly believe you could have forgotten your origin to this extent! You do not deserve to be born to the rank you have!"

"No doubt," said Valaincourt, helping Julie to get up, "she did not deserve to be born to a father like you."

He would have said more had a look from Julie not imposed silence on him, and as she went along the path toward the château, the desperate lover went away from it, cursing his fate, and nobility too. As for the Baron d'Arnonville, he was so outraged, so indignant, and in such a passion that he was unable to walk, so he sank down on the same bench Julie had been so peacefully occupying a few moments before, reading and dreaming. Having ordered a laborer who was working in the garden to fetch the housekeeper, he told her what had happened in a few words, and instructed her to make sure that Julie could not get out of her room or receive news from or about her lover. This old woman, whose name was Mademoiselle du Tour, was practically one of the château archives in her own right, and having neither heard nor seen anything other than the follies of her masters from her earliest infancy, was almost as passionate on the subject of nobility as the baron. Sharing his resentment with all her heart, she ran off to lock up and harangue her young mistress. Julie, although sweet natured, was infuriated by this harsh treatment, and as the old woman, having once explained what she had been sent to do, commenced with the words "For a young lady of your rank . . . ," Julie said, "Be silent! I have heard enough of this nonsense! Lock me up, but leave."

For two days Julie refused to listen or answer; she ate little, slept not at all, and cried a great deal. The baron, left alone on the bench, said to himself: "How could a minor aristocrat of recent date presume to ally himself to me? How could my daughter listen to him? On the one hand, what boldness! On the other, what cowardice!" He said this all alone until nightfall, then he said it to his son, he said it all night long in his dreams, and the next day while touring the portraits, he thought they were reproaching him, full of indignation. On the third day, the wind knocked down part of the dovecote, and the weather vane engraved with the Arnonville coat of arms toppled from the top of the tower into a muddy ditch in front of his eyes, and his mind was seized with the most piercing fear.[17] He went to bed, his imagination struck by these terrifying omens, and hardly had sleep scattered its sweet poppies over him than he saw the spirits of his ancestors armed from top to toe approaching his bed, looking outraged. The baron awoke with a start and asked them to appear to his daughter, but the antique shades entirely failed to do so. Julie had received a note from Valaincourt that evening, and slept peacefully; her dreams were the work of love and hope. Valaincourt had approached the gardener's little daughter about the note; Julie had always been very kind to her and she was devoted to her mistress. This girl willingly took on the commission, and asked the old jaileress if she might herself take Julie some fruit. Mademoiselle du Tour was not fundamentally unkind, and

Julie's grief was beginning to inspire her with pity, so she said yes, and after the young girl had chatted with Julie for a while she whispered to her that at the bottom of the basket of fruit she would find a letter. No sooner was Julie alone than she opened it, and this is what she read:

"Beautiful, sweet Julie, since you know what love is, there's no need to tell you what I feel, and what I suffer, and moreover, how could my pen ever express it? My aim is to assure you that there is nothing I will not undertake, nothing that I will not hazard to rescue you from the cruel grip which keeps us apart. Are you capable of not agreeing with me, Julie? Can you submit to such ridiculous prejudice? If I ever thought . . . if I thought that you could ever repent an instant, if you might be less happy . . . God be my witness that I would give up all my happiness to spare you a single regret. . . . Tell me, mademoiselle, do you fear regrets? My birth . . . excuse me, Julie, you love me, and I dare suspect your heart? Would you judge as unworthy of your hand he whom you do not judge unworthy of your affection? Is it not for me that you suffer . . . ? Trust in my love, charming Julie; we will not suffer long."

Julie believed him without really knowing why. She read and reread the charming note, and on reading it, hope and even cheerfulness were reborn in her heart. She ate, she slept; and next day she picked up her work again and her painting. Mademoiselle du Tour found her as sweet and courteous as she had ever been, and she finally had the pleasure of haranguing her without being interrupted. The following day the little girl came back with her basket while Mademoiselle du Tour was just saying: "Given your birth you can aspire to the highest in the land."

"That may well be," replied Julie, smiling.

Mademoiselle du Tour, ignorant of the secret power of the basket, thought Julie's cheerfulness was the proof of what she had experienced herself in previous times—that is, that there is no better consolation for the loss of one lover than to have another one. She therefore carried on, saying: "Your husband will be a great lord; you will have a great château, and you will be very happy."

"That may well be," said Julie, smiling even more sweetly.

Mademoiselle du Tour, believing that she'd made great progress, congratulated herself and went out to tell the baron that he needed only leave it all to her, and within two days, Julie would have forgotten her lover. But she couldn't find anyone to tell about her skill and delight. The baron had gone out to distract himself, and had left word that he wouldn't be back until the following day. Julie quickly took advantage of the housekeeper's absence to read Valaincourt's latest letter. He told her that he'd examined everything and judged that her escape would be easy; that her window was low, that this part of the moat was almost filled in; that he would wait for her in the avenue at dusk, and that a swift carriage would convey them before daybreak to a town quite far off, where they would swear inviolable love to each other at the foot of the altar.

"I no longer doubt my happiness," he continued, "since it depends on you, dear Julie; that would be to insult you. Love gives you to me; its rights are sacred. At midnight, when the moon begins to break through the shadows, leave the sad prison where barbarous prejudice keeps you locked up, and let love guide you to the arms of your lover. I ask for no reply; you told me that you loved me, and that was to promise me everything. Till midnight, Julie . . . what moments, what pleasures!"

Julie let the letter fall, and stayed quite still for a while. A completely new feeling, part surprise, part joy, suspended her thoughts entirely for some time. An elopement! That very evening! Leaving the house of her father, and giving herself to Valaincourt! Julie finally moved, and without admitting her intentions, opened the window, and in fact looked around to see how easy it would be to get out. Seeing that that side of things was not at all impossible, she picked up the letter and read it again. "It is true," she said, "that the prejudice which keeps me here is as barbaric as it is absurd. It is true that I told him I love him. Valaincourt does not doubt my consent— that would be, says he, to insult me. I am his; he will wait for me. . . ."

Is not the identical tone of authority that is so hateful in a husband compelling in a lover? With the same skill that we evade the rights of one because we hate them, we extend the rights of another because we love them. We don't want our freedom when it comes to employing it against our will. If Valaincourt had pleaded, had asked for her consent, as if doubting whether he'd obtain it, perhaps Julie would not have dared to give in; but Valaincourt demanded, and Julie did not think she could disobey. Valaincourt would no doubt have been hardpressed to explain what these sacred rights of love that he claimed with such assurance actually were. But Julie asked for no explanation, no proof; she believed his word, and she thought she was decided not so much by his passion as by a certain inviolable duty, which she nonetheless did not understand.

There she stands, almost resolved to go ahead, weeping tears over the father she is abandoning and the home in which she was born, and which she is going to leave; but she thinks about her lover, and her tears dry up. "So I will be," she bursts out, "so I will be his, forever!" Then she goes back to the window, and looking at it more carefully, she sees that at precisely the place where she'd have to climb down, there is a hole, filled with that day's fresh rainfall. She would need to fill that hole in; what should she use? Julie looks around her, and seeing the portraits of her forefathers, says to them, "You will do me at least this favor," and, laughing, she immediately jumps onto a chair to take Jean-François d'Arnonville down off the wall. As she is holding him, still up on the chair, Mademoiselle du Tour comes in—

"What are you doing, mademoiselle?"

"Dear lady . . . dear lady. . . . am I not right to send this portrait off to the painter for restoration? If I am to be married, as you believe, to a lord from an old château, I would like to be able to take the first baron of the family there."

Mademoiselle du Tour, as we will not be surprised to hear, did not disapprove of this idea, and took the opportunity to make a very long speech about the nothingness of the pleasures of love, and the solidity of the advantages of the nobility. Julie, unconquerably merry and playful, wanted to know whether this fair dame had ever experienced this thing she scorned, and du Tour told her that had her lover been cook's boy to a duke, she would have listened to him, but he was only cook's boy to a count.

Once the housekeeper had departed, Julie made a parcel of her most precious belongings, and as the day was drawing in, started to get ready for her escape. Grandpa was hurled into the mud, and he, not being sufficient, was followed by a second, and then a third. Julie had never thought her ancestors could be so useful. This new use amused her; and yet she was very agitated, and if on the one hand her heart was in ecstasies at the hope of belonging to her lover, it was also bleeding for her father. Ah! How powerful the principles of a good education would have been over a naturally virtuous soul, as yet uncertain of itself! But the arguments in favor of duty, which the father had always used, were even less solid than those of the lover in favor of love.

The little girl came to fetch her basket. Not knowing what was in the letters she had carried, and believing that a reply from Julie would give great pleasure to Valaincourt, she asked if her mistress had any orders to give her. Julie hesitated; now was the moment to destroy Valaincourt's hopes. Her face turned white, then red. "There is no reply," she said to the gardener's daughter, as she gave her a coin.

At eight o clock, her brother came to see her for the first time. After a couple of not very delicate jokes, he told her that he had condescended to play a game that he was good at with some little upstart who didn't understand it at all; and that he was so charmed to be duping someone so easily, that he had played all day long, and won a considerable sum. We are never harsher on those faults of which we feel we are completely incapable than when we feel guilty about something else. Julie told him that what he had done was absolutely disgraceful and shameful; he made some contemptuous reply, and left. "I will soon be far away from this delightful nobility," said she. "It is probably with someone like him that I would be condemned to spend the rest of my life; moreover, if his lineage was good, I would be thought only too lucky. Oh well! May these great

lords enter the Order of Malta as is their right.[18] Valaincourt
does not prevent them—I think he is happy for them to have
both honor and vows—but my heart and hand have nothing in
common with the Maltese cross."

She carried on getting ready for her departure until the housekeeper came to take her to supper. She went to bed straight
afterward so that no one would be suspicious. Once everyone
was asleep, from the young baron to his best friends the hunting dogs, she got up. She dressed quickly, without taking too
much care, without light and thus also without a mirror; she
thought that at night, by the feeble light of the moon, Valaincourt would not be spending too much time contemplating her
attire.

The moon appears, the window opens, midnight sounds,
Julie throws her parcel out, climbs up on the windowsill, comes
back down into the room, climbs up again. Something is holding her back; she thinks she can hear her father, but what can
he say to hold her back? He speaks to her of her name, her
birth, of the honor of her origin, which it is her duty to uphold.
Julie finds that none of this makes any difference, and that
there is no reason why she shouldn't be any less unhappy than
her maid, who apparently had permission to go off and elope as
she pleased. Love presents her with less feeble reasons, decides
her, and Julie jumps down lightly onto the face of one of her
ancestors, who rends and snaps beneath her feet. The noise awak-
ens the housekeeper, who sleeps not far from there, but supposing that it was one of those spirits that frequently honor
ancient châteaus with their visits, she is content to mutter a
Hail Mary and bury herself deeper in her pillows, and this time
the ghosts are useful for once.[19]

Julie advances across the ruins and goes into the courtyard.
A dog wakes up but doesn't betray the kind mistress who has
stroked him so often. She wants to go out by a little door,
which unfortunately is locked—trembling, she retraces her
steps. "God! What will become of me," says she, "if I can't
find a way of getting out?" A little old wall prevents her; she
tries to climb up on it. The bricks have been joined together

for so long that they come apart without difficulty. She's already in the avenue; now she's with her lover. . . . Let us not worry ourselves about what became of them.

The next day, when the frightful news was brought to the old baron, he fainted. Coming back to his senses after a good while, and many medicaments, he said in languishing tones: "A nobleman of recent creation! Oh my ancestors! Oh my blood! Eternal opprobrium!" It was feared that he would die of pain. In vain did a reasonable man who happened to be there represent to him that nobility is a prejudice about worth, and that recognized worth, such as Valaincourt's, had no need of prejudice; that it is impossible to lay claim to someone else's worth, and that even if it were possible, a nobleman would not often be found with more than anyone else; that the emperor who conferred the titles in the first place may well have been a dishonest man or an idiot. . . . This blasphemous speech was followed by an even longer fainting fit than the first one. I think that that would have been the end of the baron had a very consolatory letter not called him back to life. Fate compensated him for the acquisition of a rich, handsome, and generally agreeable son-in-law by offering him the most disagreeable daughter-in-law imaginable. He accepted this compensation with joy; he offered up thanks to Heaven, and admired the wisdom of Providence, which dispenses good and evil in equal measure. It goes without saying that the young lady was thoroughly noble; not her portrait but her family tree was sent, and it was such that the father did not hesitate. The son had heard it said that she had a squint and a hunchback; but the honor of uniting his arms and quarters to hers encouraged him to overlook all the rest. In any case he counted on consoling himself with less noble and less ugly creatures, and had too much greatness of soul to think that it was obligatory to love the person one marries. The marriage was therefore rapidly concluded. Julie, having heard the news, found out when the wedding day was to be. At the end of the meal, Daddy d'Arnonville, reliving the vigor of his young days, drank twenty bumpers to the excellence of the union. Once the wine had started mixing old and new nobility in his head, Valaincourt and Julie entered the room, and threw themselves at his feet. Having lost a part of what he called his reason, he felt nothing but tenderness, and forgave them. Julie was happy, and her sons were not knights, not one of them.

Letters from Neuchâtel

(1784)[1]

As the editor of these *Letters from Neuchâtel* saw neither the copy that was used for type-setting, nor the first printed pages, a large number of errors slipped into both. We flatter ourselves that this new, corrected edition will be more agreeable to read.[2]

Letter I.

Julianne C*** to her aunt in Boudevilliers.

My dear aunt,

Thank you for your precious letter telling me that you and my dear uncle are as well as ever, thanks be to God! So my cousin Jeanne-Marie will soon be wife to cousin Abram; I promise I am very pleased to hear it, having always loved her, and if they wait till springtime, me and my cousin Jeanne-Aimée can come and dance at her wedding; I would be very glad to.

And now, dear aunt, I must tell you what happened to me the day before yesterday. We had been working hard all day on the dress for Mademoiselle de La Prise, so that we were ready in good time, and my mistresses sent me to take it to her, and when I was going down by Neubourg, there were a lot of people in the street, and a gentleman who looked very kind was going by too, and he had a fine suit on. As well as the dress, I had another parcel too, and when I looked round I dropped them all, and I fell over too; it had been raining and the way was slippery. I wasn't at all hurt, but the dress got a bit dirty. I didn't dare go back to the workshop, and I couldn't help bursting into tears, because I didn't dare go to the young lady's house with her dress all mucky, and I was really frightened of my mistresses, who are already sour enough most of the time, and there were some little brats who couldn't think of anything better to do than laugh at me. But I was in luck again, because the gentleman, once he'd helped me gather everything up, wanted to come with me to tell my mistresses that it wasn't my fault. I was a bit ashamed, but I wasn't as scared as if I'd had to go all alone. And the gentleman did say to my mistresses that it wasn't my fault, and when he went away he gave me a coin—to cheer me up, is what he said, and my mistresses were all amazed that such a fine gentleman had taken the trouble to come with me, and they didn't talk about anything else all evening. And yesterday they were even more surprised, because the gentleman came back again in the evening to see if we'd been able to get the dirt off the dress. I told him yes we had, and that I wasn't so afraid of the young lady, who is a very kind young lady, and one of the kindest in all the town. So there you are, my dear aunt, that's what I wanted to tell you all about. It's another silver lining to the cloud, because the gentleman is so kind, but I don't know what he's called, nor whether he lives in Neuchâtel, because I haven't ever seen him here before; perhaps I shall never see him again.

Goodbye, dear aunt. Send my love to my uncle and my cousin Jeanne-Marie and cousin Abram. Cousin Jeanne-Aimée is well: she's still working; she sends her love.

Julianne C.

Letter II.

Henri Meyer to Godefroy Dorville in Hamburg.

*Neuchâtel, October ** , 178**

I arrived here three days ago, my dear friend, having crossed countryside covered in vineyards, and bumped along a rather unpleasant and extremely narrow track crowded with grape harvesters and all the grape harvest baggage. People say that it's all very merry; and I may possibly have found it so myself, had the weather not been so overcast, humid, and cold, such that I didn't see a single harvester woman who wasn't really rather dirty and half-frozen. I don't really like to see women working the land, other than haymaking. I find it a pity for the young and pretty ones; I feel sorry for those who are neither one nor the other, such that the feelings I have are never pleasant; and the other day in my carriage I felt like an arrogant idiot, making my way past all these poor women. The grapes, tipped and squashed down into open barrels known as *gerles*, and jolted about on little four-wheeled carts called *chars*, didn't look very appetizing either. I have to admit that I wasn't in a very good temper; I was leaving studies which I adored for a completely new occupation, one for which I may display only very mediocre aptitude. If I'd been leaving you behind me as well, it would have been a lot worse, but since you left us, I haven't felt any other strong attachment. I wasn't suffering much from regret or from any great fear of the future, for my father's friend couldn't not welcome me, but only from a bit of gloom and sadness. I won't say anything more about how I was feeling, because it hasn't changed.

Monsieur M*** was very welcoming. My lodgings are quite good; my companions, the apprentices and clerks, neither please nor displease me. We all eat together, except when my master invites me to eat with him, which has happened twice in four days. You see it's all perfectly decent, but if I'm not particularly bored, I'm not much entertained either.

I think I'll like the town more when it isn't so crowded and the streets so filthy. There are some fine houses, particularly in the faubourg; and when the fog lifts enough for the sun to shine, the lake and the Alps, already covered in snow, make for a beautiful view, but still it's not the same as Geneva, Lausanne, or Vevey.

I've engaged a violin master, who comes every day from 2 to 3; I don't have to be back at the warehouse until 3. It's quite enough to be sitting down from 8 to 12 and 3 to 7; on the days

when a lot of post comes in we have to stay even longer.[3] On
the other days I'll take lessons, either music or drawing,
because I know how to dance quite well already, and after supper my plan is to read, for I wouldn't like to lose the fruits of
the education I've been given; I'd even like to keep my Latin up
a bit. It's all very well saying that it's useless for someone in
trade: it seems to me that when a tradesman leaves his warehouse he's the same as any other man, and that there's a big
difference between your father and Mr.***.

My writing is found to be very satisfactory and my arithmetic
too. It seems to me that people are keen to keep their word to
my uncle, and make sure that I do progress, as far as possible, in
the knowledge of the profession I am learning. There is a big
difference between me and the other apprentices with respect to
the jobs they give us. Without being vain, I'd also go so far as to
say that there's a similarly big gap in our respective upbringings.
There's only one who makes me feel it is a pity that he has to
devote his attention to things which require not the slightest
intelligence and which teach you nothing at all. It would be
quite natural for him to come to envy me, but I will try to show
him every consideration, so that he is very pleased to have me
here; it'll be very easy. The others are no better than louts.

Something which I'm very grateful to my uncle for is the way
that my expenses and money are arranged for me. My board of
thirty louis is paid for me, along with half a louis a month for
laundry; I'm given ten louis for spending money, without my
needing to account for any of it, and I'm promised the same
again every four months.[4] As for my lessons and my clothes, my
uncle has promised to pay all the bills I send him for this first
year, without questioning anything. He wrote to tell me that
with this arrangement I might think myself comfortably rich,
but that that wasn't the case in the slightest; it was just that he
hadn't wanted me to lack for anything, nor to risk incurring
debts or loans, or to make a mystery about my expenses, and
that this should enable me to go my own way without denying
myself anything I wanted, so long as I'd given it a little thought.
If my mother and my other guardians have anything to say
about my expenses, my uncle will pay for them, he says, out of

the money reserved for his own meager pleasures, and won't find that pleasure the least of them all. So here you see me, a grand gentleman, my friend; ten louis in my pocket, my board mostly paid for, and great freedom to spend what I want, and I want everyone to know it. Good-bye, dear Godefroy. I'll write in a fortnight. Love your friend as he loves you.

H. Meyer.

Letter III.

Henri Meyer to Godefroy Dorville.

Neuchâtel, November **, 178*

I'm beginning to find Neuchâtel a little prettier. There have been some frosts; the streets are dry; the gentlemen, I mean the people that we all greet respectfully in the streets, and whom I hear in passing addressed as Counselor, Mayor, Mr. ***, don't look quite so careworn and are better dressed than they were during the wine harvest. I don't know why I should take pleasure in this; fundamentally nothing could matter less. I've seen some pretty servant girls and workers in the streets, and some young ladies are very well dressed and elegant—it seems to me that almost everyone in Neuchâtel has grace and lightness. I don't see as many fine people as in *** but the people look genteel; the young girls are rather thin and dark for the most part. I was told to expect something of a completely different order at the concerts. They'll be starting on the first Monday in December. I shall certainly subscribe; I might even see women acting, which will seem very strange to begin with.[5] There will also be balls every fortnight; but they're made up of various combined societies, and clerks and warehouse apprentices aren't made welcome there—and quite right too, it seems to me, for it would become a crush of yokels. Even if there are a few exceptions, that doesn't stop the rule being good, and if they apply the rule to all, no one has the right to complain; this is what I say to my companions, who find it very bad that they should be excluded, although in truth they are not at all

fit to be seen in good company. For myself, I don't mind, but I
hope I'll be allowed to play at the concert. And we've already
decided, my companion Monin, who plays the bass, Mr.
Neuss, and I, that we'll do a little concert every Sunday. My
violin master will be one of us; he will lead, and play the viola,
and he won't ask, he says, for anything other than a bottle of
red wine in return: he quite likes drinking, and knows very
well that it's better to drink a bottle at his student's house than
to risk drinking lots of them at the tavern, getting drunk, and
going home to his wife in that state. These musicians almost
put you off music; but it's important to try only to learn their
artistry from them, and not to mix with them otherwise. I'm
very good at reading music, and I get quite a good sound out
of my violin; but I'll never be able to tackle the really difficult
bits or play with real delicacy.

One thing has particularly struck me here. There are two or
three names which I hear pronounced endlessly. My shoemaker,
my wigmaker, a little boy who runs errands for me, a fat merchant, all bear the same name; it also belongs to two seamstresses whom chance made me acquainted with, to an extremely
elegant officer who lives opposite my master's house, and to a
minister whom I heard preaching this morning. Yesterday I met
a fine lady richly dressed; I asked her name, and it was the same
one again. There's another name which is shared by a mason, a
cooper, and a minister of state. I asked my master if all these
people are related; he said that they are in a way. I liked to hear
this. It must be very pleasant to work for your relations, if you're
poor, and to give work to your relations, if you're rich. They
can't experience either the same lofty elevation or the same miserable abasement which I've witnessed elsewhere.

There are of course some families that aren't so extensive;
but when people mention members of these families, they
almost always say: "That's Madame such-and-such, daughter
of Monsieur such-and-such" (who turns out also to be a member of one of the big families!), so that I can't help supposing
that everyone in Neuchâtel is related, and it's not therefore
particularly surprising that they aren't very formal with each

other, that they dress as I saw them do during the wine harvest, when I found their enormous shoes, woollen leggings, and silk knotted neckerchiefs so extremely startling.

Nonetheless, I have heard talk of the nobility, but my master said to me one day, talking about the pride of our German nobility, that he hadn't felt anything special when he got his letters two years ago, and that although he does now put "de" in front of his name, he *didn't attach anything to it* (that is his expression, and I didn't understand very clearly what he meant by it) and that he only decided to take the step of changing his signature to please his wife and sisters.[6] Good-bye, dear Godefroy, my favorite friend from work has just stepped by for some tea. I'm just off to get my violin master and Monsieur Neuss; we'll play music. I didn't think we would be starting till next Sunday, and I'm very happy to be starting this evening instead. Good-bye, I embrace you; write to me, I beg you.

H. Meyer.

Monday evening, at 8 o'clock
P.S. If those gentleman hadn't come yesterday, I should have told you all about the fair and the armorers' procession. It would be good if this ceremony had a meaning, for it has a solemnity which appealed to me.[7] But no one was able to explain where it came from nor what it is supposed to mean. I have worked hard tonight; I'm trying to do justice to the kindnesses being shown me, showing all the goodwill I'm capable of.

Letter IV.

Henri Meyer to Godefroy Dorville.

Neuchâtel, December **, 178*
Thank you, dear friend, for your long letter; it gave me the greatest pleasure.... Yes, I do believe that it is the greatest, and certainly it's the one that I was happiest with after the event, that I've experienced since I came here. You must find

what I'm saying a bit mixed up—it's no surprise that this is the case, for my thoughts are so. There are some things which I'd find ridiculous, almost bad, to tell you; but on the other hand, I don't want there to be the slightest falseness, not even the slightest exaggeration in what I say. If we were to start lacking in sincerity even once, for anything other than the most urgent necessity, no one knows, it seems to me, where it would stop; because it has to hurt a bit to lie, and each day it comes easier with practice. And then what happens to honor, the trust we wish to inspire; in a word, to everything we respect? How about that for a sermon? When we don't feel very pleased with ourselves for whatever reason, we want to make up for it elsewhere.

Coming back to your letter, it sounds as if you're leading a very pleasant life. Apart from your sister-in-law's caprices, it doesn't seem as if there's anything that needs changing. You should be careful not to court that young girl, however rich she is. Since she looks like her sister and has the same timbre of voice, she'll be like her, I think, in all things, when she dares to show herself as she really is—and you may not be as long-suffering as your brother.

I went to a concert last Monday, and thanks to Monsieur Neuss's good offices, I was allowed to play. I concentrated so hard on playing my part that I didn't notice what was happening in the hall until I heard Mademoiselle Marianne de La Prise mentioned, whom, by the greatest chance in the world, I happened to have heard praised only a few days after my arrival in Neuchâtel. Her name gave me a strange sort of pleasure, and I looked everywhere to see what had provoked it, until I saw a rather tall, very slender, extremely well although simply dressed young person get up and come to the orchestra. I recognized her dress as the same which I had picked up as carefully as I was able from a muddy pavement one day. It's a long story which I may tell you one day if it has consequences, which I devoutly hope it doesn't—particularly now I hope so.

Anyway, coming back to Mademoiselle de La Prise: she was coming up to join the orchestra, and although it was very straightforward for her to be called what she was, and to be wearing the dress which I already knew belonged to her, it seemed very extraordinary that she should come and sing next to me, and that I should accompany her, that I should watch her walk and stop, pick up her music. I watched her with such an extraordinary expression on my face, as I was told later, that it's no surprise that she flushed, for I saw her flush to her eyes. She dropped her music, without my having the presence of mind to pick it up for her, and when it came to me picking up my violin, my neighbor had to tug my sleeve. I have never been so stupid, nor so cross to have been so; I blush every time I think of it, and I would have written to tell you about my embarrassment that very evening, if my masters hadn't seen fit to employ me for the hour between the end of the concert and the departure of the post in helping get the letters ready.

Mademoiselle de La Prise sings very prettily. But her voice isn't very large, and I'm sure that no one at the back of the hall would have heard her, even if they had been making less noise. I was shocked that she wasn't given a proper hearing, but almost pleased to think that they heard her so little. I would very much have liked to have taken her hand to escort her back to her place, and I would surely have done it if my distraction and my clumsiness hadn't reduced me to such a state of confusion. I was afraid of doing yet another stupid thing. Perhaps I might have tripped going down the steps and made her fall; I shudder to think of it. I was certainly quite right to stay where I was. The symphonies we played restored me a little, but I didn't hear any other singers. It seems to me nonetheless that there was one whose voice was much stronger and more beautiful than Mademoiselle de La Prise's; but I don't know who she is, and I didn't look at her. Good-bye, dear friend; I have to work on Thursday, but I arrange things so that I can have a little leisure on Friday, which is the only day of the week on which no post arrives or departs. I am already quite used to Neuchâtel and to the life that I lead here.

H. Meyer.

Letter V.

Julianne C*** to her aunt in Boudevilliers.

178*

My dear aunt,

You're going to be rather surprised, but I promise you it isn't my fault, and I'm sure that without that Marie Besson, who has a nasty tongue, although it would have been as well if she'd held it, given that her sister and she are always up to something, none of this would have happened. You know that I told you about Mademoiselle Marianne de La Prise's dress, which fell in the mud, and how a gentleman helped me to pick it up and wanted to come back with me to my mistresses, and I told you too that he gave me a coin, which that Marie Besson had so much to say about![8] And I told you too that the day after, he called by to ask if we'd been able to get the mud off the dress, and we had been able to, really well, and my mistresses had even made a pleat where it was dirtied, which Mademoiselle de La Prise thought was very good; because I told her the whole story, and she only laughed over it, and asked me the name of the gentleman, but I didn't know what it was. And when I had told all this to the gentleman, and how Mademoiselle de La Prise was such a good young lady, he asked me where I lived, and what I earned, and whether I liked my work.[9] And when afterward he made to go, I went out to hold the door for him, and when he went past he put a big coin in my hand. I think that he even shook my hand, or kissed me. And when I got back to the room, one of my mistresses and that Marie Besson started looking at me, and I said to Marie, "What's the matter with you that you want to gawp at me?" and my mistress said to me, "and you, why have you gone so red? What harm are we doing in looking at you?" and I said, "May God preserve me!" and set back to work, half-pleased, half-cross. And the next day, as it was a work day, I ran to Jeanne-Aimée's when I had a break to tell her all about it, and we fixed together that what I would buy with my money was a gauze handkerchief, a bonnet made of gauze with a wide brim, and a red ribbon to put round it. And on Sunday when I went to church, I met the gentleman, only he didn't recognize me because of my bonnet and my ribbon; he'd only seen me on weekdays. And lots of the young gentlemen from the warehouse where the gentleman works . . . said that I was really pretty, and didn't mention that Marie Besson at all, and she was already really grumpy and it only made her much worse, and all the rest of the day she was really distant with me, and would only call me "mademoiselle." But then it was even worse on Thursday, because I'd been left in the workshop all by myself to finish some things off, and at midday I went for a little walk at the fair, and I stopped in front of a boutique, which the gentleman had just gone into, and Jeanne-Aimée and me, we were looking at some gold crosses which were really beautiful, and the gentleman saw that, and gave us one each. It was thanks to me that he gave one to Jeanne-Aimée, for he didn't know her, and mine was a bit prettier. And I went back quick to the workshop, because I saw one of the young ladies that my mistresses worked for in the distance, and I left my cross with Jeanne-Aimée so she could put a ribbon on it, and she brought it back to me in the evening. And right when I was putting it round my neck, my mistresses came back sooner than expected. They were very severe and horrible with me: they said I was a flirt, that I left my work to run after these gentlemen, seeing as I got such fine presents. And that Marie Besson, instead of helping, made it just as bad as ever she could, and one of my mistresses said so often that it was a very bad thing for her to have flirts working for her, that in the end I said I'd leave straightaway, and I packed my stuff, and went to sleep at Jeanne-Aimée's house. And the next day, I rented a little room over a cobbler's, who is Jeanne-Aimée's aunt's cousin, and I do my own housework. I know well enough how to earn my way, thanks be to God, and I've already got enough to make two skirts and three short capes for the servants of one of my mistresses' regulars, who say it's not such a big thing to get presents from a gentleman; and I also know the shopgirls in a haberdashery who will probably have shifts and wrappers needing to be made up because they're really pretty, and I'm sure that gentlemen give them really fine presents; and if I ran out of money to buy wood and candles, butter and other such things, I'd probably meet that gentleman again who wouldn't let me go without, given that it's because of him that I had to leave my mistresses. And he could come and see me here, because he's not proud. Good-bye dearest aunt. Remember me to everyone and send my fond greetings.

J.C. . . .

Letter VI.

*Julianne C*** to Henri Meyer.*

Dear Sir,

I hope Sir will forgive the liberty of writing these words to him, since I wasn't able to find him in the streets to speak to him when I went out to find him, as was my intention; and then I think Sir would perhaps not like it if I made so bold as to speak to him by day in front of everyone; and evenings would be too late for a good girl to be out in the streets all alone. But I would have said to Sir, that as I have had to leave my place at my mistresses', who called me a flirt, and only because of the cross Sir gave me—it's not as if I'm asking Sir for anything, because I am not destitute; only wood is rather dear, and winter will still go on for a long time, and the windows in my room are so bad that I almost can't work, my hands are so cold. My lodging is at the cobbler's right at the end of rue des Chavannes.

I have the honor to be, Sir, your very humble and affectionate servant.

Julianne ***

Letter VII.

Henri Meyer to Julianne C***

Dear Miss,

After what happened yesterday, which I am sure has caused you even more distress than it did me, it is extremely clear that it would not be right for me to visit you anymore. I advise you to mend matters with your mistresses; you may reassure them that they will hear no more of me. I forgot yesterday to leave you the money that I brought you to buy wood and make your room more comfortable, supposing that you stay there; but I think you need not stay there. I add a further coin to the one I set aside for you, and implore you for your own sake, to start with paying a whole month's rent, and then go back to your mistresses, or perhaps to your relations in your village.

I am, Miss, your very humble servant.

H. Meyer.

Letter VIII.

Henri Meyer to Julianne C***

Dear Miss,

I think you may have been seen leaving my rooms, and I am very distressed for your sake as well as for my own. It is not very extraordinary that I should have let myself be moved by your tears, but I nonetheless greatly regret my weakness; and when I think back to your behavior, I don't see any evidence of such great partiality that it excuses me in my own eyes. I beg you to come here no more; I told the servant who saw you depart that if you were to come back, he should not let you in. I am resolved not to visit you anymore, such that you may regard our acquaintaince as entirely terminated.

H. Meyer.

Letter IX.

Henri Meyer to Godefroy Dorville.

Neuchâtel, January 1, 178*

I had a thoroughly boring time today, my dear friend. My master was kind enough to invite me to a grand dinner, where I saw more food eaten than I ever have before in my life and where we tasted and drank twenty different wines. Lots of people got rather drunk, and weren't the merrier for it: three or four young ladies whispered among themselves in a sly way, finding it very odd that I should talk to them, and hardly uttering a word in response; all their goodwill was aimed at two young officers. Their smiles and bursts of laughter were all to do with something that had been said earlier, and which I didn't have the key to. Sometimes I doubted even that these pretty young gigglers understood what they were saying themselves, because they looked as if they were laughing to look elegant rather than for gaiety. It seems to me that people hardly laugh here, and I expect that they don't weep either, other than to look elegant. You can see that I'm in an extremely bad temper, but it's because in reality I am exhausted with all the simpering I've seen and all the Neuchâtel wine which has passed in front of me. Wine is a terrible thing! For six weeks I haven't seen two people together but they were talking of the market price. It would be too long to explain to you what that is, and I'd bore you as much as I was bored in the first place. Suffice it to say that one half of the country finds too dear what the other half finds too cheap, according to their interests; and today everyone discussed the whole thing afresh, although it was all decided three weeks ago. As for me, if it becomes my profession to make money, I will try not to tell anyone about my lust for success, as it's a disgusting thing to talk about.

Only at one point of the dinner was I at all interested, but in a painful way. One of the young ladies talked about Mademoiselle de La Prise. She could not comprehend, said she, how someone with so little voice could possibly take it upon herself to sing at a concert.

"Her pretty face," said one of the young men, "makes up for everything."

"Pretty face!" said one of the young girls. "What can you mean? But then again, she must be pretty, because I have heard that she causes people to get quite distracted."

You can imagine how comfortable I was!

From that moment on, I didn't open my mouth. When my neighbors, having nothing better to do, addressed several questions to me, I replied with the baldest yeses and nos, and the instant that we got up from table, I ran home to breathe out all my bad temper with you. May all the rest of the days of this year be sweet, agreeable, innocent! This day has been one of gloomy solemnity. I asked myself what I had made of the year just finished; I compared myself with what I was one year ago, and my reflections completely failed to cheer me up. I am weeping; I am worried. A new period of my life has begun—I do not know how to survive it, nor how it will end. Good-byc, my friend.

H. Meyer.

Letter X.

Henri Meyer to Godefroy Dorville.

Neuchâtel, January 20, 178*

I have many things to tell you, dear Godefroy, and there is a strange chaos in my head. First I have to tell you that I was brought, three days ago, two tickets for the ball: one was handed to me in the morning, and the other in the afternoon, without my knowing whom I have to thank for it. At the moment when the second one was brought to me, I was with the work companion who is my true friend, and the only one with whom I experience any real companionship. "Oh I am so pleased," I burst out. "I've already got one; you can have this one." And I gave it to him on the spot. It was no sooner done than I felt I had blundered: these tickets were sent to me, and it was doubtful whether I had the right to dispose of them as I pleased. But how could I turn the clock back? How could I tell my overjoyed friend that he should give back the ticket until I'd checked? I could never have done it; and after all, what terrible evil could result from my imprudence? My friend is a fine young man, entirely decent and a much better dancer than I. I decided therefore to take on any difficulties arising from the business and to bear them courageously. Having taken this resolve, I danced a couple of entrechats, and left the house before my doubts could weigh me down or my friend notice them.

Yesterday, Friday, was the awaited, afeared, longed-for day, and we made our way to the assembly rooms, he very pleased, and I a little uneasy. The business of the ticket wasn't the only thing that was keeping my mind in suspense: I was sure that Mademoiselle de La Prise would be at the ball, and I was wondering whether I ought to greet her, and if so, how, and whether I could ask her to dance with me. My heart was thumping in my chest; I had her face and her dress in front of my eyes, and when in fact, on entering the rooms, I did see her sitting on a bench near the door, her real self was hardly less distinct than the picture of her in my mind. But I hesitated no longer, and without thought as without fear, I went straight up to her, spoke to her about the concert, about her little aria, and about other things too; and without worrying about the big round eyes, both inquisitive and surprised, of one of her companions, I asked her to do me the honor of dancing the first quadrille with me. She said that she was already engaged.

"Well then! The second."

"It's taken."

"The third?"

"It's taken."

"The fourth? The fifth? I will not give up," said I, laughing.

"Well you'll have a long time to wait," she replied. "It is already late, and we'll be starting soon. If Count Max, with whom I am engaged to dance the first quadrille, doesn't come by the time it starts, I will dance it with you, if you wish."

I thanked her, and at the same moment a lady came up to me, and said:

"Ah, Monsieur Meyer, you did receive my ticket?"

"Yes, madam," I said. "And I am very grateful to you. I even received two tickets, and I gave one to Monsieur Monin."

"How is this?" said the lady. "A ticket sent to you . . . ! That was not the intention, nor is it in the rules."

"I did indeed fear once it was done, madam, that I had been wrong; but it was too late, and I would rather not have come here, however much I wanted to, than have taken the ticket back and come without my friend. He doesn't have the slightest idea that I have been at fault, and he came with me completely unsuspecting."

"Oh well," said the lady. "There's no harm in it happening once."

"Indeed," I said, "if we are found wanting, we will not be invited a second time; but if people are so kind as to ask one of us again, I flatter myself that it won't be one without the other."

On which, she left me, casting from afar a gaze of examination and protection over my friend. "I will try to dance a quadrille with your friend," said Mademoiselle de La Prise, in a way which I found quite enchanting; and then, seeing that everyone was preparing for the quadrille, and that Count Max had not yet arrived, she charmingly, gracefully gave me her hand, and we took our places. We got to the head of the quadrille and were about to start, when Mademoiselle de La Prise burst out: "Oh, there is the count!" It was indeed him, and he came up to us with an air of chagrin and mortification. I went up to him. I said to him:

"Mademoiselle only allowed me to dance with her because you weren't there. She will find it right, I am sure, that I surrender my place to you; and perhaps she will have the goodness to compensate me later."

"No sir," said the count. "You are too kind, and it isn't fair; it was inexcusable of me to be late. My punishment is severe, but I deserved it."

Mademoiselle de La Prise seemed equally pleased with both the count and with me: she promised him the fourth quadrille, and she promised me to dance the fifth with my friend, and the sixth with me. I was very happy; I had never danced with so much pleasure. In that moment, the dance was something quite new; I found a *meaning*[10] for it, a sense, that it had never had for me before. I would have happily gone on my knees to its inventor; I thought he must have had a great deal of soul, and a young Lady de La Prise to dance with. It must have been young ladies like these who inspired the idea of Muses.

Mademoiselle de La Prise dances cheerfully, lightly, and with decorum. I have seen other young women here dance with more grace, and some with greater perfection, but not a single one who, all in all, dances more delightfully. You could say the same about her face: there are more beautiful and more striking ones, but none so appealing as hers; it seems to me, when I see how people look at her, that all men agree with me. What I find so surprising is the sort of trust and even gaiety which she inspires in me. I sometimes felt at that ball that we had known each other forever; sometimes I even asked myself if we hadn't met as children. I had the feeling that she was thinking the same thing, and I always knew what she was going to say. So long as I am satisfied with myself, I should like to have Mademoiselle de La Prise as witness for all my actions; were I to be dissatisfied, the shame and chagrin I feel would be doubled were she to know what it is that I blame myself for. There are certain things in my conduct from before the ball which had been bothering me quite a lot, but which bother me a good deal more now. I hope she doesn't know about them; I hope more than anything that her idea never leaves me more, and prevents me from falling back down. She would be such a pretty guardian angel, especially if one could attract her interest.

I made the acquaintance of Count Maximilien de R***. He is from Alsace, a Protestant, from an ancient and noble family. He is here with his brother, who is his elder, and who will be extremely rich. They have a tutor whom I have not yet met. Both of them are in the military, and have already progressed far. They have come here to complete their education. But

Count Max, as he is known, told me that he had not found the resources in literature and the fine arts which he had been led to expect. "But sir," said a man who was sitting next to us and who hadn't looked as if he'd been listening, "how is it that you have been sent to Neuchâtel for these things which you are desirous of learning? We have some talents, but no real knowledge at all: our wives act comedies very neatly, but they haven't read any apart from those they wish to act in; not one of us knows how to spell; our sermons are barbarous; our lawyers speak the local dialect; our public buildings lack common sense; our landscape designs are ridiculous. . . . Have you not seen the little ponds at the edge of the lake? We are even more lightweight, frivolous, and ignorant than . . ." At this moment Mademoiselle de La Prise came to warn the count that his quadrille was about to commence. I rose to follow him; we each said good-bye to our caustic commentator. His gall and exaggerations made me laugh.

While the count and Mademoiselle de La Prise were dancing their quadrille, the lady who had first addressed me came up to me, asked me where I was from and who I was. I replied that I was the son of a tradesman from Augsburg.

"A merchant, you mean," she said to me.

"No, madam," said I (and I felt myself flushing), "of a tradesman. I know the difference. My uncle, my mother's brother, is a rich merchant."

The lady apparently wished to be polite; but certainly it was not particularly polite to show disdain for what my father was, to the extent of needing to suppose that he was something better. She asked me where I had learned French. I told her that it was in France. She asked me for details of the R*** boarding school, and when I told her that I had spent some time in Geneva with a minister, a friend of my parents, who instructed me and prepared me to receive Communion, she talked to me about the different political factions, the Representatives and the Negatives.[11] The end of the quadrille interrupted our conversation once more, and I was very happy that it was so, for how can one talk about a subject that one does not understand in the slightest?

After having danced the sixth quadrille with Mademoiselle de La Prise and enjoying it even more than the first one, because I was not taking another man's place, I wanted to go. I was happy, and enough things had happened in my head for one day. However, I stopped to take leave of the lady who had spoken to me. She was talking to others in a rather lively manner: I heard my name, the word *energy*, the word *friendship*. Finally, she came up to me with another lady, who had a very serious and sweet air, and they told me that both I and my friend would be welcome at the next ball. I went to look for him on the instant. We thanked these ladies very sincerely, and then we left. Mademoiselle de La Prise was then dancing with Count Max's older brother.

Good-bye, my friend. When I call Monin my friend, the word *friend* signifies something quite different from when I talk about my friend Godefroy Dorville. Monin is a fine fellow whom I am happy to oblige, who makes my life pleasant, and who deserves to be distinguished from the sullen companions who expend all their energy on making little nests for themselves, and exert themselves less in the service of their own self-advancement than in the mortification of others. In their morose combats of one-upmanship, those who are preyed on always seem slightly less stupid than those who do the preying, to me.

H. Meyer.

Letter XI.

Mademoiselle de La Prise to Mademoiselle de Ville.

Neuchâtel, ***

Well, dearest Eugénie, winter is here and starting again, a second winter of dissipation and giddiness that I will spend without a friend, and quite probably without pleasure. I miss you as much today as I did a year ago. But society, which I did not then know, promised me compensation, which it hasn't given; I believed it held charms which vanished the instant I became part of it. And yet I do need to find pleasure. My father has not been his old self since his latest attack of gout; my mother is dissatisfied with our lodgings, our servants, with everything around her; she has quarreled with my father's sister and with my cousins. Little misdemeanors come from all directions, piling up day on day, and seem to get worse with every complaint. It is the saddest thing in the world. We were obliged to sell a small piece of land that we had in the Val-de-Travers, and the vines we have in Auvernier have hardly yielded anything, for lack of fertilizer and attention. My father is coming to terms with all this in the most courageous way: he made me subscribe to the ball, get two new dresses made, and take up my old tutors. He almost orders me to have fun and be merry, and I will obey him insofar as I can. His tenderness and the liberty which he wishes me to enjoy are certainly the only things which make my situation bearable. But my father is so weak! His legs are still swollen; you would hardly recognize him.

And what are you doing? Will you winter in Marseilles or in the countryside? Is your marriage thought of? Have you learned to do without me? As for me, I simply don't know what to do with my heart. When I actually express what I feel, what I expect from myself or from others, what I desire, what I think, no one understands; I don't interest anyone. With you everything had life; without you everything seems dead. It must be that others don't have the same need as I, because if someone had been looking for a heart, they would have found mine. Do not go thinking, however, that I will always be as sad and fearful as I am in this instant. My mother sent an old servant who'd been with us for ten years packing this morning; I wanted to write to you to distract myself, but I'll only have made you sad too.

The concert does not start for another month, and the assemblies not until after the new year. We have two German counts who are said to be extremely amiable. While we wait for our gatherings to recommence, I spend my evenings hemming napkins and playing piquet with my father. He wants me to sing at the concert. If I do, it won't hurt anyone one way or the other, for no one will hear me. But I managed to become really quite a good musician this summer, and I can accompany on the harp as well as on the harpsichord; but that's all I do. As for the pieces, I'll never be skillful enough to satisfy myself. Mademoiselle *** is getting married in a fortnight—you saw her love affair begin; it has been tepid and constant. I think this marriage will do very well; they will love each other for lack of any other object. I sometimes see my older cousin, despite the quarrel; she's a good girl, cheerful and sensible, but her sister has a narrow mind. Good-bye, my Eugénie; one day I'll write you a letter that won't be so flat and so sad.

Marianne de La Prise.

Letter XII.

Mademoiselle de La Prise to Mademoiselle de Ville.

*Neuchâtel, January **, 178**

So you cried, dear Eugénie, when you read my sad letter? I cried reading yours, I was so moved and so grateful. The sympathy of two hearts made for one another is a sweet thing. If we lived together, perhaps we would not need anything more to be happy; I confess I would be angry if you got married. At the moment, it would be too selfish to demand that you be all mine.

As for me, there is not much chance that I will escape you in that way. You know how much our fortune has diminished. Despite all his lack of concern for himself, my father sometimes worries over my own fate: he said to me often that after his death, which, he says, "cannot be far off," the pension that we all live off will cease, and I will have almost nothing. My mother will have the income which my uncle settled on her, and that will be enough to take care of her, especially if she wishes to go back to her home. But enough of that. I flatter myself my father is mistaken over the situation; I have no worries insofar as it concerns me. I just wanted to tell you that, in circumstances and with prospects such as these, it is rare to get married.

The concerts have begun; I sang in the first one. I think people laughed at me a bit because of my being a little embarrassed and troubled. I don't really know why—there are a number of such trivial reasons that I wouldn't even know how to explain them to you. Each one is nothing, taken separately, or must seem like nothing, even if it were something. Good-bye, my dear Eugénie; I will write you a longer letter another time.

Marianne de La Prise.

Letter XIII.

Mademoiselle de La Prise to Mademoiselle de Ville.

Neuchâtel, January **, 178*

I seem to want to tell you something, yet when it comes to the point, I can't see anything worth telling. Every day I get ready to write to you; I hold my pen for a long time, but no word is written. All the facts are so tiny that it would bore me to narrate them, and sometimes the impression I have is so strong that I would not know how to render it, and it's too confused for me to render it well. Sometimes it seems to me that nothing has happened; that I have nothing to tell you; that nothing has changed for me; that this winter started like any other; that there are, as there always are, a few young strangers in Neuchâtel whom I don't know, whose names I barely know, with whom I have nothing in common. In fact, I went to the concert; I dropped a sheet of music; I sang quite badly; I went to the first assembly ball; I danced with everyone, among whom were two counts from Alsace and two young warehouse clerks—is there anything extraordinary in all of that, anything to make a detailed story out of? Other times I think a thousand things have happened to me, that if you had the patience to hear me out, I would have an immense story to tell: it seems to me that I have changed; that the world has changed; that I have new hopes and new fears which make me indifferent to everything that I have cared about until now, except for you and my father, and which conversely have made me care

about things which I never used even to look at or which I performed mechanically. I sense that some people guard me, and
that others attack me; my mind and my heart are, in a word,
in chaos. Allow me, my dear Eugénie, not to tell you any more
until things have disentangled themselves a bit and until I have
returned to my ordinary state, always supposing I am able to.
Not to tell you anything would have been too painful; to tell
you any more, when I don't know anything myself, would not
be possible. So good-bye. I send you fond kisses. Everything I
find out about myself, you shall find out. At least no mistrust
will keep me from speaking—the fear of seeming childish, or
of making a bad impression, could not stop me speaking; the
fear of being a bore is the only thing stopping me.

                                          M. de La Prise.

Letter XIV.

Mademoiselle de La Prise to Mademoiselle de Ville.

Neuchâtel, January **, 178*

Do you absolutely insist? Well then, I'll tell you! I wrote you a
letter which, once I'd written it, seemed quite mad. I wrote you
another to apologize for the first one, and then I discovered I
hadn't sent it anyway. I'd sealed it but then forgotten to take it
to the post. At that point I didn't know what I was doing. I'm
going to send it to you without opening it—I do not want to
read it again; I can barely remember what's in it. You will see
what I was thinking.

All the details you send about yourself are charming: you
will not love, you will never love the man being destined for
you; that is to say, you will never love him very much. If you
don't marry him, you may very well marry somebody else. If
you do marry him, you will be considerate to each other; you
may enjoy each other's company, perhaps. You will not
demand that he look exclusively at you, nor he that you look
only at him. You will not reproach yourself for having looked
at something else or having thought about something else, for

having said something which might hurt him for a second; you will explain what you meant, and it will have been perfectly straightforward, and all will be well. You and I will understand each other better; we have always understood each other, and there has been a sympathy between us which you two will never share. If it suits you, marry him. But think about it first. Look around you to see if another person might not evoke a different feeling. Haven't you read any novels? And have you never shared the feeling of some heroine? Know also that your suitor will not love you differently from how you love him. Tell him, for example, that you have a friend who loves you dearly, and that you don't love anyone as much as her. See whether he flushes or becomes angry; if he does, don't marry him. If it doesn't move him either way, don't marry him either. But if he says he regrets that he will be keeping you far from me, and that you'll come to Neuchâtel together to see me, then he will be a good husband, and you can marry him. I do not know where I get everything I'm saying to you; before now I never even thought of it. Perhaps it's not even common sense. I confess, however, that I think highly of my observations . . . not my observations, but—how can I explain it?—the light I suddenly found in my heart, seemingly shining just to show you yours. Yet don't trust what I say; ask and think. No, don't ask anyone—no one will understand you; just examine yourself. Good-bye.

M. de La Prise.

Letter XV.

Written before the twelfth letter, and enclosed, along with the sixteenth, in the previous letter.

Neuchâtel, *** 178*

Might there be a lover looking for my heart? And might I have found him? My dear Eugénie, I can just imagine how your delicacy is alarmed! I did not say *prudishness*—please admire my politeness, for your big eyes, which I see wide open and looking at me in surprise and scandal, do not deserve such courtesy. I will go my way as if you weren't a very delicate and careful person, and you can go yours, getting indignant and preaching at me, if you wish; neither of us should be the least inhibited. I am going to tell you exactly what is happening to me.

Some time ago a little seamstress dropped a dress she was bringing to me in the mud. A young foreigner picked it up for her, accompanied her back to her workshop, explained what had happened to her mistresses, and, on leaving, gave her some money. I heard the story on the very next day; I liked it. I saw goodness and a sort of bravery in it, for the young girl, pretty it is true, is so badly dressed and has such poor manners that your normal dandy would not have cared to be seen with her in the street. I asked the young man's name, but she wasn't able to tell me what it was, and I heard no more about it. The other day, at the concert, the girls sitting next to me in the gallery pointed out a young man who was playing violin in the orchestra. They told me that he was a young German, working in M***'s warehouse, and that his name was Meyer. When I walked by him on my way to go and sing, I looked at him closely. He looked at me too; I saw that he recognized my dress. And I recognized the physiognomy of the person who would have picked it up; and we were so busy contemplating each other that I dropped my music, and he forgot his violin, neither of us knowing what was happening, nor what we were supposed to be doing. He blushed; I did too, but I don't really know why, because I wasn't in the least ashamed. People teased me about his absentmindedness; I was tempted to reply that I was just the same, and then I realized that no one had perceived it. Apparently it is the done thing for a young man to be in love for a few weeks before the heroine is allowed to be the slightest bit susceptible to him.[12] I will not boast of having conformed to this decent custom, and if it turns out that Monsieur Meyer is as in love with me as I thought he was, he will be able to boast that I was as smitten as he was and from the very same instant. You see that I am completely differently disposed now than I was the last time I wrote; I confess that I couldn't be

happier. Whatever else happens to me, I think that if I am passionately loved, and if I love passionately, I would be unable to
be unhappy. It's no use my mother scolding me anymore; it
makes no dent in my happiness. My friends no longer seem so
sullen—look what I'm saying, *my friends*, but it's out of pure
overflowing benevolence, for really I have no friends apart
from you. I even prefer you to Monsieur Meyer himself, and
if you were here, and you liked him, I'd give him up to you.
Don't go supposing that we've exchanged a word yet; I haven't
even seen him since the concert. But I do hope he'll come to
the first assembly ball; our ladies, without my needing to ask
them, will be gallant enough to invite him. And then I'm sure
that we will speak, even if I have to be the first to do so. I will
be sitting near the door when he arrives. And that will decide
the question: to know whether Monsieur Meyer will be the
soul of your friend's entire life, or whether I will just have
been indulging in a pleasant dream. It'll be one or the other,
and a few seconds will decide which. Good-bye, my Eugénie!
My father is even more pleased with me than usual; he finds
me charming. He says there's nothing to equal his daughter,
and that he wouldn't exchange her for the best legs in the
world. You see that my madness is good for something at least.
Good-bye.

M. de La Prise.

Letter XVI.

To the same.

*Neuchâtel, January **, 178**

I can't wait for your reply. My last letter was so extraordinary
and so mad that I need to apologize for it. Or perhaps explain
it, because there's no apology to make. I have returned to common sense, but I'm almost sorry for it, for those four or five
days of madness were charming. Everything I did amused me.
My harpsichord and my harp were everything but a harp and
a harpsichord; they were living—I spoke and my replies came

through them. My head has returned to normal, and all I'm left with is a rather natural curiosity to know whether Monsieur Meyer is as good and decent as he seemed to be; whether he has good sense; whether he is amiable—all will be revealed and I will let you know. Do not worry that I will commit or say any folly; you know I've always had these extravagant moments and that nothing too bad ever comes of them. I believe it is the great liberty my father has given me as well as the great freedom of his speech which have prevented me from having the reserve and timidity which suit you so well. Good-bye. Please don't stop being indulgent with me, and trust me when I say I won't test you too far.

M. de La Prise.

Letter XVII.

Julianne C*** to her aunt in Boudevilliers.

Neuchâtel, January **, 178*

My dear aunt,

I went back to my mistresses seeing as you advised me to, and the gentleman too. Monsieur Meyer is what his name is; I know his name now, but what good will that do me? Yesterday it was five weeks since I saw him last, and I wish I'd never met him; but I think he thought that . . . but what's the point of telling you all this? I haven't stopped crying, and there's something he put down in his letter (because he wrote me two) which made me think as far as I could understand it that perhaps that Marie Besson did really tell him I wasn't a decent girl; but all the same, my dear aunt, apart from that horrible clockmaker that I worked for, and who was married into the bargain, there isn't a girl as good as me in all of the Val-de-Ruz, because even if I did joke with the boys when we stayed up late or when it was harvesttime, the other girls did just the same as me; and I don't know whether that would make a gentleman think I wasn't a good girl.[13] But there we are; there's no use in crying and being sorry for yourself once it's too late, and if I'm going to cry, I might as well wait until I'm sure of it. I had to beg my mistresses, but it's also because they've got a good deal of work at the moment, because of the balls and the gatherings and the concerts, and perhaps plays too; and I wouldn't know what else, would I? These ladies are all very good at enjoying themselves. Perhaps they're not as good as a poor girl who's left to cry while she works, who hasn't been to any of their lessons and boarding schools, who didn't learn to read from their beautiful books; and so that they can have bonnets and ribbons and dresses with gauze trimming we have to work all night and sometimes Sunday too; and they have all that whenever they want, from their mother or their husband, without any young gentleman giving it to them, and what difference does that make? If cousin Jeanne-Marie and cousin Abram don't know anything about the gentleman, nor that I left my mistresses, then there's no point telling them about it for the moment. I am, my dear aunt, your very humble niece.

Julianne C.

Letter XVIII.

Henri Meyer to Godefroy Dorville.

Neuchâtel, January **, 178*

You find that the style of my letters has changed, my dear Godefroy. Why don't you tell me whether it's for the worse, or for the better? But it seems to me that it must be for the better, even if I myself have changed for the worse. I am no longer a child, it is true—I almost said it is only too true; but all things considered, given that life goes on, we have to go on with it! Whether we want to or not, we change; we learn things; we take responsibility for our actions. We are no longer so carefree; our gaiety slips. If wisdom and happiness were to take their place, we'd have nothing to regret. Do you remember reading the Huron together? In it Mademoiselle de K***, I've forgotten the rest of her name, became a different person over the course of two or three days. *A person*—I didn't understand then what that meant; I do understand now.[14] I see very well that I have to pay dearly for the experience I am acquiring; but I would like it if others didn't have to pay for it too. But that is difficult, for one does nothing alone, and nothing happens to us alone.

In my last letter, I recounted what happened at the assembly ball, where I danced with Mademoiselle de La Prise. I stayed two or three days without going out at all; I didn't even go out for a walk. But on the Tuesday I was invited to dinner at my master's, there weren't so many people as at New Year; there were only men, and some were the same age as I, and among them were some who seemed very pleasant, and more than that very decent and gentle. We had got up from table and were taking coffee when the acerbic gentleman from the ball came in. We reproached him for not coming sooner. "I am obliged to you," he replied, "but I almost never eat outside my own house as I am perfectly acquainted with the wines from all of your neighborhoods, and the cheese from all your mountains." After that he came up to some of the young people, among whom I was standing, and asked me what they had been talking about when he entered.

"About some young ladies," replied one of them. "We were discussing who was prettiest, and we were arguing about it."

"Still?" he interrupted. "And who has been named?"

On which they named a good many. "Good!" said he brusquely. "That's what I expected. I see the preference goes to the dolls, the puppets, and the parrots. There is one . . ." I was next to the door; I was holding my hat. I left. "Stay," he shouted out to me. "I will not name her." I pretended not to have heard, and went down the stairs as quickly as I was able.

The Friday after that, I had settled that I would spend the evening alone reading and writing to my uncle. But Count Max came to see me, knowing, said he, that Fridays were my days of leisure. He stayed with me until seven o'clock. He is pleasant and knowledgeable; his language refreshes my ear, scoured every day by the atrocious German of Bern, Bâle, and Mulhouse.

I've forgotten my language a bit; the count criticized me for it. He will lend me German books; he spent eighteen months in Leipzig.

I admire my sangfroid in spending so long telling you what happened on Friday; Sunday was the really interesting day. Perhaps I lingered on Friday because of feeling apprehensive about Sunday. It was such a strange mixture of happy and unhappy encounters, of pain and pleasure! I think I behaved well, that is to say that I couldn't behave in any other way. You suppose that there's some big story to tell? No; the whole thing was over in a quarter of an hour. But what went before, the circumstances . . . so that you know what that is, I'll have to tell you in the end. Perhaps you'll guess what I don't say; and if you only guess the half of it, that won't be a bad thing.

It rained a lot earlier in the week. These last days it has been very cold: on Sunday morning snow fell and it got a little warmer, but in the early afternoon the cold set in again, and the water in the streets and the snow from the morning froze into black ice, worse than I've ever seen it before, and it got more dangerous with every moment as the evening air got colder. Monin and I were coming back from the ridge where we'd been for a walk to enjoy the last of the sun that had still been shining when we came out of church. We needed all our attention not to fall. Imagine the difficulty Mademoiselle de La Prise and two other young ladies were having and the danger they were in when we came on them near the town gates, going the same way we were. I stopped in front of them; I think I wanted to stop them going any farther, thinking I could already see Mademoiselle de La Prise lying on the pavement, wounded, bruised, or perhaps even worse. I don't know what I said to make them accept our help, but the two I didn't know were starting to refuse, when Mademoiselle de La Prise said sharply: "Don't be foolish, you two! We're very lucky!" At the same time, she took Monin's arm, and asked me to look after her companions.

We were walking along without a word, only thinking of keeping upright. We had only gone perhaps a hundred steps, when I saw a young girl I had previously met by chance, whom some small boys were throwing snowballs at to make her fall over. She recognized me. Her air expressed all sorts of difficulty. She was the very picture of distress, and really not knowing what she was doing, between anger and confusion, she was in real danger; she could have fallen against the edge or a corner of a building. She was the first girl I spoke to in Neuchâtel, and I helped her on a much less serious occasion. I didn't know Mademoiselle de La Prise then. Should I scorn to know her and pass by? I abruptly told the girls I was helping along and whom I leaned against Monin not to move from their place, and going toward the two little boys, I gave each a vigorous slap, and seeing a man nearby who looked decent enough, I asked him, as pleasantly as I could, to accompany the girl to where she wanted to go. After that I went back to my two young ladies and we carried on walking.

After a few seconds of silence, one of them said:

"Do you know that girl, sir?"

"Yes, madam," I replied. "I met her a few days after I arrived in Neuchâtel. . . ."

I didn't speak further. I couldn't tell my story to the end—the beginning did me greater honor than the end; it would have been a lie. One thing stopped me. When I started speaking, I looked at Mademoiselle de La Prise, as much as the ice allowed me to, and I thought I saw that her face had gone very red and that her expression was much altered. To tell you everything I felt, all the pain, the regret, the hope, the pleasure, would not be possible. Had I allowed myself to think of nothing else, the two girls would have been better off walking alone. I imposed silence on my heart; I put it off, so to speak, to another time to feel, wonder, delight at what was happening in it, for the pleasure was greater than the pain. Nobody spoke again.

When we arrived at the house where their party was, I took my leave of my two ladies without a word; they thanked me. Mademoiselle de La Prise did not speak, and satisfied herself with a deep curtsy to Monin. It was already dark beneath the porch, but I imagined she looked moved. At the same instant Count Max arrived and gave her his hand; he recognized me as I was leaving.

"Where are you going?" he cried out to me.

"Home," said I.

"And what will you do at home?"

"Play music."

"You are rather brusque," he said, laughing, "but I don't mind."

I went home. I would have preferred to be alone for at least one or two hours, but that wasn't possible. Neuss and my teacher arrived, Monin did the honors of my room, and after tea we started playing. Half an hour later, the count came in, asking us if he might listen. He doesn't like cards. Another time he'll bring his flute. At nine o'clock he made me go and have supper with him. I wanted to; it was unbearable being in that little group of companions. His tutor seems to be a sensible man, but he hardly speaks French. His older brother didn't go home until eleven o'clock; he seems very brilliant and obliging. Well what a long letter this is. I went to the concert on Monday; Mademoiselle de La Prise wasn't there. On Tuesday I only left home to go to the warehouse, and I'll write to you all about Wednesday tomorrow.

H. Meyer.

Letter XIX.

Henri Meyer to Godefroy Dorville.

*Neuchâtel, January **, 178**

Yesterday after dinner Count Max came to fetch me so we could go for a walk. The weather was very good. There isn't much choice here. We went up on the ridge and as far as the tree-lined walk. We met Mademoiselle de La Prise with one of her cousins. We asked for permission to accompany them; permission was given. After walking for a while, we turned back toward town. We talked nonchalantly about all sorts of things. The count was very agreeable. Mademoiselle de La Prise was lively. The cousin and I were almost mute. But I was happy: I listened with pleasure; I was relatively tranquil; I didn't wish for anything extraordinary to happen this time. And in fact we did not meet anyone, and no one came up to us. But as we were drawing near to Mademoiselle de La Prise's house, a light rain started to fall and it got increasingly heavy as we went along, such that it was raining quite hard by the time we reached her house. She very civilly asked us to come in, assuring us that her father and mother would be very happy to see us. We went up—there was not much to do at the warehouse that day, and the night before I had worked until quite late and missed the concert, as our masters had a lot of work on. I therefore thought I might stay if we were asked to.

Monsieur de La Prise is a military man, aged more by gout than years, and was in the service of France before his retirement. He looks as if he has enjoyed every variety of pleasure, and as if he still enjoys company; mainly, though, he looks as if he loves his daughter more than anything in the world. She resembles him. His manners are open and frank; rather free in his talk, he is pleasant and polite in his ways. I have been told that his family is one of the most ancient in the land, and that he was born to a fortune but that he has spent it all. To see him is to believe it.

I will not say anything about her mother. She doesn't look like her husband's wife, or her daughter's mother. She is French, from I don't know where. She must have been very beautiful, and still is. In her own way she was very polite to us. We were given tea, and served grapes and cakes. This little meal, which I had previously viewed as very ill conceived, seemed very pleasant yesterday. With Monsieur de La Prise and Miss Marianne, I felt as if I was part of the family. She did not offer me anything that I did not accept. She handed clusters of grapes to Count Max and me. For the first time I was no longer a stranger in Neuchâtel.

The rain having stopped and tea being over, we made as if to leave, but the father suggested we play a little music with his daughter. Straightaway I told the count that I would fetch his flute and my violin, checking at the warehouse if they could do without me, which I was almost certain they could. He thought this was an excellent idea. I dashed off and was soon back.

The little concert could not have been more agreeable. Mademoiselle de La Prise is an extremely accomplished accompanist—she is a real musician—and Count Max's embouchure is unsurpassed. The flute is a very touching instrument, and goes straight to the heart in a way nothing else can. The evening flew by, and soon it was nearly nine o'clock. Madame de La Prise conveyed this to us by nervously tidying up everything around us. Her husband entreated her to let us continue playing, and then, looking at the clock, said to us, "Gentlemen, when I was rich, I had no notion of letting people leave me at nine o'clock; even though I no longer am, I still can't bear to, and if you would like to stay to supper with us, you would give me great pleasure." Madame de La Prise said: "If only you'd thought to say so a little earlier!" And on saying this, she left the room. Her husband, leaning on his stick, followed her, and called to her from the door: "Do not trouble yourself, my wife, and don't spend too long preparing supper; they'll eat an omelet." As for us, we had neither accepted nor refused; but it was clear that we were going to stay, and we carried on playing. Mademoiselle de La Prise was, I think, very relieved that we seemed not to have heard what her mother said.

A quarter of an hour later we were told that supper was ready, and we went to sit down at the table. Supper was decent and simple. I have to confess that Madame de La Prise was not too disagreeable a hostess. Her daughter was very cheerful and bright—her father seemed delighted with her, and certainly it was the case that her guests were no less so.

At ten o'clock, a relation and his wife came to call. News was exchanged, and there was talk of a young woman from Vaud, who is to marry a rich and very difficult man while being passionately loved by a man from somewhere else who has no fortune but who is very worthy and full of spirit. "And does she love him?" someone asked. "Yes," came the reply, "as much as she herself is loved."

"Well in that case, she is very much to blame," said Monsieur de La Prise.

"But it's a very good match for her," said madam. "That girl has nothing; she couldn't do better."

"She could go begging with the one she loves," said Mademoiselle de La Prise, under her breath, who had not until that point taken any part in the whole conversation.

"Go begging with the other one!" repeated her mother. "Well there's a fine thing for a young lady to say! I really believe you must be mad!"

"No, no, she is not mad; she is right," said her father. "I think it is a fine thing, myself! It was what was in my own heart when I married you."

"Yes, well, and look what came of it!"

"It is not absolutely bad," said the father, "seeing as this girl was born from it."

At this, Mademoiselle de La Prise, who had been sitting with her hands over her eyes, head bent over her plate, slid the length of a stool which was half under the table between herself and her father, and on which he was resting both legs, and knelt down by him, clasping her father's hands in her own, her face pressing against them, her eyes welling with tears, and her lips covering them with kisses; we heard her quietly weeping. It is a scene which is quite impossible to convey. Monsieur de La Prise, without saying anything to his daughter, raised her, and seated her on the stool before him, so that her back was turned to the table. He held one of her hands; with the other she wiped her tears. No one spoke. After a few moments she went to the door without turning round, and left. I got up to shut the door, which she had left open. Everyone stood up. Count Max got his hat and I mine.

As we were going up to Madame de La Prise to say our good-byes, her daughter came back in. Her manner had returned to its normal serenity.

"You should beg these gentlemen for discretion," said her mother to her. "What will people think of you if they hear the sorts of things you say?"

"Oh, my dear mother," said her daughter, "if we don't mention it anymore, we may hope for it to be forgotten."

"Do not flatter yourself, mademoiselle," said the count. "I fear I shall not forget it for a long time."

   We left. We walked some way without talking. In the end,
the count said, "If I were richer . . . But it's almost impossible;
I mustn't think of it. I shall try not to think of it for a single
second longer. But what about you?" He turned to me and
took my hand. We shook hands, I embraced him, and we separated. Good-bye Godefroy. I couldn't sleep a wink last night; I
am going to bed.

                                                          H. Meyer.

Letter XX.

To the same.

Sunday for Monday.

                                  *Neuchâtel, February ** , 178**
I wrote to you on Wednesday, and I sent my letter on Thursday without adding anything. We worked hard, and until very
late. On Friday I had such a bad headache that I did not go
out. Monin kept me company—he read to me, and we played
music. He is a very good fellow. . . . Speaking of which, I must
tell you something which he told me that evening.
   The night before, as he was coming into the fencing school to
speak to someone, he heard some young men mention my
name. He didn't hear a word of what they were saying, but he
saw Count Max interrupt his practice with the instructor and
walk up to them. "I find it extremely regrettable, gentlemen,"
he said to them, "that you should take this tone when speaking
of such an excellent young man, and particularly regrettable
that you should do so in front of me, whom you know to be his
friend." When Monin told me this, I felt, for the first thing,
that there may be some pleasure in being a great gentleman. I
wish, Godefroy, that I were able to adopt a similar tone, and be
as imposing as the count, if he, or Mademoiselle de La Prise, or
you, ever needed to be defended. But none of you need any
defending. Who could ever say anything bad about you?

On Saturday, that is, yesterday, the count came to fetch me for a visit to Monsieur and Madame de La Prise. It was the right thing to do, after the supper we had had at their house. But Monin had made me promise not to go out at all, and stay in today too: I've got a very bad cold, and he claims that neglected colds are long-lasting and nasty this year. This excellent fellow worked an extra two hours yesterday at the warehouse to get all my work finished.

So the count went off on his visit alone, and he told me about it in the evening, sitting by my fire. Monsieur de La Prise was the only one at home, and after exchanging commonplaces, he spoke to his visitor about his daughter, saying that after his death unfortunately it was not impossible that she might need the protection of someone like him to help obtain a position at a German court. "I was young for a long time," he said. "I spent a lot of money; but nature has compensated my daughter for my foolishness with her inheritance, and in reality her lot is better than that of many. And I do not feel sorry for her. At least I do not have to reproach myself with having neglected her for an instant since she came into the world. That is hardly surprising: what father would neglect such a daughter . . . ? But, count, coming back to what I was saying before, I assure you that she is well enough born to have no difficulty in securing a position in whatever role in the retinue of even the highest princess in Europe. My ancestors came to this land with Philibert de Chalon, who was sovereign over it; our name was ***.[15] The younger branch, to differentiate itself, took the name de La Prise; the older branch, which possessed much land and wealth in Burgundy, has died out. I have extremely solid proofs of all this. I am not telling you this to boast, but so that you don't forget it, if someday my daughter needs you to make her known. Then you will be able to learn with your own eyes what I have the honor of telling you now. My daughter is amiable enough for it not to be a chore to be of service to her . . . but here she is, coming back, and as this discussion is not very cheerful, let us speak of something else." The count has a good memory, and mine isn't bad either; and you can be sure that you have here what Monsieur de La Prise said, word for word. It gave me much to think about, and if our evening was pleasant, it is because the count is truly amiable, and has real friendship for me; otherwise it was not a very cheerful one. Tomorrow I will be well enough to go to the concert. Miss Marianne will sing at it in accordance with her father's wishes. I will sit as close to her as I can so that I can hear her better and accompany her better. Good-bye, my dear Godefroy.

H. Meyer.

Letter XXI.

To the same.

Neuchâtel, February **, 178*

However am I to tell you everything there is to say? Will you blame me? Will you pity me? Or will Mademoiselle de La Prise alone strike your imagination, and banish your friend from view? But why do I even spend time in empty thought and conjecture, when my faculties barely suffice for what is happening to me and for what I need to try to tell you? Oh Godefroy, so many things have happened to me! I have been feeling so many things! Will I be able to relate it all in any semblance of order?

Yesterday at three o'clock I was still in complete ignorance, and I cheerfully made my way to the assembly rooms. I go in. I look around for Mademoiselle de La Prise. She wasn't yet in the room. But she arrived an instant later. I went to her. I found her pale. She had a serious air, and a certain solemnity which I hadn't previously seen in her. I felt myself growing paler as I greeted her, and was not immediately able to speak. I soon recovered, however, and asked her which quadrille she would do me the honor of dancing with me. She replied that she was planning not to dance, and looking around for Count Max, she said to him, once he'd come up: "Count, I have to talk to Monsieur Meyer. It may take a while, and it may give an odd impression to be saying so many things to him alone.

You are his friend. I believe you to be honest and discreet; I do not think you will be tempted to mock someone who, out of compassion for another young woman, speaks to a man about a chapter which ought to be completely unknown to her; I am sure that you will not mock me. Would you be so kind as to give up dancing this evening, like me? In a few instants, we will all sit down on this bench; you will place yourself between Monsieur Meyer and me, so that it looks as if I am talking to you both. We will often be interrupted—we must not look as if we mind; we will have to separate sometimes and leave off conversation before taking it up again. I ask your pardon for this preamble. It must make me seem strangely particular. I confess that I am distressed, and it seems to me that I have a very important piece of business to carry out. Otherwise, it is not that surprising that at my age . . . but let me speak for a little while with my friends. I will come and join you once the dancing has begun." I needed her to stop—I urgently needed to sit down; my legs were giving way under me. I was more dead than alive. She had not looked at me; she had in fact looked away from me all the time she was speaking. I leaned on the count. We went to sit down.

"But," he said, "have you guessed what she has to say to you?"

"Not exactly," I replied.

"Out of compassion for another young woman?" he asked.

I said nothing. Mademoiselle de La Prise came back and sat next to him. "But sir," she said to him, "I did not wait for your reply; are you willing to give up part of an evening which should be cheerful and amusing to listen instead to a rather sad story which has nothing to do with you?" The count assured her that he was at her service. "And you," she said to me. "Sir, I have not even asked you if you accept my meddling in your affairs." A nod was all my response.

"And do you also consent to the count knowing everything that might have happened to you since you came to Neuchâtel? I should have asked you before."

"I will consent to everything you wish, mademoiselle."

"Well then," she said, "I will tell you that there were two

seamstresses working yesterday at my mother's house with a young woman they had brought with them, who I observed was pale, sad, and agitated all day long. This young person asked me not to go out in the evening as I had meant to, but to stay in and allow her to talk to me alone, on the pretext of trying on the dresses in my room. . . ."

Here we were interrupted by a number of women. Mademoiselle de La Prise got one to sit down between her and the count. Imagine, if you can, the state I was in.

They finally left us, and Mademoiselle de La Prise, rightly supposing that we had not lost the thread of her tale, took it up where she had left off: "I said yes, and when we were alone, she told me, sir, how she had met you, how you had helped her, by what fatal stroke of fortune the acquaintance had continued; and she finally told me, in a fit of tears, that she was with child, and that she did not know what was to become of her, where to go, nor how to support herself and the child." Mademoiselle de La Prise ceased speaking. For a long time, I was unable to say a word. I tried many times; I even started— in the end I was able to make myself understood.

"Did she tell you, mademoiselle, that I had seduced her against her will, that I had forced myself upon her?"

"No, sir."

"Did she tell you, mademoiselle, when and how I stopped seeing her?"

"Yes, sir," she said. "She even trusted me to the extent of showing me your letters."

"Well then! Mademoiselle, she will not be abandoned in her hour of destitution, shame, and misery; and her child shall not be abandoned, if I am the father, if I am right to believe it. He will be cared for, brought up; I will look after him for as long as I live. But for now, please be so kind as to give me space to breathe. I am not in a fit state even to thank you. I am going outside; I will return in a quarter of an hour. This is so new! I am so young! I have known women for so little time . . . ! And now such sharp, such different interests conflict and follow on from one another! But she told you that I did not seduce her against her will, and that I have not seen her for at least two months? I must certainly help her. . . ."

As I said this, I got up and ran out into the street, where I spent nearly an hour, walking up and down, stopping short like a madman. Me, Godefroy, a mistress who is with child! Me, soon to be a father! Finally, remembering my promise, I went back in. Mademoiselle de La Prise had a softer, more smiling air. She pressed me to take some tea, and herself ensured that I was given it. The count came back to us; we sat down.

"Well, Monsieur Meyer, what do you want me to say to the girl?"

"Mademoiselle," I replied, "promise her or give her, or have her given, I mean, by some old trusted servant, your nurse or your governess, please be so kind as to give her, every month, or every week, whatever you deem suitable. I will subscribe to it all. Too happy that it should have been you . . . ! I might not have chosen you perhaps, yet, I find that I am happy that it should be you who has deigned to take this on. It is a sort of link, but what am I saying? At the very least, I shall be eternally indebted to you; and you will never be able to reject my gratitude, my respect, my services, my devotion."

"I shall not reject them," she said, and the tone of her voice enchanted me. "But it is much more than I deserve."

I said to her again:

"Will you really undertake this charge? Do you promise me? That the girl will not suffer? That she will not need to work more than suits her? That she will not have to endure insult or blame?"

"Have no fear," she said to me. "I will render up a strict account of my doings every time I see you, and I will collect thanks for my efforts and monies for my expenses."

On saying these last words, she smiled. "Then it will not be necessary for him to see her again?" asked the count. "Not at all necessary," she said, rather hurriedly. I looked at her. She saw my look; she blushed. I was sitting next to her; I bent down to the ground.

"What have you dropped?" she asked. "What are you looking for?"

"Nothing. I kissed the hem of your dress. You are an angel, a goddess!"

I got up then, and went to stand a little way from them. My tears flowed, but I did not mind, and only they could see me.

Count Max was moved and Mademoiselle de La Prise even more so: they spoke generously of me for a while. "The story would end well," they were saying. "The girl was to be pitied, but wouldn't be in absolute misery." They agreed to go and see her immediately at Mademoiselle de La Prise's home, where she was still at work. I was commanded to stay, so as not to raise any suspicion, and to dance if I were able. I gave my purse to the count, and watched them leave. And thus that strange evening drew to a close.

Saturday evening

I met our caustic commentator in the street. He stopped me with an air of benevolence. "Mister foreigner!" said he. "We are not wicked, but we are astute, and proud of it. Everyone is quick to suspect and to guess, for fear of not being the first with any news. Now, as we are barely aware of the passions, in certain cases we only go so far as to imagine an intrigue. . . . Be careful. It is so little your intention to give rise to any suspicions about an intrigue between yourself and the most amiable girl in Neuchâtel that I beg you not to agree with me." And he went on his way.

I am sending you a copy of the letter I have written to my uncle. The count found a way of reading it to Mademoiselle de La Prise; she sealed it herself and he took it to the post himself.

Letter XXII.

To Monsieur *** in Frankfurt.

Neuchâtel, February **, 178*

My dear uncle,

A young seamstress, whom I did not seduce against her will, says she is with child, and that I am the father. Various circumstances and in particular the person she confided in persuade me that she is telling the truth. I have enough to supply her wants for the moment, and as for the child, whatever my fortune is, he will never want for bread, any more than I, for as long as I live. But if I die before I am old enough to make a will, I beg you, dear uncle, to regard the child of Julianne C***, whom Mademoiselle Marianne de La Prise will confirm is mine, as being effectively the child of your nephew. I do not commend him to your care; that would be superfluous.

I have the honor of being,
My dear uncle,
Your very humble and most obedient servant.

H. Meyer.

Letter XXIII.

To Monsieur Henri Meyer.

*Frankfurt, February **, 178**

Send the girl here. Neglect nothing to ensure that she travels safely; I will pay the costs. I want her to give birth here. I will look after her. But only on condition that she depart after giving birth, and leave me the child. I will even do something for her, if I am pleased with her conduct. I know that in Neuchâtel the way in which children are baptized records their status; I do not want yours to grow up in that sad knowledge. If he learns it one day, it will be once he's happy enough with his existence not to blame you for it, and once you have proved yourself worthy, such that he prefers his birth, despite its stain, to any other birth, and that he would choose you for a father, were he to have the choice. Only by dint of virtue, Henri, can you lift this shame from your son or daughter, and only you can do it. Ask yourself if you are not obliged to do this.

Charles D.

I enclose a check for fifty louis.[16]

Letter XXIV.

To Monsieur Charles D***, Frankfurt.

Neuchâtel, February **, 178*

My dearest uncle,
     The girl has gone. What can I say? It is not thanks that I owe
you. May the heavens bless you! May my child . . .! I am
unable to say any more.

H. Meyer.

Letter XXV.

Henri Meyer to Godefroy Dorville.

Neuchâtel, March **, 178*

Here is my uncle's reply. The girl has gone. I did not see her;
Mademoiselle de La Prise, Count Max, and an old servant
of Mademoiselle de La Prise took care of everything.

Letter XXVI.

To the same.

Neuchâtel, March **, 178*

Given the remark made by my caustic protector (I'll call him
by his name, Z***), Count Max asked Mademoiselle de La
Prise how she wanted me to behave.[17] "The same as before,"
she replied (as before! She's the one who said it.). "He must
come to the balls, to the concerts; perhaps one of my relations
will invite him to her party. He will be able to see for himself
what there is to be done, or rather, to be avoided."
     The day before yesterday, the count and I were sitting by my
fireside. We were too full of thoughts to utter any of them. We

needed distraction. I suggested that he come with me to visit Monsieur Z***; I owed it to him for the mark of interest he had shown me, a significant interest, moreover, having Mademoiselle de La Prise as its object, as well as the rectitude of my conduct. The aim was no less than to spare her eternal grief, and me eternal remorse. From that day forth I have never gone past her door; I no longer go for walks; I avoid any air of daydreaming at the warehouse; I do my work more attentively than ever. My efforts are in truth their own reward: to do one's job with attention is productive of a certain zeal, which is the best distraction imaginable. But let me tell you about our visit.

I told the count that Monsieur Z*** would probably, mixed indiscriminately with other rather bitter criticisms, make some curious and interesting remarks about the country, his country, its trade, government, and mores. The count took me at my word, and we went.

We were indeed very pleased with all the information we learned. A grain of acerbity added spice to the descriptions and interest to the stories, and I at least needed that seasoning to keep me attentive. I am not calm enough to tell you what I learned, but I will try to store it in my memory for you. I will tell you only what I was able to understand of the character of the inhabitants of this land. Friendly, informal, ingenious, very talented at technical and mechanical skills, and entirely without talent for the sublime arts; the great and the simple alike are foreign to them in all shapes and sizes, so much so that they don't understand or even recognize them.

Will you not come to see me, if you come to Strasburg? Is your business in Frankfurt so pressing? Is your time so precious? Good-bye, my dear Godefroy, love your true friend forever.

H. Meyer.

Letter XXVII.

To the same.

Neuchâtel, March **, 178*

So I was indeed invited to the party held by Mademoiselle de La Prise's relation. All the high society of Neuchâtel was there. Mademoiselle de La Prise did the honors and was the ornament of the occasion. Her countenance and manners seem to me to have undergone a change: she is no less natural, but she is not so lively. I find her impressive; there is a sort of nobility and confidence in her bearing. Sometimes I think I discern sadness in her eyes, but she is calm, poised. Her movements are more solemn, like her air. It seems that her insouciance and vivacity have made way for a gentle and serious feeling of her own merit and importance. . . . Oh! I hope I'm not wrong. It is very right, that feeling! May she enjoy it . . . long may she enjoy it . . . ! May it be her reward . . . ! She saved a woman from frightful misery, from vice, perhaps from death, and a child from shame, and perhaps also from death, or from drawn-out poverty, and a young man, who thought himself decent, whom nothing should have been able to corrupt, from the same crimes as a villain.

I did not play music with Mademoiselle de La Prise; she did not play with Count Max either that evening.

On Monday there was no concert; there was a play instead. I won't tell you anything about it, other than to say that there is as much talent for singing here as for dancing, and rather more grace than is commonly found elsewhere, I believe. Otherwise, the play and the style of acting explained the tone of women in society for me: in turn marchionesses, saucy heroines, village maidens, grumpy, naive, emphatic—it is no wonder that they change their tone twenty times in the space of an hour.

Yesterday at the ball she wanted to dance with everyone, and I wanted to dance with all the ladies who were willing to dance with me. But I danced one quadrille with her. My heart sometimes felt tight in my chest, and sometimes it beat so hard it throbbed—what a contrast with the first time I danced with her in this same room! And yet my heart had already singled her out.

Halfway through the evening, Monsieur Z*** greeted me with an air of approval; and as he left he walked in front of me, and shook my hand. Caustic people are not therefore necessarily mean-spirited, or at least, they are not so in all things. But who could be nasty in all things, other than the devil? And perhaps not even the devil . . . ? Oh, what am I going on about?

Godefroy, I am waiting impatiently for you to say that you can come to see me. You would see Mademoiselle de La Prise, you would see Count Max, and your best friend would wrap his arms around you.

H. Meyer.

Letter XXVIII.

Mademoiselle de La Prise to Mademoiselle de Ville.

*Neuchâtel, March **, 178**

I was not mistaken—he loves me; there is no doubt; he loves me. He has not told me so, but he couldn't make me any more sure of it if he were to tell me a thousand times. Dear Eugénie, it has not always been so merry as it was at the beginning. I have felt grief, embarrassment, something which resembled jealousy—at least, I've felt what jealousy might be like. . . . Oh God! May I be forever preserved from it! I would prefer not to love than to have that terrible feeling to fear. Fortunately, I did not feel it, because I never had any doubts, only I would have preferred . . . But I don't want to think about all that. I am happy now; I am even pleased to have gone through that grief. I would have paid an even higher price for the happiness I feel now, for the place I hold, for now I am like a friend, like the best friend possible. I know everything about his affairs. I act for him; I know what he thinks, and we understand each other without words. We would know even in the midst of a thousand strangers that it is I who means something to him, and he something to me. We would ask each other for advice or help. To give and to receive would be equally valuable, but what would be even more so would be to have everything in common: pain, pleasures, needs . . . everything. We were certainly born for each other, perhaps not to live together—that is something I cannot know—but to love one another. You may perhaps find this letter even more deranged than the one I did not dare send you, but you would be mistaken. It isn't mad in the slightest, and I know what I'm talking about. Good-bye, dear Eugénie; I would not give him up to you any longer.

M. de La Prise.

Letter XXIX.

Henri Meyer to Mademoiselle de La Prise.

Dear Mademoiselle,

Will I dare write to you? Is it to you that I am going to write? Is it for you that I will be writing? Or will I just be relieving my overflowing heart? You love me! Is it not true that you love me? If you do not love me, I will accuse the heavens of cruelty and even injustice. I would be merely the plaything of a deceitful feeling; the connection I feel, the sympathy which attaches me, which linked me to you from the first instant I set eyes on you, would all be illusory! And yet, I feel all this. And you too—if these feelings are real, you feel them too! It seems to me that I am worthy of it, that you should not be the reward of long perseverance, and that your heart should be given in payment for mine, as mine was given. . . . Oh! If you do not love me, do not tell me. Deceive me, I beg you, for your own sake too, because you would blame yourself for my despair. Please excuse this fever, mademoiselle. If you find me presumptuous, then your heart does not understand me; it will never do so, and mine is lost. I will never be able to give it to another, and I will ask for no one else's. Young as I am, I will have lost all hope of happiness. Again I ask you not to condemn

me. What does it matter to you that I am deceived? For pity,
do not undeceive me. I may never have said a word, if I did not
have to go far from you. Happy to see you, or in the hope of
seeing you, imagining every day that it may happen, perhaps
my respect, the fear of displeasing you, and most of all the fear
that your reply may make despair follow uncertainty would
have prevented me forever, for a long while at least, from ever
asking anything of you, or saying anything. But I cannot leave
without telling you that I love you. You may not be sure of it;
is it possible that not knowing would torment you? My friend
Dorville, my oldest friend, the friend of my childhood and
youth, is ill in Strasburg; he is asking for me urgently. A letter
was sent. The express has just arrived. I leave tomorrow before
dawn. Will I be able to send you this letter? Might it be possible to secure a reply? Count Max promised to come and see
me this evening, but it is late. If only he could come! But would
he want to . . . ? Oh! There he is; I hear him. May he be able to
decipher these barely legible characters, may he take them to
you, may he find a way to have them read to you, or perhaps
he will not speak; that would be to deny me. I will not try any
other means; I would be out of my senses, totally foolhardy, to
do so. Only let him go away again, and leave me a prey to my
sadness.

H. Meyer.

Letter XXX.

Count Max to Henri Meyer.

I went to the home of ***, where I knew her to be. They had
just finished playing cards; she was still seated. I asked her out
loud to read the letter of one of my friends. She read. I went up
to her, and she took a card, and asked me for a pencil. They
were watching her; to begin with she drew a flower. Then she
wrote. Read the card; but you have already read it. Happy
Meyer! What do you do to make us love you? Or rather, with
what charms do you seduce us? I am going to a supper

engagement that I accepted long ago. When we get up from table, I will join you, and I will stay with you until you leave. If I could, I would come with you; it might be better if it were so.

M. de R***

Mademoiselle de La Prise's reply:

If you had been deceived, sir, I would be very troubled, and yet I would undeceive you.

Good people of Neuchâtel

Why be offended with a feeble satire?
It is the immortal right of every author
To lampoon people, kingdom, empire.
If what he says strikes true, then he is heard,
He is read, he entertains, and mayhap he corrects;
If he is wrong, soon rejected,
He alone is wounded by his work.
But tell me, do you claim
Not to have faults like everyone else?
Or do you want light shed only on the faults of others,
While general blindness covers your own?
The French are blamed for their mad vanity,
The Dutch for their lumpen laziness,
The Spanish for their ignorant pride,
The English for their brazen insolence.
Charming people of Neuchâtel!
Be happy with nature;
She might without injuring you
Not have accorded you all her gifts at once.[18]

Letters from Mistress Henley
Published by Her Friend

(GENEVA, 1784)[1]

Many are the marriages I have seen, &c.

LA FONTAINE[2]

First Letter.

Such a lovely and cruel little book came to us from your country a few weeks ago! Why, my dearest friend, did you not tell me about it in your last letter? It must have caused a great sensation—it has just been translated, and I am sure that *The Sentimental Husband* will soon be in everyone's hands.[3] I read it in French, and it tormented me. These past few days I have been reading it to my husband. My dearest friend, this book, so seemingly instructive, will do much injustice: the good ladies Bompré will either not recognize themselves, or not bother about it, and their husbands will blow their brains out just as much as if it had never been written. Those women who do not resemble Madame Bompré, and who are still women, will be tormented by it, while their husbands . . . Alone and reading the story of the portrait, the changed furniture, and poor *Hector*, with pain I remembered a portrait, a piece of furniture, and a dog—but the portrait was not that of my father-in-law, the dog is full of life, and my husband doesn't worry about him at all, while as for the furniture in my bedroom, it seemed to me that it ought to suit me and not the taste of my grandmothers. When I read all this out loud to my husband, instead of feeling all these differences even more acutely than I did, as I had flattered myself he would when I began, I saw him smile and sigh in turn; he said a few words, stroked his dog, and looked up at the place where the portrait used to hang. My dearest friend, they will all be believing themselves so many Monsieur Bomprés, amazed that they've been able to bear life so patiently. That particular man was completely wrong, after all, to get married. His happiness, his entire fate were too set in their groove. His wife's job was nothing other than to share feelings which were new and strange to her—she had no Nanon, no Antoine, no Hector, no neighbors to make happy, no relationships, no routines; it was not enough to fill an existence.[4] I would forgive her her books, her novels, and her boredom, without the hardness of heart, the deceitfulness, and the sinister end that they occasion. In fact, my dearest friend, I do believe that if I were to condemn her I would be condemning myself. I am not at all happy either, as little happy as that sentimental husband, although I don't resemble him in the slightest, and although my husband does not resemble his wife; he is even, if not as affectionate or as communicative, at least as calm and sweet-tempered as that excellent husband. Shall I tell you the story of my marriage, my dearest friend, and about the time before it? Shall I depict my life for you as it is today? I will be telling you things you know already so that you understand them better, or rather, so that it's easier for me to tell you the things that you don't know. Shall I tell you the thought that comes to mind? If my letter or letters are accurate at all and seem likely to you to excite any interest, just enough for them to be read, translate them and change the names, leaving out anything that you think is tedious or irrelevant. I believe that many women are in my situation. I would like at least to warn the husbands even if I can't change them; I would like to put things back in their place, and for everyone to do justice to themselves. I have a slight scruple about my project, just a slight one. I have no serious complaints to make: no one will ever recognize M. Henley, he will undoubtedly never read what I write; and if he were to read it, and were to recognize himself . . . ! Let us begin.

Orphaned from an early age, and almost penniless, I was brought up as a great heiress, and surrounded with such affection that not even a mother's love could have exceeded it. My aunt, Lady Alesford, having lost her only daughter, set me in her place, and cherished me so much and looked after me so well that she came to love me as if I had been her real daughter. Her husband had a nephew who was due to inherit his wealth and his title; I was destined for him. He was amiable; we were of the same age, and were brought up in the knowledge of what we were to be to each other. This idea pleased us both; we loved each other without anxiety. His uncle died. This change in his fortune did not change his feelings, but he was taken off traveling. In Venice he would still have been Rousseau's Lord John; he would have torn up the Marquise's ruffles.[5] But in Florence, my image was erased by more seductive charms. He spent some time in Naples, and the following year he died in Paris. I will not tell you what I suffered when that happened, what I had been suffering for some months already. In Montpellier you saw the marks of grief in my spirits, and the effect it had had on my health. My aunt was barely less distressed than I. Fifteen years of hopes, fifteen years of tending a favorite project, and nothing was left; all had been lost. I had lost everything a woman can lose.

At the age of twenty our heart allows us to glimpse remedies, and I returned to England slightly less unhappy than I had left it. My travels had molded me and made me bolder. I spoke French with greater ease; I sang better; I was admired. People paid me court, and all it earned me was more envy. Curious and critical attention followed my every move, and women found fault with me. I had no love for those who loved me: I refused a rich man with no birth and no education; I refused a lord who was both dissipated and in debt; I refused a young man whose arrogance was rivaled only by his stupidity. I was found to be disdainful; my old friends laughed at me. I came to find society hateful. My aunt, without reproaching me, told me many times that the £3,000 she was paid would finish with her, and that she didn't have even £3,000 capital to leave me.[6] This was my situation one year ago, when we went to spend the Christmas festivities with Lady Waltham. I was twenty-five; my heart was sad and empty. I began to curse the tastes and talents which had brought me nothing but false hopes, refinements which made me miserable, pretensions to happiness which never materialized. There were two men in that house. One, forty years old, had returned from the Indies with a considerable fortune. There was nothing particularly unsavory attached to the way in which he had acquired it, but neither did his reputation glow with the pure light of delicacy and disinterest, and in the conversations we had about the wealth and the wealthy of that country, he avoided details. He was a handsome man; he was noble both in his airs and in his spending; he was fond of good living, the arts, his pleasures; he liked me; he spoke to my aunt; he offered a considerable dowry, the property of a beautiful house that he had just bought in London, and three hundred guineas for my pin money. The other man looking for a wife was the second son of the Earl of Reading, thirty-five years of age, a widower of four years' standing whose wife had left him great wealth, and the father of an angelically beautiful five-year-old daughter. He has the noblest mien; he is tall, slim, with the softest blue eyes, the most beautiful teeth, the sweetest smile. There you have it, my dearest friend—that's what he is, or what he seemed to me then. I found that everything he said matched his agreeable exterior. He often talked to me of the life he led in the country, of the pleasure he would have in sharing his solitude with a companion who would unite amiability and sensibility, an honest mind and many talents. He talked about his daughter and about how he wanted to give her not a governess or a stepmother, but a mother. Toward the end of our stay he spoke even more clearly, and the evening before we left he made very generous offers for me to my aunt. If I wasn't exactly passionately in love, I was nonetheless very touched. On her return to London, my aunt made inquiries about my two suitors; she learned nothing to the discredit of the first one, but she learned better things about the other. Sense, education, fairness, perfect evenness of soul; it was generally agreed that Mr. Henley had all this. I felt that I had to choose, and you can imagine, dearest friend, that I hardly allowed myself to hesitate. It was, so to speak, the contemptible part of my heart which preferred the riches of the Orient, London, greater freedom, glittering opulence; the noble part disdained all this, and bathed in the idea of the sweetnesses of an entirely reasonable, entirely sublime felicity, of a sort that angels would applaud. If a tyrannical father had obliged me to marry the Nabob, I would perhaps have made it my duty to obey, and shaking off the thought of where my fortune had come from by the use I would have put it to, I would have said to myself, "The blessings of the poor of Europe will ward off Indian curses."[7] In a word, forced to become happy in a vulgar way, I would have been so, free from shame and perhaps with pleasure; but choose of my own free will to offer myself in exchange for diamonds, pearls, carpets, perfumes, muslins embroidered with gold, suppers, parties, I simply could not, and I promised my hand to Mr. Henley. Our wedding was charming. Witty, elegant, decent, delicate, affectionate, Mr. Henley enchanted everyone; he was a storybook hero. He seemed to me sometimes a shade too perfect; my fantasies, my moods, my impatience always came up against his reason and moderation. On the subject of my presentation at court, for example, I underwent joys and griefs that he seemed not to comprehend. I flattered myself that the society of a man whom I admired so much would make me resemble him; and I left for his estate at the beginning of spring, filled with the best intentions, and persuaded that I was going to be the best wife, the tenderest stepmother, the worthiest mistress of a house that had ever been seen. Sometimes I wanted to model myself on those highly respectable Roman matrons, and sometimes on the wives of our ancient feudal barons; other times I would see myself wandering through the countryside, as simple as a shepherdess, as sweet as their lambs, and as merry as the birds I would hear singing. But this has turned into a rather long letter, dearest friend; I will pick up my pen again at first light.

Second Letter.

We arrived at Hollow Park, an ancient, beautiful, and noble house that Mr. Henley's mother had inherited from the Astley family and left to him.[8] Everything seemed very good to me. I was moved to see white-haired servants run up to their amiable master, and bless their new mistress. They brought the child to me; I couldn't stop embracing and kissing her. I vowed in my heart to care for her unstintingly, to love her most tenderly. I spent the rest of the day in a sort of delirium. The next day I dressed the child up in the finery I'd brought her from London, and showed her off to her father, to whom I wanted to give a lovely surprise. "Your intention is charming," he said to me, "but it is a taste I would not want to encourage in her. I would be worried that these pretty shoes might prevent her running comfortably; the artificial flowers make a disagreeable contrast with the simplicity of the countryside." "You are right, sir," I said. "I was wrong to adorn her like this, but I don't know how to take the things away from her; I meant this to be a simple way of making her love me but all I've done is mortify myself and create a situation in which she is bound to feel distress." Fortunately the shoes were quickly spoiled, the locket got lost, the flowers on the hat got caught in the bushes and stayed there, and I kept the child so well entertained that she didn't have any time to miss what she'd lost. She was able to read in French as well as English; I wanted her to learn La Fontaine's fables. One day she recited "The Oak and the Reed" to her father with charming grace.[9] I was whispering the words before her. My heart was beating hard; I was flushed with pleasure. "She recites beautifully," said Mr. Henley, "but does she understand what she's saying? It would perhaps be more valuable to put truth into her head before fiction: history, geography. . . ."[10] "You are right, sir," I said, "but her nurse could teach her that Paris is on the Seine and Lisbon on the Tagus as well as I could." "Why this impatience?" Mr. Henley gently replied. "Teach her the Fables of La Fontaine if that amuses you; after all there's no great harm in it." "No," I said sharply, "she is not my child; she is yours." "But my dearest, I hoped . . ." I did not respond, and went out of the room in tears. I was wrong—I know very well; it was I who was wrong. I came back some while later, and Mr. Henley seemed not even to remember my hastiness. The child was fidgeting and yawning by his side without him noticing. Some days later I tried to set up a lesson on history and geography; both teacher and pupil quickly got bored. Her father thought that she was too young to learn music, and felt that it might bestow more pretentiousness than enjoyment. The little girl, doing nothing with me but tediously fiddling about and watching what I did with an air which was alternately stupid and inquisitive, began to annoy me; I banished her from my room almost entirely. She was no longer used to being with her nurse. The poor child is certainly more unhappy and less well brought up than before I came here. Without the measles, which she had lately and which I caught in looking after her day and night, I wouldn't know whether this child interests me more than a stranger's child would.

As for the servants, not one has had a complaint to make about me, but Fanny, my elegant abigail, caught the fancy of a local farmer, who had previously loved Peggy, the daughter of our old and excellent housekeeper, Mistress Grace, who had also been my husband's first wife's foster sister.[11] Peggy was upset and her mother outraged by this insult, and they left the house in spite of everything we could say. I make up for this loss as best I can, helped by my maid, who has a good character; if she hadn't, I would have sent her away immediately. But the whole household misses the old housekeeper, and I also miss her and the excellent preserves she used to make.

I had brought a superb white angora cat with me from London.[12] Mr. Henley found her no more beautiful than any other cat, and he often joked about how the empire of fashion decides the fate of animals, bringing them either excessive admiration or humiliating disdain, just like our dresses and hairstyles. He still stroked the angora, being good-natured, and he never refuses any creature endowed with sensation

some small token of his own. But it was not precisely the story
of my angora that I wanted to tell you. My bedroom was hung
with strips of cloth. Very dark green velvet separated pieces of
tapestry that had been hand-sewn by an ancestor of Mr. Henley's. Large armchairs that were very difficult to move but very
good for sleeping in, embroidered by the same hand and lined
with the same velvet, completed, along with a sofa that was
good and hard, the furnishing of my bedroom. My angora,
lacking respect, would sleep on the old armchairs and tug at
the antique embroidery. Mr. Henley gently put it to the ground
a number of times. Six months ago, ready to go off hunting,
and coming to say good-bye to me in my room, he sees my cat
asleep on one of the armchairs. "Ah!" said Mr. Henley. "What
would my grandmother say, what would my mother say, if
they saw—" "They would no doubt say," I replied sharply,
"that I should use my furniture as I please, just as they used
theirs, that I should not be a stranger in my own bedroom,
and from the moment I started complaining about these heavy
chairs and this dark tapestry, they would have asked you to
give me other chairs and different hangings." "Give! My dear
life!" replied Mr. Henley. "Can one give to oneself? Does one
half of oneself give to the other? Are you not the mistress? In
the past this has been thought extremely beautiful. . . ." "Yes,
in the past," I retorted, "but I live in the present." "My first
wife," replied Mr. Henley, "loved this furnishing." "Oh my
God!" I cried, "If only she were still alive!" "And all this for a
cat to whom I do no wrong?" said Mr. Henley in a soft and
sad tone, with an air of resignation, and he left. "No," I cried
out, "it's not the cat!" But he was already far away, and a
moment later I heard him calmly giving orders while mounting his horse. This sangfroid provoked me even more; I was
beside myself. I rang the bell. He had told me that I was the
mistress; I had the armchairs carried to the drawing room,
and the sofa put in a lumber room. I ordered a footman to take
down the portrait of the first Mrs. Henley, which faced my
bed. "But, madam!" said the footman. "Obey or get out" was
my reply. He no doubt thought, and you probably do too, that
I resented the portrait. No, in truth, I don't think I did; but it

was attached to the tapestry, and wanting to take that down, the portrait had to be taken off first. The tapestry followed; it was only hanging from hooks. I had it cleaned and rolled up carefully. I had cane chairs put in my room, and installed a cushion for my angora myself, but the poor animal did not stay to enjoy all this pampering: overwhelmed by all the fuss, he ran off into the grounds, and hasn't been seen since.

When he returned from hunting, Mr. Henley was surprised to see the portrait of his wife in the dining room. He went up to my room without a word, and wrote off to London to have the finest Indian wallpaper sent to me, the most elegant chairs and embroidered or woven muslin for the curtains. Was I wrong, my dear friend, other than in the way I did it? Has age greater worth than newness? And those people who seem so reasonable, are they doing anything other than soberly setting their own prejudices and tastes against other more vehemently expressed prejudices? The story of the dog is not worth telling; I was obliged to make it go out of the dining room so often during meals that it doesn't come back anymore, and eats in the kitchen. The question of his relations is more serious. There are some whom I entertain as best I can, because they are not well-off; but I yawn all through the visit, and never call on them of my own accord, because they are the most boring people in the world. When Mr. Henley says to me quite simply, "Let's go and pay a visit to my cousin such-and-such," I go. I either go in the carriage or ride with him; this could never be disagreeable to me. But if it happens that he says: "My cousin is a good woman," I say, "No, she likes to hold forth; she is envious and quarrelsome." If he says that Mr. so-and-so his cousin is a gallant gentleman whom he respects, I reply that he is a vulgar drunkard, and I speak the truth; but I am wrong, for I cause him pain. I get on very well with my father-in-law; he has a modicum of wit and lots of good humor. I embroider his jackets and play the harpsichord for him; but Lady Sara Melvil, my sister-in-law, who stays with him all summer long, is so proud with me that I can't bear to stay in the great house any longer, and I only go very rarely. If Mr. Henley were only to say to me: "Put up with her pride for

love of me; I would only love you the more. I feel it as you do,
but I love my father; I love my brother—and your coldness will
separate them from me bit by bit, and you would be upset
yourself at the decrease of happiness, of tender and natural
feelings, that you would have caused," I would inevitably
reply, "You are right, Mr. Henley. I feel already, I have often
felt the regret that you mention; it will only get worse. It pains
me, and pains me more than I can say. Let us go to stay with
my lord; one affectionate look from you will give me greater
pleasure than all Lady Sara's absurd disdain can give me pain."
But instead of that, Mr. Henley has seen nothing, cannot
remember. . . . "Now that you say it, my dear, I do seem to
remember vaguely . . . but even if it is the case, what does it
matter! How could a reasonable person be bothered by it . . .
and is Lady Sara not excusable? Daughter of a duke, and wife
of the future head of the family." My dearest friend, punches
would be less distressing than all this reason. I am miserable; I
am bored; I have brought no happiness and found none; I have
caused disturbance without making things any better for
myself. Everyone admires Mr. Henley, and congratulates me
on my happiness; I reply: "It's true; you're right . . . what a difference there is between him and the other men of his rank
and age! What a difference between my fate and that of Mrs.
so-and-so, Lady such-and-such." I think it, I say it, and my
heart doesn't feel it; it swells or tightens, and often I go up to
my room to cry in freedom. At the moment tears, whose source
I barely understand, are mixing with the ink on this paper.
Good-bye, dearest friend; I will write again very soon.

P.S. On rereading my letter, I find that I was even more in
the wrong than I had thought. I will restore the portrait of the
first Mrs. Henley to its old place. If Mr. Henley thinks it is
better in the dining room, where in fact he sees it in full light,
he need only take it back there; I will call the same footman
who took it down. Once he's put it back, I'll tell him to bring
the carriage round, and I'll go and see my father-in-law. I will
only need to tell myself, on behalf of Mr. Henley, what it is I
wish he'd said, and I'll be able to bear Lady Sara Melvil.

Third Letter.

You are right, my dearest friend, it wasn't my place to resent the injustices that *The Sentimental Husband* caused. All the same, I was in good faith, and still today my ideas on all this are not very clear. Whether it's because of his patience, indifference, virtue, or temperament, I do not think Mr. Henley has been unhappy. That he felt each one of my faults, I do not doubt; but as he never displayed any bitterness, and as he also never tried to prevent new faults by behaving in a way that might bind my soul closer to his or my pleasures to his, I have had grounds for believing that he had learned nothing from any of it. He lived and judged me, so to speak, from day to day until Monsieur and Madame Bompré came to make him more pleased with himself, and more displeased with me. I have had much grief since I last wrote. One day when I was deploring my inadequacy with respect to household chores, my slow progress, and the highs and lows in my zeal and efforts in this area, Mr. Henley listed, perfectly honestly and smilingly, all the things that had been going less well since Mistress Grace's departure. "Let's try and get her to come back," I immediately said. "I've heard that Peggy is now well placed in London, and that her mother is living more or less happily with that cousin she went to." "You could try," said Mr. Henley. "I doubt you would succeed, but there can be no harm in trying." "Would you like to talk to her?" I said. "The sight of her old master and the attention paid her would make her forget all her resentment." "That would not be possible," he replied. "I have business; but if you want, I will write." "No, I'll go myself." I ordered the carriage, and went; it's four miles from here. Mistress Grace was alone; she was very surprised to see me. Behind the cold way in which she tried to receive me, I could see her emotion and a sort of embarrassment whose cause I was unable to guess. I told her how much we had all lost when she left, how much we missed her, how much her absence was regretted. "Would you like to come back?" I said. "You would be welcomed with open arms; you would see how much respected and beloved you are. Why blame us all for the inconstancy of a young man who was not worth Peggy's regrets, seeing as he abandoned her? Perhaps she has forgotten him herself—I heard that she is placed in London." "Placed!" Mistress Grace cried out, joining her hands and lifting her eyes to Heaven. "Have you come here to insult me, madam?" "God preserve me," I cried out in turn, "what can you mean?" "Ah! Madam," she took up again after a long silence, "harm cannot be repaired as quickly as it is done, and your Fanny, with her lace, ribbons, and town airs, let my Peggy and her poor mother in for griefs that will not end with us." She wept bitterly. Pressed by my caresses and entreaties, weeping, she told me the story of her sorrows. Peggy, hurt by the loss of her lover, and bored by life with her mother and cousin, left without a word. They searched for her for a long time, and believed that she must have drowned herself; in the end they had learned that she was in London, where her youth and freshness had made her welcome in a house of ill repute. You can imagine everything the mother added to this sad tale, everything I would have said, everything I had to feel. At the end of it, I repeated my first proposition. Despite a thousand natural and just objections, whose force I accepted fully, I engaged this poor woman to return with me to Hollow Park. "Nobody will mention your daughter; you don't have to see Fanny until you've told me that you want to. Come, good Mistress Grace, seek consolation, and finish your days in the home where you spent your youth and which I should never have let you leave." I put her in the carriage, not wanting to run the risk that while packing up, new thoughts would prevent her from coming. On the way she did not stop weeping, and I wept too. A hundred paces from the house I got down from the carriage, and told the driver not to go forward until he received the order to do so. I returned alone, therefore; I spoke to Mr. Henley, to the child, to Fanny, to the other servants. Finally I went to fetch Mistress Grace and, giving her my keys, I asked her to take up her post immediately. Five or six days passed, Fanny obeying me to the letter: she ate and worked in her room. One day when I had come to see how her work was getting on, Mistress Grace came up, and after having thanked me for my generosity, asked me kindly to allow Fanny to eat with the others from then on, and to live in the house as before. Fanny was moved, and wept for Peggy and her mother. Poor Fanny! Her turn was soon to come.

Mr. Henley asked me to come down, and to bring her with me. We found the father of the young farmer with him, in his study. "Madam," said he, "I have come to ask Mr. Henley and you to furnish my son with references for the Indies; it is a country where people get rich quickly, so I've heard. He can take the young lady with him, or come back and marry her once he's a rich gentleman. They can do what they want; but as for me I will never receive an idle flirting town doll in my house, besides which I believe I would be bringing down a curse from Heaven in introducing to my family the person whose foul wiles instigated my son's inconstancy and poor Peggy's ruin. My son can do what he wants, miss, but I declare before God that he will have neither father nor paternal home if ever he sees you again." Fanny, as pale as death, made to leave but her legs gave way beneath her, and she leaned against the door for support. I ran to her immediately, and took her up to her room. We met Mistress Grace on the stairs. "Your daughter is avenged," Fanny said to her. "Lord, what is the matter?" Mistress Grace cried. She followed us. I told her what had happened; she swore to us that she'd had no part in any of it, and swore that she hadn't even seen the farmer or his son since her departure from the house. I left them; I went to lock myself in my room. There I thought bitterly about the deplorable fate of these two girls, and of all the harm I'd done; then I wrote to my aunt that I was sending Fanny back to her, asking her to find her a good place, either with a lady or in a boutique; and after having told the coachman to get the horses harnessed as quickly as possible, I went back to Fanny, and got her to read my letter. The poor girl burst into tears. "But what have I done?" she asked me. "Nothing, my poor child, nothing that can be condemned; but we absolutely have to separate. I will pay your wages to the end of the year; I will also give you extra money and clothes that at the moment you'd rather not accept from a mistress whom you find unjust. I will write to your parents to send me your young sister; but you have to come with me straightaway, so that I can take you to where the stagecoach will be passing in an hour. Mistress Grace and I will take care of everything you leave here, and you will receive it in two days' time." The carriage was ready; I got into it with her, and we arrived at the coach stop, almost without opening our mouths. I waited for the coach; I asked the people in it to look after her, and came back sadder than I can say. "There!" I said to myself. "That's what I came here to do! I have caused the disgrace of an innocent girl; I've made another one unhappy; I've got a father and son at loggerheads; I've filled a mother's soul with bitterness and shame." Walking across the park, I wept for my angora; going into my room, I wept for Fanny. Since then, Mistress Grace has done the work of a lady's maid for me. Her sadness, which she tries to overcome, is a continual reproach. Mr. Henley seemed surprised by all this commotion. He has been unable to understand why I sent my maid away so suddenly. He thinks that the old farmer did very well to oppose the marriage of his son. "These women, used to town life," said he, "never take root in the country, and are no good for anything." But he thinks that we could have made his son see reason, and that I could easily have kept Fanny on; that "they would even have become more distant from one another by continuing to see each other, instead of which the young man's imagination will now be lingering over the chimera of love, and he will perhaps make it a point of honor to stay faithful to his persecuted mistress." What will happen is God's will, but I did what I thought I had to do, and spared myself scenes which would have affected my health and temper. Fanny left a fortnight ago. Lady *** will keep her until she's found a good place for her. Her sister is arriving this evening. She has only ever been in London for as long as it took her to learn to dress hair, and since then she's spent a further year in her village. She is not pretty, and I will make sure that she is not elegant. Good-bye, my dearest friend.

P.S. My letter couldn't be sent the other day—seeing that I was going to seal it up, they told me that it was too late.

Fanny's sister is dirty, clumsy, lazy, and impertinent; I will not be able to keep her. Mr. Henley continually tells me that I was wrong to send off a girl whom I loved, and who served me well, and who was blameless. I should not have taken literally what John Turner's anger made him say—think of the mad idea of sending a boy to the Indies who doesn't know how to write. He is amazed that we passionate people could be so taken in by each other's allegations and exaggerations. In his opinion, we should know how much to disregard of what passion makes us imagine and say. He says that I mistook an action that caused me pain for a generous one, without considering that what would be disadvantageous to me might still nonetheless not be advantageous to others. It would have been better if I had not brought the girl with me. He believes he hinted as much at the time, but that "since she was here and since she wasn't to blame, I should have kept her." Could he be right, my dearest friend? Could I be wrong again, always wrong, wrong about everything? No, I don't want to believe it; it was natural for me to keep her with me after my marriage. I did not understand Mr. Henley's hint at all.

I did not know that it was supposed to be difficult to live in the countryside; I was coming to live here myself. Fanny might easily have appealed to someone who lived in the countryside— she might have married him; she is sweet and amiable. I did not know that it would be a grief to her family and a misery for him. I wasn't at all wrong to send her away—I couldn't become either her jailer, preventing the young man's visits, or her accomplice in encouraging them. I shouldn't take either their griefs or their faults on myself. In time, if she forgets her lover, or if he gets married or moves away, I could take her back; my aim is not ever to abandon her.

I do think, however, that I was too hasty. I could have waited one or two days, consulted Mr. Henley, consulted her, seen what would come of her courage and his respect for his father. I allowed my impetuous nature to overcome me. I dreaded the spectacle of unhappy love and humiliated self-respect too much. God protect Fanny from misfortune, and me from repentance.

I'll write to my aunt again, and will commend Fanny to her again.

Fourth Letter.

I am talking to you about things that are really not at all interesting, my dearest friend, and at such length, in so much detail! But that's how they are in my head, and I would think I wasn't telling you anything if I wasn't telling you everything. It is the little things that upset me or make me impatient, and which put me in the wrong. Here's another heap of little things.

Three weeks ago there was a ball at Guildford.[13] Mr. Henley was one of the subscribers. A relation of Mr. Henley's who has a house there had asked us to go and stay with her the day before, and to bring the child. We went; I wore the clothes I wanted to wear: a dress that I had worn to a ball in London eighteen months ago; a hat, feathers, and flowers that my aunt and Fanny had specifically chosen for this party, and which I had received two days before. I hadn't seen them until the moment came to put them on, as I hadn't opened the box. I was very pleased with them; I thought I looked very fine once I was dressed, and I put some rouge on, like most women do. One hour before the ball, Mr. Henley arrived from Hollow Park. "You look very fine, madam," he said to me, "because you would be unable to look anything else, but I find you a hundred times better in your simplest dresses than in all this finery. It seems to me, moreover, that a woman of twenty-six should not be dressed like a girl of fifteen, nor a decent woman like an actress. . . ." Tears came to my eyes. "Lady Alesford," said I, "did not think she was adorning a girl of fifteen nor an actress when she sent me them, but her niece, your wife, whose age she does know. . . . But sir, tell me if this costume vexes or displeases you, and that I would give you pleasure in not appearing dressed in this way, and I will immediately give up the ball, and with a good grace too, I hope."

"Would it not be possible," he said to me, "to send a rider to get a different dress or hat?" "No," I replied, "it wouldn't. My maid is with me here; no one would be able to find anything; I haven't got anything suitable; my hair would be completely messed up." "Oh, never mind!" said Mr. Henley with a smile. "But I do mind!" I cried sharply. "Tell me that I shouldn't go to the ball, that I would oblige you in not doing so; I would be happy to oblige you." And half from pique, half from emotion, I started to weep in earnest. "Madam, I am distressed to have upset you so much. I will not stop you from going to the ball. You have not found me a very despotic husband up till now. I wish for reason and decency to govern you, and not for you to give in to my prejudices. Since your aunt considers this dress appropriate, you must stay as you are . . . but put your rouge back on; your tears have messed it up." I smiled, and kissed his hand out of pure joy. "I see with pleasure," said he, "that my dear wife is as young as her hairstyle, and as flighty as her feathers." I went to reapply the rouge. Lots of people came, and once it was time for the ball, we went. In the coach I pretended to be merry, so Mr. Henley and I might actually be so—I did not succeed. I couldn't tell whether I had or hadn't done the right thing. I didn't like myself; I was uncomfortable.

We had been in the room for a quarter of an hour when all eyes turned toward the door, attracted by the noblest figure, the simplest, most elegant, most magnificent dress. People were asking and whispering, and everyone said: "Lady Bridgewater, wife of Governor Bridgewater, lately returned from the Indies and just knighted."[14] Forgive my weakness; this was not a sweet moment for your friend. Fortunately another object of comparison presented itself: my sister-in-law came in with a spot of rouge, and many more feathers than I! "You see!" I said to Mr. Henley. "She is not my wife," he replied. He went and handed her to her chair. "Others will have the same indulgence for me!" I thought to myself. A feeling of vanity slipped into my heart, and I shook off my sorrow and tried to be more agreeable for the rest of the night. I had a reason not to dance, which I do not want to tell you yet.

After the first country dance, Lady Bridgewater came to sit down next to me. "I asked who you were, madam," she said in the most graceful way. "Your name alone makes me feel I know you, and that we're almost friends. It would be too vain to tell you how much your face plays a role in this prejudice; my husband, Sir John Bridgewater, has often spoken of you, and told me how much I look like you." All this sweetness and frankness won me over. Everything should have contributed to my envy, and yet I stopped feeling any. It yielded to sweet sympathy. It may well be, in fact, that Lady Bridgewater does look like me, but she is younger and taller, her waist is narrower, her hair is more beautiful—in a word, she has the advantage over me in all the things that one can delude oneself about, and as for anything else, I have none over her, for it would be impossible to have more grace, or a tone of voice that goes more directly to the heart.

Mr. Henley was very attentive to Miss Clairville, a young lady from this county who is very fresh-faced and cheerful as well as modest and not pretty in the slightest. As for me, I chatted with Lady Bridgewater and her brother, Mr. Mead, to whom she introduced me, all night long, and, all things considered, I was very pleased with myself and everyone else.

I invited them to come and visit me; Lady Bridgewater was very sorry to have to be leaving the county the very next day to go back to London and thereafter to travel up to Yorkshire to join her husband, who was standing for election. As for Mr. Mead, he accepted my invitation for the day after next. We separated as late as we could.

I went to rest for a few hours at the house of Mr. Henley's relation, and after lunch, we climbed into the carriage, my husband, his daughter, and I; the nurse and my maid had already left. My head was full of Lady Bridgewater, and after having pictured her agreeable face in my imagination, and seeming to hear her words and accents, I said to Mr. Henley, "Admit that she is charming." "Who?" he asked. "Can it be true that you don't know?" I asked him. "Apparently you're talking about Lady B.? Yes, she is amiable; she is a beautiful woman. I thought in particular that she was very well dressed. Otherwise I can't say that she made a great impression on me." "Ah!" I retorted. "If small blue eyes, red hair, and a country-woman's air count as beauties, then Miss Clairville certainly has the edge over Lady B. and all the others like her. My opinion is that after Lady B. the next most agreeable person I saw at the ball was her brother; he reminds me of Lord Alesford, my first lover, and I invited him to come to dinner with us tomorrow." "Fortunately I am not jealous," said Mr. Henley, with a half smile. "It may be fortunate for you," I retorted, "but it's not fortunate for me, for if you were jealous, at least I'd know you feel something; I would be flattered; I would feel precious to you; I would feel that you dreaded losing me, that I still please you, that at least you think I am still capable of pleasing. Yes!" I added, agitated both by my own liveliness and his unalterable sangfroid, "The injustice of a jealous man, the anger of a violent man would be less distressing than the phlegm and aridity of a wise man." "You will make me believe," said Mr. Henley, "that it is true that Russian women like to be beaten. But my dear, restrain your vivacity in front of this child, and let us not set her a bad example. . . ." "You are right," I burst out. "Forgive me, sir! Forgive me, dear child!" I took her onto my lap; I embraced her; I drenched her face with my tears. "I set you a bad example," I said. "I should be a mother to you; I promised you I would be, and I don't look after you, and I say things in front of you which you are lucky not to understand much of!"

Mr. Henley said nothing, but I don't doubt that he was touched. The little girl stayed on my lap and showed me some affection, which I returned a hundredfold, but with a feeling that was much more painful than tender. I felt bitter regret; I formed all sorts of projects; I promised myself to become her mother, finally—but in her eyes, that is to say, in her soul, I saw that it would be impossible. She is beautiful, she is not naughty in the slightest, she is not false; but she does not have much liveliness or sensibility. She will be my pupil but not my child; she won't want to be.

We arrived home. At my request the Henleys from the great
house were also invited for the next day. Miss Clairville happened to be there; she came. At table, I placed Mr. Mead
between her and Lady Sara Melvil, and the day was neither
vexatious nor remarkable. The following day I wrote a letter
to Mr. Henley; I enclose a draft with all its crossings-out.
There are almost as many words crossed out as left in, and you
won't find it easy to read.[15]

Sir,   .

You have seen, I hope, how ashamed of my excessive liveliness
I was the day before yesterday. Do not believe that either on
this occasion or on any other the worth of your patience and
sweetness has escaped me. I can assure you that my intentions
have always been good. But what are intentions when they are
never met with any response? Your own conduct is such that I
can blame nothing, however much I may sometimes wish to
justify my own. And yet you have been wrong in one thing,
which is in doing me the honor of marrying me. You believed—
and who wouldn't have!—that, finding in one's husband everything that is amiable and respectable, and in one's situation
honest pleasures, wealth, and respect, a reasonable woman
could not fail to be happy. But I am not a reasonable woman,
as you and I have seen too late. I do not combine the qualities
which would have made us happy with those you seemed to
find appealing—you could have met with both sorts in thousands of other women. You were not asking for glittering talents, since you settled for me, and there is certainly no one
who requires the more difficult virtues less than you. I was
only sour about Miss Clairville because I felt painfully that a
girl like her would have suited you much better than I. Accustomed to country pleasures and occupations, active, hardworking, with simple tastes, grateful, cheerful, and happy—would
she have left you any time to remember what might be lacking?
Miss Clairville could have remained among her relations and
all her old habits. She would have lost nothing and only
gained . . . but it is too late to linger over a chimera . . . the

past cannot be called back. Let us speak of the future; let us speak in particular about your daughter. Let us try to order my conduct so as to repair the greatest of my faults. In the beginning, when you opposed what I wanted to do for her, you did nothing that was not just and reasonable; but it was tantamount to blaming everything that had been done for me, and scorning everything that I knew and everything that I was. I was humiliated and discouraged; I lacked flexibility, and true willingness. In the future I want to do my duty, not according to my own fantasy, but according to your judgment. I do not ask you to draw me a plan; I will try to guess your ideas so as to submit to them—but if I guess ill or go about it the wrong way, be so kind as not just to blame me, but to tell me what you would like me to do instead. On this point as on all others, I sincerely wish to merit your approbation, to regain or to gain your affection, and to reduce the feeling of regret in your heart for having made the wrong choice.

S. HENLEY.

I took my letter to Mr. Henley in his study, and withdrew. A quarter of an hour later, he came to join me in the drawing room. "Have I complained, madam?" he said, embracing me. "Have I mentioned Miss Clairville, have I thought of any Miss Clairville?" At that instant his father and brother entered; I concealed my emotion. It seemed to me that during their visit Mr. Henley was more attentive, and looked at me more often than normally; it was the best way to reply to me. We have not spoken of it again. Since that day I have been getting up earlier; Miss Henley takes her meals with me. She has a writing lesson with me; I give her one on geography, some elements of history, some ideas of religion. Ah! If I could only learn it by teaching it, if I could only convince myself and fill my heart with it! How many faults would disappear! How many empty vanities would fade away when confronted with truths whose object is sublime and whose usefulness eternal!

I will not relate my success with the child. We have to wait and hope. Nor will I relate everything that I am doing to make the countryside interesting for me. This place is like its master:

everything is too good; there is nothing to change, nothing that requires my activity or my care. An old lime tree blocks a rather fine view from my window. I wanted it to be cut down, but when I looked at it up close, I saw with my own eyes that it would be a great pity. What makes me happiest in this brilliant season is to watch the leaves appear and unfurl, the blossom come out, a crowd of insects flying, walking, and running in all directions. I know nothing about it, I learn nothing about it; but I contemplate and admire this full and animated universe. I get lost in this wholeness which is so astonishing and I won't say so wise as well; I am too ignorant. I do not know its ends; I do not know its means or its aim; I do not know why so many flies are given to this voracious spider to eat; but I watch, and hours pass without me thinking about myself or my childish griefs.[16]

Fifth Letter.

I am no longer in any doubt, my dearest friend, I am with child; I have just written to tell my aunt, and have asked her to tell Mr. Henley, who has been in London for a few days. My joy is extreme; I will redouble my efforts with Miss Henley. For over a year I have been nothing to her; for two months I've been a mediocre mother. I must avoid becoming a stepmother. Goodbye. You won't get anything more today.

Sixth Letter.

I am not very well, dearest friend. I won't be able to tell you everything I'd like to all at once. The task is long and not very agreeable. I will take a rest when I get tired. It doesn't make any difference whether you get my letter a few weeks sooner or later. After this one I don't want to write any more like it. A note will tell you from time to time whether your friend is still alive or not.

My situation is a sad one, or else I am a being without reason or virtue. Caught in the grievous choice of either blaming fate, which I cannot change, or blaming and despising myself, whichever way I turn, the scenes which present themselves to my imagination, the details which weigh down my memory daunt my courage, make my existence somber and painful. What is the point of my narrative bringing impressions back into painful life, of going back over scenes which cannot be too quickly nor too entirely forgotten? For the last time you will see my heart; after that I will forbid it from uttering any complaint—either it must change or never open more.

When I was sure that I was with child, I asked my aunt to tell Mr. Henley. He only came back eight days later. In that interval I had not stopped wondering whether I should or shouldn't feed my child myself.[17] On the one hand I was overwhelmed by the fatigue, the relentless burden, the privations that I would have to accept. Shall I admit it? I was also worried about the damage that feeding a child has on a woman's figure. On the other hand, I also dreaded the immense humiliation of being judged incapable and unworthy of fulfilling this duty. But, you will say, is there anything to you apart from vanity?[18] Can you not imagine the immense pleasure of being everything to your child, of attaching him to you, of attaching yourself to him by every possible link? Yes, no doubt, and that was my most constant impression; but when one is alone, and always thinking about the same thing, what does one not think?

I resolved to talk to Mr. Henley about it, and it was not without pain that I introduced the subject. I equally dreaded him approving my plan as a necessary thing which went without saying, and which I was wrong to hesitate over, and also that he might for reasons I would find humiliating reject it as something absurd.

I escaped neither of these pains. In his view, nothing could dispense a mother from carrying out this first and most sacred duty, other than the danger of some temperamental fault or character defect which might endanger the child, and he told me that his intention was to consult a friend of his, Dr. M., to find

out whether my extreme vivacity and my frequent hastiness
meant that a stranger should do it instead. Of me, my health,
my pleasure, not a word was said; there was no question of anything other than this child which did not yet exist. This time I
contested nothing. I did not fly into a passion; I was only sad-
dened, so much so that my health was affected. "What!" I said
to myself. "Will none of my impressions be divined? None of
my feelings shared? No pain spared me? Everything I feel is
absurd, then, or else Mr. Henley is insensitive and hard. I will
pass my entire life with a husband in whom I inspire nothing
other than perfect indifference, and whose heart is sealed!
Good-bye to the joy of my pregnancy; good-bye to joy in general." I fell into a profound depression. Mistress Grace realized first, and spoke to Mr. Henley, who had no idea where it
came from. He thought that my state was making me fearful,
and offered to engage my aunt to come and see me. I embraced
this idea with gratitude. We wrote, and my aunt came. Tomorrow, if I can, I'll take up my pen again.

I said nothing about it to my aunt, and didn't so much seek
consolation in her affection as distraction in her conversation.
Emotion plunged me back into anguish; in order to escape, I
had to escape myself, divert myself, forget myself, forget my
situation.

The intrigues of court, the news from town, the affairs, the
weddings, the positions bestowed—all the futility and frivolity of high society restored me to my own frivolity and even to
a sort of gaiety; dangerous blessing! Its usefulness was only
temporary, and stored up new chagrins for me.

Soon I was no longer thinking of my son or daughter other
than as a prodigy of beauty whose glittering talents, cultivated
by the most astonishing education, would excite the admiration of the entire country, or even of Europe as a whole. My
daughter, more beautiful even than Lady Bridgewater, would
choose her husband from among the highest in the realm. My
son, if he took the path of arms, would become a hero and
command armies; were he to devote himself to the law, he
would be at least Lord Mansfield or the Chancellor, a perma-
nent chancellor whom the King and the people would be

unable to do without. . . .[19] Having my head filled with this
extravagant nonsense, I couldn't prevent myself entirely from
showing some of it to Mr. Henley. Nonetheless I laughed at my
folly, for I wasn't completely mad. One day, half-joking, half-
rational, or supposing myself so, I described my fancies . . . but
setting them down has agitated me so much, that I am obliged
to put down my pen.

We were alone. Mr. Henley said to me: "Our ideas are very
different; I desire my daughters to be raised simply; that they
should attract few glances, and not think about attracting
them; that they should be modest, sweet, reasonable, obliging
women and vigilant mothers; that they should know how to
enjoy opulence, but more important, that they should know
how to do without it; that their position in life should be more
apt to strengthen their virtues than to thrust them into the
public eye; and that if all this cannot be united in one person,"
said he, kissing my hand, "I will be content with half the
grace, charms, and refinement of Mistress Henley. As for my
son, a strong body and a healthy soul; that is to say, free from
vices and weaknesses, the strictest integrity underpinned by
extreme moderation; this is what I ask of God on his behalf.
But, my dear love," said he, "seeing as you give such importance to everything which glitters, I do not want you to risk
finding out from someone else something that happened a few
days ago. In the first moment of surprise, you might be too
affected by it and, initially upset, show in public that husband
and wife do not share a single soul, and do not have the same
way of thinking or feeling. I was offered a place in parliament,
and a position at court; I was permitted a glimpse of a title for
me and a position for you. I refused it all."

"Nothing would seem more natural to me, sir," I replied,
pressing my forehead into my hand for fear of betraying my
emotion, and speaking slowly in a voice I forced to sound natural. "Nothing would seem more natural to me, if these offers
were attempting to persuade you to vote against your principles; but you support the measures being taken by the current
Ministry, do you not?" "Yes," he replied, "I am attached to
the King, and I support what the Ministers are doing today.

But am I sure that I will support what they will be doing tomorrow? Is it certain that these Ministers will stay in place? And will I run the risk of seeing myself removed from a position which has nothing in common with any political system, by a cabal, by my peers? Sent back here to this place which has always been agreeable to me, would I not be running the risk of finding it spoiled, changed, because I would myself have changed, and because I would be bringing back to it wounded vanity and frustrated ambition, passions which until now have been foreign to me?" "I admire you, sir," I said to him, and in effect I had never admired him so much; the more it cost me, the more I admired him—I had never seen his superiority so distinctly. "I admire you; but still, public usefulness, the duty to work for one's country—" "That is the pretext ambitious people use," he interrupted, "but the good one can do in one's own house, among one's neighbors, friends, relations, is more secure and more indispensable. If I do not do everything I should do, it will be my fault, and not my situation's. I have lived too long in London and in the cities of the Continent. There, I lost sight of the occupations and interests of country people. I have no talent for conversation; nor am I able to learn anything instructive from them, or be as active as I would like. I would carry these defects into my public duties, and I would be guilty of choosing that place myself, instead of staying here, where Providence has placed me."

"I have nothing further to say, sir," I said to him. "But why did you make a secret of this business?" "I was in London," he replied to me. "It would have been difficult for me to detail my reasons to you in a letter. If you had set your reasons and tastes in opposition to me, you would not have shaken me, and I would have had the distress of causing you sorrow that I could have spared you. Even today, I am vexed to have to speak to you about it, and had I not learnt that the thing has become public, so to say, you would have been informed neither of the offer nor of the refusal."

A moment passed after Mr. Henley stopped speaking. I wanted to say something; but I had been listening so carefully, I was so torn between the respect that so much moderation, reason, and uprightness in my husband forced from me, and the horror of seeing myself so foreign to these feelings, so totally excluded from his deliberations, so useless, so isolated, that I was unable to speak. My head was worn out and confounded with all these efforts; I fainted.[20] The care that has been taken of me since prevented the consequences that might have followed such an accident, but I am still not properly well again. Neither my soul nor my body are in a natural state. I am only a woman—I will not kill myself; I haven't the courage. If I become a mother, I hope I never want to; but grief can also kill. In one year, two years, you will hear, I hope, that I am reasonable and happy, or that I am no more.

The End.

Letters Written from Lausanne: Cécile

(1785)[1]

To Madame la Marquise de S***[2]

If these letters, instead of displaying the usual mixture of
passion and reason, weakness and virtue, such as is normally
to be found in society, depicted nothing but virtues as pure
as yours, the Editor would have ventured to adorn them with
your name, and boldly proclaim his homage to you.

Letter I.

November 30, 1784

You are quite wrong to complain! Your son-in-law may not be
worth much, but your daughter married him without distaste.
She has an establishment which you yourself consider advantageous, although you were barely consulted about it! What
does that matter? Why do you mind? Your husband, his relations and matching fortunes did it all. So much the better. If
your daughter is happy, will you feel her happiness any less? If
she is unhappy, will it not lessen your grief not to have been
responsible for her fate? You are so romantic! Your son-in-law
is mediocre, but is your daughter's character or mind so distinguished? You are being separated from her, but was it really so
pleasant to have her with you? She will live in Paris; is she

sorry to be living there? In spite of your rants about its dangers, seductions, illusions, delusions, frenzy, and so on, would you be so sorry to live there yourself? You are still beautiful, and you will always be amiable; I am much mistaken if you would not eagerly wear the chains of court yourself, were they to be offered to you. In fact, I think that they will be offered to you. On the occasion of this marriage, people will talk about you, and it will be felt how much the princess who attaches a woman of your merit to her service would have to gain: you are well-behaved without being prudish, as sincere as you are polite, and modest despite your many talents. But let's see how true this all is. I have always found that this sort of merit exists only on paper, where words never fight, however contradictory they may be. Well behaved and not at all prudish! You are certainly not at all prudish; I have always known you to be very well behaved—but have I known you in every situation? Have you told me the story of every moment of your life? A woman who was entirely well behaved would be a prude; at least I think she would be. But let's pass over that. Sincere and polite! You are not as sincere as it is possible to be, given how polite you are, nor perfectly polite, given how sincere you are; and you are only one or the other at the same time because you are only a little of each at any given moment. Enough of this! My harangue is not directed at you—this is a topic which has been weighing on me, and I needed to unburden myself.

My daughter's guardians periodically torment me on the subject of her education: they tell me and then they write to me that a young lady must acquire knowledge which the world will find agreeable, without thinking about trying to be agreeable. Where the deuce will she find the patience and the application for her harpsichord lessons if she doesn't mind whether she succeeds or not? They want her to be both open and reserved. What does that mean? They want her to fear blame without desiring praise? My love for her is heartily praised, yet it is felt that it would be better if I were not quite so busy shielding her from pain and bringing her pleasure. This is how words which let themselves be put next to each other combine to construct sorts of characters, legislation, education, and domestic happiness, all of which are impossible. They are used to torment women, mothers, young ladies, all the imbeciles who allow themselves to be moralized over. Let us come back to you, who are as sincere and as polite as anyone needs to be; to you, who are charming; to you, whom I love tenderly. The Marquis of *** told me the other day that he was almost sure that you would be dragged out of your country retreat. So! Let yourself be placed at court, without complaining about your family's demands. Allow yourself to be governed by circumstances, and be happy that in your case there are circumstances which govern, relations who make demands, a father who marries off his daughter, and a daughter who is not very sensitive or very thoughtful who lets herself be married off. If only I were in your place! When I look at your destiny, the temptation to find fault with my grandfather's religious fervor is almost overwhelming! Had he, like his brother, consented to go to mass, I don't know whether he'd be happier in the other world, but I would have been in this one.³ My romantic cousin is complaining, but it seems to me that in her place I would not be.

Today I am complaining; I sometimes think I have a lot to complain about. My poor Cécile, what will become of her? She turned seventeen last spring. I had to introduce her to the world so that she could see it, and so that young men could see her, and perhaps consider her. . . . Consider her! What a ridiculous expression to use on this occasion! Who would consider a girl whose mother is still young, and who after the death of this mother will have twenty-six thousand of this country's francs! That's about thirty-eight thousand French pounds. We have an income, my daughter and I, of fifteen hundred French francs.⁴ So you see that if anyone marries her, it will not be because they thought about her, but because they saw her. So I have to show her off; I have to amuse her, allow her to dance. But I shouldn't show her off too much, for fear of wearying the eye of the beholder, nor amuse her too much, for fear that she can no longer do without it, for fear too of her guardians berating me, for fear of the other mothers denying that any understanding has been reached. She has so little money! What a lot of time wasted in getting dressed, without counting the time spent being in society, and then all her finery, modest as it is, never stops costing money: her gauzes and ribbons, and so forth, for nothing is so precise, so long, or so detailed as the criticism of women. I can't let her dance too much either; dancing makes her hot and that doesn't suit her: when her hair, rather poorly dressed by her and by me, comes down, it makes her look unkempt; she gets too red, and the next day has a headache or a nosebleed. But she is passionate about dancing—she is quite tall, shapely, agile, and her ear is perfect; to stop her dancing would be the same as stopping a doe running. I have just told you what my daugher's height is like; now I will tell you about the rest. Imagine a pretty forehead; a pretty nose; black, rather deep-set or hooded eyes, which, although not very large, are shining and soft; lips which are rather big and very red; healthy teeth; a beautiful brunette's skin with vivid coloring; a neck which is getting bigger despite all my pains; a bosom which would be beautiful were it not so highly colored; passable feet and hands; that's Cécile for you. If you know Madame R***, or if you have ever seen the beautiful country-women of Vaud, then you would have a more accurate idea. Do you want to know what the whole of her appearance pro-claims? I would say that it is health, goodness, gaiety, suscepti-bility to love and friendship, simplicity of heart, and uprightness of spirit, but not extreme elegance, delicacy, subtlety, or nobil-ity. My girl is a beautiful, good girl. Good-bye; you are going to ask me a thousand things about her, and why I said, "Poor Cécile! What will become of her?" Well, ask then! I need to talk about it, and there's nobody here I can talk to.

Letter II.

Well yes. A handsome young man from Savoy, dressed up as a girl. That's more or less it. But don't forget, so that you can picture her as pretty as she is, a certain transparency of color-ing, a satiny, bright sheen that I can't describe, and which often gives her a light glow—it is the opposite of matte or dull; it's the sheen on the red sweetpea flower. That's exactly what my Cécile is at the moment. If you didn't recognize her on meeting her in the street, it would be your fault. Why a fat neck, you ask? It's an illness particular to this part of the world, a thickening of the lymph, a swelling in the glands which no one has been able to explain to this day.[5] It has long been attributed to water that is too cold or which has too much tufa in it, but Cécile only ever drinks spring or mineral water.[6] It must come from the air, perhaps from the cold blasts of certain winds which can suddenly halt the summer heat. There aren't any goiters up on the mountains, but the narrower and deeper the valley the more goiters you see and the bigger they are. They are particularly frequent in the places where you see the most cretins and the most scrofula.[7] Remedies have been found, but nothing to prevent it yet, and it does not seem entirely clear to me that the remedies completely cure the illness or are without side effects. I will redouble my efforts to make sure Cécile is never subjected to the cold evening air, and I won't do anything other than this, but I do wish that the sovereign would offer prizes to those who discover the nature of this deformity and who would indicate the best ways of protecting oneself from it.[8]

You ask me how it happens that anyone gets married when all they can scrape together is thirty-eight thousand francs, and you are amazed that I am not richer, given that I am an only child. The question is a strange one. People get married because men and women like each other; but that aside, I will tell you the story of my inheritance. My grandfather, as you know, left Languedoc with nothing; he lived on a pension that your grandfather made him, and from another one paid by the English court. Both ceased with his death. My father was a captain in the Dutch army. He lived off his salary and his mother's dowry of six thousand francs. My mother, in brief, was from a bourgeois family of this town, but so pretty and amiable that my father never felt poor or mismatched with her; and she was so tenderly loved by him that she died of grief after his death. Cécile takes after her, not after me nor her father. May her life be as happy, although longer! May her fate be as happy even if her career is no longer! The six thousand

francs my mother left me is all my wealth. My husband had
four brothers. His father gave them each ten thousand francs
when they were twenty-five years old; he left another ten thousand to the four youngest, and the rest to the eldest, along
with land valued at eighty thousand francs.⁹ He was a rich
man for this country, and who would also have been so in
your province, but when you have five sons, who can become
neither priests nor go into trade, it's not easy to leave enough
for them all to live on.¹⁰ The income from our twenty-six or
thirty-eight thousand francs is enough to give us all the pleasures we wish for, but you see that no one will ever marry
Cécile for her fortune. And yet I could have had her settled
already if I'd wanted . . . but it wasn't only up to me; I would
never have been able to do it, and she wouldn't have wanted to
herself. There was a young minister, related to her through my
mother, a little, pale, thin man, spoiled, cultivated, and adored
by the whole family. He is supposed, on the basis of a few bad
lines and a couple of unfeeling speeches, to be the first man of
letters, the first genius and orator of Europe. We were staying
with his family, my daughter and I, about six weeks ago. A
young lord and his tutor, who are boarding there, spent the
evening with us. After tea, we played word games, then we
played blindman's buff, and then lotto. The young Englishman is from the same sort of mold as Cécile; he's as handsome
a young English villager as she is a pretty Vaud peasant. He
did not excel at the word games, but Cécile was much more
indulgent of his bad French than of her cousin's tired witticisms; that is to say, she ignored her cousin, and acted as tutor
and interpreter to the other. At blindman's buff, as you might
imagine, there wasn't any difference in their skill; at lotto, one
was economical and attentive, and the other distracted and
magnificent. When it was time to go home, his mother said,
"Now Johnnie, you take our Cécile home, but it's cold out, so
put on your overcoat and do up all the buttons." His aunt
brought him his galoshes. While he was buttoning himself up
like a piece of luggage and looking as if he was getting ready
for a long journey, the young Englishman ran up the stairs
four steps at a time, came back down in a flash with his hat,

and offered Cécile his arm. I couldn't help laughing, and I told the cousin he could unswaddle himself. If previously it had seemed as if his fate with Cécile was unclear, that moment decided it. Although he is the only son of rich parents and will be inheriting from five or six aunts, Cécile will not be marrying her cousin the minister; it would be like Agnes and the dead body, but instead of resuscitating, he'd only ever get deader.[11] This dead body has a very lively friend, also a minister, who fell in love with Cécile after seeing her two or three times at the house of his friend's mother. He's a young man from the Joux lake valley, handsome, blond, robust, who can easily walk ten leagues in a day, who hunts more than he studies, and who strides off to the chapel one league from his home every Sunday to do his preaching.[12] In the summer he takes no parasol and in the winter he takes no overcoat or galoshes; he could carry his little pedant of a friend if he had to. If this husband suited my daughter, I would willingly go and live with them in a mountain parish; but he has only his ministry stipend to live on, and that's not even the greatest difficulty: I am afraid of the cunning those mountain dwellers have, and Cécile would be less well-adapted to it than any other woman. Moreover, my brothers-in-law, her guardians, would never consent to such an alliance, and I'd only consent to it with difficulty. Nobility, in this country, is worth absolutely nothing at all, confers no privilege, right, or exemption; but if that makes it all the more ridiculous in those people who are inclined to claim to be noble, it is all the more precious among a small number of the others. I admit that these people exist more in my head than in my actual acquaintance. I imagine people who can't become canons or Knights of Malta; who pay all their taxes; but who feel all the more bound to be brave, disinterested, and true to their word; who see no possibility of ever acting in a cowardly way; who believe that they have inherited from their ancestors, and must bequeath to their children, a certain flower of honor, which is to virtue what elegance is to movement, what grace is to strength and beauty, and who tend to its luster ever more carefully the harder it is to define, and who themselves do not have a clear idea of what it can stand without being destroyed or withered.[13] This is how one safeguards a delicate flower or a precious vase. This is how a really proper good friend never leaves anything to chance where his friend is concerned, and how a truly faithful wife or mistress even watches over her thoughts. Good-bye; I am going to enjoy thinking of these beautiful and delicate things that I have just been telling you about. I hope they give you sweet dreams too.

P.S. Perhaps what I've just been saying is as old as the hills, and in fact its nature is such that it wouldn't be new anyway, but never mind; it gave me so much pleasure to say it that it gives me pain not to return to the same idea, and go into more detail. This privilege of nobility, which would consist in nothing other than a further, stricter, and more intimately felt obligation, which would speak to the young man louder than his conscience and make him scrupulous in spite of his desires, and also to the old man, giving him courage in spite of his weakness—this privilege, I say, enchants, captivates, and seduces me. I can't bear it that this class, idealized as it may be, should be neglected by the sovereign, that it should be left forgotten in idleness and poverty; for if it marries for money, or gains wealth through commerce or financial speculations, then it is no longer what it was, and nobility becomes common, or to speak more accurately, my fantasy evaporates.

Letter III.

If I were King, I don't know if I'd be more just, although I'd want to be; but this is what I'd certainly do. I'd have a list drawn up of all the highest noblemen in the country. I'd give these nobles some not particularly shining distinction that would nonetheless be very distinct, and I wouldn't allow anyone else into this elite class. I would take responsibility for their children if they had more than three. I would grant a pension to all the heads of families if they fell into poverty, like the King of England gives to all the lords whose fortunes have decayed.[14] I would form a second class for officers who had reached certain grades and for their children, and for those who had had certain employments, etc. In each province, this class would be free to admit such-and-such a person who had distinguished himself through a fine deed, or a foreign gentleman or a rich businessman or the author of some useful invention. The people would name representatives, and that would be a third order in the nation; this one would not be hereditary. Each of the three would have certain distinctions and the task of taking care of certain things, apart from the posts which would be given to individuals along with all the rest of my subjects. Deputies would be chosen from each of the three classes and, gathered together, would form the nation's council; they would live in the capital. I would consult them about everything. These councillors would be appointed for life; they would all take precedence over the nobility. Each of them would name his own successor, and he couldn't be a son, a son-in-law, or a nephew, but the nomination would need to be examined and confirmed by the sovereign and by the council. Their children would enter the noble class by right. This would be the way of replacing families who died out. Every man would, on marrying, enter his wife's class, and his children would also belong to it. This arrangement is for three reasons. First, because children are more truly the wife's than the husband's. Second, the very first things, the very first prejudices we learn, all come more from our mothers than from our fathers. Third, I would think that this would help increase emulation among men, and facilitate marriage for those girls who may be supposed to be the best brought-up and the least rich of all marriageable girls of a country. You see that in this superb political arrangement, my Cécile has not been forgotten. I started with her; I return to her. I suppose her to belong to the first class: beautiful, well brought-up, and good as she is. At her feet, I see all the young men of her own class who don't want to slip rank, and all those of an inferior class who have ambition to raise themselves. Really, only this sort of ennoblement could content me. I hate all the other ones, because a sovereign cannot confer along with his title this bias, this feeling of nobility which seems to me to be its single advantage. Supposing that here the man were not able to acquire it on his marriage, the children would inherit it from their mother. Well, that's quite enough of politics and of reverie.

Apart from the two men I told you about, Cécile has another suitor from the bourgeois class, but he would be the sort to bring her down to his level; he wouldn't rise to hers. He gets into fights, drinks too much, and regards girls in the same way as the German nobles or the few English lords that he frequents; other than that, he is handsome and quite amiable, but his morals frighten me. His idleness bores Cécile, and although he does have some wealth, by dint of imitating those who have more than he, he may well soon find himself ruined. And there's another one too. He's a sensible, gentle, and amiable young man who is talented and destined for commerce. Elsewhere he could make something of it, but not here. If my daughter had a predilection for him, and if her uncles set no obstacles in her way, I would agree to go and live with them in Geneva, Lyons, Paris, wherever they wanted; but it may be that the young man does not love Cécile quite enough to leave his native soil, and it is in fact the most agreeable land in existence, with its view over our beautiful lake and its pleasant banks. You see, my dearest friend, that among these four suitors, there is no husband. And I haven't got any others that I could offer Cécile apart from a certain very noble cousin who lives in a sad château where, from one generation to the next, they read nothing but the Bible and the newspaper. And the young lord, you will say? I would have many things to say on that subject! I will keep them for another letter. My daughter is insisting that I go for a walk with her. Good-bye.

Letter IV.

A week ago, my cousin (the mother of the little theologian) being ill, my daughter and I went to keep her company. The young lord, having discovered this, gave up a picnic that all the young English people in Lausanne were going on, and asked if he would be permitted to visit my cousin. Apart from at mealtimes we hadn't seen him since the galoshes evening. He initially received a rather cold welcome, but he was so careful to walk about on tiptoes and speak quietly, he offered his services so gracefully, and so prettily brought his French grammar to Cécile so she could teach him pronunciation and how to say his words precisely like she did, that my cousin and her sisters quickly melted. But this all annoyed the son of the house to the precise extent that it charmed everyone else, and he developed such a grudge that, by dint of complaining about the noise over his head interrupting either his study or his sleep, he persuaded his good-natured, silly mother to request Milord and the tutor to seek lodging elsewhere. They came to tell me, and to ask if I would like to have them as lodgers. I refused straightaway, without waiting for Cécile to find out or to formulate a wish. Later they dug their heels in, asking me for a floor of my house which they knew to be empty. I refused again.

"But only for two months," said the young man. "For one month, for a fortnight, while we find another lodging elsewhere. Perhaps you will find us so discreet that you will keep us on. I am not as noisy as Mr. S. says; but even if I were naturally that noisy, I am sure, madam, that you and mademoiselle your daughter wouldn't hear my footsteps, and apart from the favor of coming here sometimes to learn a little French, I wouldn't insist on anything else."

I looked at Cécile. Her eyes were fixed on me. I saw very well that I was going to have to refuse, but in truth I felt almost as much pain as I caused. The tutor discerned my reasons, and prevented the young man from saying any more. The latter came round this morning to tell me that having been unable to persuade me to take him in, he had found a lodging as near to our house as he could, and he asked my permission to come and see us sometimes. I gave it. He went away. After taking him to the door, Cécile came to embrace me.

"You are thanking me," I told her. She blushed; I embraced her tenderly. Tears slid from my eyes. She saw them, and I am sure that she read in them an exhortation to be sensible and prudent, and that it was more persuasive than the most eloquent speech would have been. My brother-in-law and his wife have just arrived; I must break off.

I can tell you what happened in an instant. My brother-in-law has learned that I had refused to rent rooms which are worthless to me for a very high rate. He is my daughter's guardian. He rents rooms in his own house to foreigners, and sometimes he rents the whole house. Then he goes to the countryside, or he stays in his own rooms. He therefore found what I had done quite extraordinary, and rebuked me at length for it. The only reason I gave him for not renting it out was that I had not considered it appropriate to do so. This reply seemed insufferably proud to him. He started to get truly angry, when Cécile said that I probably had reasons which I hadn't wished to give, that he should suppose them to be good ones and not press me any further. I embraced her in thanks; this time it was her turn to have tears in her eyes. My brother- and sister-in-law left without knowing what to make of either mother or daughter. I will be held up for the censure of the whole town. Only Cécile and perhaps the young lord's tutor will be on my side. You probably don't understand what I'm talking about with all this renting to foreigners or why my brother-in-law should be so vexed with me. Do you know Plombières, Bourbonne, or Barège?[15] According to what I've heard, Lausanne is quite similar. The beauty of our countryside, our academy, and Monsieur Tissot bring us visitors from all countries, of all ages and characters, but not of all fortunes.[16] Only the rich can afford to live away from home. What we mainly have is English gentlemen, the wives of French financiers, and German princes, all bringing money to our innkeepers, to the local peasants, to our tradesmen and artisans, and to those who have houses to rent in either the town or the country. They impoverish the rest of us by driving up the cost of provisions and labor, and they give us a taste for the luxury they enjoy, which is ill adapted to our fortune or resources. The people of Plombières, Spa, and Barège do not live with their guests, and do not imbibe either their ways or their morals. But we, whose company is more enjoyable and whose birth is often as good as theirs, we live with them, we are agreeable to them; sometimes we mold them, but they ruin us. They turn our young ladies' heads, they make our young men who keep their simple ways look gauche and common; those who ape their behavior just look ridiculous and often squander both money and health. Homes and marriages don't fare any better for having their gatherings adorned by elegant French women and beautiful English ladies, handsome English men and agreeable French rakes. Even supposing that this didn't harm marriages, it certainly prevents a good number from taking place. The young women find their compatriots insufficiently elegant. The young men find the girls too coquettish. All dread the economies that getting married entails, and if they have any inclination to take mistresses or lovers, nothing is more natural or reasonable than to feel apprehensive about a cramped and constraining situation. For a long time I found it extremely unfair that the morals of a merchant's or lawyer's wife should be judged more harshly than a tax farmer's or duke's.[17] I was wrong. The former is corrupted further, and does much more harm than the latter to her husband. She makes him look more ridiculous, because she makes his house unpleasant for him, and unless she manages to deceive him completely, banishes him from it. Now, if he allows himself to be banished, everyone takes him for a blockhead; if he allows himself to be cheated on, then he looks like an idiot—in one way or another he loses all respect, and is no longer able to do anything successfully. The public pity him, and find his wife hateful for having turned him into an object of pity. Among the wealthy and the mighty, in a huge house, no one can be pitied. The husband has mistresses if he wants to, and it's normally he who initiates the disorder. He is too respected to seem ridiculous. The wife doesn't appear hateful, and isn't. She treats her servants well, brings up her children, can do charitable works, and can invite people to dance and eat in her house. Who would complain, and how many people in fact feel pleased with themselves? The fact is that in this world, money can achieve anything. It even makes it possible to keep one's virtue in the midst of disorder, to indulge in vice with the minimum of drawbacks. A time comes, I admit, when money can no longer give these people what they desire, and when men and women, corrupted over a long period by its intoxicating possession, find it intolerable that it can no longer give them another moment of health or life, of beauty, youth, or vigor—but how many there are who die before its inadequacy makes itself so painfully felt! This is a very long letter. I am tired with writing. Good-bye, my dear friend.

I realize that I have only discussed unfaithful women, be they rich or poor; I could say the same thing about the husbands. If they aren't rich, they give their mistresses money their wives can't do without; if they're rich, it is spare money, and the wives are left with a thousand pleasures, resources, and consolations. To allow my daughter to marry a man without a fortune, I'd want them to be passionately in love; if it is a question of a great rich lord, I might look a little less carefully.

Letter V.

So your husband finds my legislation completely absurd, and went to the trouble of drawing up a list of the disadvantages of my project. Ungrateful wretch! Why doesn't he thank me for having occupied his thoughts with a thousand interesting objects, and made him think more in a week than he had perhaps done in his whole life? I am going to respond to some of his objections. "Young men would expend too much effort trying to attract those women who could raise them to a higher social class." Not more than they currently expend in seducing and cheating on all women from all classes.

"Husbands, raised by their wives to a higher class, would be too indebted to them." Apart from the fact that I can't see that this sort of gratitude has any great disadvantage, the number of indebted people would be very small, and it wouldn't be any worse to owe one's nobility to one's wife than to one's fortune, which is the sort of obligation which we see being contracted every day.

"Young ladies would not bring the most deserving people into the noble class, but only the most handsome." Young ladies would be dependent on their parents just as much as they are today, and even if every so often they did ennoble a man whose only value were to be found in his face, would that matter so much? Their children would be better-looking, and the nobility would have greater beauty. A Spanish lord once said to my father that "if you ever come across a man in Madrid who is very ugly, small, weak, and unwholesome, you can be sure that he is one of the highest in the land." A joke and a caricature do not constitute an argument, but your husband will agree that in every country there is some foundation to the Spaniard's point of view. Let us return to his list of disadvantages.

"A gentleman who fell in love with a beautiful and virtuous young woman of the second class wouldn't be able to marry her." Excuse me, but he would marry her. "But he would be lowering himself." No, everyone would cheer his sacrifice. And would he not be able to climb back even higher than his own class by meriting nomination as a member of the council to both nation and king? And wouldn't that be a way of bringing his children back up to their original class? And couldn't his children enter it anyway through marriage? "And what would be the functions of this national council? What would be its business? What affairs would it judge?" Listen, Sir Cousin: the first time a sovereign asks me to explain my project, with the intention of doing something with it, I will explain it in every detail to the best of my ability, and if, on examination, it is found to be as ill imagined and as impracticable as you suppose, I will bravely abandon it. "It certainly is a woman's project," you say. Well, indeed, I am a woman, and I have a daughter. I am biased in favor of the old nobility, and I have a weak spot for my own sex; it may well be that I am only an advocate of my own cause, rather than a balanced judge, working for the cause of society in general. And even if that were so, wouldn't it be forgivable? Would you not concede that the Dutch are more likely to feel the disadvantages that allowing free navigation of the River Scheldt would bring than the arguments of all their adversaries in favor of the rights of all nations over all rivers?[18] You remind me that this Cécile, on whose behalf I would like to create a completely new sort of monarchy, would only be in the second class, according to my proposals, given that my father would have become part of his wife's class, and my husband of mine. Thank you for having replied so seriously. You do me more honor, I won't say than I deserve, but than I had hoped for. Good-bye, cousin. I return to your wife.

You find Cécile enchanting and you are entirely right. You ask me how I've managed to keep her so robust, so wholesome and healthy. She has always been with me, she has always slept in my room, and when it was cold, in my bed. I love her and only her, and that makes me very farsighted and attentive. You ask me if she has ever been ill. You know that she had smallpox. I wanted to have her inoculated, but the illness was too quick for me, and it was long and violent.[19] Cécile is subject to very bad headaches, and every winter she has chilblains on her feet that are so bad she has to keep to her bed sometimes. I thought that would be better than completely preventing her from running about in the snow, so we warm ourselves up afterward if she gets very cold. As for her hands, I was so worried they might become ugly that I have managed to save them from that fate.

You ask me how I brought her up. I never had any servant, other than a girl brought up in my grandmother's house, who waited on my mother. It was with her, in her village, in her niece's house, that I left Cécile to come and spend a fortnight with you in Lyons, and when I came to see you at our old aunt's house. I taught my daughter to read and write as soon as she could speak and wiggle her fingers, thinking, along with the author of *Séthos*, that we don't properly know anything that we haven't learned mechanically.[20] From the age of eight to sixteen she had lessons in Latin and religion every day, given by her cousin, the father of the pedantic jealous little lover, as well as music lessons with a very accomplished and aged organist. I taught her as much arithmetic as a woman needs to know. I showed her how to sew, knit, and make lace. I left the rest to chance. She learned a little geography by looking at the maps that hang in my withdrawing room, she read what she came across when it amused her to do so, she listened to what was being said when she was curious, and her curiosity was never any trouble. I am not very learned; my daughter is even less so. I didn't make a point of keeping her busy all the time; I let her get bored when I couldn't keep her amused. I didn't hire any expensive tutors for her. She is completely unable to play the harp. She can't speak either Italian or English. She had only three months of dance lessons. You see, she's nothing particularly marvelous, but in truth, she is so pretty, so good, so natural, that I don't think that anyone would want to change anything. Why, you ask, did I have her learn Latin? So that she understood French without my needing to correct her endlessly, to give her something to do, to get rid of her and be able to rest for an hour every day; and it cost us nothing. My cousin the professor had more wit than his son, and all the simplicity he lacks. He was an excellent man. He loved Cécile, and up to his death, the lessons he gave her were as agreeable to him as they were profitable for her. She nursed him in his final illness as if she were nursing her own father, and the example of patience and resignation that he gave her was a last and more important lesson than all the rest, and made all the others more useful. Whenever she has a headache or her chilblains stop her from doing what she'd like to or anyone tells her about any epidemic disease threatening Lausanne (we are rather subject to epidemics here), she thinks about her cousin the professor, and she doesn't allow herself to complain, get impatient, or be excessively terrified.

You are very good to thank me for my letters. I'm the one who should thank you for being so kind as to give me the pleasure of writing them.

Letter VI.

Is there no drawback, you say, to letting her read and listen as she pleases? Wouldn't it have been better to, and so on? I'm summarizing and not transcribing your sentences in full, because they gave me pain. Perhaps it would have been better to teach her more or less, or something else; perhaps there were disadvantages, etc. But don't forget that my daughter and I are not a novel like Adelaide and her mother, nor a lesson or an example to cite.[21] I love my daughter and only her; nothing, or so it seems to me, ever shared my attention, or weighed against her interest in my heart. Suppose that despite all this I did it badly, or insufficiently. Blame the parents. If you have faith in education, blame the parents, from children to fathers and mothers, back to Noah or Adam, who, bringing up their children badly, transmitted their bad education from father to child all the way down to Cécile. If you have more faith in nature, go back even further, and consider that whichever system it pleases you to adopt, I could not have done better than I did. After receiving your letter, I went to sit down opposite Cécile; I watched her working with skill, activity, and cheerfulness.[22] My mind filled with what you had written to me, tears came to my eyes, and Cécile started playing the harpsichord to cheer me up. I sent her to the other end of town, and she went and came back without ill effects despite the fact that it's very cold. Tedious visitors called; she was sweet tempered, helpful, and cheerful. The little lord begged her to accept a concert ticket; his offer gave her pleasure, but, with a glance at me, she gracefully refused. I am going to go to bed in peace. I will not believe that I have brought her up badly. I will not blame myself. The impression your letter made has almost worn away. If my daughter is unhappy, I will be unhappy; but I will not blame the tender heart of a mother devoted to her child. Nor will I blame my daughter; I will blame society, fate, or even nothing at all; I will not complain; I will submit in silence and with patience and courage. Do not apologize for your letter—let's forget it. I know perfectly well that you didn't mean to give me pain; you thought you were consulting a book or interrogating an author. Tomorrow I will continue in a more peaceful frame of mind.

Your husband does not want me to complain about the foreigners in Lausanne, saying that the number of people that they benefit is greater than the number of people they harm. Maybe, and I'm not complaining. Apart from this generous and considered reason, habit makes the company of strangers quite agreeable. It is more cheerful and more gay. It also seems like a sort of homage that the universe is paying to our charming country, and unlike the universe, which has no vanity, we receive this homage with pride. Moreover, who knows if all the girls don't secretly see a husband and their mothers a son-in-law in every carriage which arrives? Cécile has a new adorer who is from neither Paris nor London. He is the son of our bailiff, a handsome young man from Bern, all milk and roses, and the nicest child in the world.[23] After having met us two or three times, I don't know where, he has been visiting us with great assiduousness, and he hasn't concealed the fact that he's doing it secretly; he finds it so obvious that his Bernese parents would be appalled to see their son become attached to a subject of the Pays de Vaud. Let him come, poor lad, secretly or otherwise; he won't do Cécile any harm, nor damage her reputation, and Mr. and Mrs. Governor won't have any seduction to reproach us with. He's just coming in with the young lord. I will leave you to welcome them. Here's the little dead minister and the quick one too. I'm also expecting young Faraud and the young shopkeeper, and many others. Cécile is receiving friends. Some young ladies are also coming to us, but they will be in less of a hurry than the young men. Cécile has begged me to stay at home and do the honors of her day, as much because she feels more at ease when I am with her as because she thinks it's too cold to let me go out.

Letter VII.

So you would, in your enchantment with Cécile and pride in your relations, have me banish the governor's nephew from my home? You are wrong; you are unfair. The richest and best-born girl from the Pays de Vaud is a bad match for someone from Bern. If he were to marry someone from his own city he would gain more than wealth; he would gain support and connections, and the ability to enter government. He would put himself in the way of distinguishing himself, of making his

talents useful to himself, his relations, and his country. I
applaud the fathers and mothers for feeling all this and for
safeguarding their sons from the traps that could be set for
them here. Moreover, it's all very well for a girl from Lausanne
to become the wife of a bailiff or even of a councillor—in
Bern she would miss Lake Geneva and its charming shores.[24]
It's as if you took a girl from Paris to be a princess in Germany.
But I would like it if the women of Bern married the men from
the Pays de Vaud more often and if there were greater equality
and openness between us, if we stopped complaining, sometimes unfairly, of their sullenness and proud reserve, and if they
stopped providing us with the slightest justification for our
complaints. It is said that the kings of France have been obliged
for good political reasons to weaken their great vassals and
make them less able to cause trouble. Doubtless, they did the
right thing; to guarantee the peace of the state is the most
important thing of all, yet I feel that I would have been incapable of carrying out this policy of which I approve. I love
everything which is beautiful and prosperous so much that I
would be incapable of pruning a single branch from a fine tree,
even if it were to give more food or sun to trees that I had
planted myself.

Everything appears to be going as well for me as before, but
I fear that the wound in my daughter's heart is deepening
every day. The young Englishman does not mention love; I
don't know if he feels any, but his attentions are wholly hers.
She receives a beautiful posy on ball days. He took her for a
sleigh ride. He always wants to dance with her. He offers his
arm either to her or to me whenever we leave an assembly. She
says nothing about it to me, but I can see that she is either
happy or thoughtful, depending on whether she does or does
not see him, and according to how marked his preference is.
Our old organist has died. She begged me to devote this hour
to teaching her English instead. I consented. She will be profi-
cient very quickly. The young man is amazed at her progress,
and doesn't consider that it is because of him. They have
started being paired together at card games wherever they
meet. I did not want her to play. I said that a girl who plays as

badly as my daughter should not play, and that I would be vexed for her to learn so soon. Whereupon the young Englishman had the tiniest checkerboard made with the tiniest pieces and carries it about everywhere in his pocket. How can I stop these children playing! When checkers starts to bore Cécile, he will, he says, get a miniature chessboard. He does not notice how unlikely it is that she will get bored. The delusions of self-love are endlessly debated, but in fact it is very rare for anyone to realize how much they are loved when they are truly loved. A child does not see how much his mother continually thinks about him. A lover does not notice that his mistress has eyes and ears only for him. A mistress does not suppose that she does not utter a word or make a gesture that does not cause her lover pleasure or pain. If they only knew, how much they would watch each other, out of pity, out of generosity, out of interest, so as not to lose the inestimable unthinkable good of being tenderly loved!

The young lord's tutor, or the person I have called his tutor, is a cousin of his from an older but untitled branch of the family. This is what the young man tells me. He is not much older, and there's a certain something in his physiognomy, in his whole appearance, which I have never seen in anyone else. He would not mock my ideas on nobility like your husband did; he may find them trivial but he wouldn't find them obscure. The other day he was saying: "A king is not always a gentleman"— in sum, whether my ideas are fanciful or not, they exist in other imaginations as well as in mine.[25]

Good God, how preoccupied I am with what is happening here, and how anxious I am about how I ought to behave! Milord's cousin (he is Milord par excellence, although there are many others, because I do not want to name him, and I do not want to name him for the same reason that I do not sign my name or name anyone; the accidents which can befall letters always frighten me)—Milord's relative is sad. I don't know whether this is because he has undergone some misfortune or whether it is his natural disposition. He lives two paces from us, and has started coming every day. Seated by the fireside, stroking my dog, reading the gazette or some newspaper, he lets me run my household, write my letters, direct Cécile's work. He says he will correct her essays once she is able to write them, and will give her the English newspaper to read so that she can become accustomed to everyday familiar language. Should I send him away? Am I not allowed to encourage him to view favorably what would be a brilliant and agreeable establishment for my daughter by letting him see what mother and daughter are like from morning to evening and obliging him to speak well of us to the father and mother of the young man? Must I push aside something which might secure for Cécile the man who pleases her? I don't yet want to say the man she loves. Soon she will be eighteen. Nature perhaps more than the heart . . . will it be said that the first woman a young man is attracted to is the one he loves?

You would like Cécile to learn chemistry because in France all the young ladies are learning it.[26] This reason does not seem decisive to me, but Cécile, who's heard it being discussed often enough, will be able to read what she wants to about it. For my part, I do not like chemistry. I know that we owe many useful discoveries and inventions as well as agreeable things to chemists, but their operations give me no pleasure. I consider nature as a lover; they study it as anatomists.[27]

Letter VIII.

Something happened the other day which upset and alarmed me greatly. I was working, and my Englishman was gazing into the fire without saying a word, when Cécile came back from paying a visit looking as pale as death. I was very frightened. I asked her what was wrong, what had happened to her. The Englishman, almost as frightened as I was, almost as pale as she, begged her to speak. He wanted to leave, saying that it was no doubt his presence that was stopping her from speaking; she stopped him by holding on to his coat, and started weeping, or rather sobbing. I embraced her and caressed her; we gave her a drink; her tears continued to flow. Our collective silence lasted for more than half an hour. In order to allow her to calm down, I picked up my work again, and he started stroking the dog again. In the end, she said, "It will be very hard for me to explain what has affected me so much, and my grief is giving me more pain than the thing which caused it in the first place. I don't know why I am so upset, and more than anything I am vexed with myself for being upset. What does this mean, Mama? Will you be able to understand me when I can't understand myself? I am calm enough now to tell you what the matter is. I will say it in front of monsieur. He has gone to too much trouble on my behalf and shown me too much compassion for me to show him any reserve. You can both laugh at me if you want—perhaps I'll laugh at myself with you—but promise me, monsieur, to tell no one what I'm about to say."

"I promise you not to, mademoiselle," he said.

"Repeat *no one*."

"No one."

"And you—you, Mama, please do not ever speak to me about it unless I mention it first. I saw Milord in the boutique opposite here. He was talking to Madame de ***'s lady's maid."

And she did not say any more. We said nothing in reply. An instant later Milord came in. He asked her if she'd like to go for a sleigh ride. She said, "Not today, but tomorrow, if there's still enough snow." Then, having come close to her, he noticed that she was pale and that her eyes were swimming. Tentatively, he asked what the matter was. His cousin replied firmly that we could not tell him that. He did not press us. He remained thoughtful, and a quarter of an hour later, when some ladies arrived, they both left. Cécile recovered quite well. We have not returned to the subject. Only when she was getting into bed she said, "Mama, in truth, I do not know whether I want the snow to melt or not." I did not reply. The snow did melt, but we have been seeing each other as much as before. Nonetheless, Cécile has been looking a bit graver and more reserved. The lady's maid is pretty and so is her mistress. I do not know which one she was worried about, but from that moment on I fear that all this has become quite serious. I haven't got any time to write more today but I will write soon.

Your man must have finally heard me if he said that "if a
king can be not a gentleman, then a yokel can be a king."
Granted, but I suppose, in favor of nobles by birth, that nobility of feeling is more often to be found among them than elsewhere. He wants the king of my kingdom to ennoble the heroes,
the Ruiters, the Tromps, the Faberts—exactly![28] Quite right!

Letter IX.

This Latin really is important to you, and you do not forget it.
"Do you know Latin?" you ask me. No, but my father told me
a hundred times that he was vexed not to have made me learn
it. He spoke French very well. He and my grandfather did not
let me speak it very badly, and this is what makes me harder to
please than others. As for my daughter, one sees, when she
writes, that she has a thorough knowledge of her language,
but she speaks it very incorrectly. I let her speak. I like her negligent lapses, either because they're hers, or because they are
agreeable. She is stricter: if she sees me making a spelling mistake, she pulls me up. Her style is much more correct than
mine, and therefore she writes as little as she can; it's too much
trouble. You ask if her Latin doesn't make her arrogant. Good
God, no. What we learn when young seems no more strange
or difficult than breathing and walking. You ask how I come
to know English. Do you not recall that we had an aunt, you
and I, who had to retire to England for religious reasons? Her
daughter, whom the Bretons would call my aunt, spent three
years in my father's house when I was young, soon after my
journey to Languedoc. She was a person of great spirit and
worth. I owe her almost everything I know, as well as the practice of thinking and reading. Let us return to my favorite subject and to my habitual details.

Last week we attended an assembly, to which Monsieur Tissot had brought a Frenchwoman; her face was charming and
she had the finest eyes possible, as well as all the grace which
confidence and social ease can bestow. She was dressed in the
excesses of fashion, without looking ridiculous. An immense

cadogan went below her shoulders, and great ringlets floated on her bosom.[29] The little Englishman and the man from Bern were ceaselessly attentive to her, more out of astonishment than admiration, at least that was the case with the Englishman, whom I was watching closely. So many people pressed round Cécile that if she was affected by their desertion she didn't have time to show it. Except that when Milord wanted to play checkers, she said to him that she had a slight headache and preferred not to play. The rest of the evening she stayed close to me, and cut out paper shapes for the child of the house. I do not know whether the little lord sensed what was happening in her, but, not knowing what to say to his Parisienne, he left. As we went out of the room, he was waiting at the door with the servants. I do not know whether Cécile will ever have a more agreeable moment in the rest of her life. Two days later he was spending the evening at my house with his cousin, the man from Bern, and two or three girls, cousins of Cécile. The French lady came under discussion. The two young people mercilessly praised her eyes, her waist, her bearing, and her dress. Cécile said nothing; I didn't say much. Finally, they praised her forest of hair. "It's not real," said Cécile. "Ha ha, Mademoiselle Cécile," said the man from Bern. "Young ladies are always jealous of each other. Admit it! Isn't it true that you're envious?" I thought that Milord was smiling. I became really angry.

"My daughter does not know what envy is," I told them. "Yesterday she praised the foreign lady's hairstyle, as you just did; she was at the house of an acquaintance of mine whose hair was at that moment being dressed. Her hairdresser, who had just come from the Parisienne's house, told us that her big cadogan and great ringlets were false. If my daughter had been a few years older, she would have said nothing; at her age, and having a real forest on her head, it's natural enough to speak out. Only yesterday," I continued, turning to the man from Bern, "were you not telling us with great animation about how you have the biggest dog in the country? And you, Milord, did you give us any room to doubt that your horse was much finer than Mister such-and-such's or Lord what's-his-name's?"

Cécile, embarrassed, smiled and wept all at once. "It is too good of you, Mama," she said, "to defend me so vigorously."

But in fact I was wrong; I would have done better to keep quiet. I was still angry. "Sir," I said to the man from Bern, "every time a woman seems jealous of the way you praise another woman, far from reproaching her for it, in your heart, you should be thanking her. You should be flattered." "I do not know," said Milord's cousin, "whether there would be grounds for being so. Women wish to please men, and men women; nature has ordained it so. That one might wish to enjoy the advantages of the gifts we have received, and not allow a usurper to benefit from them at our expense, still seems so natural to me, that I cannot see how anyone could find it bad. If someone was being praised to these ladies for something that I had myself done, I would certainly say that it had been I. And then, there is a certain truthful spirit which makes itself heard instantly, without thinking about the disadvantages or benefits to itself. Supposing mademoiselle had had false hair, and that it had been admired; I am sure she would immediately have said that it was false." "No doubt I would, sir," said Cécile, "but I can see that it's not right to say it about someone else." At that point, chance brought us visitors—a young woman, her husband, and brother. Cécile started playing allemandes and country dances on the harpsichord, and everyone danced.[30]

"Good night, my mother, my protectress," said Cécile when she went to bed. "Good night, my Don Quixote."[31] I laughed. Cécile is growing up, and becomes more lovely with every day that passes. May she not buy her charms at too high a price!

Letter X.

I'm afraid I think Cécile may have made a new conquest, and if that's so, I will be reconciled, I think, to the partiality she has for her lord. Indeed, if it is no more than a partiality that she has, she may be insufficiently protected. The man in question, a cousin of mine, is very amiable. He is a gentleman from this region, a Captain in the service of the French army, who has just got married, or rather allowed himself to get married in the worst way in the world. He had no fortune. A distant cousin of the same name, heiress to a fine estate which has long been in the family, said that she'd marry him more willingly than anyone else. His parents thought this was admirable, and thought she was a charming girl because she is lively, bold, talks a great deal at great speed, and passes for a wit. He was at his garrison. He was written to. He replied that he had counted on not getting married but that he would do what was wanted of him, and things were so well managed that having returned on October 1, he was married by the 20th. I think that by the 30th he would already have wanted no longer to be so. His wife is vain, jealous, and haughty. What mind she has is nothing more than a sort of sharp and pretentious inanity. I went without my daughter to congratulate them two months ago. They have been back in town for a fortnight now. Madame wants to be in the center of everything, to shine, to please, to play a role. She considers herself rich, amiable, and pretty enough for all this. The husband, ashamed and bored, avoids being at home, and as we are distantly related, it is in my house that he has sought refuge. The first time he came, he was very struck by Cécile, whom he hadn't seen since she was a child, and finding me almost always alone with her or only having the Englishman, Milord's tutor, for company, he has become used to coming every day. The two men are well suited and like each other a great deal. Both are educated men, both have subtle minds, are discerning and tasteful, polite and gentle. My cousin is indolent, lazy; he is no longer so sorry to be married because he's forgotten that he is. The other is quietly sad and contemplative. From the first day they have behaved as if they had always known each other, but my cousin seems more preoccupied with Cécile with every day that passes. Yesterday while they were discussing America and the war, Cécile whispered to me, "Mama, one of these men is in love with you."[32] "And the other with you," I replied. Upon which, smiling, she started to consider him. His appearance is so noble and elegant that if the little lord weren't there, I would be worried indeed. I should never tire of being vexed about it at present,

but there are so many things happening that I can't take them all to heart. My cousin and his wife will have to get along as best they can. He hasn't noticed the young lord yet, he being less of a fixture in the house than his cousin, far from it. But whenever he finishes lessons at the college, he comes to look for his cousin here if he can't find him at home. That's what he did the day before yesterday, and knowing that we were due to spend the evening at the cousin's where he had first lodged, he begged me to take him too, saying that he couldn't bear still to be on bad terms with them, after all the kindness he'd received in that house. I said I would be happy to. The two pillars from either side of my fireplace came too. My cousin the professor's wife, convinced that in all word games her son would shine way above everyone else, wanted us to fill in rhyming couplets, and then make speeches on eight words, then write out questions on a card. You jumble the cards; everyone takes one at random and writes a reply beneath the question. You rejumble and write until all the cards are filled. I was asked to read them out loud. There were some very flat things and others which were very pretty. I should add that everyone scratches and scribbles so that no one's handwriting is recognizable. On one card this is what had been written: "To whom do we owe our first education?" "To our nurse" was the reply. Under the reply had been written: "And the second?" Reply: "To chance." "And the third?" "To love." "You were the one who wrote that," one of the company said. "I give my consent for you to suppose it," said I, "for it is a pretty thought." M. de ***
looked at Cécile. "She who wrote it," said he, "already owes much to that third education." Cécile blushed more than she ever had in her life. "I would like to know who it is," said the little lord. "Might it not be yourself?" I said to him. "Why do you want it to be a woman? Do men not need this education as much as we do? Perhaps it is my cousin the minister." "Go on, tell us, Johnnie," said his mother. "I think it must be because it's so pretty." "Oh no," said Johnnie, "I finished my education in Bâle." This made everyone laugh, and the game stopped there. On our way home, Cécile said to me, "It wasn't me, Mama, who wrote that reply." "So why did you blush so much

then?" I asked her. "Because I thought—because, Mama, because . . ." I never found out why, or rather, she didn't say any more.

Letter XI.

You want to know whether Cécile's guess about my friend the Englishman is correct. I do not know; I do not think about it; I haven't the time to pay any attention to it.

Yesterday we went to a large assembly at the castle. A nephew of the governor, who had arrived the night before, was presented by him to the ladies he wished to single out. I have never seen a better-looking man. He serves in the same regiment as my cousin. They are friends, and when he saw his brother officer chatting with Cécile and me, he came to join the conversation. I was, in truth, extremely pleased with him. It would be impossible to be more polite, to speak better, to have a better accent or air, or to have nobler manners. This time the little lord might have felt pained. He did not seem anything other than a pretty child of no importance. I don't know whether he was pained, but he certainly kept very close to us. As soon as the question of playing cards came up, he asked me if it would be as proper to play drafts at the governor's residence as elsewhere, and entreated me, should I deem it suitable, to arrange for him to play reversis with Cécile.[33] He claimed that he knew no one but her in the entire assembly, and that he played so badly he would bore the ladies he was partnered with to death. The more attentive to Cécile the most remarkable men present became, the better pleased he seemed to know her. He really did make more of a fuss of her. She seemed to notice, but instead of laughing at him for it, as he deserved, she seemed pleased. Happy to make a favorable impression on her lover, she was content with the reason, whatever it might be.

You are amazed that Cécile goes out by herself and is allowed to receive young men and women in my absence—I see that in fact you blame me for it, but you are wrong. Why not let her enjoy the liberty our customs endorse and which she is so little tempted to abuse? Circumstances have separated her from the companions she knew as a child, and the only close friend she has is her mother, whom she leaves as little as she can. We do have mothers who, whether from caution or vanity, bring their daughters up in the same way as fine Parisian young ladies are brought up, but I don't see what they gain from it, and hating fetters of any sort, and hating pride, I am careful not to imitate them. Cécile has cousins from my mother's side as well as from my husband's; she has male and female cousins in every quarter of the town, and I consider it a good thing that she live with all of them, as they do, and that she be dear to them all.* In France, I would do as the French do; here, you would do as I do. Good God! How ridiculous, how odious is a haughty and scornful young lady who weighs up her own reception, tone, and curtsy in contrast to those of the people she encounters! That humble vanity which consists of being so very afraid of compromising oneself that one seems to be admitting that the slightest thing would be sufficient to make us forfeit our rank is not rare in our little towns; I've seen enough of it to be disgusted with it.†

Letter XII.

If you hadn't been pressing me so generously and earnestly to continue these letters, I would be hesitating today. Until now it has been a pleasure and a relaxation for me to write them. Today I think it's going to be the opposite. Moreover, to

---

* Author's footnote: In Lausanne there are some quarters not frequented by high society.

† Author's footnote: Some people deem it bad that these letters do not give a more exact idea of the behavior of the most distinguished inhabitants of Lausanne, but apart from the fact that Mme de *** is not an outsider who would watch their behavior and consider it worthy of observation, of what interest could it be to her cousin? People of the first rank resemble each other everywhere, and had she said something that was specific to those in Lausanne, would we be pardoned for publishing it? When one only praises as much as one must, one flatters little, and is even often offensive.

narrate it accurately, I would need a letter which I can't recall
from memory alone. . . . Aha! There it is, in a corner of my
desk. Cécile, who has gone out, will no doubt have been worried that it would fall out of her pockets. I might copy it out, as
I don't dare send it to you. Perhaps she'll want to reread it one
day. This time you do owe me thanks, as I'm giving myself
quite an arduous task.

Starting with the jealous moment I told you about, whether
because she's sometimes cross and remains suspicious, or
because having seen into her heart more clearly, she has condemned herself to greater reserve, Cécile has never wanted to
play checkers in company. She has been working or watching
me play. But at my house, once or twice, they have played, and
the young man undertook to teach her how chess works the
other evening after supper, while his cousin and mine (I mean
the officer from ***) were playing piquet together. Seated
between the two tables, I was working and alternately watching the two men and the two children play—that evening they
were behaving even more like children than they normally do.
Cécile was endlessly getting the name and moves of the chess
pieces wrong and provoking pleasantries in response which
were as cheerful as they were lacking in wit. One time the little
lord grew impatient with her inattention and Cécile got cross
at his impatience. I turned my head. I saw that they were sulking at each other. I shrugged my shoulders. A second later, not
hearing them speak, I looked at them. Cécile's hand lay unmov-
ing on the chessboard. She was leaning forward, her head lowered. The young man, also leaning down toward her, seemed
to devour her with his eyes. Everything else was forgotten; it
was ecstasy, abandon. "Cécile," I said softly, for I didn't want
to frighten her. "Cécile, what are you thinking about?" "Nothing," she said, hiding her head in her hands, and suddenly
pushing her chair back. "I think this wretched chess has tired
me out. For the last few minutes, Milord, I've been even less
able to tell them apart than before, and you will have even
more cause to feel displeased with your pupil, so let's stop."
She got up, in fact, left the room, and didn't come back until I
was alone. She sank to her knees, laid her head on my lap, and

taking my hands, drenched them with tears. "What is it, my Cécile?" I said to her. "What is it?"

"But I'm asking you, Mama," she said. "What is happening inside me? What have I been feeling? Why am I ashamed? Why am I weeping?"

"Did he notice your distress?" I asked her.

"I don't think so, Mama," she replied. "Perhaps vexed with his own impatience, he grasped my hand and kissed it when I tried to pick up a pawn which had fallen over. I withdrew my hand, but I was so happy we were no longer quarreling! His eyes seemed so tender to me! I was overwhelmed! At that moment, you said quietly, 'Cécile! Cécile!' He might have thought that I was still angry because I wasn't looking at him."

"I hope so," I told her.

"I hope so too," she said. "But Mama, why do you hope so?"

"Do you not know, my dear Cécile, how much men tend to think and speak ill of women?"

"But," said Cécile, "if there were grounds here for thinking and speaking ill, he could not accuse me without accusing himself even more. Did he not kiss my hand, and was he not as troubled as I was?"

"Perhaps, Cécile; but he will remember the impression you made much more clearly than what he was doing. He will have seen a sort of sensibility or weakness in you which may carry you very far, and decide your fate. His own feelings are no doubt not new to him, and are of less consequence. Still filled with your image, if he encountered a girl of easy virtue in the street . . ."

"Oh Mama!"

"Yes, Cécile, do not allow yourself to be deluded: a man will seek to instill in every woman and secure for himself the feeling which often he has for the entire species. Being able to satisfy his inclination everywhere he looks, that which for us is only too often the great affair of our life, for him is almost nothing at all."

"The great affair of our life! What! It happens to some women that they devote their thoughts to a man who barely notices them?"

"Yes, it happens. It also happens to some women that they think about men in general. Whether they lead abandoned lives, or whether they do not give in to their inclination, it is still the great, the single affair of these unhappy women. Cécile, in your religious lessons, you were told that you needed to be chaste and pure. Did you attach any meaning to these words?"

"No, Mama."

"Well, the moment has come for you to practice a virtue, to abstain from a vice which you could have no idea about. If this virtue comes to seem difficult to you, think that it is the only one which you must rigorously observe, vigilantly practice, with scrupulous attention to yourself."

"The only one!"

"Examine yourself, and read the Ten Commandments. Will you need to watch over yourself so as not to murder, steal, or bear false witness? No doubt you never even thought to remember that you were not allowed to do these things. You will not need to remember, and if you ever were inclined to covet something, it would be the lover or husband of another woman that you would desire for yourself, or rather the advantages that attract to someone else the husband or the lover whom you want for yourself. What is known as *virtue* for women will be the only virtue you won't be able to have, the only one which you will practice as a virtue, and the only one about which you will be able to say when practicing it, 'I obey the precepts that I have been taught are the laws of God, and which I have received as such.' "

"But, Mama, have men not received the same laws? Why are they allowed to flout them and thereby make it difficult for us to observe them?"

"I really do not know what to say in reply, Cécile, but either way it is none of our business. I have no son. I do not know what I would say to my son. I have only thought about the daughter I do have and whom I love above all other things. What I can say to you is that society, which dispenses men and does not dispense women from a law which religion seems to have given equally to all, imposes other laws on men which are not perhaps any easier to observe. It requires moderation, delicacy, discretion, and courage of them, even in debauchery, and if they forget these laws, they are dishonored and avoided, their approach is feared, and everywhere they go they meet with a welcome which says to them: *we had given you privileges enough, but they did not satisfy you; society will use your example to inspire fear in those who might be tempted to imitate you, and who in imitating you would disturb everything, reverse everything, and take away all security and confidence from the world.* And these men, punished more harshly than women ever are, have often been guilty of nothing worse than imprudence, weakness, or a single moment of frenzy, for men of determined vice, of true wickedness, are as rare as perfect men and perfect women. They are rarely seen elsewhere than in ill-imagined fictions.[34] I repeat that I do not consider the condition of men even in this respect to be so excessively unlike women's. And then, how many other painful obligations society imposes on them! Do you believe, for example, that if war is declared, it would be particularly pleasant for your cousin to leave us in March to go and and risk being killed, maimed, or infected with the germs of an illness from which he may never recover, caught from lying on damp ground and living among diseased prisoners?"

"But Mama, it's his duty and his profession; he chose it. He is paid for everything you just said, and if he distinguishes himself, he will win honor, maybe even glory. He will advance in his profession and perhaps be honored wherever he goes—in Holland, France, Switzerland, and even by the enemies he has fought against."

"Well, Cécile, it is the duty of every woman to be decent. She won't have chosen it, but most men don't choose theirs either. Their parents and circumstances make the choice for them before they're old enough to understand and choose. A woman is repaid only by being a woman. Are we not almost always dispensed from arduous work? Do men not protect us from heat, cold, and fatigue? Are there many men so lacking in politeness that they don't make way for you on the pavement, or give you the least rocky path, or the most comfortable seat? If a woman protects her morals and her reputation from attack, she would have to be odious and disagreeable indeed not to meet with attentions everywhere she goes, and then is it nothing, after having attached an honest man, to get him to settle, to be chosen by him and his parents to be his companion? Those girls who don't behave as they should are even more attractive; they drive men to delirium, but it is rare that this delirium prompts them to marry, and rarer still that these girls, once married, are not punished for their erstwhile seductiveness with humiliation and repentence. My dear Cécile, one moment of that sensibility, which I would like you not to give in to ever again, has often deprived amiable girls who were in no way given to vice of an advantageous establishment, of the hand of the man they loved, and who loved them."

"What! That sensibility, that feeling which they inspire and which they try to inspire, estranges them?"

"It frightens them, Cécile. Until the instant the question of marriage arises, they want their mistress to be feeling and responsive and will complain if she isn't responsive enough. But as soon as it is a question of marriage, supposing that they haven't lost their head completely, they judge as if they were already husbands, and a husband is such a different thing from a lover, that the one judges nothing as the other had done. They remember refusals with pleasure; they consider the favors they received with anxiety. The bold trust displayed by a girl who is too tenderly affectionate no longer appears to be anything other than the sort of indiscretion she might be led to by anyone who gave her encouragement. The warmth of her response to her lover's marks of affection will come to seem like nothing other than a disposition to love all men. Imagine the displeasure, the jealousy and pain of her husband, for the desire for exclusive ownership is the most acute feeling remaining to him. He will quickly console himself for not being loved enough, so long as no one else is. He is jealous even when he himself no longer loves, and his anxiety is not as absurd and unfair as you may at present suppose. I often find men odious for being so demanding and for being so demanding of women, but I do not think that they are so mistaken in fearing this particular thing. An imprudent girl is not often a prudent and decent woman. The girl who did not resist her lover before marriage is rarely faithful after it. Often she no longer sees the lover in her husband. The latter is as negligent as the former was insistent. The former thought everything was good, the latter everything bad. She barely considers herself obliged to keep the promises to the second which she made to the first. Her imagination also promised her pleasures which she did not find, or no longer finds. She hopes to find them outside marriage, and if she did not resist her desires as a girl, she won't resist them as a woman. She gets used to being weak, and duty and modesty become accustomed to giving way. What I say is so true that society finds the decency of a beautiful woman courted by many men as admirable as the discretion of a girl in the same case. We recognize that temptation is more or less the same and that resistance is as difficult. I have seen women get married in the grip of violent passion and yet have a lover two years later, and then another and another, until the moment when, despised and disgraced, they—"

"Oh Mama!" Cécile burst out, getting up. "Have I deserved all this?"

"You mean, do you need all this?" I said, pulling her back onto my lap, and with my face wiping away the tears that flowed down hers. "No, Cécile, I do not believe that you needed to hear such an appalling account, and even if you had, would you be any guiltier, less praiseworthy, less lovely—would you be any less dear or precious to me? But off you go to bed now, dear daughter; off you go, and don't forget that I did not blame you for anything, and that I really did need to warn you. I'm only going to do it this once. Off you go." And off she went. I sat down at my desk, and wrote:

My Cécile, my dear daughter, I promised you that just this once you would be tormented by the solicitude of a mother who loves you more than her life: thereafter, knowing everything on this subject that I know, everything that I've ever thought, my daughter will judge for herself. I may remind her from time to time about what I tell her today, but I will never repeat it. So please allow me to finish, Cécile, and pay attention until the very end. I will not be saying to you what I would have said to many others; that is, that should you fail in decency, you relinquish all virtues, that as a jealous, duplicitous, coquettish, flighty woman, you would soon have love only for yourself, and would cease to be a daughter, a friend, or a lover. On the contrary, what I will say is that all the precious qualities which are in you and which you could never lose would make the loss of decency more painful, by increasing its misery and troubles. There are women whose flaws somehow make up for vice and cover it up. They retain a decent and impressive exterior however depraved they are. Their hypocrisy saves them from the scorn that would have rebounded on everyone around them. Imperious and proud, they make the yoke they themselves cast aside weigh down on others all the more. They set and maintain the standard; they make the women who imitate them tremble in fear. To hear them judge and condemn others, anyone would suppose them to be prudes.[35] Their husbands, little though chance has served them, believe them to be prudes, and their children, far from blushing at them, cite them as examples of austerity. But if it were you, what would you dare say to your children? How could you dare reprove the servants? Whom would you dare censure? Hesitating, interrupting yourself, blushing at every word, your indulgence for the faults of others would reveal your own. Sincere, humble, and just, you would only dishonor those whose reputation depended on yours all the more. Disorder and debauchery would gather around you. If your husband had a mistress, you would discover that you were happy to share a home with her that you considered you no longer had any right to, and perhaps you would permit her children to share the inheritance destined for yours. Be good, my Cécile, so that you can enjoy your lovely qualities. Be good—you would risk being much too unhappy if you weren't. I will not say everything to you that I might. I will not depict the regret of having given too much love to someone who did not much deserve it, the despair of blushing for your lover even more than for his weaknesses, of being amazed in cold blood that you could ever have committed a crime for him. But I have said enough. I have finished, Cécile. Benefit from my advice if you can; but if you do not follow it, never hide yourself from a mother who adores you. What would you have to fear? Rebukes? I would never rebuke you; that would upset me even more than you. The loss of my attachment? I would perhaps love you even more if you were to be pitied and ran the risk of being abandoned by everyone else. To make me die of grief? No, I would live; I would try to prolong my life so as to assuage your troubles, and to force you to respect yourself despite the weaknesess that would still leave you with a thousand virtues and in my eyes a thousand charms.

When Cécile got up she read what I had written. I arranged for some needlewomen we needed to come straightaway. I tried to occupy and distract Cécile and myself, and I succeeded. But after dinner, as we were all at our work together, she interrupted the general silence. "One word, Mama. If husbands were as you have described them, if marriage has so little point, would it be a great loss?" "Yes, Cécile—you see how sweet it is to be a mother. Moreover there are exceptions, and each girl supposing that she and her lover are an exception will be sorry not to have been able to marry him, as if that were a great disaster, even if it weren't. One word, my daughter, in turn. I have been thinking about what I was going to say to you for more than an hour. You have heard women who are well-known for their loose morals, being praised, and perhaps it was wrong to praise them in your presence, but these were women who could not have done what we admire them for had they been decent women. Adrienne Lecouvreur would not have been able to send the price of her diamonds to the Maréchal de Saxe had she not been given them, and she would not have known him if she hadn't been his mistress.[36] Agnès Sorel could not have saved France if she had not been Charles VII's mistress.[37] But would we not be angry to learn that the mother of the Gracchi, or Anthony's wife, Octavia, or Cato's daughter, Portia, had had lovers?"[38] My erudition made Cécile laugh. "Dear Mama," said she, "I can tell that you've been thinking hard about what to say, and you had to go back quite far—" "It is true," I interrupted, "that I haven't found anything in modern times, but we can replace the Roman dames with Madame Tr., Mlle des M., and Mlle de S. if you want."[39]

The young lord came to see us earlier than usual. Cécile barely raised her eyes from her work. She apologized for her lack of attention the night before, said it was very natural that he should have become impatient, and blamed herself for having been ill tempered. She requested him, after having asked my permission, to return the following day to give her a lesson that she would no doubt learn much more from. "What! Is that what you remember about it?" he said, drawing near to her and pretending to look at her work. "Yes," she said, "that's right." "I flatter myself," said he, "that you were not angry with me." "Not angry in the slightest," she replied. He left undeceived—that is to say, deceived. Cécile wrote on a card: "I deceived him, but it was really not very agreeable to do it." I wrote: "No, but it was necessary, and you did well. I am an interested party, Cécile. I wish it was only up to you to marry this little lord. His parents would not find it too good, but as they would be wrong, I do not care. For that you have to try to deceive him. If you succeed in deceiving him, he may say: 'This is an amiable, good girl; she does not have much of that sensibility which a husband so fears; she will be decent; I love her, I respect her, I will marry her.' " Cécile gave me back the two cards with a smile. I wrote on a third one: "As for the rest, I only say *deceive* so as not to have to do deceiving. If I am curious to read a letter which is entrusted to me, to the extent that I am sometimes tempted to open it, is it being deceitful not to open it and not say unless necessary that I had been tempted to? So long as I am discreet, the confidence others have in me will have been deserved as well as advantageous to them." "Mama," said Cécile, "say everything you want to me, but as for reminding me of what you have said or written, there is no need. I am unable to forget it. I didn't understand it all, but the words are graven in my mind. I will explain the things you said with the things I see and read, and with those that I have already seen and read, and those things I will explain in turn with the things you told me. Everything will illuminate everything else. Help me sometimes, Mama, to apply it as you used to when you would say: 'Look at that little girl: that's what we call being clean and tidy. Look at that one there: that's what we call being unkempt. The first one is nice to look at and the other is displeasing and disgusting.' Do the same for me on this new chapter. That is all I think I need, and now I don't want to do anything but my work."

The young lord came as he had been asked to. The game of chess went very well. Milord said to me once during the evening, "You will find me very odd, madam; the day before yesterday I was complaining about mademoiselle's inattention, and this evening I find that she's too attentive." It was his turn to be distracted and thoughtful. Cécile seemed not to notice or hear anything. She asked me to buy Philidor for her.[40] If this continues, I will admire her. Good-bye; I repeat what I said at the beginning of this letter: this time you really owe me thanks. I have completed my task more thoroughly than I thought I would. I copied the letter and the cards. I remembered what was said almost word for word.

Letter XIII.

Everything's going quite well. Cécile is being extremely careful. The young man sometimes looks at her with an expression which says: "Was I wrong, are you completely indifferent to me?" He tries harder to please her with each day that passes. We no longer see my cousin the young minister, nor his mountain friend. The young man from Bern, perhaps feeling too cast into the shade by his cousin, no longer honors us with his visits. But that cousin does come to see us very often, and still seems very amiable to me. As for the two other men, I call them my Penates.[41] Your gentlemen made me laugh a good deal. The one who was amazed that a female heretic should know what the Ten Commandments are reminds me of the Frenchman who said to my father one day, "Sir, I understand your being Huguenot by day—you distract yourself, go about your business, and think of nothing; but in the evening, getting ready for sleep, in your bed, in the dark, you must get very worried, because, when all is said and done, you might die in the night," and another who said to him, "I know perfectly well, sir, that you and the other Huguenots believe in God. I have always said so, and I don't doubt it; but what about Jesus Christ?" As for the judge, who cannot understand how a woman who has some education and some knowledge of the world could dare to speak of the Ten Commandments, and of religion in general, he's even more amusing or more pitiful. He wanted to reason: he said, like so many others before him, that without religion we would not have less morality, and he cites some atheists who are honest people. Tell him that to be able to determine this, one would need to wait three or four generations and have a whole atheist people, for if I have a father, a mother, and teachers, all of whom are Christian or deist, I will have contracted ways of thinking and behaving from them that I will not lose for the rest of my life, whatever system I adopt, and that will influence my children whether or not I want it to or even know that it is happening. Such that Diderot, if he was an honest man, may well have owed it to a religion which, in good faith, he maintained to be false.[42]

You had no need to reassure me that you would never say anything about my letters which could cause the slightest harm. Would I write them if I didn't know so? I am very pleased to hear you are so satisfied with Cécile. You find me extremely indulgent, although you don't know why; in truth, I don't know either. There would have been no justice or prudence, it seems to me, in a more rigorous approach. How can one be protected against something which we can neither know nor imagine, foresee, nor fear? Is there any natural or revealed, human or divine law which says "the first time your lover kisses your hand, you will not feel any emotion"? Should I have threatened her that

. . . all misbehaving wives shall dwell

In ever-boiling cauldrons down in Hell.[43]

Should I have made my displeasure clear, and estranged her from me, encouraging her to say like Telemachus: "O Milord! If Mama abandons me, I will have no one but you."[44] Supposing that anyone were mad enough to say to me, "Yes you should," I would say that not having either indignation or estrangement in my heart, such conduct, which would not have seemed right or sensible to me, would also not have been possible.

Letter XIV.

What would you say of a scene which so overwhelmed us yesterday, my daughter and me, that we've barely opened our mouths today, not wishing to talk about it and unable to talk about anything else? That in any case is what keeps my mouth shut, and I think it is what keeps Cécile's shut too. She still seems completely terrified. For the first time in her life she did not sleep well, and I find her very pale.

Yesterday, Milord and his cousin being due to dine at the château, I had only my cousin from the *** regiment after dinner. My daughter asked him to sharpen her pencil. He used a penknife to do it; it happened that the wood of the pencil was very hard and his knife very sharp. He cut his hand deeply, and the blood flowed so abundantly that I was frightened. I went out to fetch sticking plaster, a bandage, and water. "It is very strange," said he, laughing, "and absurd, but I feel sick." He was sitting down. Cécile said that he turned very pale. I called out from the door, "Daughter, use your eau de cologne." She quickly damped her handkerchief with it, and used one hand to hold it to M. de ***'s face, which was completely covered, while with the other, she tried to stanch the blood with her apron. She thought he had almost fainted, she said, when she suddenly felt him pulling her toward him. Leaning over as she was, she was unable to resist, but fear and surprise stopped her thinking. She thought he was mad; she thought that a convulsion had made him move involuntarily, or rather, she didn't think anything at all, her ideas were so rapid and confused. He said to her, "Dear Cécile, charming Cécile!" At the same instant that he was ecstatically kissing her forehead, or rather her hair, from the way in which she'd fallen on him, I return. He stands up, and seats her in his place. His blood was still flowing. I call Fanchon, show her my cousin, give her what I was carrying, and usher my daughter out without a word.[45] More dead than alive, she told me what I have just told you. "But, Mama," she said, "how come I didn't think to throw myself aside or push his head away? I had two hands; he only had one. I didn't make the slightest effort to remove the arm that was round my waist and was pulling me against him. I kept on holding my apron round his hurt hand. What would it have mattered if it had bled a bit more? He must have a very strange idea of me! Isn't it dreadful that you can lose your judgment at the exact moment you most need it?" I said nothing in reply. Equally fearing the damage I might cause by imprinting something which was already causing her so much pain too deep into her imagination, or by encouraging her to treat it as a common, ordinary event that she shouldn't worry too much about, I did not dare speak. I didn't even dare express my indignation against M. de ***. I said nothing at all. I ordered the door to be closed to visitors and for them to be told that Cécile was indisposed. We spent the evening reading English. She understands Robertson quite well.[46] The story of the unfortunate Queen Mary caught her attention a bit, but every so often she would say, "But Mama, wasn't it strange? Was he mad, then?" "Something approaching it," I would reply, "But read, daughter; it will distract you, and me too." But here he is! Doubtless he has avoided having himself announced for fear that he would be sent away again. I cannot speak to him or look at him. I see Cécile make him a deep curtsy. He is as pale as she is, and does not seem to have slept any better. I must stop writing. I mustn't leave my daughter in embarrassment.

Monsieur de *** came up to me when he saw me laying down my pen.

"Will you banish me from your house, madam?" he said. "I do not know myself whether I deserve such a cruel punishment. I am guilty, it is true, of forgetting myself in the most inexcusable manner, but not of any wicked design, not of any design at all. Did I not know that you would come back? I love Cécile; I say it today to excuse myself. Yesterday, coming to your house, I felt I would never be able to say it without committing a crime. I love Cécile, and I couldn't feel her hand against my face, my hand in hers, without losing my mind for a moment. Tell me now, madam, do you banish me from your house? Mademoiselle, do you banish me, or do you both generously pardon me? If you don't pardon me, I leave Lausanne tonight. I will say that one of my friends has asked me to take his place in the regiment. It would be impossible for me to live here if I cannot come to your house, or to come and be treated as you must feel I deserve."

I said nothing. Cécile asked my permission to reply. I said that I agreed in advance to everything she would say.

"I forgive you, sir," she said, "and I entreat my mother to forgive you too. It is primarily my fault. I should have been more careful, given you my handkerchief and not held it against you and untied my apron after having wrapped your hand in it. I did not know what the consequences of all this would be; now I will know for the rest of my life. But, seeing as you have made me a confession, I will also make one to you and perhaps it will be useful, and will explain why I am not worried about continuing to see you. I also have a preference for someone."

"What!" he cried out. "You are in love?"

Cécile did not reply. In my life I have never felt so moved. I thought she was, but to know, and to know that she is sure enough of her love to say it, and to say it in that way! To feel that it is a protection and that she does not fear other men! In that moment, glancing at M. de***, I felt compassion, and I forgave him everything.

"The man you love, mademoiselle," he said to her in an altered tone, "does he know his happiness?"

"I flatter myself that he has not guessed my feelings," replied Cécile in the softest, the most expressively modest tone she has ever used.

"But how is that possible?" said he. "For, loving you, he must study your every word, your every gesture, and then he must perceive—"

"I do not know whether he loves me," interrupted Cécile.

"He has not told me so, and it seems to me that I would see whether he does or not, for the reason that you indicate."

"I would like to know," he started again, "who is the man lucky enough to please you and blind enough not to know it?"

"And why would you like to know?" said Cécile.

"I believe that I would not wish him ill, because I do not believe he is as deeply in love as I am. I would speak to him about you with so much passion that he would pay you greater attention, appreciate you more, and place his fate in your hands; for I cannot believe that he is unhappily tied down, as I am. I would at least have had the happiness of serving you, and my consolation would be in thinking that no one else would be as happy as I could have been in his place."

"You are generous and amiable," I told him. "I also forgive you with all my heart." He wept, and so did I. Cécile bent her head and took her work up again.

"Had you told your mother?" he asked her.

"No," I said, "she hadn't told me."

"But you know who he is?"

"Yes, I can guess who it is."

"And if you were to stop loving him, mademoiselle?"

"Do not hope for that," I said. "You are so amiable that if that were to happen, I would have to banish you."

Visitors arrived, and he fled.

I told Cécile to stay with her back to the window, and I had coffee brought in, which I asked her to pour, even though it was hardly the right time for coffee. All this kept her busy and hidden, and she had few questions about her pallor or her indisposition of the previous day to endure. The only person whom nothing escaped was our friend the Englishman.

"I met your cousin," he said to me in a low voice. "He would have avoided me if he could have. What a look he had! Ten days of illness could not have changed him more than he has since the day before yesterday. And he said, 'You think I look very pale. Believe it if you can,' he said, and he showed me his hand, 'this pin prick, deep though it is, was responsible for the change.' And he told me that he'd done it at your house with a penknife, sharpening a pencil, that he had lost a lot of blood and felt unwell. And he said that it was so ridiculous that it made him blush. And in fact he did blush, and then turned even paler than before. I saw that he was telling the truth but not the whole truth. Coming in here I find you with an air of emotion and pity. Mademoiselle Cécile is pale and dejected. Permit me to ask you what has happened."

"Because you have already been confided in once," I replied with a smile, "you want to continue to be; but there are some things which cannot be said." And we spoke of other things. We worked, took tea, played piquet, whist, and chess in the usual way. The chess game was very serious. The man from Bern had Cécile playing chess in the Philidor style, as I had obtained his book for her.[47] Milord found this very unamusing, gave up his place, and asked to play a rubber of whist. At the end of the evening, seeing her work, he said to Cécile:

"All winter you have refused to make me a purse or note-case. But I will need to take something to remember you by when I depart, and you must permit me to leave you something of me."

"Not at all, Milord," she replied. "If we are not to see each other ever again, we would do very well to forget each other."

"You are very firm about it, mademoiselle," he said, "and you say *not see each other ever again* as if you were saying nothing."

I came up and said, "There is firmness in the way she expresses herself, but you, Milord, there was firmness in your thought, which is much stronger."

"Me, madam?"

"Yes, for when you spoke of departure and remembering, you were thinking of an eternal separation, were you not?"

"That is clear," said Cécile, forcing herself for the first time in her life to take on an air of pride and detachment. And I think that even if the detachment was limited to her air, in her heart there was real pride. The tone in which he had pronounced *when I depart* had wounded her. And he was wounded in his turn. Is it not strange that we only worry about being loved when we think we aren't; that we feel its loss so much, and its possession so little; that we trifle with the wealth we have, and that we only value it from the moment we no longer have it; that we inflict wounds without thought, and that we are offended and aggrieved at the effect the wound has; that we push away the thing that we then wish to get back for ourselves?

"What a day!" Cécile said to me as soon as we were alone. "May I ask, Mama, what struck you most?"

"It was the words *I also have a preference for someone.*"

"I was not mistaken, then," she replied, embracing me. "But do not fear, Mama. I do not think I have anything to fear. I find that I have some firmness, as he said, and I very much want not to give you grief! This morning you know we hardly said anything. Well, all the time we were silent I was busy thinking about how best to adapt to the way you want me to live for a while. It will be a bit troublesome for you, and very sad for me, but I know that you would do much more difficult things."

"How should we live, Cécile?"

"I think we should not be at home as much, and that these three or four men should not find us alone as often. The life that we lead is so sweet for me, and so agreeable for them; you are so amiable, Mama; we are too comfortable, nothing is awkward, we think and say what we want. Although we risk being bored, it would be better to go more into society. You will command me to learn to play cards, and there will be no question of chess or checkers. We will get less used to one another. If we love each other, we can show it, and finally say it. If we don't love each other, this will become more evident, and I will no longer be able to deceive myself."

I held her tight in my arms. "How lovely you are, and how reasonable!" I cried out. "How happy with you I am! How I glory in you! Yes, my daughter, we will do everything you wish. Let no one reproach me for my weakness or blindness. What would have happened if, being as you are, I had required you to follow my reasoning, and that instead of having your own soul, you had only had mine? You are worth more than me. I see in you what I thought it would be impossible to unite, as much firmness as sweetness, as much discernment as simplicity, as much prudence as uprightness. May this passion, which has developed such rare qualities, not make you pay too dearly for the good it has done you! May it dwindle away or make you happy!"

Cécile, who was very tired, asked me to undress her, to help her get into bed, and to have supper in bed. In the middle of our supper, she fell asleep. It is eleven o'clock, and she has still not got up. From this evening I will start to put Cécile's plan into execution, and I will tell you in a few days how successful we find it.

Letter XV.

We live as Cécile asked us to, and I admire the welcome we are given in society, seeing that previously we neglected it a great deal. We are a sort of novelty. Cécile, who has gained in countenance, ease of manners, civility, and modesty, is assuredly a very agreeable novelty, and what is more important, we are returning four men to society which it is not sorry to receive. The first few times that Cécile played whist, the man from Bern wanted to teach her as he had at chess, and his assiduousness has kept the young lord at a distance. People have also lost the habit of constantly pairing him with Cécile in card games as they did at the beginning of winter. In the course of a single day we have had a succession of different, rather curious scenes, as well as quite cheerful moments. Cécile had been for dinner at the house of a cousin who is ill, and at three o'clock I was by myself when Milord and his cousin came in.

"These days, we have to come very early to hope to find you at home," said Milord. "Before this change, we spent six weeks which were much more agreeable than these last eight or ten days. May I be permitted to ask, madam, whether it was you or Mademoiselle Cécile whose desire it was that you should start going out every day?"

"My daughter's," I replied.

"Was she getting bored?" he asked.

"I don't think so," I said.

"But then what is the point," he continued, "of rejecting a

way of living which was so comfortable and agreeable, to adopt one which is irksome and insipid?"

"I think that . . . it seems to me that," his cousin interrupted, "that Mademoiselle Cécile may have had three reasons for doing it, each one of which would do her honor."

"What three reasons?" asked the young man.

"First, she may have feared that this way of living which we miss might give rise to talk, and that some women, vexed not to see these two ladies among them, and envying them the attentions of all the men whom they so kindly tolerate, might make some unfair and malicious remark. Now, a woman, and young women even more so, cannot be careful enough to ward off mischievous gossip and the attitude which gives rise to it."

"And your second reason? Let's see if I find it any better than the first," said Milord.

"Mademoiselle Cécile may have inspired a feeling in one of the people coming here that she did not believe it was right to respond to, and which, in consequence, she did not wish to encourage."

"And the third?"

"It is not impossible that she may herself have felt the stirrings of a preference to which she did not wish to yield."

"Men will thank you for the first and the last conjectures," said Milord. "It's a pity they're so completely without foundation, and that we have so few reasons to suppose that we are subjecting these ladies to envy or that we are inspiring love."

"But my lord," said his cousin with a smile, "since you wish to be so humble about ourselves, permit me to say that two men come here who are more amiable than we are."

"Here comes Mademoiselle Cécile," said Milord. "I don't think you would be very pleased if I told her about your conjectures, however honorable they may be, would you?"

"As you wish," he replied.

Cécile came in. Her eyes sparkled with pleasure.

"Shall we play a little game of chess without anyone else interfering?" asked Milord.

"I would like to," said Cécile, "but it is not possible. In quarter of an hour I have to go and have my hair dressed and change my clothes for Madame de ***'s assembly" (the wife of our cousin, to whose house we had been invited). "I would prefer to talk for a little while than play half a game of chess."

And in fact she started chatting with us so calmly, thoughtfully, and serenely that I had never found her lovelier. The two Englishmen stayed while she was at her toilette. She came back simply and agreeably attired; we all admired her a little, and then went out. At the door of the house we were going to, Milord's cousin said that he mustn't come in with us, and wanted to pay another visit.

"Will these ladies also be envied," Milord said, "the happiness of having been accompanied here by us?"

"No," said his cousin, "but our own happiness may be envied, and I would not wish to give pain to anyone."

We went in, my daughter and I. There were many people present, and Madame de *** had expended a lot of care on a dress which was meant to have a careless effect. Her husband did not stay long in the drawing room, and had already left when two young Frenchmen were presented, one of whom looked very alert, the other very sullen. I only caught glimpses of the first; he was everywhere. The other stayed immobile in the place which chance had first led him to. Our Englishmen arrived. They asked Madame de *** where her husband was.

"Ask this young lady," she replied in a teasing tone, indicating my daughter. "He spoke to no one but her, and content with that happiness, he left straight after."

The Englishmen therefore approached Cécile; she said, without being disconcerted, that her cousin had complained of a headache and had proposed a hand of piquet with General d'A. in a study far removed from the noise. On this I left Cécile to look after herself, and went to find my cousin, to ask him whether he had a headache as he had claimed to Cécile or whether he had found the situation too embarrassing.

"Is it possible that you are being so cruel as to tease me?" he asked (I should add in passing that the worthy General d'A. is a little deaf). "Never mind, I will make you my confession. I did have a headache; my health has not recovered since my cut"—he showed his hand—"although that wouldn't have been enough to force me to retire. But I felt that I would be very embarrassed, and then, I have always felt that a man looks very awkward in a big assembly at his own home, and I was vain enough not to want you to see me stupidly walking from woman to woman and table to table paying my compliments. These sorts of assemblies are on the contrary the triumph of the mistresses of the house, and I wanted Madame de *** to enjoy her ascendancy, and not risk spoiling her pleasure by annoying her."

I teased him for all this refinement, when one of the Frenchmen put his head round the door of the study. Opening the door wide as soon as he saw me, he greeted me and said, "I would wager that you are the sister, the aunt, or the mother of a pretty person that I have just seen in there."

"Which one?" I said.

"Ah! You know very well, madam," he replied.

I said, "Well then! I am her mother; but how did you guess?"

"It's not because of her features," he replied. "It's more her countenance, and her physiognomy. But how can you leave her prey to the malice of the mistress of the house? I begged her not to drink a cup of tea which she had given her, and to say that she had seen a spider fall into it, but mademoiselle your daughter only shrugged her shoulders and drank. She is either brave, or she believes in virtue like Alexander's,[48] but me, I believe in Madame de ***'s jealousy. Your daughter must have carried off either her husband or her lover, but I think it's her husband, because the lady looks more vain than tender. I would love to see him. I am sure he is very amiable and very much in love. Moreover I heard it said here and in the town where his regiment is garrisoned that he is the most amiable as well as the best knight in the world. But, madam, that is not the only situation which mademoiselle your daughter is providing for spectators to consider. She also has two men from Bern, a German, and an English lord by her; the lord is the only one she doesn't talk to much. He looks very discouraged by it. I don't think he can be subtle at all. I think that in his place I would be flattered. To be distinguished in one way is as good as being distinguished in any other."

"Your scenarios seem to be the creations of your imagination

alone," I said, smiling, although in fact I was extremely per-
turbed. "Let's go and see what's happening." I closed the door
of the study behind me.

"Do you realize, sir," I said, "that you were speaking in front
of the master of the house? The one who was playing cards."

"What! Him? I am in despair. I didn't think he would be so
young," and immediately opening the door again and pulling
me back to the card game, he said to my cousin, "What, sir, can
a brainless young imbecile do for a gallant man who has been
so kind as to pretend not to hear the idiocies that escaped him?"

"What you are doing, sir?" said M. de ***, rising. With a
good grace, he shook the hand that the young foreigner was
holding out to him, drew up a chair, and begged us to be seated.
He then asked for news of many officers from his regiment, and
of other people which the young man had seen more recently
than he. In my turn, I put some questions to him. He is related
to your husband; he has seen you and your daughter, but only
in passing, such that I couldn't find much out from him on this
interesting subject. He is more closely related to the Bishop of B.
than the Abbé de Th. whom we know here, and he has a little
of his fine and lively physiognomy. I asked what his brother
does. "An officer in the artillery," he told me, "full of talents
and application, but not merely that."

"And you?" I asked.

"A thoughtless scatterbrain and mischief maker, but also
not merely that. I thought that this profession would suffice
me to the age of twenty, but although I'm only seventeen, I
want to quit it henceforth. One day it will be too late."

"And what profession would you choose instead?"

"I have always promised myself," he replied, "to be a hero
once I stop being a madman. By the age of twenty I want to be
a hero. I want to spend the next three years preparing myself
to carry out this new trade better than I could if I dropped my
current one straightaway."

"Thank you very much," I said to him. "I am very happy
with you and your replies. Let us go and see what my daughter
is doing." I begged the apprentice hero to remember that loyalty, prudence, and discretion toward ladies were part of the

profession, as practiced by his most famous predecessors, whose exploits and loves the troubadours of his country sang. I implored him not to utter a word about my daughter that was not worthy of the most discreet of valiant knights.

"I promise you," he said. "Not.in jest, but in truth. I cannot be too scrupulously careful after the impertinent wildness with which I spoke."

We were then in the drawing room. My daughter was playing whist with children—princes, in truth, but the scruffiest little bears in the world nonetheless.

"You see," said the Frenchman, "the English lord and the handsome man from Bern have been placed at the far end of the room."

"Make no observations," I said.

"May I then be permitted to point out my brother to you? He is sitting where we left him, bombarding the same town— Gibraltar, for example—with his cannon fire. This table is his fortress, or perhaps it's Maastricht that is in need of defense."

This babble would never have ceased had I not requested to be allowed to play. I was just finishing my game when my cousin came back into the drawing room. He came up to me.

"Did that scatterbrain have to see in one instant what I was unable to see despite all my pains? Did he have to come and drag me out of an uncertainty whose full value I now know?"

He sat down sadly beside me, not daring to approach my daughter, nor sufficiently resolute to go up either to his wife or to the young lord.

"I will do nothing to stop you believing it," I said to him. "If you had suspicions of someone else, it might have been even more vexatious, for I do not think that child has a particularly distinguished face or mind. But still, ask yourself whether it is truly reasonable to have such faith in the observations which a young scatterbrain made in the space of half of a quarter of an hour."

"That scatterbrain, did he not comprehend my wife?"

We withdrew; I left my cousin plunged in sadness. The Englishmen took us home, and Milord pressed me so insistently to allow their supper to be brought to our house that I could not refuse. They related all the barbed words our cousin's wife said, and all her malicious glances. This was the explanation of the cup of tea the Frenchman had not wanted my daughter to drink. We talked of the game that she had had to play. To all of this, Cécile said not a word, and pulling me aside, said, "Mama, please let's not complain, and let's not mock her; in her place I might do as much."

"Not out of self-love, like her," I replied.

Supper was cheerful. I thought the little lord seemed very pleased that he had no one from Bern or France or anywhere else to compete with. As he left, he told me that this once he would adopt his cousin's behavior and not say a word about the supper party for fear of making people envious of him. I wouldn't have asked him to keep it a secret, but I wasn't sorry that he suggested it himself. I feel extremely sorry for my cousin. The Frenchmen leave tomorrow. They have caused a great sensation here, but in admiring the talents and application of the elder, it is regretted that he doesn't speak a bit more, wasn't a bit more like someone else, and in admiring the vivacity of mind and kindness of the younger, it is thought that it would be better if he spoke a little less and were a little more circumspect and modest, without considering that then there would be little to admire or criticize in either of them. No one recognizes sufficiently that among us humans, the flip side of the coin is as much a part of our essence as the good side is. Change one thing, and you change everything.[49] In the balance of faculties you will find mediocrity just as much as wisdom. Good-bye. I will send you, via your husband's relatives, my daughter's silhouette.

Letter XVI.

I am going quickly to copy a letter from the man from Bern that my cousin has just sent me.

"Your cousin Cécile de *** is the first woman that I have ever desired to call my own. She and her mother are the first women with whom I have ever thought I might be happy to spend my life. Tell me, dear friend, you who know them, am I mistaken in the thoroughly favorable opinion I have of them? And please tell me also (this is my second question), tell me, without feeling obliged to give your reasons, whether you advise me to attach myself to Cécile, and ask her mother if I may have her?"

Beneath this my cousin wrote, "To your first question I respond without hesitation *yes*, and yet to your second I reply *no*. If what makes me say *no* should change, or if my opinion on that matter changes, I will tell you without delay."

Inside the envelope he wrote: "Be so kind, madam, as to let me know whether you and Mlle Cécile approve of my reply. Supposing that you do not, I will keep this one, and respond as you dictate."

Cécile is out; I am waiting for her before I reply.

She approves it. I said to her: "Think carefully, dear child."

"I am thinking carefully," she replied.

"Do not get angry with my question," I said. "Do you find the Englishman more amiable?" She said she didn't. "Do you think he is more honest or more loving, gentler?"

"No."

"Do you think he is more handsome?"

"No."

"You would live here, at least in the summer. Would you rather live in an unknown country?"

"I would prefer a hundred times more to live here, and I'd prefer to live in Bern than in London."

"Would you be indifferent to entering a family which would not welcome you with pleasure?"

"No, I think that would be very distressing."

"If there are secret ties and sympathies, are there any here, my dear child?"[50]

"No, Mama. At the very most, I only occupy his thoughts when he sees me, and I don't think he likes me any better than his horse, his new boots, or his English whip."

She smiled sadly, and two tears glittered in her eyes.

"Do you not think it would be possible, dear daughter, to forget such a lover?" I said.

"I think it's possible, but I don't know whether it will happen."

"Are you sure that you can find comfort in staying unwed?"

"I'm not at all sure, and it's one of those things that cannot be known in advance."

"And so the reply?"

"The reply is the right one, Mama, and please write to my cousin to tell him to send it."

"You write it," I said.

She made an envelope for the letter and wrote inside: "The reply is the right one, sir, and I thank you for it. Cécile de ***."

Once the letter had gone, my daughter gave me my work and took up her own. "You asked me, Mama, whether I could bear not being married. I think it would depend on the sort of life I could lead. I have thought many times that if I had nothing to do but be a spinster and live among husbands, lovers, wives, mistresses, children, I might find that very sad, and sometimes covet, as you were saying the other day, the husband or the lover of my neighbor; but if you thought it would be a good idea to go to Holland or England and run a shop, or a hotel, I think that, being always with you and always busy, and not having any time to go into society or read novels, I wouldn't be yearning for or missing anything at all, and that my life could be very pleasant. What would be missing in reality, I would be able to hope for. I would flatter myself that I might become rich enough to buy a house with its own field, orchard, and garden, somewhere between Lausanne and Rolle or Vevey and Villeneuve, and spend the rest of my life there with you."

"That would be a good idea," I said, "if we were twin sisters; but, thank you, Cécile. Your project is charming and touching. If it were more reasonable it would not be so touching."

"People die at any age," she said, "and perhaps you will have the sorrow of surviving me."

"Yes," I replied, "but there is an age when you can no longer live, and that age will come nineteen years sooner for me than it will for you."

Our words stopped there, but our thoughts did not.

Six o'clock chimed, and we went out, for we no longer spend

our evenings at home, unless we have real guests; that is to say, women as well as men. I had never gone out so little as I did last month, and never so often as I have this one. Our retired life was the result of chance and of disposition; dissipation is rather an arduous occupation. If I didn't spend half my time in society feeling acutely anxious, I would be bored to death. The intervals between anxiety are filled with boredom. Sometimes I rest and regain my spirits by taking a walk with my daughter, or as I did today, sitting by myself and looking through an open window over the lake. Thank you mountains, snow, and sun for all the pleasure you give me. Thank you Creator of everything I see, for having made these things so lovely to look at. Laws on which the preservation of the universe depends make this snow fall and this sun glow. When the sun melts the snow, it produces torrents, waterfalls, and fills them with rain-bowlike color. These things are the same where there are no eyes to see them; but as well as being necessary, they are also beautiful. Their variety is also necessary, but is also no less lovely, and prolongs my pleasure just as much. Striking, lovely beauties of nature! Every day my eyes admire you; every day I feel you in my heart![51]

Letter XVII.

My dearest friend, you give me even more pleasure than you think when you say that you like Cécile's silhouette so much, and that the account the Chevalier de *** had given you of us had made you want to see the daughter for the first time, and the mother again. Well then! It's up to you to see them! My daughter is losing her gaiety, now that she imposes so much constraint on herself. If this were to last much longer, I fear that she might lose her bloom, and even her health. For some days I have been meditating on how to forestall a disaster which I find it dreadful to contemplate and which I would be unable to bear. I was no longer able to receive compliments on her grace or praise for her education without wanting to weep, and I have not always been able to suppress it, and all the time

I was alone, I spent thinking about how to distract my daughter, how to make her happy again and keep her in health and in life, for my fears had no limits. I found nothing which satisfied me. It is too early to go into the countryside. If I had rented a house this season, and gone to it, imagine what people would have said! And even if later I had rented a house near Lausanne, apart from it being very expensive, it wouldn't have been enough of a change of scene; if it had been farther away, up in the mountains or in the Lac de Joux Valley, the fact that my daughter was no longer in public view would have exposed her to the most unjust and grievous conjectures. Your letter has arrived. All uncertainty has ceased. I have told my daughter of my plan. She courageously accepts. And so we will come to see you, unless you forbid us; but I am so convinced that you will not do so that I am going to announce our departure, and rent our house to foreigners who are looking for one. The regiment of *** is in your vicinity. I cannot be vexed about this for my cousin, because he will be very happy himself, and I am very pleased for the man from Bern. If the young lord allows us to go without saying anything; or at least if, after our departure, he doesn't run after us, feeling what he has lost, does not write to me, does not ask his parents their permission to bestow Cécile on them as a daughter-in-law, then I flatter myself that Cécile will forget a child who is so little worthy of her love, and that she will do justice to a man who is superior to him in all respects.

End of Part One.

LETTERS WRITTEN FROM LAUSANNE; SECOND PART.[52]

Announcement from the Editors.

Supposing that this second part is as kindly received by the public as the first, we shall try to obtain more of the letters which these people whom we have made known must have since written to one another.

Continuation of the Letters Written from Lausanne.[53]

Letter XVIII.

We are waiting for your reply in a pretty house which I have been lent, three quarters of a league from Lausanne.[54] The foreigners who wanted to rent mine, and now have, were in a hurry to take possession. I left all my furniture, and so we had neither fatigue nor bother. If the snow either does not melt or melts too quickly, it is possible that we will be unable to depart as soon as we would like. At present, it makes no difference to me, but when we were leaving Lausanne, I would have preferred to have farther to go, and newer objects to occupy the mind and imagination of my daughter. However much affection one has for one's mother, I thought that being alone with her in the month of March might have seemed a little melancholy. It would have been the first time that I would ever have seen Cécile getting bored with me, and wanting our intimacy to be interrupted. I confess that I dreaded this mortification, and had done everything to avoid it. A portfolio of prints that Monsieur d'Ey*** lent me, *Thousand and One Nights*, *Gil Blas*, the tales of Hamilton, and *Zadig*, had all gone ahead, along with a pianoforte and supplies for our work.[55] Other things which owed nothing to my forethought have worked much better than they would have—Milord, his cousin, an unfortunate dog, a poor negro . . . But I should take up my tale from an earlier point.

After I wrote to you, I made preparations to go to a house where I would find all the fine society of Lausanne. I advised Cécile not to come for another half an hour, until I'd offered my house for rent and announced our departure, but she told me that she was interested in seeing what impression I would make.

"You will see," I said, "that this arrangement won't make you miss anything other than the first surprise and questions."

"No, Mama," she said. "Let me see their whole reaction, whether it give me pleasure or pain. At your side, resting against your chair, touching your arm, or only your dress, the most powerful as well as the most amiable protection, will make me feel strong. You know very well how much you love me, Mama, but you don't know how much I love you, and that, having you, I would be able to give up everything, renounce everything. Come on, Mama, you are too much of a coward, and you think I'm much weaker than I am."

Do I need to tell you, dear friend, that I embraced Cécile, that I wept, that I pressed her to my heart; that walking down the road I leaned on her arm with even more pleasure and affection than normally; that when we went into the room, the first thing I did was to secure a chair for her, and place it a little behind mine? Oh! surely you can imagine, you can see all this; but can you also see my poor cousin, and his friend the Englishman, approach us with an anxious air, searching in our eyes for the explanation to I know not what new or strange thing they saw there? My cousin, in particular, watched Cécile, and seemed both to want me to speak and to fear that I might, while the other, seeing how agitated he was, divided his attention between him and us, sometimes mechanically putting his arm around him, sometimes laying a hand on his shoulder, as if to say, "I am truly becoming your friend; if someone tells you something distressing, you will find a friend in this foreigner, in whom until now you have only seen sympathy, and a certain affinity of character or circumstance." As for me, all day long I had not thought of your letter or my reply other than as it affected my daughter; all day long I had thought only of her and her feelings, and now, suddenly, I was so moved by what I could see of one man's passion, and the other's tender compassion, by the feeling and familiarity which had grown up between us all, and by the sort of leave that we were going to have to take of them, that I started to weep. Ask yourself whether they were reassured by this, and whether my daughter was surprised.

Our silence became unbearable; their anxiety was mounting, and my cousin's face was draining of color. Cécile pressed my arm and whispered to me:

"But, Mama, what is it? What's the matter?"

"I am very foolish," I finally said to them. "What is this all about? A journey which is not taking us out of the world and not even to the end of the world. Languedoc is really not far. You, sir, travel, and so I may hope to see you again, while you, cousin, are going in the same direction as I am. We want to visit a truly amiable relation, and one who is very dear to me; she also wants to see us. There is nothing to stop us, and I have decided to leave soon. Please, cousin, will you go and tell Monsieur and Madame *** that my house will be available to rent for a period of six months?"

He told them. The Englishman sat down. My daughter's guardians and their wives all came running up. Milord, seeing us engaged in answering their questions, leaned against the mantelpiece, watching from a distance. The man from Bern came to express his pleasure at discovering that he would be spending the summer nearer to us than he had supposed. Then the foreigners came up, and rented my house on the spot. The only question that remained was where to stay while we wait for your reply. We were offered accommodation in a country house which some English people left vacant in the autumn. I accepted eagerly, and thus everything was arranged and made public within a quarter of an hour, although the manifestations of surprise, the questions, and the exclamations went on all evening. Those who were most concerned with our departure spoke the least. Milord was satisfied with finding out how far away our new lodgings would be, and declaring that the road to Lyons would not be fit for women for a long while yet, he then asked his cousin whether, instead of proceeding to Bern, Basel, Strasburg, Nancy, Metz, and Paris, they might not decide to start their journey through France by going first to Lyons, Marseilles, and Toulouse.

"But would it be any easier to leave Toulouse once you get there than it now is not to go at all?" he was asked.

"I don't know," he said rather weakly, and with a less meaningful air than I would have liked.

"Once you have spent six weeks in Paris," his cousin said, "you may go where you like."

Cécile asked if she could sit with me while I played cards, saying that she couldn't think of anything other than the journey, and that she would be useless as a player herself. After the card game had finished, I asked Monsieur d'Ey*** whether he would lend us some prints and books; my cousin offered his pianoforte, which I accepted, as his wife is no musician. The man from Bern, who has his horses and carriage here, begged me to make use of them for our journey into the countryside, and to allow his coachman to inquire from a dairy maid who came into town every morning whether I needed him during the day.

"It shall be I," said Milord, "who, whenever the weather is clement enough, will go to discover any orders these ladies may have, and who will bring them to you."

"Quite right!" said his cousin. "Poor foreigners have nothing to offer but their zeal."

The man from Bern then told us that he would not long enjoy the pleasure of being of service to us, as he needed to return to Bern to seek election to the Two Hundred, having obtained six months' leave from the military for the purpose.[56] As his father is dead, and he has no uncle who is a councillor, he was asked whether he would be marrying a girl with a baretly. The Two Hundred is the sovereign council of Bern; a baretly is the hat which one wears when attending the council, and the label "girl with a baretly" is given to a girl whose father's support can secure a place on the Two Hundred for the man who marries her.

"No, certainly not," he said. "I have no heart to give in exchange for a baretly, and I would not want to take without giving."

The elections were discussed. Amazement was expressed that Monsieur de *** was already twenty-nine years old. He is thirty. The governor talked about the senate and the senators in Bern.

"Senate, senators, dear uncle!" exclaimed his nephew.

"Why not call them that? I have been told that the burgomasters of Amsterdam were sometimes known as consuls by their clients, and that they sometimes called themselves by the same name."[57]

"And you, my dearest uncle, should we in fact not call you the Asian pro-consul, resident in Athens?"

"Nephew, nephew," said the governor's wife, who has some wit, "with jokes like these, you'll need to marry two or three baretlies to be sure of getting elected."

Madame ***, my cousin's wife, seeing everyone gathered around us, drew near toward the end of the evening, and said to her husband, "And you, sir, now that these ladies are leaving, you will finally gather courage to leave; you will stop having letters to write every day, and pretexts to think up. For eight days now," she added, pretending to laugh, "his bags have been packed and secured to his carriage."

No one spoke.

"But really, sir," she continued, "when are you leaving?"

"Tomorrow, madam, or this evening," he replied, turning pale, and running toward the door. Having shaken his friend's hand, he left the room and the house. In effect, he did leave that same night, his way lit by moon and snow.

The following day, which was Monday, and the day after that, I was busy and received no one, and last Wednesday at midday we were in the carriage, Cécile, Fanchon, Philax, and I, on our way to Renens.[58]

Orders had been sent to open our rooms and to light a fire in the dining room, and we planned to eat milk soup and eggs for our dinner. But when we drew near, we were surprised to see much movement and life about the place—all the windows were open, and big fires in all the bedrooms competed with the sun to dry and heat the air and furniture. Once we had reached the door, Milord and his cousin assisted us to get down from the carriage, and carried the boxes and packages into the house. The table was laid, the pianoforte tuned, a favorite melody open on the music stand; there was a cushion for the dog near the fire, and flowers in the vases on the mantelpiece—nothing could have been more gallant or better conceived. An excellent dinner was served; we drank punch, and were left with provisions: a pâté, lemons, rum. Permission to allow our friends to come and dine with us once or twice a week was urgently requested.

"As for taking tea, madam," said Milord, "I do not ask your permission, as you would deny that to no one."

At five o'clock their horses were brought. They left them to the care of their servants, and as the weather was fine, although very cold, we accompanied them to the main road. Just as they were about to leave us, a Great Dane suddenly appeared, coming toward us, pushing his muzzle through the snow with a last great effort. A bank of snow impedes him; he anxiously tries to get through it, totters, and collapses at Cécile's feet. She stoops down. Milord shouts out and tries to stop her, but Cécile persists in stroking the dog, declaring that it is not rabid, that it has simply lost its master, and is a poor dog half-dead with fatigue, hunger, and cold. The footmen are sent back to the house to fetch milk and bread, whatever can be found. They are brought; the dog eats, drinks, and licks the hands of his benefactress. Cécile wept with pleasure and pity. Taking great care of him, bringing him back to the house, matching her pace to the weary animal, she barely looks at her lover, who is now leaving; the whole evening was spent warming up and comforting the new guest, thinking up a name for him, wondering about his misfortunes, considering how best to prevent Philax from getting upset and jealous. When my daughter retired for the night, she made a bed for him from the clothes she was taking off, and this unfortunate creature is now the happiest dog on earth. Instead of reasoning and moralizing, we should give someone who is in love something to love; if love is dangerous, love shall preserve her; if loving gives her unhappiness, loving will be her consolation—for anyone who knows how to love, it is the only occupation, the only distraction, the only pleasure in life.

And so Wednesday passed, and there we were, installed in our country retreat, Cécile looking incapable of being bored (she has not had recourse to half her resources; books, work, and prints have all stayed in a drawer).

Thursday arrives, and the flowers, dog, and piano are enough for the morning. After dinner she goes to visit the farmer who lives in part of the house; she caresses the children, chats with his wife, and sees milk being taken out of the kitchen. She discovers that it's for someone who's ill, a negro dying of consumption whom some English people, whose servant he was, left in this house. They urged the farmer and his wife to take very good care of him, and left orders with a banker in Lausanne to pay them more than enough to enable them to do so for as long as he should live. Cécile came to tell me this information, and begged me to come with her to visit the negro, speak English to him, and ask him whether there was anything he might like which we could give him.

"They told me, Mama, that he doesn't know any French. Who knows," she said, "whether these people, in spite of all their goodwill, really understand his needs?"

We went. Cécile spoke her first words of English ever to him—what love taught her, humanity made use of. He seemed to feel some pleasure in hearing them. He was not in pain, but he had barely any life left in him. Mild, patient, calm, he did not seem to wish for or regret anything. We gave him a bit of wine or soup from time to time. I was sitting next to him, with my daughter, on Sunday morning when he died. We stayed there for a long time without moving.

"So is this how we end, Mama," said Cécile, "and how what feels and speaks and moves, ceases to feel, hear, or move? What a strange fate! To be born in Guinea, sold by his parents, grow sugar in Jamaica, serve English people in London, and die near Lausanne![59] We brought some pleasure to his final days. Mama, I am neither rich nor clever, and will never do much good, but if only I were able to do a little good wherever fate leads me, just enough for me and anyone else to think that on balance it's better that I should have come than otherwise! This poor negro! But why call him a poor negro? Whether one dies in one's own country or anywhere else, lives a long or a short time, has more or less pain or pleasure, in the end it all comes to the same thing: the King of France will be like this negro one day."

"And me too," I interrupted. "And you . . . and Milord."

"Yes," she said, "that is true. Let's go out of this room for now. I can see that Fanchon is coming back from church; I will tell her."

She went to meet her, and embraced her and wept, and came back to pamper her dogs, still weeping. Today we are burying the negro. What we have seen on this occasion is death alone, without anything else; nothing frightening, nothing somber, nothing pathetic. There is no family, no grieving, no regrets, either sincere or feigned, and so the impression it has made on my daughter has not been mournful. She has gone back to sit with the body two or three times every day; she obtained permission for him to be left covered and untouched in his bed, and for his room to continue to be heated.[60] She spent time reading and working there, and I had to be as reasonable as she was. Oh! How pleased I am to see that she does not have that sort of sensibility which leads her to avoid the dead, the dying, and the miserable! Nor do I see her actively seeking them out, and I confess that I am very happy to see that too. I would not like to see anyone do that other than a penitent Magdalene—the sinning Magdalenes should not, themselves, do any good other than very quietly; otherwise it would look as if they were not buying forgiveness so much as indulgences, both from people and from God. . . . I say no more! I say no more![61] And I have already said too much. What does it matter to the poor who are being relieved how we behave when we relieve them? Should any of those women I am discussing ever read this, I would say, either pay no attention at all to my rash words, or pay them complete attention; continue to do good, do not deprive yourselves of the blessings of the wretched, and do not bring down on me either their curses or the condemnation of he who tells you that charity covers a multitude of sins. I have urged you to give alms in secret. Secret charity is what is most agreeable to God and most satisfying to our hearts, because what motivates it is much simpler, purer, and kinder, less mixed with that vanity which is the torment of our lives; but in this case the action is more important than the motivation, and perhaps a good act will make the motivation better, because the sight of a poor person, suffering and distressed, the sight of the gratitude of a poor person who has received relief may touch your heart and change it.

Letter XIX.[62]

Dear Sir,

You seemed so sad yesterday that I cannot prevent myself from asking you what is causing you so much sorrow. Perhaps you will refuse to say, but you cannot resent my asking—since yesterday I have had nothing but your image in my mind. Milord comes to see us almost every day. It is true that he is normally with us for only a moment. Is it your impression that people have noticed in Lausanne, and that I am blamed at all for receiving him? You know him as well as any young man can be known; you know his parents, and their way of thinking. I do not doubt that you have read Cécile's heart, so please tell me how I should conduct myself. I am, sir, your very humble and obedient servant.

Letter XX.[63]

It is true that I am very sad. I am so far from resenting your question that I had already determined to tell you my story, but I will write it down for you; it will be a way of keeping me busy and distracted, indeed the only way liable to interest me. All that I can tell you, madam, regarding Milord, is that I know him to have no vice. I do not know whether he loves Mademoiselle Cécile as much as she deserves, but I am almost sure that he has no interest in any other woman, and that he has no liaison of any other sort. Two months ago I wrote to his father that he seemed to becoming attached to a young woman without fortune, but whose birth, education, character, and appearance left nothing to be desired, and I asked him whether he wanted me to find some pretext to encourage his son to leave Lausanne, for to try to remove him directly from you, madam, and from your daughter would have been tantamount to telling him that there is something better than beauty, goodness, grace, and wit. I had more reasons than another not to burden myself with such a hateful and absurd task. His father and mother both wrote to me to say that so long as their son loved, and was loved in return, so long as he was marrying for love, and not for honor, love having already faded, they would be very happy, and that from the way in which I spoke of the person to whom he was becoming attached, and of her mother, it seemed as if nothing of that sort was to be feared. They were absolutely right, no doubt, and yet I depicted to the young man the shame and despair that he would feel were he to be obliged to dissolve an engagement in cold blood which he had contracted in a moment of complete intoxication. I did not want to think that such a thing might even be possible.

I do not believe, madam, that anyone sees anything odd in his visits; he declared in front of everyone that he would be making them before your departure. He is seen to be assiduous at his lessons, and is in female company almost every evening. I have had news from Lyons from your cousin: he came to no harm despite traveling night and day, and despite the fact that the roads are more blocked with snow than they have ever been at this season. He is not happy.

I will start writing this evening, perhaps. I have the honor of being, madam, etc., etc., William ***.[64]

Sequel 2[65]

From Milord's father to the Englishman.

I am sorry but not surprised; that is what determined me to send him traveling eighteen months ago. I feared from his appearance and his liaisons that this winter we were just entering would be spent aping the latest fashions and adopting frivolous tastes as well as imitating dissipated behavior—and all of this without having any appetite for the pleasure of being noticed, or for wine, or for women. He was very young, and yet I feared that by spring he would be a sort of old man if I kept him in London, and because of that I would have sent him to Brunswick with an old and trusted servant or to Vienna to stay with our envoy, who is a friend of mine, if you hadn't acceded to my request. That was much the best, and I am eternally obliged to you. He has employed his time well and we have gained eighteen months during which his temperament has strengthened such that he has at least had time to become a man, and if he hasn't acquired that energy that I would have liked him to, it's because apparently it cannot be acquired; it has always been clear to me that he was not born with it, which only made me regret more acutely the two little boys and a pretty daughter who died in their infancy. But all is not desperate, as milady is with child. To return to my son, I had begun to have a little hope this winter when you wrote to me that it looked as if he were falling in love. Apart from the fact that I hoped this might make him find in his soul a new soul, I would have very much liked this Cécile for a daughter-in-law and I would have very much liked my son to marry for love. It's all very well saying that it's madness; one has to be determined by something on this occasion as on all others, and it is more natural that it should be by love rather than money, and in any case my son has no need of money or of support. Moreover, I like races to be crossed and nations to mix, and in my view the children that result from it are cleverer than others, and their families are more interesting and stimulating—my wife and I, who hardly go out, and less these days than ever (for to tell you in passing I think she is turning Methodist), my wife and I, we would have held a great party to give a fitting welcome to the mother-in-law of my son, and to our daughter-in-law.[66] It would have been a great pleasure to bestow wealth on her, to entertain her, to make her happier and better attended to, if that were still possible, if being in Paris he had very much wanted to go to Toulouse. . . .[67]

Sequel 3[68]

Berne April . . . 1795.[69]

Cécile to her mother.

We did everything we should have, dear Mama, so we must not be sad or complain, although this separation is very cruel.

Letters do not take the place of people whom I love dearly as much as they might for someone else. I have never liked writing, and have never paid much attention to what was happening other than to you or me, which thank God has never been and never will be anything other than the same person. It is impossible to tell you the extent to which my husband is devoted to you, and as for me, I would be ashamed to tell you anything about my love and affection; that would be to suppose that you did not know either me or yourself perfectly, and that you did not know what you deserve or what I am capable of—how could you possibly be unaware of anything in this respect? Has there ever been the slightest reason to doubt, the slightest distraction or cloud between us? No, you know very well that there are no limits to my gratitude or to my attachment to the best and loveliest of mothers. This is the second letter I have written you in my life. Do you remember the first one? If your journey has gone well, tomorrow you will be going past the convent from which I wrote it. It was the day after I had declared to Milord *** that I wished to see him no more. I was still feeling great emotion when I wrote it. . . .

Eaglonette and Suggestina,
or, On Pliancy

A Story

(1791)[1]

An obscure writer, his pen as free from malice as from
sycophancy, wrote a sketch of what should have been the
fate of King WELL-BORN.[2] The poor prince will not have
read it. His ministers must have robbed him of his story, for
they were so unhappy with it that they sent the bookseller
to prison; fortunately, a woman took pity on him and had the
duration of this harsh punishment reduced; and as for the
author, neither minister nor public knew who he was.[3] Let us
see whether he will be able to draft a few lines that distress
no one, and perhaps please her to whom they are most particularly addressed.

In a great empire, to a great queen and to the husband whom
she had raised to great heights, a princess was born, destined
by the heavens to play a great role.[4] All the good fairies rushed
to her birth. One gave her beauty, another grace, another intelligence, another courage. The fairy who gave her this last gift
was rather proud, and on seeing the quiet and modest arrival
of a little fairy whom she regarded as of second rank, she said

rather spitefully, "I expect you are bringing the gift of pliancy; but Eaglonette," for this was the name she'd been given, "Eaglonette will need none of that. Remove yourself; you may taint the gift I have just bestowed on her. Yielding is incompatible with strength and courage."

"You are mistaken," replied the gentle little fairy with a smile.

"Even if that were true," rejoined the other, "admit at least that your present is useless. With beauty, grace, wit, and a strong and generous soul, one can make everything bend before one, and never need to bend oneself, particularly when one is raised above the common people by wealth and rank."

"Are wealth and rank completely unsusceptible to attack? Is beauty unchanging? Without pliancy is it always possible to rise to the spirit of the moment or occasion? For, even supposing that we did not ourselves change, it seems very likely that many people and things around us would change, and that we would not always be viewed in the same way . . ."

"To doubt her happiness is already to lack courage," cried the proud fairy. "Remove yourself; I fear that you will shed a little of your wariness on Eaglonette, which is nothing other than faint-heartedness, or a little of your pliancy, which is nothing other than shameful weakness."

The little fairy curtseyed and withdrew, saying, "If one day I am needed, I will return, for the child's prettiness touches me."

This pretty child became the most beautiful and amiable princess in the world. The idea that to lack pliancy might be a misfortune never occurred to her. The queen, her mother, had never needed it. She governed her husband and her empire without contradiction, and could have said as Louis the Magnificent did that "I have laid down the law at home and sometimes elsewhere."5 For example, she was able to ally her daughter in accordance with her ambitions to a neighboring state, despite age-old prejudice, and despite some quite good reasons that, in that state, prevented many people from looking kindly on such an alliance. The mother overcame prejudice and reasons alike with her powerful politics, and no sooner had the daughter made her appearance than any dislike was forgotten, transformed into adoration. The court that was soon to be hers gave itself over entirely to celebration. It became intoxicated by, among other things, the fragrant vapors of wit. Which is not to say that wit is tasteless or unrefined, but its assault on the senses, breathed in by the great like incense at mass, never ceased, whether at the theater, while walking or dressing, or among their close circle. They were never allowed to breathe pure air, and it is no surprise that they ended up intoxicated. And then, unjust humans, unjust subjects, you harshly judge her whom you deprived of the very possibility of thought and self-knowledge!

Everything that beautiful Eaglonette did was painted in flattering colors. Yes, I cannot now say without being moved that what has since been dubbed criminal prodigality was then called beneficent liberality, that what has since been qualified as excessive freedom and indulgence was then described as amiable affability and lofty scorn of constricting etiquette. The public's estimation and judgment of her behavior had already shifted without the language of the courtiers changing in the slightest. Blind that they were, they thought that Eaglonette was only too right to persist in conduct that, dangerous for her, disagreeable to everyone else, they felt was so preeminently advantageous *to themselves*. How wrong they were! I see them tumbled headlong into an abyss from which they will never emerge. We should not insult their misfortune: sad victims of their sycophancy, they have done themselves greater damage than their misguided mistress, for her ill luck is not without remedy, unlike theirs.

If her rank has sunk under the weight of its own privileges, her courage has remained. If beauty has altered with grief, grace endures. Her mind . . . has had to stretch and grow. Does trouble not bring reflection? Does censure not force us to examine our conduct? If one does not openly proclaim one's guilt, there are nonetheless things that one does not openly justify: one colors, eludes, differentiates, and therefore measures, judges. I repeat, courage and grace remain, and one is on the way to acquiring that capacity of mind that one had been used to suppose so inappropriate, when, instead of being enlightened by experience, one was ceaselessly blinded by flatterers.

These new acquisitions, far from compensating the princess for what she no longer has, have only aggravated the sense of loss. She has only become unhappier as she has seen more clearly. Apart from anything else, it was extremely painful to learn that those she had supposed to be true friends were nothing other than greedy courtiers.

How long, princes, will you carry on thinking you have friends! For as long as there are good people on the globe, you will be able to have faithful servants and virtuous councilors; but friends! Consider that, to have friends, you have to be a friend yourself. You have to listen to confidences, and yet you find only your secrets important; share sorrow and pleasure, and yet you find only yours interesting; tolerate inequality, want, depression of mind and body, and yet you want everyone to be always ready to listen to you, reply, and run around with you or for you. You need an automaton that you wind up every hour, and that is pretty much what a courtier looks like on the outside; but in actual fact, it's he who's doing the adjusting and winding, he who's resetting the mechanism and holding the wires; for it is you who are the machine.

And so the princess was very unhappy. Sometimes religion inspired patience in her; at other times a sort of internal justice that not even the great can always silence said to her: "You are expiating your harsh and vengeful behavior, the persecution you initiated or allowed to happen." And then a sort of lugubrious resignation took the place of bitter resentment; but her grief, however much it varied, was still grief.

One day, unusually, one of the people attending her encouraged her to take part in some entertainment or other that was on offer. "I could," said Eaglonette, "if my mind were only a little more pliant . . ." No more was needed. The little fairy, repulsed in former times, slipped into the room. She was not presented, but she had so much grace, and her little dose of timidity was so seemly, that the princess hadn't the heart to look disagreeably surprised: on the contrary, she came up to the stranger, and spoke with her about the weather in the most natural way in the world.

"Who are you, madam?" the princess finally said. "You seem as polite as any of the people in my court, except for the fact that you take nothing to excess. Your dress is not so thoroughly modeled on the ones I have been seen to praise; your attentions are moderate; everything you do and say is measured and appropriate in a way that I have never encountered before now."

"But how obliging and kind you are!" burst out the fairy. "You are indeed that Eaglonette in whom I took such a tender interest even as a baby! I am a fairy. My name is Suggestina. As I can't walk very fast or speak very loud, I arrived a bit late when you were born, and allowed myself to be repulsed by other fairies who are more imposing than me. I was bringing you pliancy; I was assured that you had no need of it. Now that you desire it, you have only to say the word."

Eaglonette blushed. "The fairies who prevented you giving your present were not completely in the wrong," she said, "and I should not have needed your gift. Even today I would be ashamed to accept it, not believing that it is proper for me to use it. The reed agrees to yield . . ."

"And the oak snaps," completed the fairy.[6] "Yes, you cannot know in advance that the winds will gust with such redoubled intensity, it happens too rarely."

"Is it up to the oak to calm down the winds?"

"Perhaps not, but—it is always good to know how to give way, because we may have no other resource."

"Is it not finer," replied Eaglonette proudly, "is it not finer to snap than to yield like a coward?"

"Like a coward!" repeated Suggestina with a smile. "That flower of rhetoric is too common and unworthy of a princess of your intelligence. An epithet of that sort decides the question before any light has been shed on it. Without doubt, anything is better than to do something like a coward. I could, imitating this way of arguing, ask in turn. . . .[7] But no; let us leave exaggeration and epithets behind us. The question at hand is to know whether we must always stiffen further when the blows of fortune strike us, or whether sometimes we should yield, particularly when it looks unlikely that our resistance will meet with any success."

"My friends," said Eaglonette, "those who demonstrate the most eagerness for my glory, tell me never to relent, and consider that I could not do so without shame . . ."

"What!" said the fairy. "Courtiers use expressions like that! Oh, do not believe them. What they call *your glory* is in fact *their interest* . . . Moreover, even if they were in good faith, they are the worst judges of shame and glory in the world. Self-prostration is the only way they know how to yield; they walk bowed down."[8]

"But whom should I listen to, whom should I believe?" replied Eaglonette. "Must I consult my detractors, my implacable enemies?"

"No," said the fairy, "no, beautiful Eaglonette; consult only experience, which you will find filling the annals of history, and when you have done that, listen only to your own judgment."

"Oh well," said Eaglonette, "without needing to go further back in history, my mother was unhappy, and yielded never. I accept that the circumstances were very different, and I am judicious enough to not infer anything from the success her courageous perseverance won her. My brother never yielded . . ."[9]

"And what did he succeed in?" asked the fairy.

"Let's leave my family aside," said Eaglonette. "Does Dionysius the tyrant not look ridiculous in his schoolroom?"

"Yes, a bit, but that's because of the ferule that took the place of the iron scepter he was unable to hold on to."[10]

"Queen Zenobia, *degraded*, as a celebrated author says, *to the status of a Roman matron*, inspires me with nothing other than contempt and pity."[11]

"We differ a great deal there," said the fairy. "A different, more tragic end to her glorious adventures might have looked better in a book. But for Zenobia, who would never have been able to read it, this would have been a meager recompense that she did very well to reject in favor of several pleasant and peaceful years, and the merit of leaving her daughters content with their fate. Change the times a little in your imagination, beautiful Eaglonette; make Zenobia live in Rome, not under despots and with slaves, but with the Gracchi, their mothers, and wives, and you will no longer pity her."[12]

"Good God," cried Eaglonette. "What are you saying? Are you comparing the *** to the Gracchi and Mad. *** to Cato's daughter?"[13]

"No more than you are comparing yourself to Zenobia. You are not falling so low or from such a height. She was a true heroine."

"You are adopting, madam," said the princess, blushing, "the fashionable tone, the republican tone. Should beings who are superior to human nature let themselves be governed by circumstances and imitate people they should despise?"

"We are not imitating anyone," replied the fairy; "but nor do we fear anyone, and we tell the truth to the great when they are worth the effort, and we think that they are disposed to hear it. In accordance with my own naturally gentle and obliging temper, as well as the inclination I have for you, I would much prefer to have nothing but flattering truths to tell you. If I do otherwise, then blame fate that is stronger than you or me, or rather, submit to it, and accept the advice I give you in your interest alone."

The fairy stopped speaking. The princess meditated. Two charming children came in. Suggestina started joking with the younger. "And you, will you deign not to be unhappy?" she said to him. Eaglonette's eyes filled with tears.

"Good-bye, madam," Suggestina said to her. "If you do not wish me to be useful to you, you must surely find me impertinent."

"No, stay, please stay," said the princess. "You have acquired an influence over me that I can no longer destroy. Whatever I do, I will no longer be able to pursue my resolves with the same confidence and self-approbation as I had felt before your visit."

"Would you like *pliancy*?" said the fairy. "I offer it to you for the last time; later you would not be able to use it with the same grace. What will be admired today, will be scorned tomorrow. No one will be impressed if you wait until you are forced to come down to our level. You must still have the choice of yielding or resisting before you for yielding to be a virtue."

"Give it to me," said the princess. "I do not promise to use it, but give it."

No sooner were these words spoken than the fairy vanished from the room, but the princess was left with a different spirit, a different heart, or rather, with a new faculty that she was moved to put to use from that moment, even if only to try it out and persuade herself that she did indeed have it. That is what she did, but with so much discretion and prudence that she had already taken many measures, written many letters, interfered, hindered, countermanded many things, before anyone around her had noticed any change, and this spared her an infinity of objections against which she would have found it hard to stand firm. One morning, however, she pretended to fall asleep while reading a news sheet that every day for two years had mentioned the august Eaglonette and her illustrious mother. "I cannot be the only person that this man sends to sleep," said she, opening her eyes, "and I do believe that he does me more harm than service, because he makes these tributes to me so excessively boring. Find out from him what profit he makes from it over six months: I will pay him that sum on the condition that he goes traveling for that entire time, and that when he comes back he writes in a different way." This was executed on the spot, and from that time on another scribbler, who is no less vulgar and insolent than the other was dull and overemphatic, has been at a loss to know how to fill up the pages intended for insulting Eaglonette. Bit by bit the hacks and windbags of both parties have been lowering the pitch, and the result is that though she may not be praised as much, she is also no longer ripped to shreds.

Oh how hard and painful were some of the sacrifices that she felt compelled to offer up to circumstances! But just like the naturalist who sees nothing but insects, fossils, stones, and metals wherever he looks, becoming more knowledgeable with every step he takes, the princess saw everything in terms of its resistance or its flexibility, and was ever more aware of how precious her present was. Whether it was chance or providence, on one single day she saw a gold ingot get thinner and thinner without losing any of its value, another gold ingot be divided into round shavings and stamped with a pattern that gave it new beauty, and also a whole treasury of glassware smashed with a child's stick. The same day that she saw a high wall, rotted away by stagnant water, collapse, crushing animals and children as it fell, she also saw feeble bullrushes lift their modest heads above the rushing waters of a furious torrent. The same hen she saw yesterday courageously battling a fearsome enemy who was threatening her young brood, today she sees gathering her chicks and hustling them away as she covers their retreat, for the sparrowhawk she espied high in the sky is too strong; to wait and fight him would not only be madly imprudent for herself, but also an atrocious cruelty toward those whom it is her duty to protect. History teems with examples that spoke even louder once she lent them her ear. Society alone, consulted properly, would have sufficed, for each house is a state and each family a nation.

One day, a courtier, hoping to entertain her, told her about something he had just seen at the house of a lady he knew. She and one of her friends, both beauties, had recently suffered an attack of smallpox, and had just recovered their health. He had managed to make one of them let him pay her a visit, although not without difficulty. There was little daylight. One beautiful hand, which had entirely escaped the wreck, continually concealed the forehead and cheeks that had been completely destroyed. The other friend arrived. She was barely recognizable. The first one cried out; the other laughed.

"Where are you going when you leave here?" asked the first.

"To the theater," replied the other.

"What, to your box?"

"Yes, as usual. I may no longer have the pleasure of being admired, but I am still able to look and listen, and I am not fool enough to give up everything if I can keep something."

When this courtier saw that the princess, content with the reputation she could have and happy in the pleasures that remained to her, was gaining new respect for her ability to forget past splendor, he was stunned. He ventured to blame her, and she reminded him of the two friends.

Many people complained loudly of her ingratitude. "You guided me so badly," said Eaglonette to them, "that you are lucky I am pardoning you at all. Try to follow my example, and do not hope that I will sacrifice myself for you."

Émigré Letters

(PARIS, AUGUST 1793)[1]

Letter I.

Germaine to Alphonse.

London, April 19, 1793[2]

I can't hold out any longer, my dearest Alphonse; boredom, distress, and indignation have got the better of my obedience. My submission has lasted much too long, because my father . . . but please, my dearest Alphonse, do not take sides against me, or believe that I have turned into a rebel daughter, full of insolence—no, no, not at all, and I am still the person you loved. I was saying that my father should not have forbidden me to write to you, and that he no longer has the right to, after everything he repeatedly told me, and after the relationship he'd had with you for so long. He came to have a father's authority over you; he did not allow your marriage with a cousin to be thought of; he prevented you from following many of your inclinations—these were so many promises, without counting the one I believe to have been formally given to your parents. And what has changed for me now to be forbidden what I used to be allowed, and which I was even ordered to do? Was I not charged with writing everything to you which my father wanted you to know? Were your replies not addressed to me? Were our letters read? Did anyone distrust us? So what has happened? We are adrift and unhappy, divided from each other, so why forbid us our only possible pleasure? I say *us*, my dearest Alphonse; God forbid that I am not mistaken about you! My father has not written that you have formed any tie which could upset me or displease him. The only reason that he cites for his change of behavior toward you is that *you do not evince the sentiments of a gentleman*, that *you betray your name*, that *you are not what my husband and his son-in-law must be*. I would have shuddered, I would have supposed that you had been guilty of some low or wicked action, had I not known the real meaning and value of all these words. You are still in *** and are not with Condé's army; you are not seeking admission in M. de La Châtre's regiment; nor are you in the Vendée; you were not in Maastricht during the siege—this is what my father reproaches you for.[3] I am more likely to praise you for it, and I no longer wish to model my conduct on his, seeing as I no longer share his sentiments; I do not want you to forget me, and no longer wish to be deprived of your letters. In God's name, make up for this overlong privation! May this pleasure so long, so continually desired be finally restored to me, and may it help me bear my troubles more easily! I will tell you all about them another day. If I were to embark on all the detail, I might forget the time and miss the post. Address your reply to *Mistress Sparrow, Mantua Maker, Covent Garden Street, London.*[4] Despite our misfortune, the *Mantua Maker*, that is to say the duchess's dressmaker, holds such a significant position in this household and is such an important and precious person, and one moreover whom we rarely spend two days without seeing, that you could choose no better letter box: even were Mistress Sparrow to be discovered in the act of handing me a letter from you, people would pretend not to have noticed; it would be impossible to quarrel with such an essential person, and the storm would fall entirely on me, which is what I want. My poor Victoire would also have received your letters, but she has a brother in the national guard, and is herself slightly tainted with democracy. A pretext is being sought to take her away from me, and nothing could be sadder, as she is really the only reasonable person there is for me to talk to. The duchess . . . you know what she's like, and her son is an automaton. But there I go, having promised not to get involved in the long chapter of my troubles. Perhaps you will tell me that I should learn English, extend my sphere of conversation and be released from French stupidity, for you can guess, I am sure, everything I have to hear from morning to night and from one end of the week to the other, and perhaps you hear the same where you are. So, yes, I do learn English, but it's not for the pleasure of learning and spending one or two hours free from the usual chat, for our English circle is so choice that it's just like being at home, and I prefer them to murder our language than make them speak their own; perhaps they don't even want to. It's a stupid English thing to want to speak French—I don't believe that it extends any further than high society, among the lords and ladies; but do you think I am ever allowed to see anyone else? Good bye, dearest Alphonse.

Germaine.

P.S. I started my letter indignantly; I am angry with the duchess and others like her, but assuredly not with my father, although I find his conduct very surprising and distressing. Even more upsetting is that I hear no news of my stepmother or of my sisters—the whole of the Vendée is ablaze.[5]

Letter II.

L. B. Fonbrune to Alphonse.

From the Vendée, April 24, 1793

I could date my letter more precisely but I would have made your heart beat faster. I am writing to you from exactly the same place that you once wrote to me, in the time before émigrés and Jacobins existed.[6] You have joined one group, and I've joined the other, and yet we are still friends. Yes, *soyons amis, Cinna, c'est moi qui t'en convie.*[7] Which of us is Cinna? Which of us is Augustus? Which of the two is the conspirator? Who will be the master, able to be merciful toward the other? In truth, I have no idea; I've lost my head, and I no longer know who I am or what I want. I loved you, although you are the only one of your arrogant caste whom I have ever been able to tolerate. Your cousin C*** could have told you what my master, brave Truguet, had to endure from your upstart so-called gentlemen;[8] judge from that how I was treated, an upstart myself, as brave as any of them, better educated than most of them, but lacking prudence and experience, having done nothing which could make them respect me. And so I hated them, and they deserved to be hated. My brother has gathered enough support to be appointed to the Legislation; he was a Girondin, he was a Jacobin, and today he presides at the Convention.[9] He never went as far as many others. Has he not already gone much too far, and am I not part of an unjust and cruel war here? I don't know any more, as I told you. At the moment, although on the winning side, I am out of action, and in a poetic sense I am beaten and forced to burn *de plus de feux que je n'en allumai*.[10] My wound (you will think I'm still speaking poetically, but no, I have a very real, very ragged wound in my left thigh) has put me out of action, and on the pretext that I needed to be left here to contain mutineers and fanatics, I have been granted permission to stay with the loveliest angels in paradise—in Heaven, I should say. Until now, I have enjoyed the company of angels so little that I did not even know where they lived, but now I know where their elite is; it is surely here. I had already caught a glimpse of your Germaine's stepmother and of her half sisters before the last fight; they were staying at a cousin's estate. Our troops moving into that area, they came back to their own home, and now we're troubling their repose again. Repose! What is repose? Nothing other than boredom. Beautiful Pauline, would you not rather have me in your home, dressing my wounds (this is pure poetry for the moment, as Pauline does not touch me even with the tip of her little finger), than vegetate like a flower in the meadow which no one looks at or admires?[11] Beautiful Pauline, don't you already love me a little bit? My grandfather was a baker at the beck and call of everyone; yours was Lieutenant-general of the King's armies: my father is an attorney, although a very decent man; yours, although also very decent, is in the army of a very mediocre prince who does not love his country, a man who was a fawning courtier before he became a minor conspirator, currently executing military statutes under the command of a mistress who is past her best, and whose pedigree army has still not slaughtered a fly, and only makes any noise at all in the wretched gazettes. . . .[12] But where is my sainted patriotism leading me? Beautiful Pauline, I forgot you, I forgot myself; and yet I'm not talking about anything other than you and me. We don't want to make our grandparents live together; if they had to, I accept that the former should devote himself to making bread for the latter, who would eat it in a very dignified manner. We don't want our fathers to live together—they would heartily loathe one another and would make a very unhappy household—but you and me, why should we not be living together? I only see between us the differences that there should be. You are beautiful; am I so ugly? You are gentle; am I ill-tempered or brutal? You are chaste . . . well then, you've been chaste for both of us, but if I become your husband and you love me, I will be faithful to you—yes, completely faithful. Today, Pauline, what did you ask me for? To write to Alphonse; I am writing to him. To send him a letter to forward to your father; I enclose it here. To send another one for your older sister to my brother the president, so that he can have it sent to England; it is already done—my letter has been written, yours is enclosed; I am going to seal it and send it all. Adieu, dear Alphonse. Write to me; send me your letter to this address. Aaaghh! These damned pains! And I'll be having them for a long while. Write to me, do you hear? Please hurry up. Sometimes we get better quicker than we want to; a second of distraction will make me forget to limp at all.

L. B. Fonbrune.

P.S. Yesterday I spoke a bit sailorlike and sans-culottishly about the holy mysteries:[13] "Sir," Pauline's maternal grandmother said, "if you have a father, would you like to hear him spoken ill of? If you thought you had a friend you had never met but of whose existence you had no doubt, would you like it if someone, for no reason other than to tease, said that he had never existed, that he was a phantom creature, or that he is unable to do the good you had hoped he would?" I blushed, Alphonse, and said nothing.

Letter III.

Germaine to Alphonse.

London, April 19, 1793

I want to give wings to the letter I have just sent you, and for your reply to have them too, but the packet boats and mail coaches will only go at their ordinary speed. Good God! How slow it all is; I will have to wait for three weeks before I get anything! I must write to you; that will calm my impatience, and the long chapter of my woes alone will keep me busy enough. Pity me, my dearest Alphonse; you will see that I deserve it.

Imagine first of all what it is like to have a thousand little annoyances imposed on one in the name of decorum by a woman who violates all decorum, from morning to night and night to morning. I will not allow myself to tell you what I am forced to see against my will, but in truth it is extraordinary that my father entrusted me to this woman's care. Could he have foreseen the effect that her example has on me? It is not an effect, dearest Alphonse, which should vex you; on the contrary, our wise convent teachers could not make me love virtue half as much as the duchess makes me hate vice. It reminds me of something witty that an Englishwoman said to one of our gentlemen: "Sir, are you paid by the French patriots to bring the aristocracy into disrepute?" But where was I? To begin with I wanted to tell you how I am restricted in a thousand trivial ways, such that I cannot take a step, say a word, or tie a ribbon as I want to; and then I started talking about the duchess, and then about the aristocracy that aristocrats make hateful in the same way that the duchess makes vice hateful, or to put it differently, how prudes supposedly make virtue hateful.

Oh! We are very good at inciting hatred, and without the frenzied democrats who serve our cause, as we serve theirs, I do not think any foreigner would ever want to fight for us. Do you want to know why I say all this? I am going to tell you; it will be the same as telling you my troubles. You will see if I am not right to be alternately ferociously indignant and incredibly bored. In truth, it is enough to test the patience of an angel to hear people always reasoning and joking so badly. . . . Reasoning . . . no, that's not what it is, or anything close to it. To reason, even to reason wrongly, requires a certain amount of patience and application, whereas in three minutes here we shout, bemoan, curse, then laugh or pretend to, in such a way as to rout any reasoning and discourage any reasoner. The result is that the English people in our circle, even those who try to be as frivolous as we are, are stupified by our jumps, leaps, and sudden digressions. No sooner do they prepare to console us for the woes we complain of than we have already comforted ourselves, and there's nothing left for them to do other than join in with our noisy mirth, except that they shouldn't even think of it; we've already stopped laughing. Half of our delightful company tease me for my taciturnity, others gravely criticize my dress, and the wisest of them all compare the duchess's cook with such-and-such an English or French lord's, and discuss what they've been eating today, and what they'll be eating tomorrow. This is one of my greatest grievances, dearest Alphonse: is it not disgraceful that we should allow ourselves to keep a real gourmet's table, while we see our poor compatriots, driven from their country by the same scourges, and calling on the same god, worshipping in the same way, begging, suffering, and almost dying from hunger? If the English were unaware of what we were like in France before the Revolution, they know now, and this is yet another way of justifying our enemies, and they may thank us for it. Happily for the honor of the nation, such depravity is not widespread; I know that there are some compatriots who share what they have with the indigent, and please believe, dear Alphonse, that despite the duchess's surveillance, Germaine finds ways of not spending everything that is given her on knickknacks. Victoire

and I know the poor émigrés, and they are as welcome here at
the duchess's town house before daylight as others are elsewhere the rest of the day. And that's what it was like in France;
there were some very good people. If there had only been Ger-
maines and Alphonses, I don't think there would have been a
revolution. This is what Victoire tells me every day. Her brother
was in service with you and certainly was not unhappy. Why
can we not come back to France, you and I and everyone like
us, and leave the duchesses, their cooks and friends to fast as
they please! I'm being called; I must go.

The 20th

A ridiculous scene has just taken place, but at least I have got
a very good discovery out of it. The duchess wishes she had
kept quiet, but her regrets are of no use to her; I know what I
know. This is how it happened. A Roman Catholic lord from
Ireland has been visiting us often enough for the duchess to
have thought it worth her while to find out how wealthy he is.
He is very rich. She took it into her head to marry her idiot son
to the daughter of this Irishman—the daughter is rich, even
beyond her father's wealth, because of what she has inherited
from an uncle. This project is a few weeks old, and it gave
birth to another one, which is to marry me to the father, who
seems to find me to his liking. The duchess no doubt thought
that if she gave me to the father, she would be granted the
daughter. This was being plotted so secretly that I barely noticed
anything. But today it was judged wise to alter the approach.
Here's the conversation, word for word.

Milord: Her Grace goes extremely well, I hope.[14]

Duchess: Oh dear God, my lord, how can anyone be well
when we fear for everything that is most precious to us? I have
received letters which inform me of appalling decrees being
passed and atrocious things happening. People are being
denounced, arrested, massacred; all justice, honesty, and taste
is finished. Can you believe that my china has just been sold
for nothing? For nothing I tell you, superb pieces of china and
charming furniture; among other things was my Boulle table,
which was absolutely one of a kind.[15]

Milord: What is "boule," Your Grace? Is it the same as "bouleau" [silver birch]? Is it out of this wood that are made the tables?

Duchess (laughing merrily): Oh Good God no, milord. Comte, do you hear milord's question?

The comte: Boulle, bouleau, quite right! Milord would call la rue du Roule la rue du Rouleau, and why not, so long as everyone understands each other![16]

Milord: I don't understand; but I do not leave from pitying you greatly, madame.

Duchess: Oh milord, it cannot go on; the turn of these upstarts will soon come, now that your generous nation has embraced our quarrel. But let us talk of something more interesting. Beautiful Germaine, come closer. Would it not be a kind thing, milord, to make this beautiful exile forget her atrocious country?

"What a touching sentiment," I retorted angrily, "but I neither can nor want to forget my country."

Duchess: She has character, milord; you see that she has character, and that must please a proud Englishman a great deal.

Milord: A proud Englishman, duchess? Who are you calling a proud Englishman? Not me, I hope.

Duchess: Oh milord, I mean the nation, the national pride.

Milord: I think that mademoiselle, with the face she has and the good character you give her, for I suppose that her character is a good one, must please everyone.

Duchess: No doubt, milord, and he who makes this excellent acquisition will be very happy and no doubt much applauded. [Milord, whom she was regarding fixedly, looked very embarrassed, and as for me, I flushed with anger.] Ah Germaine, are you blushing? What charming modesty! You see, milord, you see—you like modesty, do you not, milord? And this modest beauty is in possession of a fine château and an estate estimated at 45 thousand pounds per year.[17]

Me: You forget, madam, that the château is half burnt down and that the land has been destroyed, not omitting that it will be sold and all proceeds go to the nation as soon as there are any buyers.[18]

Duchess: Good! Would anyone dare buy it? And will the château not be rebuilt and the sans-culottes pay for it?[19] [I laughed and shrugged my shoulders.] But mademoiselle, even if my hope were as much of an illusion as your disdainful and contradictory smile implies, do you not also have beautiful estates in Holland and in Brabant?

Me: In Holland and Brabant! Is this the plot of a novel? I feel as if I'm listening to a tale from the *Thousand and One Nights*.[20]

Duchess: No, no, it is neither a novel nor a fairy tale. Your father kept it hidden from you and forbade me to tell you, but I am forced to respond to a young person who in ironic tones, tones which are fast becoming her habitual tones, dares to accuse me of inventing fairy stories: know then, young woman, that your grandmother, born in Brabant of a Dutch family, left you an estate in each of those countries. You have administrators who send the money which you spend here to a banker in the city; it is not a quarter of what these estates bring in. "It is not fair," your father said, "that my daughter, who is rich in spite of all our troubles, should lack for anything, and so that she can marry as well as possible, I want the excess to accumulate." If you doubt my word, look at this letter.

"What!" I exclaimed. "I am rich, and my father, who must have great difficulty finding any money, is not using any of my revenues? This must be settled at once; I must write to him, beg him—" I had already got up when the duchess took hold of my dress. "You must certainly not do that," she said to me. "It would compromise me." And I was forced to sit back down, but for me the conversation was over—there was no milord or duchess for Germaine in the room or in the world; I saw only my father and Alphonse. Bit by bit my young sisters and my lovely stepmother came back into my thoughts. So, Alphonse, I could live with you, and help the others to live. If everything was taken or sold or destroyed, we would still have your parents' wealth as well as mine, and we'd have enough for us all to live on! Oh! Let the duchess say what she wants today! Supposing that I listen, or that without listening I hear, she has done me too much good for me not to forgive her everything—yes, everything.

She takes the permission I gave her too far. First of all, I was subjected to a long exhortation to encourage milord's advances; and after my very clear and decided refusal this morning, instead of finding, as she did this morning, that I had *character*, she is now scolding me for contradicting her.

"What suits other people perfectly," she said, "is no good for you; you wouldn't look kindly on my son, and now that I am trying to match him with a young woman whom you could help me obtain for him . . ." At this point I looked at her so fixedly that she blushed and continued no further, which dispensed me from replying.

April 21st

Listen to how unbelievably indiscreet the duchess can be! Milord visited today again, and the duchess, seeing that I was hardly in the mood to make him any advances, which is what she truly wants, got up from her place, pulled him aside, and said, loudly enough for me and the comte and two or three other people to hear: "Do not let these little ways put you off, milord; she was engaged to marry a young man whom her father no longer approves of, and she thinks that her heart must stay as romantic and faithful as before, but it will pass, I guarantee it." Everyone looked at me; some smiled and others seemed disagreeably affected. But I, without being disconcerted in the slightest, I said with a curtsy to the duchess, that I thanked her, and that supposing that milord had done me the honor of thinking of me, although nothing had made me think he had, he would surely no longer do so, and with that I left the drawing room and shut myself in my room to write to you. But already I am being interrupted. There will be neither pleasure nor repose for me, I see.

22nd

The duchess was uncomfortable: Her son was alone with her, and refusing to talk to her, and it was to break up this

disagreeable tête-à-tête that she had me called down. She
wanted us to go shopping or to the park, even though it was
quite cold. Fortunately Lady Caroline Delmont was announced,
the most agreeable of our acquaintances (I don't know why I
say fortunately, for it would have been much better to quarrel,
freeze, and get colds—anything would have been better than
what that visit caused yesterday and today). Our gentlemen,
who had departed for only a moment, all returned to a silenced
duchess and her sulking son, oblivious to the fact that the scene
had already changed. All except the Vicomte des Fossés, a
handsome boy age twenty-three, witty, well brought up, with a
slight tendency to tell coarse jokes, but all things considered,
very amiable.[21] They have all noticed that Lady Caroline shows
signs of preferring him to everyone else, but they have decided
to pretend the opposite to the vicomte, who, they say, already
enjoys too many advantages. I have seen them play many little
tricks on him about this, denying that Lady Caroline had asked
for news of him when she had, throwing an invitation that they
found in his lodgings into the fire before he saw it. I would
have told him about it a thousand times, if Victoire, to whom I
tell everything I see, hadn't prevented me. Yesterday Lady Caroline asked where he was, and whether they would be seeing
him that evening; they replied with sly grins, talking in discreet
and mysterious tones of good luck, of actresses, of a beautiful
Englishwoman and a pretty Frenchwoman. Finally our detest-
able count started saying what a pity it was, you couldn't deny
his wit, grace, talent or bravery. . . .

"What is a pity?" Lady Caroline interrupted.

"A total lack of principles, disgraceful treachery," said the
count. "He comes from the same province as I, he served in
my regiment; and everywhere I have encountered him he has
seduced women whom no one had heard of, and boasted of it
with the most revolting self-satisfaction."

"This is disgusting!" exclaimed the Chevalier de Neuveville.[22]

"It distresses me a great deal," the comte continued, "for I
love him; he is lovable—but I cannot tolerate such deep-seated
vices in my best friend."

"Wicked man!" I thought to myself. "You describe yourself perfectly."

"These words," said Lady Caroline, whose eyes were fixed on a picture on the ceiling, "these words sound strange together. Deep-seated vices in one's best friend . . . You are unfortunate in your best friends, my lord comte, if they have vices of the heart that have to be tolerated or not tolerated."

The comte was embarrassed for a reply, and the interfering duchess interrupted everything with loud exclamations about Lady Caroline's dress.

"We really would take you for a Frenchwoman," she said. "You have the taste and the elegance for it. Did your mother spend any time in Paris before your birth?"

A thousand stupid remarks on this subject then ensued, all while arranging a game of three of a kind, but Lady Caroline, no doubt worn out and exasperated, ordered her sedan chair, and left.²³ A little afterward M. Des Fossés returned. He had seen her but hadn't been able to get her to notice him; he was very sorry not to see her. I hastily said that she had also been sorry not to see him—I was in a horrible mood, and although I wouldn't want to answer for what the comte said as being completely false, I would have wagered and I would wager anything in the world that at the very least he greatly exaggerated it. But I am still only halfway through my story. Today, toward evening, the duchess, who continues to be ill at ease when alone with me, suggested that we visit Lady Caroline. I asked for nothing better. She received us politely but coldly. Nonetheless I had begun to melt the ice with a thousand fond remarks, when the Comte de *** and young Des Fossés were announced.

"Run and say that I am not in," said Lady Caroline. They were already at the door, and heard what she said; they withdrew. The duchess showed her surprise.

"How can you be surprised?" said Lady Caroline with much emotion. "After what I heard yesterday at your house, either one or the other or both are extremely bad company."

"Good God! What is all this?" said the duchess. "If the vicomte is a bit conceited or if the count is a bit jealous that

you don't prefer his favorite Monsieur de Neuveville, it's a fine
thing to fly into a passion about!"

"What do you mean, madam, jealous?"

"Yes, jealous . . . you only have eyes for him, beautiful lady,
and our men are a bit wicked. Those who are not present are
always in the wrong; yesterday they didn't want you to be only
thinking about someone who wasn't there. Oh! If we inspected
everything that closely, we would live alone and be very
bored."

"Before you, madam, and your friends arrived in London, I
was only alone for as much of the time as I wanted to be,"
replied Lady Caroline proudly. "And I would much prefer to
be alone forever than to be in such bad company, even if it
wasn't very often."

"Oh! You are angry," said the duchess, rising. "I will tell
Monsieur Des Fossés, and perhaps he will be flattered, and
tomorrow you will come and dine with us and make peace
with everybody. Do you promise me to come?"

"Not at all," replied Lady Caroline. "I leave for the country
this evening."

"Then we will come and see you. Where in the countryside?"

"Very far away," replied Lady Caroline with an air which
showed us the door forever. We were going out. The duchess
caught some part of her clothes in the door or the lock. I took
advantage of this mishap to go back a few steps into the drawing room and say to Lady Caroline as I embraced her: "You
know the proprieties better than I do; may I speak to the
vicomte?"

"No," she said, "but I will write to you. What address?"

"Mistress Sparrow is my dressmaker as well as yours," I
said aloud as I rejoined the duchess.

"What are you talking about Mistress Sparrow for?" said
the latter ill-temperedly. "And why have you kept me waiting?
I do believe in truth that you have tears in your eyes. Are you
so attached to that conceited woman that you are weeping to
see her go?"

"Yes" was all I said in response, and I let her rail to her heart's
content at all English women, at silly-minded women, at Lady

Caroline, and at me, without uttering a word in reply. On returning to our house, I went straight up to my room. I will go to bed so as to avoid having to eat supper with those people; they can tell the vicomte what happened in their own way. . . . No, I will go down—my presence will embarrass them.

They weren't able to keep quiet, and they didn't want to tell the truth.

"There's Germaine; she will tell you if it didn't all happen just as I said!" exclaimed the duchess as soon as she saw me. She launched back into a story that was half-true and half-false, with the comte saying from time to time, "Oh but yes, that's exactly it—I was joking: I said that you were a terrible conqueror, and who is the conqueror who doesn't allow fame to say a little word about his triumphs?"

The vicomte looked at me fixedly, the duchess called on me, but it was all very well her treading on my toes and making faces at me—I said nothing, no, not a single word. They are going to hate me as much as I despise them.

My dearest Alphonse, be so bold as to write to my father. Send him my letters, if you want; he will forgive me for disobeying him, and will take me away from these infernal people. The vicomte told me as he left that he had no wish to make a stir but that the following day he would be leaving London. Lady Caroline is a widow, she is young, she is rich, and there is no one but her that I liked here. I do believe that the vicomte is really deeply in love with her. Good-bye. My letter will go off tomorrow morning; I am going to seal it. If I had my father's address, I would write to him myself.

P.S. I reread my letter; do I not go into minute detail and describe everything at great length? This *boule* or *bouleau*, will it make you smile or yawn? That really depicts our people and their conversations very well! For while they know not a syllable of English, they think that all English people ought to know our proper names, our sayings, and all the little trifles as well as we do. And then we laugh with great intelligence and wit. About the Commandant de Landau, one day we sang, *Gillot, Gillot, how that name interests me!* . . . Good-bye.[24] If Alphonse weren't French, I wouldn't want to be French.

Letter IV.

L. B. Fonbrune to Alphonse.

April 30, 1793

I wish that a certain head could be taken around the entire surface of the globe, or at least Europe, or at the very least those countries inhabited by the French. . . . A head![25] Oh have no fear, dear Alphonse, never think that I am having cruel thoughts, never believe that I have turned into a bloodthirsty monster. No, I swear to you, I have never applauded these horrors that are defiling France. Too rarely, alas, have I ever been able to prevent what I loathed. Oh France! Oh shame! Why can I not be rid of certain atrocious memories? Often they make my existence unbearable. I dream horrible dreams, and then wake up yelling, all covered in sweat, my heart beating. A few nights ago I woke Pauline, even though her bedroom is not very close to mine. She thought it worth sending someone who, on opening my door, asked me if it was my wound that was causing such violent pain. . . . It is worse than that, compassionate Pauline: it is ghosts and bloody corpses. Ah! How much worse than I some people must sleep! I don't know whether I hate them more than I pity them. I know that I avoid them, for if I see them smile, I am tempted to stab them; if they look thoughtful or sad, I think I see a vulture devouring their heart. The head I'd like to take around with me is Medusa's; I want her to stop all the blows, all the screams; I want the arm that is raised ready to strike a blow to stay forever motionless, the mouth that is open ready to curse to remain silent, and that every Frenchman, left with nothing other than the faculty of thought, were forced to use that faculty without stopping for a long time, the only object of his thoughts being these two single questions: "What can I do?" and "What do I want?" Ponder these questions if you prefer, mettlesome, vengeful aristocrat. Satisfy yourself first, enumerating your cruel desires to yourself. You want to beat us, humiliate us, crush us, exterminate us—but can you? What do you want, then? To become richer and more powerful than ever! Can you? Consider your means and ours; recognize the goodwill of those who aspire to support you; appreciate also their strength, and if you are not completely mad, in the end you will want to be reconciled with your compatriots on conditions which may not be satisfactory but must nonetheless be accepted and even proposed, because they will be the best you can obtain. And you, anarchists, what do you want, and what can you do?[26] But I am using a senseless word, for no one calls himself an anarchist, for although anarchy is only too real and some people cause it to be born or prolong it, nobody wants it; it is nobody's project. Everyone has a master or mistress in view, be it the people that they want to control, or d'Orléans or Robespierre, whose minister or favorite they hope to become— once they've decided what they want, let them ask themselves whether they can achieve it.[27] No doubt a few days' reign will not suffice, either for those they'd like to set on a throne or for themselves. Well then, how many months could such a reign last or keep its credibility, a reign of the people as they understand it, an unrestrained reign of sans-culottes over this disorderly people? How many days would the reign of a d'Orléans or a Robespierre last?

Once they've compared in cold blood (which is what Medusa's head will make even the most inflamed of them do) what they want and what they are able to achieve, many of them will be happy to return to their original obscurity and there enjoy the indulgence or the oblivion of their fellow citizens, keeping what they've acquired, without anyone asking how they acquired it. But the decent people, the decent Jacobins, what do they want? The republic, and order in the republic. Can they, must they hope to achieve that which they have so desired and steadfastly continue to desire? Let them never waver; let them persevere and obstinately persist in their hope— Medusa's head should not change their courageous intentions; on the contrary, she will enable them to realize their goals, for she will cool the frenzy on both sides, and each party will submit and act as ordered, placing the public good in their hands. Have you noticed, my dear Alphonse, that a class of people exist whom I have not even mentioned? Medusa's head will have no effect on them, for they seem not even to be aware of it—they are the cowards and the egotists. They do not even have any esprit de corps to embolden them or take the place of any other sort of spirit. They remind me of a besieged Rome, and the old invalid senators who, quaking less than everyone else, waited in stillness for the Gauls, and for death.[28] If those people, instead of being struck by Medusa and turned to stone, could be made to move again, and if they then asked themselves, "What do we want?" they would reply, "To live and not be ruined." And when they asked, "But what can we do?" they would reply, considering their prodigious numbers, "We can do a great deal; we can do everything," and they would rise up and march to join the brave Republicans, who by force or will would triumph over everyone still unconvinced by ideas alone.

There, dear Alphonse—these have been my political dreams since love and compassion came to soften my heart. When I can't be with Pauline, I ask her for a book, and she brings a table covered with everything that occurs to her up to the bed in which I am forced to lie prone; sometimes it's Montesquieu, sometimes *The Imitation of Jesus Christ*; yesterday she gave me *Esprit de la Ligue*, and today Jean-Jacques Rousseau and good Rollin.[29] I am vexed not to see a good big republic any-where I look, but what does not exist yet, may yet come to exist. I dislike federalism: "single and indivisible" seems very beautiful to me, in the abstract, but I confess that when I try to work out the details, I get lost.[30] I hope that others will be cleverer than I am, and will know how to arrange it. I would consent to two chambers, with 43 deputies in each, as I would not want more than one deputy for each department; lots would be cast to divide the 86 deputies into the two chambers.[31] The responsibilities of each chamber would be different, but each would regulate the things which in the first instance had been decided by the other. This council would be renewed every year. The deputies would sit in Versailles, as Paris is too crowded and there is too much entertainment, and any farther away the knowledge and lights of Paris would be lacking. I say that there is too much entertainment there, but if I were the master, there would be less of it. Productions would be confined to the opera, which would be very expensive, and to a single carefully supervised play, which would be free for everyone. Immediately we would say good-bye to all the revolutionary and licentious plays.[32] To reform the government at the same time as corrupting morality seems too impossible to me, and unless we ever become both better and more sober, we will never be anything other than half-broken puppets, who go completely wrong at the slightest movement. As for the ci-devant princes, they could live wherever they pleased, so long as it wasn't in France.[33] The nobility would stay abolished, but noble aristocrats could come home, after a more or less lengthy period, depending on the amount of damage they had inflicted on their country. Each person's trial would be done *pro Deo*, we would request the lawyers to be brief, and one hour would be enough to lay out the case and to judge it. As for compensation, the state would grant none; they would have to ask for it from their friends and family. Oh how many nobles would reveal their villainy and let their own flesh and blood cower in abject poverty! And do you know what I would want to do with young Capet?[34] Bring him up very simply, but very well, far from Paris and Versailles, from Marseilles, Bordeaux, and the borders. If after fifteen years my republic had nothing in it of any worth, but he, age twenty, was worth something, I would make him king without a second thought.

Another day I will speak to you about Pauline and me—the cold and my insomnia are delaying my recovery; my blood was bitter and boiling; I have been given remedies which weaken me. I will admit to you, Alphonse, and you will not betray me: I don't know where I could find the resolve to take up arms here again; at the frontiers I'd fight as much as I was told. Ah! If I could make Pauline's father my prisoner, you can be assured that he would die neither at my hands nor beneath the blade of the guillotine.

L.B.F.

Letter V.

The Abbé des *** to the Marquis de ***

We have read this letter, which has been lost, not in going from Cress . . . or from Neuch . . . to Condé's army, but on a shorter journey.[35] *In it, the abbé recounted how he found Alphonse on first arriving, and how sad the young man was. He told Germaine's father everything he thought might change his opinion and behavior toward him. He described Alphonse's reasons for not joining the enemies of his country on this second occasion at great length, and also laid out his own political ideas in no less detail. He wanted the state to have a king, but no princes or privileged classes, maintaining in a way that was at least plausible that the nobility, if allowed back in as nobility, would no longer be able to agree among themselves. Himself a persecuted priest, he desired there to be limitless tolerance in religious matters, and seemed to think that the believers of each sect should pay for and support their clergy. He would have liked to reestablish the natural tithe, as the least onerous of all taxes. With this portion of the revenue of a propertied man, he seemed to think it as easy as it was just and natural to feed the indigent sick, the poor orphan, the poor old man, as well as the man who devoted his time to handing out alms, to teaching and public instruction, who, having no time left over for his own affairs, might lack anything to live on were he not also to be provided for.*

Letter VI.

Alphonse to Germaine.

In N***, May 6, 1793[36]

What a surprise, my sweet love, what a treasure these two letters are, both landing in my hands at the same time! The first one traveled very slowly, given that it arrived at the same time as the second. Should I be angry? I waited a little longer; the unhappy silence that reigned between us, lasting so long, and failing to make me any more accustomed to it, endured a few days more, but look how rich I am today! I can see all your thoughts and all your heart. Here I am moved with you, there I admire you, at the same time as feeling enraged at the odious duchess and at that man who is so entirely worthy of her. I will accord a little interest to young Des Fossés, once I am less preoccupied with myself and you. Poor Alphonse! Poor Germaine! One is desolate, the other tormented, and yet how happy they could be! May my Germaine at least be as free of unjust suspicions as I have always been! Perhaps you are surprised that the reply you must have been wishing for has not come sooner. Oh, do not blame me! Know yourself, and know your lover. I do not believe that any man in my place could have forgotten or neglected Germaine, but what I am doing, what I swear, is that Alphonse has not one moment of distraction to reproach himself with. I will deliver not only your letters but also my reborn courage and restored spirits to the Abbé des ***. He has seen so much, and has so affectionately shared my sorrow, that he must have his part in my joy. I will travel two leagues, and look as if I'm traveling alone, but in fact I shall have delightful company. Keep back, unwelcome companions! Do you not see that Germaine is with me? My eyes are wet, yet I laugh and run—my face and expression must look completely different than before, for I have a different heart. Let us be off, dearest letters; let us be off, Germaine— we shall go and find the abbé.

May 7th

The abbé was on his way to see me and we met half a league from here.

"What is it? What's the matter with you, Alphonse?" he said to me when I flung my arms round his neck. "Have you by any chance heard from Germaine?"

A spring cloud was raining great drops of water on us. What to do! How could I show him the letters without running the risk of the beloved characters being washed away before our eyes? I wish you could have seen me, Germaine, sometimes hiding my treasure against my chest and trying to recite what you had written instead of reading it, sometimes worrying that I was changing a few words, and unfolding the paper, despite the rain falling even more heavily. Never was any predicament greater or more precious. Finally there was a break in the rain, and the two letters were read from beginning to end. The abbé was calmer than I and grasped the details of your affecting descriptions better than I did. What you say about the duchess did not surprise him at all. "If the marquis had known her as I do, he would never have entrusted Germaine to her," he said. He confirmed what the duchess's indiscretion revealed to you, but he pointed out to me that the richer you are, the less pressure I must put on your father, and we decided that because of this, I should neither send him your letters nor write to him. Tell him what you think is right, dear Germaine. We think you should address your letters to Mannheim—Condé's army will not be far from there. When we came to M. Des Fossés, the abbé said, "And that is what comes of certain misdemeanors that we suppose to be harmless. The role the comte played is odious, I agree, but he would never dare speak as he did had the young man been completely irreproachable. He loses, perhaps forever, the heart of an amiable woman and the hope of an honorable establishment. . . . Take care, Alphonse, never to deserve to lose Germaine."

"No, dear abbé, do not fear for me. To lose her without having deserved it would make me despair, but to lose her and know that it was my fault . . . with grief like that in my heart, I would be unable to live."

"Is it not distressing," said the abbé, once we had started walking back toward his home, "is it not distressing to see these unhappy French compromise their reputation among strangers through their frivolity, indiscretion, and spiteful gossip? It will be supposed that they are incorrigible, and who will feel sorry for these people whose misfortune does not give them pause for thought, whose nobility, while demanding respect, shows itself to be without dignity or generosity, without anything that might make it worthy of respect? Among themselves, individuals tear each other apart, disparage each other, while as a mass, they claim they deserve to be honored! What might the dignity of a body be which does not derive from the dignity of its individual members? If I, a gentleman, do not respect you as a gentleman, how can I hope that this title will win us respect from anyone at all?"

"I think we hope that the foolishness of people who do not know us as well as we know ourselves will be what allows us to be respected," I said.

"Oh well, yes," said the abbé, laughing. "I think that's what it is," and this thought, not as serious as our other reflections, led us to reread your letters with some hilarity, looking for all the absurdities and follies you describe. It's better to read about them than witness them, dear Germaine—we laughed, but you suffered. Write to me, I beg you, to tell me whether the duchess still sometimes intends you to wed her stupid son and sometimes to be the prize that will win him a different bride. What! How is it possible that she could have such an idea? Using you to trade with! You, dear Germaine, the companion of my childhood and the hope of my heart—warn your father so that he can take you away from the hateful hands to which he has entrusted you! I spent last night at Cr*** and did not get back until late because of the terrible weather, not until four o'clock. If it wasn't time for the post to go, I would write more, although in truth my life is so uniform and my thoughts so monotonous that I can have nothing to tell you about myself— I only ever think of you; it is always you who occupies me.

Alphonse ***

Letter VII.

The Marquis de *** to the Abbé des ***

Headquarters of Condé's army, May 6, 1793

Why, Reverend Abbé, did you not take the famous oath?[37] You would now be a bishop and preaching to your flock, instead of to me, who requested no sermons. It seems to me that you are constitutional, monarchic, and in general a very fine man, but

not at all a good Frenchman or a worthy descendant of your
noble ancestors, any more than you are a worthy minister of
the old church.[38] I repeat, I wish you had taken the oath.
Amphibian beings are what I like least in all creation; your
dear Alphonse walks in your footsteps.[39] Good God, how well
it suits a young man of twenty-two to declaim instead of fight!
He would fight, says he, in the Vendée—well, that costs nothing to say as the guillotine blocks his way, but he could fight
on the frontier, instead of which he stays by your side, reasoning, making fine distinctions, and holding forth like a veritable
Cato.[40] But you say that he is missing my daughter—well, why
does he not fight to win her back? This reason alone should
suffice: even if he had no love for royal blood, no hatred for
abominable brigands, still he should fight next to Germaine's
father, and strive to deserve her by wanting what I want, looking for honor where I say it is to be found. Allow me, Reverend
Abbé, to believe that in matters of honor I am as good a judge
as any. Please God that I may not accuse my old friend's son of
being deaf to the call of honor, but he has befuddled his mind
with too much study and with philosophizing, which has
nothing in common with the vocation and duties of a brave
gentleman. I believe, Reverend Abbé, that you have played a
part in this education of which I have never approved. I came
upon you refuting books with him that needed not refutation
but removing from him and burning. Has Germaine not also
been infected with this accursed mania for reasoning about
everything? If you wish to do me a service and expiate to some
extent the evil you have done us, then write to my family and
tell them to make a great bonfire of all the modern books that
may have found their way into my house; let my wife's mother
go through them and let her spare nothing that has a whiff of
this century's damnable philosophy. As for Alphonse, let him
become a member of a learned society, if that will allow him
to live a soft and indolent life, for that is what he needs. I do
not suspect him of lacking the courage to fight, but rather the
courage required to endure all the privations and fatigue. Those
he experienced last year disheartened him, and fortunately for

him he found some sophisms in his head which allowed him to make a virtue of what suited him. The fine proposition you put to me, Reverend Abbé, to live with him and Germaine in some peaceful retreat! Know, Reverend Abbé, that for as long as there is one brave gentleman left to fight for King, Nobility, and Faith, in me he will find a brother in arms and also a friend whom no danger will shock, no fatigue weary. God having granted me no son, I wanted a son-in-law who could be a son to me, and I thought I had found such a person in my best friend's son; but philosophizing and faintheartedness have taken him away from me. Tell him that I do not hate him, but that he must think of my daughter no more. I did not take the trouble to mull over your ridiculous plans, and I shall not describe either the projects or the hopes we harbor, and which would make you despair. You talk of the people, and in times past I wished more than anyone to see them less burdened with work and taxation, but how can I ever be interested again in these cannibals? And in any case, what is to stop the regent from reforming certain abuses in the King's name? Let us save the house that the brigands have set alight, and when the master of the house is safely installed once more, he will be able to turn his mind to improving it.

The Marquis de ***

Letter VIII.

*Alphonse to Laurent B*** F****

*N***, May 11, 1793*

How surprised and pleased I was to receive your letters, my dearest Laurent! Laurent B*** in R*** sur ***.[41] I'll wager the room you have is my old one, from which you can see the clear little river advance toward the steep rock and then, as if repulsed, tear away at great speed and fling itself at the bosom of the sea. I loved Germaine with more hope and security than you love Pauline, and yet now I am further removed from

happiness than you are. The marquis detests amphibian
beings, or so he says, and in his eyes I am one of these foul
creatures. He likes bravery even more than nobility; he cannot
deny you have that, although he almost denies that I do. He
will suppose that a noble and valiant race starts with you and
ends with me. Perhaps I will owe Germaine to your interces-
sion. Will I love her any the less for it? Oh no, Laurent! And
I will love you the more for it, and we will equally benefit
from my obligation to you. Between Laurent the Jacobin and
Alphonse the aristocrat, how much sympathy, how many true
links can I see, and how well they'd live together if fate wanted
them to be brothers! Is the difference of opinion so great when
hearts are equally true, and minds equally upright?

Living near me there is a deported priest who, like you, is
full of plans about how to govern. He wants a king at the head
of your republic, and that is the sum of the difference between
your plan and his; he even only wants a king to smooth the
path of the republic, and if you were able to prove to him that
it didn't need one, he would abandon the idea, for it is not for
the sake of any kingdom or monarchy that he plans, nor in
the name of the so-called grandsons of Henri IV. Henri IV's
son was too weak; his real grandson was too egotistical, too
entranced by sumptuous grandeur.[42] Can a family renew those
traits which are thought to characterize it by moving ever farther from their source? No, the abbé expects neither more
nor less from the Bourbons than from any other family, and he
only prefers to have them on the throne because he can see
no reasons to choose any other family. Five working senses,
a more or less robust health, a good education, consisting less
of lessons than of examples—this is all he asks of a king, and
he would exclude from the throne any prince who was too
doddery, inept, or depraved to occupy it with dignity. He nonetheless thinks that a king is necessary to bring together a
machine the size of the French Republic, and also to inspire
confidence and awe in foreigners. He thinks that a king is the
only Frenchman who is French from every part of France, the
only Frenchman who cannot be wrenched apart without us all

being affected, and finally, the only Frenchman who could bring together his own glory and that of his descendants, monarchy throughout the ages and his own reign, thereby embracing posterity in everything he does for his contemporaries. Not hiding from himself what is to be feared of a king or minister, he also thinks that anyone to whom people give power is to be feared. In effect, Laurent, what is the inherent wrong, the incorrigible flaw in a king or minister? It's nothing other than being human, and this same wrong or flaw is also to be found among the people who elect, and in the representative who is elected. Weakness, corruptibility, lack of application, sensuality, love of domination, hatred of constraint, even of that which reason alone imposes—who is the man, who is the class of men among whom you do not exist? Without your lures and easy temptations, the rich man would do good, and the poor man be decent: Worries, work, and paternal cares would fall to those who govern, grateful prosperity would be the lot of those who are governed, and one need fear neither being oppressed by the great nor robbed by the poor, for wealth would not harden nor poverty degrade. Sometimes I admire the naïveté of the man who inveighs against the rich and similarly the person who rails against the people; it is tantamount to saying, without realizing, "If I were a great man, I would have such-and-such a vice, and if I were a man of the people, I'd also have my vice"—the great lord admits that he is weak enough to be degraded by poverty, while the man who is not a great lord admits that he is weak enough not to be able to resist the lures of gold and vanity. If such were the case, why do they not hold their tongue, and forgive those people to whom they feel so similar? I am not so modest, although I used to be very inclined to ask God to *give me neither poverty nor riches*, for that is the best way to keep one's integrity, as well as to be happy. I would dare to be *great and rich*; I would dare to be *poor and of the people*, and never condemn what characterizes these two situations of man in society, because in recognizing the obstacles to virtue, I still see nothing which would make it impossible. But what is this horror of rich people, this persecution of them, that the people are currently indulging in, and which its teachers, supposedly wise men, are not ashamed to applaud? Alas! It is the vilest and also the most odious of human weaknesses; it is the crime of the strong over the weak, of the conqueror over the conquered. Oh French people! Too long oppressed, do you not now blush to outdo your oppressors in savage despotism? To justify day after day the tyrants that your rage punishes? Your games, your songs, your tortures are a thousand times more barbarous than their barbaric lack of concern: they let you suffer while they indulged in their pleasures, but you make them suffer and you insult them, and take pleasure in their sufferings. But this power which they did not use well, and which you in your turn are abusing, are you so sure that you will be able to keep it forever? How can you not fear that the retributions which you mete out day after day will not set a savage example?

Tell me, my dearest Laurent, will these horrors be over soon? Could reason not have the same effect as the head of Medusa? Could decent men not come together, consult, and understand one other? Never mind whether it's a republic or a monarchy, we must all accept order and peace, under whichever denomination they are offered. I am the same as the abbé: I would like a king as the mainspring of the republic, but if you can find me another sufficiently active spring, I would like that just as much. Would you like it if, every year, before being dissolved, each of your chambers chose from within the other the man who had displayed the most wisdom and virtue, the two men duly selected exercising for the duration of the following year the power that I would want to invest in a king? One of these two consuls or kings would be randomly chosen to be at the head of the republic as a whole; the other would lead the military forces, command the armies, and nominate the generals. . . . Let no one laugh at the presumption of either young Laurent B*** or his even younger friend Alphonse. We too are French, and have as much right as the primary or constituent assemblies to reflect, deliberate, make plans, and express hopes.[43] How fervent, how selfless are the hopes I have for my country!

Letter IX.

The Duchess de *** to the Marquis de ***

London, May 21, 1793

I watch so carefully, my dearest marquis, over the precious treasure entrusted to me, that nothing concerning Germaine escapes me. This morning, a workwoman I hire to keep myself decently dressed, which is the most that can be expected of us in these days of calamity, seemed a little more urgent about going up to see your daughter than there was any reason for. I stopped her, and with presents and promises managed to extract a letter that she was taking up. Here it is; I have no time to do anything other than put it in an envelope. I assume that it is from that old suitor, and I fear that despite your injunction and my care, Germaine has been writing to him. I will do everything in my power to prevent it happening again. It would be highly desirable that she should lose all hope on that side; it would make her reject those who venture or may venture to pay homage to her with a little less violence. I hope that the consequence of this letter having been so happily intercepted will be to make her accuse her lover of being graceless, faithless, and unworthy of any further thought. The duke is still in Spain. What cruel separations we are forced to endure, and how bizarre and frightful is this time that we live in! Good-bye, Monsieur le Marquis. I prostrate myself at the feet of the hero to whom fate has linked you; present my respects to his worthy companion.

Victorine de ***

Letter X.

Germaine to Alphonse.

London, May 21, 1793

My God, how anxious and wretched I am! According to calculations which I have done over and over again, I should have had a reply to my first letter some days ago, and by now even one to the second. And yet not a word from you for unhappy Germaine. Could Alphonse have forgotten her? No, no, a hundred times no. I have not really felt the doubt that my question seems to express—no, in truth, I have not. I doubt you no more than I doubt myself. Our hearts were not made for unjust fears, and if I had any which were founded, I would not have the strength to say so. I would die, Alphonse; I think I would die. Nor do I have the anxiety of supposing you to be ill. The duchess received news that the Abbé des *** had been deported and was going to join you. He would have written on your behalf, if you had received letters from me that you were not well enough to reply to. Perhaps you are traveling around Switzerland—that is the best and most natural thing to think, and I look forward to hearing from you as soon as possible. I had news from Pauline in the last few days. It was thanks to Laurent B***. He must have written to you. Between you and me, Pauline seems to be a bit infatuated with him. "Dear sister," she writes, "I assure you that for all that he's a Jacobin he is far from being harsh or cruel, and I have to remind myself endlessly that he's a Jacobin to stop myself from simply treating him like a decent gentleman." Pauline straightforwardly recounts the terrors that she and Minette have felt, the resignation of her grandmother and the courage and sweetness of her lovely mama. There are Jacobin troops in the village, but only Monsieur B. F*** is in the château. He seems, Pauline says, like one of those wounded prisoners that you hear about in novels, and she would ask nothing better than to dare keep him company—I expect she does dare it sometimes, the little rogue. Oh if my father only knew! If he discovered how this letter found its way to me, what ranting there would be! What! To owe something to such miserable curs . . . ! I have reminded these gentlemen about certain passports, and that shut their mouths. Good-bye, dear Alphonse. I am completely unsettled by having received nothing from you, but I will be brave, and whether I receive any news from you or not, I will send a long letter in a week; in the meantime and to give today's packet a little value and consistency, here's a letter Lady Caroline wrote to me along with one from Monsieur Des Fossés. Good-bye.

P.S. Victoire saw Mistress Sparrow coming out from the duchess's room looking very flustered. What can this mean?

Letter XI.

Lady Caroline Delmont to Germaine.

Do not suppose, mademoiselle, that I mistake Germaine de *** for the people by whom she is unfortunately surrounded. No, I am not that blind. I admired in you a combination of charms, each of which deserves admiration in itself. At the age of nineteen, your bloom and the simplicity of your manners make you look no more than sixteen, while your sense is such that any woman of any age would be lucky to resemble you. But what struck me more than anything is the courage that you seem to draw from your candor. You are unable to speak anything but the truth, and you always do speak it, whatever the consequences may be. Your conduct, never deviating from your words, is uniformly upright and noble. That is something, mademoiselle, which is very fine, very lovely, and unfortunately all too rare. Why are those around you so different from you? Without you, I would be very unhappy to know them! Humanity and compassion drew me to your duchess; I felt that a woman far from her husband, her family, and her country, whose rank and wealth was being reduced to nothing, was very much to be pitied, and that she could not be made too welcome in the country in which she had taken refuge. The first visit that I paid her allowed me to retain all these impressions, but without you and the pleasure I took in seeing you, the second visit would have been the last. It is not that I no longer pity the duchess, but that contempt is now mixed with pity. I therefore only received her in my house and only visited her because of you, whom I regarded as a beautiful and pure pearl surrounded by glass and lead beads. Soon the Vicomte des Fossés came to adorn this society in which until that point you had shone alone. I believed that he had sought you out, and I harbored wishes for such an amiable couple, but when I perceived that your heart was principally absorbed in some fond memory and that you treated the vicomte more as a brother than as a lover, I admit that I did desire to occupy that place which you did not want. My husband was the most honest man in Great Britain, but his duties demanded so much attention from him that he had little left over for me. My friends have husbands who passionately love either their horses or hunting or gambling or the speeches they make in the House of Commons; not one of them resembles the sort of husband that I would so love to have, and yet marriage does suit a woman who is neither a flirt nor dissipated. I did think that I would be happy with Monsieur Des Fossés, who is neither a hunter, a gambler, nor a great politician, who has a lively mind and whom I believed to be an honest man. I thought that I would be happy to become a Frenchwoman with him, if ever he were able to return to France, and that it would give me pleasure to see him become English with me, if a return to his own country were to be eternally forbidden. This is how I was thinking, and I was seduced by superficial graces to which I should have paid less attention, but if I was foolish and ridiculous, my excuse must be that an amiable Frenchman is the original on whom all our elegants model themselves, and when so many women allow themselves to be seduced by the misshapen copy of an agreeable model, can I not be forgiven for having been predisposed in favor of the model itself? The predisposition has been destroyed, the charm has been broken, and I owe it to a wicked man, who no doubt invented half of what he said, but even if no more than a quarter had been true, that would still be more than enough to stop me thinking of the vicomte. It would be pointless for him to display a flattering preference for me; the distrust that has been inspired in me would poison everything he could possibly say, and I would see nothing more than a cruel game in his most fervent advances, for I am as little able to limit my distrust of people as my confidence in them, and the man who has cheated once is to me a cheat forever. There, mademoiselle, is the story of all my sentiments, and Caroline Delmont is henceforth as transparent to you as she is to herself. It is with regret that she has fled your company. Terror hastened a flight which would have been less precipitate had cool prudence been able to advise her. I shuddered at the thought of being in the company of people who ridicule everything, and who might have seized on my mistakes and pain as an opportunity for merriment. I despise them for it, but I forgive them. They spend all day talking, and so they need to look for and latch onto something to talk about. They are incapable of being alone, and so they are obliged to use witty, lively, and light conversation to attract and hold on to one another. Do not linger with them, mademoiselle; there is no safety there, and the least dangerous risk that you are running is to become like them. Oh what a pity that would be! I dare at once to offer you some advice and to make you a request: write to the marquis your father, and ask him for permission to come and spend the summer with me. I am sure that in speaking of me you would flatter me in many respects, but whatever you might say about the affectionate and pure interest that I take in you, you could only weakly render the feelings of your devoted servant,

Caroline Delmont
Lone Castle, Derbyshire, April 28, 1793

Letter XII.

The Vicomte des Fossés to Germaine.

From a vile inn, April 25, 1793

Will this letter escape the Argus-eyed surveillance? I do hope so. Sometimes they sleep and at other points their blunders or general dullness are as good as sleep. Accursed people! They have chased away first an amiable woman of feeling and then a young man, who by her side and yours too was beginning to be reborn into happiness, reason, and virtue—now they are

far apart. But, mademoiselle, have I ever been completely dead
to virtue? When I first knew you, was I not touched by your
charming face? When I dared to tell you how lovely I found
you, did I not subside into respectful silence the instant you
confided that you loved a deserving young man? Have I betrayed
you, distressed you, tried to make you inconstant? Were it possible for the duchess and her worthy cicisbeo to utter anything
other than calumnies and black slanders, they would tell you
how often I have justified to them what they call your intractable and stubborn humor;[44] they would tell you that it was none
of my doing that they have offered you in turn a mindless child
and a decent Irishman for a husband—the latter, only half
understanding our language, would be completely incapable of
appreciating you. But were they to give me as much help as they
have done me damage, this man and this woman that I hate,
there is nothing that they could say which could set me right in
your view. How would they be able to realize that there was anything to say? How would they be able to understand how important it is for me? The pleasure of being respected by someone we
respect is beyond their understanding—for them there is no vice
or virtue; the only good things are a rich marriage, a position at
court, advancement in the service, and certain sorts of success
in society, and the only evils are absence, want, and the loss of
those first things. They are currently reduced to intrigues over
nothing, and I, a young man, whom they would barely have
deigned to notice when they were caught up in their great whirl,
have become worthy of their malevolent attention. Listen,
mademoiselle, I am ashamed to say that it is only too true that
every time I sang you some feeble ballad or accompanied your
pianoforte on the violin, I saw your displeasure, and I, stupid
child, I found it amusing; it made me sing and play better. They
and I were as ridiculous as each other, only they are wicked,
and I am merely a little too vain . . . no, much too vain, or at
least I used to be, and that is what has provided them with the
weapons they are now using so cruelly. I don't really know
what there is to say about me, but I judge from how Lady Caroline has proceeded that they have much exaggerated my misdemeanors. I must expiate them and keep silent; I will not

allow myself to indulge in recrimination. Even if my detractor were worth much less than I, would I be worth any more? My youth, the bad example I was set, and my regrets are all that I will cite in support of my claims to the indulgence of good people. It is above all yours, mademoiselle, that I now entreat you for, and if I obtain it I venture to hope that one day you will say to Lady Caroline: he was not entirely unworthy of your regard.

H. Des Fossés.

Letter XIII.

Germaine to Alphonse.

May 24, 1793

You wrote to me; the letter arrived, but I did not receive it. There's no great harm done, for my anxiety is allayed, and whatever you wrote, I am not sorry that my father should see it. You are entirely incapable of saying anything that could injure us! Perhaps it may even serve our cause. But I want to tell you quickly what happened. Yesterday, Mistress Sparrow came to fit a dress for me, and I said to her: "What, madam, is there still nothing for me?"

"No, mademoiselle; since the letter that came, I think, from Derbyshire, there has been nothing for you."

"Dear God, how wretched that makes me feel. But you seem sad, Mistress Sparrow. What is the matter? What is upsetting you?"

"It's my daughter, mademoiselle. She is in love with a completely unsuitable young man. He lacks morals, prudence, and stable employment. Because I refused to let her go to live with my mother in Hackney for a month, a place where she could have seen him every day, she is miserable, angry with me, and often tearful. She is no longer my sweet Sally, but a little rebel whose head has come loose. She no longer says or does anything that isn't completely senseless."

"Dear God, Mistress Sparrow, I am very sorry for you! But

do not cry. Would you like to send her to me? Perhaps I can help her see reason. Victoire and I will be able to distract her; sometimes it takes very little to distract a young woman. Here's an embroidered kerchief I brought with me from France—send me your daughter and we will show her how to make an identical one for herself."

Mistress Sparrow was very touched. "How good you are!" she said, bursting into tears. "It's not my daughter who is distressing me at the moment, even though everything I told you is perfectly true. I am weeping because . . . listen, I have to admit that . . . you need to know that . . ."

Eventually, after a quarter of an hour of hesitating, she told me that the duchess, suspecting the other day that she had something special to tell me, had stopped her, subjected her to questioning and flattery, saying, "Madam Sparrow, you have a daughter. If anyone made it their business to help her exchange letters with someone whom you were anxious to prevent becoming her husband, what would you do? What would you say?"

"Me, madam duchess?"

"Yes, you, Madam Sparrow; you who are a very affectionate and careful mother, would you not think that that was very wrong and very dreadful?"

That was to attack her on her vulnerable side, for her daughter was already causing her much anxiety, and the duchess did it so well, dear Alphonse, that Mistress Sparrow gave her the letter I had been waiting for with such impatience. It passed from the seamstress's hands to the duchess's without my ever having seen or touched it. When she first confessed all this, I neither spoke nor moved for a while. Having recovered a little, I then asked: "And what did the duchess do with this letter?"

"She sent it to your honored father."

"Are you sure of that?"

"Oh, very sure, because she quickly wrote something, made an envelope, sealed it up, and then asked me to take the packet to the post."

"Did you see what the address was?"

"No, mademoiselle; I only noticed the name, which is the same as yours. I didn't know whether I'd done the right or the wrong thing, and I was sorry to have betrayed you, so I was as eager to get rid of the letter as if it had been a great weight. Are you angry with me, mademoiselle?"

"No, madam. I was very worried, but I no longer am, and as for my father reading the letter before me or instead of me, there's no harm in that at all. So you see that this correspondence of mine is not reprehensible at all."

"Oh yes, mademoiselle, I see, and that inveigling woman the duchess looks much more as if she's plotting something wicked than you do. Oh! I do hope that a letter arrives from the same person extremely soon. I will bring it to you directly."

"You give me great pleasure, Mistress Sparrow, and I am more touched by your goodwill than I was hurt by the trifling wound you dealt me. Send me your daughter, and Victoire and I will still show her how to embroider a kerchief."

"How good you are, mademoiselle!"

"Did the duchess reward you for your compliance with some pretty present?"

"Oh no, mademoiselle, but I wouldn't ask her for one. If she wanted to pay for the work I do, I would be very satisfied."

I gave Mistress Sparrow a guinea and sent her away. It was time to dress and Victoire got me ready as if I were a wooden doll, and I noticed nothing at all. I tried to remember everything that I had written to you, and to imagine everything that you might have said in reply, and after writing myself a letter from you, and clearly seeing the fold, the margins, the handwriting, and the signature, then I saw my father open it, become angry, read, consider, and calm down bit by bit. May the duchess be punished for the harm she has tried to do us! May this letter damage her alone! May my father take me away from her and restore his esteem and affection to Alphonse!

Once the doll was dressed, it was taken down and sat at table. There were a great many people present, and they were already seated. The duchess had saved me a place between herself and Lord O'Battle, whom I had not seen since it had been decided to tell him my secret. Toward the end of the dinner, a footman brought me a letter.

"A letter!" said the duchess, reaching forward. "Oh look at that!" The letter had rapidly passed from one hand to the next and disappeared into my pocket. The duchess flushed. "So your letters are not all addressed to Mistress Sparrow?" I said nothing. "Well look at that! What a tone, what arrogance!"

"Oh, how can I have a tone when I say nothing?"

"Mademoiselle . . . if I were to demand that you gave me that letter immediately—"

"I would ask you, madam, what you planned to do with it."

"I do not think I would be obliged to tell you."

"Forgive me, madam—if you were to tell me that you would be sending it to my father, you would not frighten me at all; but I would ask if I could envelope and address it straightaway, in your presence, and I would give it to milord, and ask him to be so kind as to post it himself."

"And why not give it directly to me?"

"Why, madam?"

"Yes, why?"

"Because to send a letter which may be about us to a third party, without knowing what was in it, would be a blunder that someone of your intelligence would not want to commit twice in a week."

"Keep your letter, mademoiselle," said the duchess, with marked embarrassment. "And another time, do not reply so clumsily to what was nothing more than banter."

Without this evidence of her falsity, so natural to her now that she was unable to hold it back despite her evident confusion, I would have felt sorry for the wounds dealt to her pride. Everyone fell silent; the comte himself, sitting opposite the duchess, lowered his eyes and found nothing to say. In the end I broke the silence myself, asking how I should address a letter to an officer in Condé's army.

"Very simply, I think, to Condé's army," said a young Englishman. People immediately started talking of this army and of the exploits it would carry out, so as to persuade me that no other address would be needed.

"My lord comte, would you put anything else?"

"Oh yes . . . I am very careful myself, painstakingly prudent; I would put the town or village, the road if I knew it, and even the name of the inn."

"What, to one of the general officers?"

"Oh yes, even to the general. I would put: to HRH the Prince of Condé, General of the Noble Army of the Same Name, in such-and-such a road, such-and-such a house—"

"But an army must be well known far in every direction!"

"Not at all; this one seems to retain a sort of disguise," at which all our immoderate fools started roaring with laughter. The English were stunned.

"Seriously," I said to the duchess, "if you had to write to my father, how would you address your letter to him?"

"I don't know," she said (how she lies!). "I'd have to look it up in the newspapers and see where our heroes are currently encamped."

I did not have time yesterday to send for the newspapers, as I had to stay in company so as not to look dissatisfied. This morning I've only had time to write you, and I still had to get up very early, for fear of interruptions. Good-bye, dear Alphonse; I'm being called to receive visitors. I will leave Victoire to make a packet for this letter and for the one I received yesterday from M. Des Fossés, which is the very one which closed the great events of the day.

Germaine.

Letter XIV.

The Vicomte des Fossés to Germaine.

Friardale, Hertfordshire.

May 22, 1793

Yet another letter, mademoiselle, yet another importunate call on your notice from an unhappy creature, a fugitive twice over. Consider that there is no one apart from you in the world on whose concern I can venture to count; consider moreover that I need urgently to know whether the letter which contained an admission of my guilt more than any justification, and was very painful to write, did get to you. Before, I could ask you for no word in reply, having no address to give you; today I ask that at least Mademoiselle Victoire tell me whether my letters have been given to you, supposing that they in fact have been; and if I receive nothing, I will conclude that you have received nothing, which will be desperate for me.

I am settled here in a way that would seem comfortable enough, were my memories more agreeable. Perhaps I'd still need a smiling future on the horizon, however unclear and as if veiled by fog. . . . But no, too busy trying to work out this cloudy object of possibly misleading hopes, I would not pay enough attention to what I do have at present, to the fact that in my possession are some truly precious things. My health is very good, the season is beautiful, the countryside around me is fertile, I am with people who seem well disposed in my favor, and what is worth even more than all this, I am learning to know myself much better, and I find that I have resources that I didn't know about, and am easily able to do without things that I believed I was very used to. You will be able to judge, mademoiselle, whether what I have just said is true, or whether it is yet another feature of my self-love.

After having spent a number of days with my trusty La Flèche sadly wandering along the Thames, and then as far as the Welsh borders, I ended up in a pretty little valley in Hertfordshire.[45] We went all along it without thinking that night was closing in and that we were not sure of finding somewhere to stay. Night did fall, but in its train came some auspicious lights which rescued the imprudent travelers from their difficulties. I do not mean stars, which would not have told me where I could stay, but common firelight, in the form of *lamps and candles*, which glowed through a clump of trees and told me that on the other side I would find people and houses. Less insubstantial than light, we had to go around this little forest. It was already very late, and some lights were beginning to be extinguished as we passed beneath their windows. La Flèche thought the best thing would be to knock at the first house that was still lit up, and he immediately hastened to carry out this wise plan. But what was less wise was that he addressed himself to the poor servant girl in French, as he always does in similar cases, with the result that instead of understanding what he wanted, she was completely terrified. I then stepped up with my three or four words of bad English, and the master having appeared, it turned out that this was the village priest's house. He, half in Latin and half in French, very kindly offered me hospitality. I dined well and slept even better, and the following day, having considered my host, his house, his children, and having learned a bit more about how things are done here, I requested that we might be allowed to stay, and proposed the terms of the contract I wished to draw up. My host asked for three days to think about it, and at the end of three days it was decided that La Flèche and I would earn our board and lodging with our labor. La Flèche's will be to plant, sew, and prune when the weather is fine, cut wood when it's raining, and do all the cartwright's jobs, which is very valuable, because before they had La Flèche, who is very skilled at it, they had to go quite far to mend the carts and plows. As for me, I help with everything in the garden and the meadow, but apart from that, I give French, mathematics, and drawing lessons to the priest's two sons, pretty children of thirteen and fifteen. He has no daughters, and his wife is a very clean but very simple housewife. He is clever and well educated, and seeing that I was having a great deal of difficulty with a volume of Horace that I had taken down from his shelves, he offered to go over all my classical books with me, and that's how we entertain ourselves after supper.

What do you say, mademoiselle, about the hitherto frivolous des Fossés? Is he rising at all in your esteem? And what would Lady Caroline say of the man whom people forced her to run away from as if he had been evil? Do you not think that my simple and hardworking life might reconcile her to me a little? Would she not be inclined to think that the person who could prefer Friardale and a village priest to London and the duchess, innocent children to corrupt and sneering posers, is not yet a member of that perverse breed? How happy I am that I no longer need to request money to be sent to me; those who had to send it will no longer be in danger! To receive what belongs to me after so much trouble and circuitousness that it feels as if I had stolen it was extremely disagreeable, and the reduction of my needs allied to my work spares me that unpleasantness for a long while. Good-bye to my cravats and to their indispensable width; I will no longer pay to be suffocated in three ells of muslin.[46] Good-bye to my powder, pomade, and the oh-so-simple white waistcoat which had to be put on fresh every day. The greater part of my wardrobe is still in London, and sometimes I have to borrow from La Flèche, who is more or less the same size as his master. *His master* . . . He's the one who will not stop calling me that, even though it is rather ridiculous, given that we both work for other people at the same tasks.

We only get the papers here once a week. The news from France is out of date and of doubtful authenticity, or so it seems to me. What does it matter? To be better informed about things doesn't change them, and it suits me to distract my thoughts from a country in which I am no longer wanted, and may not call my own. But can I really be exiled for good, forever? Is it possible that a young man traveling abroad with his ailing and fearful mother, who does not return to France by the fatal date because his mother is dying at that point, can be forever associated with the enemies of the fatherland?[47] Yes, mademoiselle, that is my story. My mother died in Dover on the very day after which it was no longer possible to return. I have never taken up arms against France, but all those others who have, all those young people who have obeyed their parents and joined the émigré princes, are they more blameworthy than I? Your own Alphonse spent two months in Coblenz and was present at the flight of the Prussian army.[48] Is he any more to blame for that? The French people would be lucky to have many aristocrats of his stamp among their numbers; they would never tyrannize the people like their so-called friends do. But again, does France want to be rid of, or perhaps rather deprive itself of excellent citizens like Alphonse and me, from whom, I venture to say, more good than harm can be expected, and of thousands of others like me, and a few others like him, heroes to whom the empire or republic might owe its protection, happiness, and glory? Are there so many enlightened and courageous people of integrity that their loss is not an important thing? Honest people were not any rarer in times past than they are now, and yet would Athens and Rome have been what they were without an Aristeides and a few Cincinnatuses?[49] But we are still treated as citizens, since we are treated as rebels and punished as traitors; were we foreigners we would only count as ordinary enemies. Cruel contradiction! Frenchmen who have been stripped of all their rights as Frenchmen are allowed in certain cases to become French again, but only to be led to the guillotine! No, this cannot last; no, this absurd cruelty will end. If it were not to end, if it were to be the case that the character of my compatriots turned savage once they ceased to be oppressed, without the experience of liberty being able to restore human feeling to them, I in turn would disown and revile them; I would want my abominable country to become the prey of greedy foreigners—but let such a wish keep far from me for as long as I retain the slightest glimmer of hope!

For pity, mademoiselle, accord some friendship and a word in reply to your devoted servant,

Henri Des Fossés.

Letter XV.

The Marquis de *** to Germaine.

From the headquarters of Condé's army, June 4, 1793
I so dislike to open a letter addressed to anyone but me, my dearest daughter, that Alphonse's remained unopened in my desk for two days. In the end I did open it, and neither you nor your lover come off any the worse for it. I have to be fair; this letter is from a very honest young man. I enclose it here, and cannot summon up the courage to scold you for it. To write to

him was to disobey me, but to desire him to send me his letters was to repair your disobedience, and in your conduct I perceive a candor which disarms me. I have no idea how to thank the duchess for her zeal; to intercept a letter, turn it from its path, and make it take such a different one would never occur to me, and, as you know, it is hard to praise properly that which diverges from our own habits. Tell her what you wish on this subject, or if you prefer, do not talk to her about it at all, and simply present my respects to her. Live with her as well as you can, but only imitate those parts of her conduct that you respect. You have had good models: your stepmother and her mother are worthy women, and you must rely above all on the good sense which God has given you to tell the difference between good and bad, and to attach yourself to one and eschew the other. In the choice of a husband you must as in all things see with your own eyes, and then not make a decision unless you have my consent. I confess that despite my grief at Alphonse's weakness and inaction, it would not be without difficulty that I could ever give you to someone other than him. I will consider all this. His letter does him great credit, as well as his abbé, whom I may have judged rather hastily. Be patient, my daughter; I will think about you, and will not leave you where you are for long.

Le Marquis de ***

Letter XVI.

The Marquis de *** to Germaine.

June 6, 1793

I have received your letter, my dearest daughter,* and I am losing no time in giving you the consent you ask for. Go with Victoire to Lady Caroline as soon as you can, but avoid being

---

* Author's footnote: We do not have this letter in our hands, but it is clear enough from the marquis's reply what his daughter must have written to him.

abrupt or rude to those you are leaving behind. Your anxiety
and insistence about how much money I have are very kind,
and I do not have much difficulty in understanding why. I
know from Alphonse's letter what the duchess told you about
your fortune, but although I am sorry for her indiscretion, we
must forgive her, as I forgave your disobedience. When the
consequences are good and the intentions were not reprehensible, how can anyone be very angry about it? The duchess's
indiscretion prompted evidence of my daughter's affection and
generosity, which in truth do not surprise me in the slightest
but nonetheless give me great pleasure. I promise to become
your debtor in preference to anyone else, although a tutor
should be very careful about borrowing from his pupil. Write
to tell me whether Lady Caroline would be the sort of woman
who would travel with you to Holland. You could spend the
winter in your own home with her, and I could come and see
you there. Our affairs are not going as well as I could wish.[50]
Good-bye, Germaine; I embrace you fondly.

My respects to the duchess. Again, be respectful with her;
separate from her respectfully. I have no idea how the granddaughter of the brave *** could have become such a scheming
courtier.

Letter XVII.

Alphonse to Germaine.

June 8, 1793

This time your two letters did indeed arrive, but I was cast
down by the first of them, and so distressed at the delay or loss
of my letter that I was unable to write before receiving more satisfactory news from you. They arrived the day before yesterday,
in the evening. So it is not the devil in person who is meddling
in our affairs, it's only the duchess. I am very pleased to hear it,
because although she's as wicked as he, she's not as clever. I
agree with you that she will not have done us much harm.

My state of mind is singular. Apart from the abbé, I spend

most of my time in the company of people who are not here. It
is principally you, Germaine, as you may very well suppose,
whom I constantly see and hear, but I can also imagine Monsieur Des Fossés very distinctly. I am with him when he writes
to you sadly from some sordid inn; I accompany him across an
unknown land; I finally arrive at Friardale, and I see him settle
there, as I attached a little boat that the abbé and I had taken
out on our lake to a willow tree the other day when the wind
got up. Our shelter was a bad one, *Mais où mieux? Jean Lapin
s'y blottit.* [But where else was any better? John Rabbit hud-
dled there.][51]

We stayed there until the lake became calm again. Des Fossés is waiting for a favorable glance from love and fortune. If
none comes for either him or me, I may well go to join him. I
love his character for that indescribable simplicity and naïveté
that he has. In Friardale there must be some ruins of an old
convent; will Germaine and Caroline never make a pilgrimage
there? Instead of the monks of yesteryear, they will find one
young hermit, perhaps two; we will offer them fruit and milk,
and barely venture to look up at them, but we will be so
respectful, so eager! Besides, am I not immensely good and
immensely foolish to liken the inclination of a few days to the
devotion of Alphonse to Germaine? It may be a joke, but it
offends me. Once I've spent a long time dreaming about England, I transport myself to the Vendée. What extraordinary
letters I do receive from my old companion! He is full of sensibility, mobility, passion, honor, and courage; he loves Pauline
and will die for the convention. Yet another triumph for maratism, I predict that he will be made destitute and his brother
forced to flee.[52] Perhaps we'll see them at Friardale as well. . . .
As soon as we've learned our profession of cultivators, you
will write on our behalf to your manager in Holland, and we
will come to work for you. I fear Laurent may be a fairly bad
journeyman, but I will work hard enough for two, and his
vivacity will beguile me out of my melancholy. Seriously, I prefer a thousand times to go and work your fields and look after
your sheep to leaving the continent without you and seeking
refuge in America like so many others.

In the Western desert my ennui would know no limits.[53]

I can't wait to hear whether your father will allow you to go to Derbyshire as I'm sure you must have asked to do. Try, if you have to stay in London, to make the acquaintance of one of our countrywomen, of whom I have heard many good things. At the age of nineteen, she was asked to become one of the governesses of the royal English princesses, and she fulfilled the duties of her place for ten years as well as her weak health allowed her; by the end of that time, well behaved, modest, and prudent, having neither flattered nor maligned anyone, made any noise or any money, she had friends at court who are still her friends. She is now married, and lives in retirement, bringing up her own children. From time to time the princesses, to whom she has remained genuinely attached, seek her out, and she is invited to visit the Queen herself, she being of all queens the one who has been most solicitous and careful of her children's education. I have met this Mistress C***'s sister on two or three occasions and it is she who gave me the address which I am sending you. She unites a thousand talents, and more than anything she sings exquisitely.[54] Everyone says she is amiable and reasonable, but she would be very angry if people who know them both preferred her over her sister. It is in the heart of a privileged family such as this, it is with reason and the arts that one might sometimes be able to forget one's sufferings. But I will not try to forget anything; the sweetest memories are mingled with my very saddest ones. Like the exiled Jews, I have no wish to cease lamenting and singing the praises of my unhappy country.

Alphonse.

Letter XVIII.

From the same to the same.

June 11, 1793

How sad I was last Saturday once I'd sent you my letter! Do you know what I did to cheer myself up a little? I reread yours.

Initially absorbed by their general tone and reaping a plentiful harvest of regrets, I sometimes find, combing through them again, things which cheer me up. I laughed, I do admit, at the comte's witticisms about that Condé's army of ours. He has a brother in that army, and if it weren't for the duchess he'd be there himself. I am sure that I'm right, and I only find his witticisms the wittier for it. The English would have said: those people laugh at themselves rather than not to laugh.[55] Besides, it's not only the French who have that tendency. I have met someone here a couple of times, a Swiss man who has a very quick and subtle touch that nothing escapes, on whom nothing is lost.[56] The harmful and amusing sides of a single object both strike his mobile organs in turn; he becomes distressed by the first and laughs at the others with equal facility. At the moment he has no feeling which I do not share. He is often amused at his own expense, and even if it were at mine, I would be unable to take it amiss. I live too quiet a life, my darling Germaine, to think of telling you about what is being done and said in society, but here is a fine witticism that I must relate. A democrat went for dinner recently at the house of a bizarre and contradictory woman.[57] He was laying out his principles, and she was defending the cause of the aristocracy, which in fact she does not care about in the slightest.

"What, madame, do you approve of there being superiors and inferiors? Is it then permissible in your view for the strong to oppress the weak?"

"I do not know, monsieur," said she, "what may be permitted or forbidden. I do not know, for example, whether it is acceptable to have the chicken killed that I have the honor of serving to you, and whether I may not be very much in the wrong to harness one of my horses to a cart while the other only draws a light chase."

"But madame, how can there be any comparison between man and beast, between a rational creature and a base animal?"

"Monsieur, it is not, or so it seems to me, because it is rational but because it is sentient that every living creature demands to be well treated."

Let us live together, Germaine. Together let us doubt, believe, be rational and irrational, and let us never leave each other even at death.

Alphonse.

Letter XIX.

L. B. Fonbrune to Alphonse.

May 25, 1793

Consuls . . . !⁵⁸ So be it. My mind is in such chaos that all my efforts to clear it are in vain. There is something about the projected order of things that I find shocking. We talk about equality as if we were in the youth of the world, while repressive laws, such as are hardly needed other than in periods of great corruption, proliferate. We seem to want to move nearer to nature; nature is constantly appealed to, and yet we weaken all natural bonds. Soon fathers will have nothing in common with their children. Divorce not only separates spouses, but makes them more tepid with regard to the children they share in common, and the abolition of all unequal legacies between children leaves them so independent of their father and mother that, along with obedience, respect is also lost.⁵⁹ What century has ever resembled the one that we are making for ourselves! What country serves as model for the new France! In the books of Moses, the songs of Homer, in all history or fable, there is nothing similar to what we would like to establish, and I do not see how our constitution and our laws, our morality and morals, our social system and social customs, our citizenship and financial speculation can work side by side for a year, a month, or even a day. But let us leave all that aside; let's talk about ourselves, our loves, and our affairs.

My wound has almost healed, and I must go back to fighting. It will be with reluctance, but there's no other way. The day before yesterday I succeeded in preserving the château and environs from a whirlwind of sans-culottes who wanted to raze everything to the ground, and in two days' time I will have to put myself at the head of a few batallions of the same people, and brave death, giving or receiving it, when I would much rather spare, save, love, and therefore live. "Arrange," wrote Admiral Russell to James II, "arrange for the French fleet to avoid coming up against the one I command, for although I am on your side, I will fire on the first vessel I see, even should you be on deck."[60] I would say the same. Please God that I do not come up against any of the friends from this hospitable house which it gives me so much pain to leave . . . ! Let us see, however. I could snatch them from death as well as victory. . . . But no, let's not meet them. The war here is not one that can be made generous; the slightest leniency on my part would endanger my reputation and my brother's safety. Whoever is less than ferocious passes for a traitor. I would like to conquer with such glory that in the future I would be dispensed from fighting or being killed or captured. The war I am waging is intolerable to me from now on. Remember what I say, Alphonse, or keep my letter to show Pauline's father one day. Let him know that whether I live or die, let him know that I respected his wife, that I adored his daughter, that I would have risked my life for his devout mother-in-law and for his kind naive little Minette more willingly than I would for the indivisible republic, the invisible liberty, or the impossible equality.[61]

Do you want to hear, Adolphe, the story of how I cooled down toward these fine things? It wouldn't do me any honor with a philosopher but it will move a friend; besides, if a fable can be what it wants, history is what it can be, and I am so far from wanting to assert my rights to any undeserved esteem that I would rather expose my weak points than tell you my reasons. So, then, I have acquired a taste for the nobility and a respect for it. There is something rather graver, more delicate, more romantic, more antique, simpler in this family than I have seen among our bourgeois families, be they engaged in commerce, finance, or the law. At table, everyone takes their knife out of their pocket in the same way it used to be done everywhere, fifty or a hundred years ago. Pauline goes to fetch the wine from the cellar, and were it not as good as it is, I

would still find it better. Minette feeds the newborn chicks
with the bread crumbs which are left on the tablecloth, and
this careful little rural economy suits her beautifully. It's all
very well for Germaine to write that her hats and dresses
should be worn and her linen shared out, the wardrobes of our
older richer sister, only daughter of a rich heiress, remain firmly
closed, and the little presents she sends are respectfully, gratefully shown to me. What do you expect? Alphonse, all this
is practically nothing; there are no grand interests, no pure
and heated citizenship, no people rising up en masse; but it all
attaches me, touches me, encircles me. In my heart, Roche sur
L*** is France, the world.

But listen to some more details, which will show you the
extent of my bewitchment. An old servant used sometimes to
say when talking to Mme ***, "Madame la Marquise," and to
her mother, "Madame la Baronne"; they pulled him up, and
he corrected himself.[62] One day I said, "Why torment yourself
to change old habits which are basically very unimportant?"
And since then, when we are alone, I say like old Youthful,
"Madame la Marquise" and "Madame la Baronne."[63] In the
château there are some very bad old portraits. Well, I ask for
the history of their subjects. This one was killed at the Battle
of Lens, that one got that prominent scar in the Siege of Barcelona, and the marquis's uncle, *our* neighbour, who comes visiting almost every day, had his right arm blown off at Krefeld at
the same time that the young Comte de Gisors received his
fatal injury.[64] I also have an uncle with an almost identical
wound, but before him no B*** had ever received a scratch
of this sort. And what made him go to war? The taste for lib-
ertinism and the eloquence of the army recruiter, or rather
the brandy he was lavishly plied with. And me, what made
me brave wind and wave, cannon, bomb, and boarding? I was
bored with writing; I was ashamed somehow that despite being
strong and alert, I was nothing more than an attorney's clerk.
I have to admit it, to be brave, to run all sorts of dangers, to
fight like a true hero was the hereditary profession of our nobles,
and whatever we say or do not say about our ingratitude, without them the *one and indivisible* that we are so proud of would

be very small, indivisibly small. The other day, as I was request-
ing the invalid chevalier to arrange for the farmers to stop
insulting the small garrison that I keep in the village, he said
to me, holding out his remaining hand, "I give you my word as
a gentleman." He corrected himself straightaway. "My apolo-
gies, sir."

"And for what, monsieur le chevalier? It is a very fine right
to be able to promise on one's word . . . ! Never give it up,
monsieur le chevalier, for as long as you live. For the first time
I envy you your prerogative, and the more I envy it, the more I
feel that I must not take it away from you. It is the price of
your arm, the price of that young brother whom you loved so
much and whom a bullet cut down by your side. I am not a
gentleman, and I have long loathed vain, proud, and insolent
gentlemen, but I am learning from you to respect the rank
which I mistakenly associated with some individuals whose
flaws should have been blamed on nothing worse than their
youth. Had I been less young myself, I would have judged them
better. In this house, from you, I am acquiring new ideas and
impressions."

"Which may be false," interrupted the chevalier. "Falser
than the initial ones. I gratefully receive the compliments you
pay me, my nieces, and their mother in what you say. I will
even accept that they are neither exaggerated nor deluded, and
I would go so far as to say that you would find that many
noble families are almost the same, but as we have agreed to
speak the truth, word of a gentleman"—and here the old chevalier smiled with grace and nobility—"I will tell you that the
Revolution has done our minds good just as much as it has
harmed our fortunes. The persecuted Christians of the first
centuries were much better Christians than the happy Christians of following centuries, and nobles who are alive now
have more sense and are much better than those happy
ci-devant nobles who preceded them."

"What, sir?"

"Yes, sir; please believe a confession which is too humble
not to be regarded as sincere."

"But sir, where did you learn your habits, and where did the marquise's mother learn hers?"

"Sir, there are exceptions to all general truths, and besides, my cousin and I have always been persecuted. We were in love once. . . . You see how your questions take me back into times past! I was the victim of a father and a brother who were extremely vain, and she was sacrificed to the views of an ambitious family. Was it possible for us to indulge in irregularities which would have cost us our happiness? The baroness brought up her daughter very well, and has helped her to bring up hers more or less reasonably. This is why, if I am not mistaken, they are the way they are, and why you are able objectively to approve and honestly praise them. I have no doubt that you could have found the same, even before the Revolution, in some noble families, but in how many others have you not observed the flattest idleness, the most stupid ignorance, the most puerile pride? You would have been amazed, bored, disgusted . . ."

Is that really true, Alphonse? You must know whether it is. If it is really true, what should we conclude from it? Must I now renounce my youthful enthusiasm for that caste which has grown old and is now reviled and despised? I cannot do it yet. Let us destroy the courtiers; not only do I consent to it, but I want it. They mix vice with disgrace. I endorse stripping all nobles not only of their privileges but also of their titles, coats of arms, and mottoes, all of which allude to things which were destroyed or forgotten long ago, and no longer have any sense, grace, or pertinence. But after that would it not be permitted to retain a secret brotherhood, an association of nobles who had never stolen from the regimental treasury, pilfered soldiers' pay, made a false oath, trafficked or speculated in any way? Few émigrés would be part of this band, but Alphonse should be. Honor would be the mobile secret and the single statute. *Honor* is the delicacy of virtue. *Honor* is something less vague than the love of a country as vast as ours. People ceaselessly invoke Rome, but Rome was a small town, and love for one's country was part of the religion, while this small town was as unlike the capital of France as the first Brutus was unlike the Citizens Pétion, Santerre, Chaumette, etc., etc.[65] So there is the chaos of my mind, my dear Alphonse, not so much cleared as laid out in part before you. In a field of corn ready for harvesting, have you ever seen single scattered blades growing, not yet ripe, impossible to bind into sheaves because they would start fermenting if they were sealed away . . . ?

Yet another brawl, yet more sans-culottes who wanted better clothes, and more than anything else wanted to eat and drink too much at the expense of the worthy family which took me in, looked after me, healed me, which has been lavish with the help it has given to all our sick, and has concealed from me, their commander, many of the stupid things our libertines have been doing. It was not to be borne; I vigorously restrained them.

"Sir," the chevalier said to me, as I was running for my sword, "see these women! You are a man of honor, a brave military man!"

"Sir," the marquise said, "preserve my children from insult."

On her knees, her mother prayed to God, and glanced at me once or twice. Pauline cried out, "For God's sake, do not run so fast—your wound will reopen! For God's sake, don't get yourself killed."

On the stairs, in the hall, I continued to hear the same words. Do you hear them, Alphonse?

Everything is over and calm at present. The marquise and her mother have been persuaded to retire to bed early. The chevalier has gone home despite Pauline's insistence that he stay at the château. "They'll think I'm afraid," he said.

I can hear Pauline . . . she is alone. I think she is trying to make herself heard without quite daring to call me. I am coming to find you, Pauline. . . . Alphonse, I promise you, on my word, not as a gentleman, but on my word as your friend, on my word as someone who considers himself worthy of being your brother-in-law, nephew of the chevalier, son-in-law of the marquise, I promise you, Alphonse, to respect Pauline.

I reminded her that all her fears had been for me, and she agreed without demur.

"It would have been better to see the house burn down," said she, "than to have to weep for your loss. . . . A house is only a house, but you, sir . . ."

I don't quite know whether she blushed when she said this, because it was quite dark in the room where we were, but it seemed to me that her voice was a little changed.

"I have no wish to make you feel pity for me, mademoiselle," I said to her, "and I would be in despair if I caused you to utter a single word or undertake the slightest shadow of an engagement that you may later regret, or for which your parents would blame you, were they to know about it, but please condescend to reply to one single question: would you marry me if your parents consented?"

"But would you want to have me as your wife?"

"Yes, I passionately desire to become your husband."

"Well then, I would be your wife, but on one condition."

"What is it?"

"It is that we should be married forever, and that we would never be able to divorce."[66]

"That is enough, dearest Pauline . . . say no more, I am too happy; I am too fortunate."

"You would renounce the right to leave me one day?"

"I would renounce it. Please God that it wouldn't be living with you that I was called upon to renounce."

"Why would you renounce it, sir? I do not say I will renounce it myself."

"Say no more, Pauline; promise nothing. Me, I promise to have no other wife than you, for as long as you are unwed. Will you take this ring as proof of my word?"

"Yes, I will; give it to me."

"Would you allow me to give you a kiss?"

"Yes."

She received it on her forehead, and returned it less cautiously, but not without innocence, nor with any disadvantage . . . to herself; and I withdrew immediately, and tomorrow morning

I leave without seeing her or anyone else. Good-bye, Alphonse.
I am going to try to sleep for an hour or two.

I am sealing up my letter and leaving it here. Pauline will
surely see it, and send it to you. Good-bye.

Laurent B***
Your friend, your brother.

Letter XX.

Germaine to Alphonse.

June 18, 1793

Everything went smoothly, my dearest Alphonse. Your delightful letter has been in my hands for two hours. It's rather late to
receive a reply to what I first wrote two long months ago
tomorrow, but no matter; I forget my hardships and feel nothing but my joy, which is extreme. My father expresses himself
on your account and mine with the greatest generosity. Present
my respects to Monsieur l'Abbé des ***, and thank him for the
interest he has been so good as to take in me. If only he were
here, instead of certain bishops whom I heartily wish elsewhere! I have no time to say more now. Good-bye, dear
Alphonse.

Germaine.

Letter XXI.

From the same to the same.

June 21, 1793

Another letter from my father. Here it is, my dearest Alphonse.
The duchess is extremely piqued and asks nothing better than
to see me leave without further ado. And yet what will she do
when I am no longer part of her household? Expenses will be
much less diminished than the means of sustaining them.

Victoire is busy distributing some relief to various indigent and obscure émigrés—I have no wish to assist other people to live in luxury, and I do hope that the duchess doesn't make any requests, for I wouldn't know how to refuse her, and yet would only give most unwillingly. Good-bye. I am very sure that Lady Caroline will ask for nothing better than to accompany me to Holland. Ah! if only my father would ask Alphonse and the abbé to join us there! My heart tells me that this will happen. My father is what I venture to boast I am; he is never generous by halves. I will write to you from Lone Castle as soon as I have arrived. I received a few lines from the vicomte a few days ago. I had already replied to his long letter, as you may imagine. His conduct is not slipping, and he seems fairly content with his situation. I had imagined I might have a reply from you by now to one of my letters from May 21 and 24, or at least to the first. The post is slowing down when we would like to hurry it up.

Germaine.

Letter XXII.

Laurent B*** F*** to Alphonse.

La Roche sur Yon, June 28, 1793

My friend, I fought like a tiger. It was not my fault that Saumur passed into the power of the Christian army. Abandoned by the troop I commanded and whom I persisted in trying to rally, I was surrounded and taken.[67] I could go to Paris, having signed the oath which as you know is being demanded, but I did not hesitate to take the road to which my heart steered me, although in obedience to prudence and delicacy, I turned slightly to the right, and stopped in La Roche sur Yon, from which I make frequent visits to the other Roche.[68] I am treated there as I was before; I am as happy as it is possible to be and do not think I suffer much boredom on those occasions on which I force myself not to go. I study the theory of the state. Books of mathematics and astronomy instruct me in the morning; tales of traveling entertain me in the evening. I could vary my reading more, but I cast from me those novels of quality, in which entirely plebeian writers introduce no characters who are not comtes, marquises, and duchesses, and lacking any real knowledge of them, paint their most ordinary actions with a gloss of deceit, a pretend elegance, whose model exists nowhere. I despise libertine novels even more, dishonest webs of error and seduction, in which every young man is depicted with the strength of Hercules and the grace of Adonis, in which the meanest wh*** is a Laïs or an Aspasia.[69] This should all be burnt; particularly now, when none of us know what fate holds in store for us; now, when, as new athletes, possibly confronting misery and death any day, we need to seek illumination and strengthen our minds with the most manly elements our studies contain and by dint of the most severe reflection.[70] Oh how I revile your counterparts, who parade their insipid nonchalance as they idle their time away, who trill, jest, and ridicule as if they were still the same privileged zeros as before . . . !

Do you know, dear Alphonse, what came into my mind? Suppose that the French Republic is consolidated, that we do become a true nation once more, then build up a warlike, valiant, and formidable fleet, that I find a way to take you on board, that you fight, risk danger, distinguish yourself, and that soon after I show you covered in scars and laurels to your fatherland. If, then, it does not see you as a hero but only as an émigré, as an enemy instead of one of its most deserving offspring, then I will perish with you, and on a single day one tomb will receive both Laurent and Alphonse.

But before then, is there no other way of seeing each other, of living together again? I am a prisoner. Are prisoners who leave their country listed as émigrés? In truth I do not know, and I do not wish to ask—I would be told that the oath I made to the rebels is void; I would be told that I have to fight here in the very place where I know both terrain and enemy. I would certainly disobey. One of these days I may well go round La Rochelle or Rochefort and see my sailor, seafaring, and other friends who might do something for me. I used to enjoy great

popularity in our little floating cities. Good-bye, my dear
Alphonse; write to me in La Roche sur Yon. Do not delay writing to me. Pauline charged me yesterday with saying a thousand tender things to you from her. You would cherish her, if
you saw with what good faith and security she loves your
friend. I think she only knows about love from old novels fur-
tively extracted from some old bookcase, and not seeing any
similarity between herself and Clelia or with the lovers of
Cyrus or Faramond, she doesn't believe she's in love.[71]

Letter XXIII.

The same to the same.

July 2, 1793

Ask your abbé a question which is bothering me. For a long
while I have been hearing people excusing or comforting themselves about the troubles that the Revolution has inflicted on
the nobility and priesthood with the thought that there are no
more than half a million French being sacrificed to 25 million,
and I have never contradicted them. Now, seeing these troubles extending across all classes, with the number of unhappy
people augmenting every day, we say the current generation is
being sacrificed for posterity, while a foreigner, predicting our
destruction, has recently said that "France is sacrificing itself
for the inhabitants of the rest of the universe." This time, the
holocaust seemed too great, and revising my opinion, I asked
whether all human sacrifice is not more worthy of the priests
of Moloch than of the fathers of a people and the legislators of
a nation.[72] Considering first those whose sufferings we may
wish to alleviate, I can only see individual suffering, however
great the number, and although I feel pity for each and every
person who suffers, my pity does still not augment, for there is
no greater intensity of pain than the suffering of one unhappy
man. A hundred suffer like one; one does not suffer like a
hundred. I would in truth be more disturbed by the moans of
a hundred people than of one, and I could indeed make one

person unhappy in order to be rid of a hundred unhappy people, but it does not seem to me that I have any obligation toward the hundred who suffer, nor any right over the person I condemn to suffering. If this obligation and this right did exist, if it were a case of one and a hundred, they would still exist if it were a case of one and ten, or one and two, or two and three, and nothing should stop me sacrificing my father, my friend, or myself to a certain number of foreigners or strangers. This is a thoroughly revolting consequence of that principle which had already seemed wrong to me in itself for the reason which I gave, for the reason that men do not suffer collectively but individually.

Ask your abbé what he thinks, dear Alphonse; ask him if he has ever when meditating on the inevitable troubles of the human species justified the Creator by means of an argument similar to the one the revolutionaries use. If we adopt this way of reasoning, we must stop condemning the human sacrifices certain peoples perform as injustices, and only condemn them for their foolishness. The Athenians could send a victim to the Minotaur every year and children be sacrificed to Moloch without our being permitted to say a word against it, for although it was not useful, it was not barbarous either.[73] If they were sinning against philosophy, they were not sinning against humanity.

I am deliberately not including any other question with this one that I want to disentangle. I am not asking the extent to which sacrificing you is useful to France, nor the extent to which sacrificing France is useful to the universe. I am not comparing the misery which is being destroyed with the misery which is being created. I do not differentiate between external circumstantial troubles and those of private feelings.[74] Most of all, I am being careful to avoid talking of the happiness that we claim to bestow, as I also avoid talking about the troubles from which we claim we are delivering a great people, for do we know what happiness is? I therefore confine myself to this question: do I have the obligation and the right to relieve the troubles of a certain number of men at the expense of a smaller number of men? I beg the abbé to meditate on this, and to resolve the question if he can.

Christian and non-Christian troops are flooding the country; disorder, terror, and suspicion reigns on all sides. As you may imagine, no one at La Roche sur *** is calm; I was there yester-day and I return tomorrow. I wish I could be there all the time. I am staying for a few hours in Rochefort. If in need, I would be able to obtain a great deal from some of my old friends.

Letter XXIV.

*The Marquis de *** to the Abbé des ****

In Gernsheim, July 2, 1793

Certain events and reflections have much softened my spirit, Reverend Abbé, toward you and Alphonse; the proof is that I ask a favor of you. You both have friends on all sides and in all classes. Please use them to try to get a message to my wife and daughters. I am increasingly worried about them and want them to find a safe person in La Rochelle or Rochefort and go by ship to Holland, where Germaine will also join them. If our affairs are no better in two months than they are today, I may well be able to join them, and if that happens, I want you and Alphonse to come and see us there.

I foresee that my mother-in-law, whom nothing frightens, will wish to stay where she is. So be it; let her be kept safe by the respect in which everyone holds her. Let Minette stay, if she cannot bear to leave her grandmother. I commend her to my uncle and to God. But as for the marquise, whose fragile health may be threatened by fear itself, without counting actual dangers, and as for Pauline, whose age, liveliness, and appearance endanger her in more than one way, let them leave as soon as possible. You see, Reverend Abbé, that I am not intractable. May I die if I were ever to owe the preservation of everything I hold dearest to someone whom I did not respect! My anger with you yielded to the proofs I have of the perfect

honesty and delicacy of your sentiments, and I am, with my
previous respect, your servant and friend.

The Marquis of ***

P.S. Could you suggest or find a prudent, honest, and brave
guide for my wife and daughter? I would never forget the service
he had done me; he would have every right to all the marks of
gratitude which it would be in my power to give him. If it were
only possible to convey the two fugitives as far as Calais or
Dunkerque, perhaps they would then be able to find a way to get
to Ostend, where you and Alphonse could meet them. And yet,
how can they get out of France alone? I am defeated. I would like
them to make the journey in complete safety, but on the other
hand, I would also be very distressed to endanger anyone.

Good-bye, Reverend Abbé.

P.P.S. Is there any hope that the enemies of the anarchists in
Lyons, Marseilles, Bordeaux, and Normandy may save France
by joining those whom the anarchists dub the Rebels of the
Vendée?[75] Tell me what you know or conjecture on this subject.

ÉMIGRÉ LETTERS.

Sequel.[76]

Germaine to Alphonse.

*Lone Castle, Derbyshire, July **, 1793*

Here I am in the noblest, most solemn and solitary of retreats.
Dispense me, dear Alphonse, from describing it to you; the
description would be pleasing enough, only it would be a little
long, and too much like a novel. Truly it is a very novel-like,
romantic place to stay. If you were to take two children, twins,
identical in every way, and bring one up in Lone Castle and
the other in the Palais Royal, for all you gave them the same
books and the same education, they would grow up to be very

different men, I think, even though neither of them would have known the world in any way other than from their window.

Anyone else would enthuse about a natural waterfall which cascades from its rock a quarter of an hour from here. I admired its rainbows, I let myself be soaked by its sparkling, colorful droplets, but the noise it makes stops me sleeping, and until I have got used to it, I will be unable to mention it without being ill tempered. On the other hand, I am in love with the two straight and well-kept walks which more than one imitator of nature has tried to destroy. One of these old walks is made from old oaks replaced here and there with young lime trees. It is there, in the morning and again in the middle of the day, walking in the shade, without effort or fatigue, that I dream of you. The other one has a sort of thick wall of hornbeams which traps every importunate ray of the setting sun. A double row of poplars is planted on the other side and as well as letting in the breezy air, it also reveals vistas of meadowland on which your gaze can linger. This is where I received and read a thousand times over one of your brief letters. What lovely things you say to me! How sweetly alluring your projects are! And your thoughts have something lovely about them, even when they're sad. The only thing that shocked me a little was that you should have been amused by the comte's jests about Condé's army. We may blame those who are enlisted, but they are too much to be pitied for it to be acceptable to laugh at them. In any case, their inaction is in no way ridiculous, since it is involuntary, for they are certainly not running away from danger. On the contrary, they are being kept away from it, for fear that they have any part in the promised victories or in the hoped-for gains.[77] After having pretended to fight with them and for them, they are rejected, exiled from camps as they have been exiled from their country. Unhappy people! If they had only stayed in it! They would have fought or surrendered, but in one way or another they would have been spared the mixture of ill luck and scorn to which they are condemned. Excuse me for being so earnest and solemn, dear Alphonse. I do not know whether it comes from the small amount of Dutch blood which flows in my veins, from the air we breathe at Lone Castle, or whether I am finally taking the side of the chivalrous little army because my father is one of its knights.

Talking about seriousness, the lady of this noble manor is so reserved that I cannot tell whether the vicomte is ever present in her silent reveries. I read her his letters. "We shall see," said she, "whether the regeneration continues." I did not dare ask the slightest question. Lady Caroline is very impressive without being exactly proud. She is much respected in this county, and people come from afar to visit her, each visit being a respectful homage. I have seen hunting, drinking gentleman, or so their appearance and a certain something about them seemed to declare, barely venture to touch the wine they were served, no doubt for fear that they would not be sufficiently able to control what they said. They nonetheless seemed to be amused, but in a way that seemed most extraordinary. Half-obscure allusions provoked long bouts of laughter—sorts of puns which are more ingenious and profound than our own, and where the idea is played on as much as the word. The laughter they provoke seems kinder and more sincere, so to speak. Here it is not a subtle smile underpinned by malicious gossip; it's a great gust of laughter which makes me laugh too. In time perhaps I'll laugh at the joke directly, once I can understand how a hunting or sailing term applies to politics or marriage a little more promptly. It would be impossible for Lady Caroline to select a husband from among the laughers that I have seen, and I hope that if the vicomte deserves her, he will win her.[78] I will wait for a few days more before broaching the subject of our journey to Holland. She needs to be reassured that I am as serious as she is, and that my company will never be a burden to her. Her extreme circumspection dictates that she wait for the proof of experience. She could be sure that here I would not be able to behave too freely, but she was so frightened by what she saw of the French in London that she fears to set off with me for some less wild and solitary place.

Good-bye, my dearest Alphonse; I will not wait long before writing again. I have heard nothing from the duchess since I left London. So much the better—the best thing she could do would be to slip into oblivion. Victoire is a bit bored with Lady Caroline's women. Some of them are as upright and stiff as the yews that I see from my window. The others are as giddy as little lambs dashing about in the fields. They jump, run, shout, fight, and tickle each other—this is called *romping*, and many young Englishwomen of a different rank apparently amuse themselves in the same way. So modesty has its own way of refreshing itself. Perhaps the stricter it is, the more important it is to relax it from time to time. Lady Caroline is never tired and never needs to relax; it is absolutely natural to her to be decent. She is very consistent and amiable. Good-bye; I hear the bell announcing dinner.

Germaine.

P.S. Had I remained in London, I would have made every effort to become acquainted with Mrs C. But why did you tell me what that bizarre woman said?[79] Not only do I no longer touch what has lived or seems destined to do so, but I barely dare pick a rosebud for fear I may hurt or distress the rosebush.

Letter XXV.

The Abbé des *** to Laurent B. Fonbrune.

In Cr***, July 4, 1793

Your question interests and engages me very much, sir, as it is a question put by one honest man to another, where both understand each other perfectly on *right* and *obligation* without thinking of defining them. Nothing being so difficult as definitions of this sort, we are very lucky when we feel that they are superfluous. Neither you nor I perhaps is particularly well-informed about the rule by which we are claiming to judge, but our knowledge and our ignorance are equal. Religion, education, and custom are common to us both, consisting for you and me in similar morals and consciences, and that is why any discussion of the sort that you are proposing is so clear and satisfying for us both.

As by chance you start considering this question in relation to us clergy and nobles, I will start with us, and the question as you formulate it at the end will be resolved as we go along to the extent that I am able to resolve such a thing in a letter and without any prior meditation.

As he removed the privileges of the clergy and nobility, the revolutionary may have said to himself:

1. A hundred men are suffering. One man will suffer, so I will get rid of 99 percent of the human species' suffering.
2. What I strip the victim of will not deprive him of everything he had, and the distress that I cause will therefore be less than the complete destitution of many of those to whom I sacrifice him. I am therefore individually relieving those that I relieve more than the person whom I inflict suffering on will suffer.
3. If the regrets that the victim feels are excessive and lead him to behave in such a way as to lose what I wanted to leave him with, then he is a mad egotist, whose regrets, ruin, and downfall should be disregarded.

Like you, I see no force in the first argument, and I entirely agree with what you say about it. But the same does not apply to the two other ones, and I can see very well that any person who has not only developed or adopted such views but also feels incensed that we do not all hold them would, in his indignation, regard us as guilty parties, against whom it would be necessary first to draw up and then to enact harsh laws.

Yet I have myself never been this man, this revolutionary, whom I cannot resolve to blame. I think that in my youth I would have been that person—I was as trusting as I was generous spirited, and it would never have occurred to me to mistrust the people with whom I would have needed to associate to bring about this act of national justice. I would have been that person if, knowing that my undertaking was bound to fail, my own intentions had been in any doubt either to myself or to anyone else. This last aspect was so important to me that the Duke de la Rochefoucauld is the only revolutionary with whom my heart has been fully in sympathy.[80] I reject that supposedly more sublime virtue which soars above sinister interpretations and degrading rebukes. To risk your life, give up your fortune, and renounce your rank, I understand all this because I would have been capable of it, but to allow oneself to be accused of being a greedy, ambitious, and therefore hypocritical man, despite all one's protestations of pure zeal for the public good, I cannot and do not want to understand it.

Despite being young and confident, despite being sure of myself and without fear for my reputation, I would perhaps have decided not to become the man that I hypothesize, if refusing to be that man and refusing to act had not counted as an action in itself, if vigorous attacks on that vicious and oppressive social existence had ever looked as if they might not actually improve it. Striking blows is so painful for those who are not born cruel and malicious! To admire what the second Brutus did, I have to remind myself that Caesar was on the brink of calling himself King, and Rome on the point of being condemned to perpetual bondage. . . . Rome was not free! Antony and the civil war made Brutus's anguished heroism redundant! Brutus plunged a dagger into the breast of a great man who loved him and who was supposedly his father, and he had done nothing for his country . . . !

Let us return to our question, and, to protect ourselves from any emotion which might propel us in the wrong direction, let us apply it to objects which are further from us.

Let us imagine a mother with only one child, sheltering from an icy wind under a roof, the only shelter which I have at my disposal, and another mother with six children, coming to seek refuge under it. If the two mothers and seven children can all shelter at the same time in the same space, then there is no difficulty. But imagine that the lack of space or some other reason requires me to decide between the two families: will I dispatch the mother of one child to make room for the mother of six? No, and for the reason that we have both agreed on, you and I, which is that the cold suffered by two is as painful as the cold suffered by seven, or a hundred, for the number cannot affect the situation. Moreover, perhaps possession produces a sort of idea of property in me, and my repugnance to dispossess the person who possesses affects my decision in some way. In brief, I will *leave* the seven to be cold rather than *make* two cold, and far from feeling any obligation, perhaps I will barely feel I have the right to do anything other than this.

Now I will imagine that I am the father or master of six almost naked children, and of one child who has more clothes than the other six put together. Should I take away everything that is not strictly necessary from this child to cover the other six? Yes, and if that child becomes so cross that he throws off the rest, I will let him do it. In this case it is not the number that influences my decision, and I would also have taken away from six children what they could have done without to give it to a single child. *Number* only counts when it presents itself in the guise of *strength*. If a vase of flowers gives pleasure to a party of twenty people, but those same flowers makes one of them ill, will anyone hesitate to remove it? How many serious reflections may be drawn from this puerile example! If the person who feels unwell throws the flowers away in some violent manner, she will perhaps be blamed; should her lover do precisely the same thing, he will receive applause. If the entire assembly unites in a prompt expulsion of the flowers, they will all congratulate themselves for their kindly impulse. Why is man only capable of such tiny sacrifices that it is almost embarrassing to mention them? Why are our best feelings so weak, so easily alarmed and overwhelmed by fearful selfishness, while there is nothing bold and enterprising that cupidity will not dare to do, fearing neither peril nor remorse?

La Marquise de *** to Alphonse.

July 3, 1793

I know, sir, that you retain all your friendships, and that even those people of whose affection you are currently least sure are nonetheless still dear to you. Rest assured, they will return to you, and in the meantime, continue to prove to them how worthy you are of their attachment. To tell them what it is important that they know is a service that you will surely not refuse to render them.

I am going to tell you about a rather strange adventure. A wife who had reason to believe that she would oblige her husband by leaving France with her older daughter and who was urged by everyone around her to do so finally resolved to do it. There were some quite strong reasons for it, for if she was to stay in the least safe part of France, she would have a great deal to fear from the patriots, since she had previously been noble, and also from the nobles, since she had treated the patriots decently. A neighboring aristocrat, who had been a great admirer of her daughter, had even seen fit to become extremely jealous of a Jacobin who, being both wounded and on the winning side, had been taken into the house previously known as a château and had there come to be treated with great respect in recognition of his rare and amiable qualities. Note that this jealous and vengeful lover was one of the leaders of the currently victorious Christian army. It was therefore decided that flight was necessary, and accepting generous offers, mother and daughter set off accompanied by an old servant who had lived in the house all his sixty years. Wide trousers and a long coat disguised the young person I will call Pauline decently enough; her mother insisted on keeping her own clothes. "My daughter," said she, "is unknown in the place where we will board our ship, but I am very well known there, and were I to be recognized despite my disguise, what mockery and scenes I would be subjected to! Jokes of the most insulting sort would circulate; my respectable mother would blush for me, and my husband may even come to hear of it. I prefer to risk worse dangers than ridicule such as that."

The two travelers with their faithful servant arrived where they were expected. Pauline walked in front of her mother with the man who was risking his own safety to help them, and they were near the port when the mayor of the town, crossing the square, recognised the marquise, and politely greeted her. She signaled to Pauline to keep going and went into a store, which was luckily empty. The mayor and the servant followed her. When she saw that the former was not leaving, she said to the latter: "Dear clerk, sir, time is precious; do not waste it. I will wait here for the mistress of the store—go where your business takes you." The servant understood her and left; the mistress of the store arrived, and the marquise, who knew her, chatted to her about matters that had nothing to do with business. The mayor, however, beginning to look suspicious, asked her what was the reason for her journey. "I would like to make some purchases," she said, "but I have left my purse at home and find myself without a single promissory note.[81] Would you be so good, monsieur mayor, to lend me what I need and take me to a linen draper's? If not, come with me and help me hire a carriage to take me home straightaway."

The mayor was flustered by the first of these two propositions and wished to prevent it from being repeated. He therefore seized on the second with alacrity and rushed off by himself to fetch a carriage. If then the marquise had had anyone to guide her, she could have gone to the port straightaway and found the boat which was due to carry her daughter away! But it was too late. Perhaps they had already weighed anchor and set sail. She made some wishes . . . how ardent they were!

The chaise arrived and she was helped in. "But it's very strange!" said the mayor. "To come so far to make your purchases and yet not to have brought anything with you to do it!"

"Do you want me to empty my pockets, monsieur? You will see that I am telling the truth."

"No, citoyenne; I believe you, but it is strange."

"Yes, but it's true."

In fact the marquise had given all the necessary money for the journey to their guide and rescuer the night before. She returned home and is not thought to be worried about her daughter. "The love that put her in danger will save her," she said. "And the person who is looking after her feels love of the very highest stamp." If, however, she could find any way to join her daughter, you may rest assured that she would take it. But she does not think it very likely.

This letter will reach you quicker than L.'s will. For greater safety and speed I will have it sent from the post office in Paris. Write as soon as you possibly can but do not forward my letter, as certain expressions may have escaped me. It is not easy to be equally impartial.

Marie Julie de ***

Minette and her grandmother and the uncle of her father are all very well and send you friendly greetings. My respects to the abbé. When will we be able to see you both?

Letter.

*The Abbé des *** to the Marquis.*

Cress., July 13, 1793

I was preparing to carry out your orders when I received the letter from Madame la Marquise that I am copying here, removing certain disguises which were necessary for its journey across France. I will nonetheless imitate her reserve on one point: I will not name the man who is accompanying your daughter, but I can tell you that he is a gallant man in every sense of the term. Alphonse knows him personally, and I know him from his letters, and neither we nor the marquise have any anxiety about Pauline. Nor should you, Monsieur le Marquis. You must not; would we wish to deceive you?

A summary of the preceding letter follows.

We will send you any news we hear from your daughter or from her zealous and honest liberator as soon as we hear it. I cannot express how happy Alphonse was to hear that you have returned to your old sentiments toward him. Such a return is entirely worthy of you, Monsieur le Marquis; it is frank, and touchingly generous.

The Abbé des ***

Letter.

Leopold Nieuwermeulen to Alphonse.

Amsterdam, July 16, 1793

I am asked to tell you, monsieur, that Pauline—just Pauline; she wishes to be called by no other name—very fortunately arrived at my father's house last night, accompanied by an old servant. She refuses to say which French port she left from, who her guide was, and which Dutch vessel he transferred her to, not wishing to compromise people who have treated her extremely well and toward whom she has the greatest obligations. Despite the ignorance to which such reserve confines us, and without having any idea who she is, it is very clear to us what sort of a welcome we should give her. She named an excellent friend of ours who is established in Smyrna as being the friend of friends, and she spoke of you, monsieur, and a priest who is with you in such a way as to prove that her heart and habits have given her very pure and delicate notions about everything. Nothing more is needed to confirm everything which a charming face says in her favor. I have the honor of being, etc.

I forgot, monsieur, to tell you that the beautiful fugitive has enough money not to need any of the money I would be very ready to lend her for a long time. . . . Here she is, just coming into the study.

"What did you call me?" she asks me.

"Just Pauline."

"Neither madame nor mademoiselle."

"No, but I would be grateful if you would tell me what I must say and what you wish to be called in the house."

"Advise me."

"But what are you?"

"I am mademoiselle but I would be preferred to be believed to be madam."

"Why?"

"Because it would be useless to think of me as mademoiselle."

"Have you given your word?"

"I was not allowed to give my word, but my decision is taken."

"With no hope of change?"

"No."

"Let's say Madame Pauline, then. Madame Pauline does not sound very good. . . . Do you and your family not own any lands whose name you might take?"

"Of course, but we are no longer allowed to bear those names."

"In Holland that does not matter."

"And you don't think it would trouble a French citizen?"

"Not at all."

"Well then, I will call myself Madame Pauline de . . . No, I can't bring myself to do it; it may bring trouble on my parents and displease a man whom I would wish to please forever."

To me no to her that [. . . .] replied.[82]

Fragments of Two Novels
Written in English[1]

Translator's Note

"A Correspondence" and "Letters of Peter and William" are not translated; they are simply transcribed from Charrière's original (unpublished) English. Nothing, from spelling and grammar to syntax or repetition has been altered, the point being to allow the reader to savor the original.

A Correspondence

(1796)[2]

Letter the First

Emily Fontaine to Harriet Denizet

June the 10th 179*

At last I have heard of my Harriet! God be praised my dear! I know you are well tho' you happened to be at Geneva in one of its worst moments. You health has not sufferd in the least from the fright, witness your complexion as bloomy as bright as ever. I know also your Uncle got safe out of France with at least a considerable part of his fortune bringing home to his niece the fond affection he always bore her.—I was even told near which town of the *Pays de Vaud* you likely must be at present, but as this part of the information was not very clear I begged a Lady who goes that way to find you out more accurately and to have this letter given you by a sure hand.—Pray, my dear, let me have quickly a long letter with your direction in it. You shall direct yours to *Mlle Emilie Fontaine chez Madame Peacock à Tavanes.* Till I know every thing that can be known about you, till I know what you have done, what you now do, what you intend doing, and where and with whom you are, I am resolved not to say a word of me. It was *you* my dear who deserted our correspondance. Perhaps you were forced to it, but why not write again When you could have written? You must now atone for that, my Dear, to your ever loving friend, and pray make haste.

Letter the Second

Harriet to Emily

Mont venoge June the 22th

To be sure you shall have it, that *long letter* you sue for, my
dearest, precious, friend. But to satisfy altogether your friendly
demands would require a whole book and it is but a letter you
desire. Do not require I should relate minutely the circumstances which have in a short time changed altogether my fate
and put me in the situation I am now in. This rehearsal would
be more painful to me than interresting to you, and it would
awake some recollections which I wish might sleep for ever,
lest they should make me unable fully to enjoy the happiness I
am now blessed With.

By my uncle's testamentary disposition and his death which
happened two months ago, I am almost free and independant,
I am the mistress of my self and of a fortune which considering
my wants and my expectations could be call'd considerable.
I said I was almost free and independant but I might have said
altogether for the two guardians to whose care my uncle trusted
me don't middle at all with what I am doing and a Maiden
aunt who lives with me for decency's sake is so complacent so
simple, I could say so weak, that she has no thought, no will,
but what her niece inspires.

I must acknowledge this situation is not without its danger
for such a young and unexperienced girl as I am; but having
no guide now but my self how cautiouly shall I seek my way!
How much shall I reflect before I act! Now my dear that gravity you some times laugh'd at me for, will be perhaps of some
use. But Notwithstanding natural gravity and designed caution I fear I shall err Very often—Oh! May it not be in a manner that would keep me long without knowing of the error.
There is one advantage in my independancy. There is one
advantage in my independancy. I shall have no body to blame
but my self for each desagreable effect of a false step and I

think experience must be quick and effectual in proportion of its being mortifying.

Hitherto I have done nothing very foolish, and I hope I have shunned most dangerous follies by chusing for my abode a solitary country seat where I am happier than I ever was since I left Neuchatel and you. Let me give you an idea of its beauties; I'll take infinite pleasure in describing the house, its comodious appartmens the drawing room, the parlour, . . . You are safe My dear; you escaped the description for here is one of my guardians. I cannot the whole day think of my letter but just to seal it and to send it off. The post passes through the nearest village at midnight. You'll write (and pray don't tarry and do talk of your self now) to *Mlle D. a Mont Venoge par Marsin route de Moudon à Lausanne.*

Letter the Third

Emily to Harriet

June the 29th

I wish you joy dear Harriet and tho' I can hardly conceive how you could forget your friend while you suffered and not seek some comfort in displaying your sorrows to her, tho' I still less can account for your remaining silent when you began to find your self happy, I will force my thoughts to be employed in no other manner than an agreable one when on you they dwell. I will suppose discretion with regard to people you must have complained of bereft me from my friend's letters when she was in affliction, and a thousand new embarassing affairs when she was become an heiress; so all will be settled, & I shall love her as much as ever.

My situation is also changed but not for the better like yours. My mother married, not long ago, a widower with four children of which I am now, shall I say the governess or the slave? Oh! what blinding fondness produces such a marriage especially in women! I think that late tribute pay'd to charms they thought decaying, impresses them with an extraordinary gratitude. My mother has no eyes but for her husband and would have me think of nothing but his troublesome babies. She will certainly scold if she sees me write and not for them. I am tired to death with stories they will have me invent and write down. Soon tho' I'll get rid of this fatiguing task. *The Tales of Mother Goose, Young Misses' Magazine, The Conversations of Emily* will do just as well as my performances.[3] I have wrote for all those young books and so my poor head shall soon get repose. Adieu my Dear. I hear my Mother. The flock of Children is with her. They'll rush in this moment, . . .— Be quiet Betty, be gone Nancy. Dear William draw a little while, or be so good as to cut a pen or two for me. I must needs write some more lines to my friend Harriet.

My Dear, beware of growing romantick in your solitary abode. I dread nothing for you but an imagination, which I think is apt to build to it self a fantastic world in a manner as not to permit one ever to know the real world. Beware of groves; of lonely walks; or romantick songs. I fear not your heart should beat for an unworthy object, but I fear Werther's love, a love that was never felt and tore no heart but only adorned a sheet of paper, might endanger your reason, your happyness.[4] You were fond, already at school and when but 12 years old, of *strong sentiments*, of *striking ideas* Don't nurture that disposition. *Ideas*, my dear ought to be *right Sentiments* when they are such as cannot likely make us happy ought to be subdued and then the weaker they are the better. . . . Here is my uncle the Dean, who you know is my oracle, I am talking and writing; he talks of you and grumbles about me. Now he is saying: Young girls speak too much of being *happy*, of making one self or other people *happy*! I know that *good luck* is. *Fortune* can be run after *Affluence* can be got. a nation may be blessed with *prosperity*, a man may enjoy *pleasure* and *diversion*—But thou, *happiness*, most airy most whimsical of all fantastick or real beings where art thou? and who could grasp at thy shadowlike substance?

Now my dear I am left to my self and must descend from that high tuned string to vulgar expressions. The thing I have to say is this: If you happened to think of having me with you don't tell me. It would be too painfull to refuse too wicked to accept. My father's fortune is now my own, and my mother married so imprudently that she wants what I pay for boarding with her.

Farewell my dearest Harriet.

Letter [the] 4th

Harriet to Emily

July the 4th

It were both my guardians that came to me on a visit and not a short one for they were here three days—let me rather say three nights.

All day they were about business of their own; the one buying and letting grounds, the other trying and buying horses. It was one so eagerly employed about two bushes of hay amongst which he was to chuse for a provision he intended to secure I could not help asking why he did not taste them. Both these my *soi disant* guardians forgot my concerns in the pursuit of their own, and had only chosen their wards house as a place whence they could do commodiously the business they had in this part of the country.⁵

As it is possible however they might have one day or other some influence on my fate I endeavoured to get acquainted with their disposition, but could discover nothing but what is seen in the first moment one meets them. M. Menil is low bred, ignorant and good natured. He loves money and an only son he has & who joined him here of a morning when he was to depart the afternoon. Born to a small fortune this man by his menagement has raised it to a large one. Mr Du Roset is said to be still richer . . . . . . But here I have a letter of yours. Oh! you are kind!

You are kind! I cannot too much feel nor to often repeat it: your gentle indulgence prevents the excuses I could have made. My friend pleads for me to her self. Oh how happy I feel to find I am acquited tho' perhaps not quite innocent. Oh how much I am obliged to my advocate who perhaps in some measure seduced my judge!

I am then forbid to make you a proposal so natural and that it had been so much my interest you should have accepted! I obey my dear, but remember 'tis with reluctance, and at all times look upon my home as your own.

I have a mind to return warnings by warnings, admonitions by admonitions, and first of all I must tell you that if your way of talking of your mother and her betrothed children is that which is usual among those reasonable people, whose *ideas are right*, whose *sentiments are likely to make them happy*, I wish to remain as long as I live the foolish, the romantick thing I am. Out of what corner of your heart, dear Emily, you who are generally sweet and mild did you call forth that harshness, that unkindness and such expressions of disdain? How could you laugh at your Mother's innocent and virtuous affections? How would you talk of *decaying charms*? The person is decaying when her form is altered. I know that cruel for bode.—I have lost a fond mother. But if your ill humour is in some measure excusable, when it has for its object her who took from you part of her affection to bestow it upon a second husband and his children these at least are not to blame they are innocent of the mischief. Poor Children! They had lost a mother. My dear, be their friend, be their sister; be the superior, the mother-like-sister, Werther's Charlotte was.

I thank you my dear for your solicitude about me. I am in some danger, if that word tho' is not misaplied here, of becomng quite romantick.

It was always said 'twas my turn, and now I may live without controul a romantick life, adding thus habit, to a natural disposition. But where is the harm of all that—if that makes me happy and does not pervert those few good qualities by which I could well value my self since they won your heart. I remember to have seen your uncle at Neuchatel. He said seeing our amusements. *You do well. Be Chearful.*—'*tis wisdom to be thus Childish.*—*one must enjoy all the innocent little pleasures Nature and fortune puts in one's way.* Well my dear if I can make my self happy by romantick *rêveries*; if Werther and his exalted feelings carry my fancy to an imaginary World which appears to me finer than the real one, I do just what your uncle advised us, I enjoy an innocent pleasure.[6] Why should I trouble my head by teaching my self another way of being happy than that which I was naturally led to follow? As to what you say that Werther's love shall turn my head, Is it not much safer to love an imaginary object than an unworthy one? I had a mind to say a *real* one.

Of how many afflictions is not real love the cause which imaginary love can never produce. I have read some where *Love puts our happines totally in the power of another.* There, there, is *danger* true *danger.*—As long as I love no body but Werther no dangerous comand shall be exerted over me. Farewell my dear friend. I am for ever your loving Harriet.

Letter the Fifth

Emily to Harriet

Very well my dear. First you censure me, secondly you admire your self. In answer I shall tell you the babies are not my brothers and sisters nor my mother's own Children but those of Mr Peacock and of the first Mrs Peacock the silliest woman on earth. Then I grumble against them and call them some times by harsh names but I am for ever telling and writing stories to the eldest of them, and washing the dirty little face and fingers of the little one. As your and Werther's Charlotte never existed her example is nothing.

[First version of *A Correspondence*]

Letter the 2

Emily to Harriet

I wish you joy dear Harriet and tho' I can hardly conceive how you could forget your friend while you suffered and not seek some comfort in displaying your sorrows to her, tho' I still less can account for your remaining silent when you began to find your self happy, I will force my thoughts to be employed in an agreable manner only, when you shall be the subject of them; I'll suppose discretion delicacy, bereft me from my friend's letters when she was in afflicted, and a thousand new and embarrassing affairs when she was become an heiress.

So all will be settled in my mind & I shall love you as much as ever.

My situation is also changed but not happily. My mother married a widower with four children of which I am now, shall I say the governess or the slave? Oh! what blinding fondness produces such a marriage, especially in women! I think that late tribute pay'd to charms they thought decaying impresses them with an extraordinary gratitude. My mother has no eyes but for her husband and would have me think of nothing but his troublesome babies. She'll certainly scold if she sees me write and not for them. I am tired to death with stories they'll have me invent. I'll get get rid tho' of this *ennui*. Les contes de ma Mere l'oye, Le Magazin des enfans, will do just as well.[7] I have wrote for all those young books and so My poor head shall soon get repose. Adieu my Dear. I hear my Mother. The flock of Children is about her. They'll rush in this moment. Adieu. However I must needs add some more lines, Let them say what they please. My Dear Harriet be ware of growing romantick in your solitary abode. I dread nothing for you but an imagination that paints to it self a fantastic world so as never to permit one to know the real one. Beware of groves, of lonely walks, of romantick songs. I fear not your heart should beat for an unworthy object but I fear Werther's love, a love that never was felt, might turn your head. You was fond already at School and when but 12 years old, of *Strong sentiments*, of *striking ideas*. Don't nourish too much that disposition.[8] *Ideas* ought to be *just* still more than to be *striking*. *Sentiments* must be likely to Make us happy. If that were not the case the weaker they were, and the easier subdued would be the better.

Farewel.

Letter the Third

The same to the same

My uncle the Dean who you know is my oracle, ask'd me yesterday if I had at last heard of you. I told him of your letter and of my answer. Young girls speak too much, he said, of being happy of making one Self happy &c. Happiness is not an absolute thing, and ought not to be looked upon as a thing that could ever be complete. To avoid great misfortunes great sufferings of body or mind, a total want of money, a knowing self reproach and to injoy all the innocent little pleasures that nature and fortune puts in our way is all we can do, all we must try to do for ourselves. Wisdom it self could not make us completely happy. I saw people of great piety be resigned, but some of them were far from being happy. Tell all this to your young friend. I obey Harriet without examining if my uncle is right or wrong. If you happened to think of having me with you don't tell me; It would be too painfull to refuse such a proposal and I must not accept of it. My father's fortune is all my own now and my mother married so imprudently that she wants what I pay for boarding with her. I'll stay therefore if my situation grows not altogether intollerable.

You are indeed in the Right, Madam; as to the Valais Your arrangement is much better; But pray, let me put Harriet near Tavannes, and Emily near near Lausanne.⁹

Letter the Fourth

Harriet to Emily

You are kind; I cannot too much repeat it. Your gentle indulgence prevents the excuses I could have made to you—Let us, my dear, my amiable friend, forget my past wrongs—and my gratitude shall still encrease my tenderness for you.

You can think that I pity you—Your Situation is desagreeable indeed—Why did you refuse before hand the proposal friend-ship could inspire to me, to mend your fate? I dare say, that if you would grant me the favour to come and live with me, you should have no reason to repent of it—and how much would the presence of so beloved a friend add to my own happiness?

Don't take it amiss my dear if I return you your warnings and admonitions which by the by I don't all reckon as worthy of my railing me altogether. If your way of feeling is that of all reason-able and sensible people, *whose ideas are just, whose senti-ments are likely to make us happy*, oh! pray, let me remain my whole life a foolish, romantick thing.—How can the sweet and mild Emily speak of her own mother in a manner so unkind, so disdainful? How can she laugh at that Mother's innocent feel-ings, instead to rejoyce at her happiness—How unworthy of your disposition are your jokes over your Mother's *decaying charms*—If you think to have some reason to be discontended with your Mother's marriage, are her husband's children not altogether innocent of that mischief—Poor little babies! Why, my dear, did you not like them? Be neither their slave, nor their tyrannical governess, but their friend, their teacher, their true sister—They shall in return of your tender cares, love, respect you—and these *troublesome babies* will procure you delightful enjoyments. If you had read Werther, dear Emily, as often as I did, you should not want all I am saying to you;—you would think yourself happy to be put in a situation, which offers to you all the pleasures the amiable Charlotte enjoyed among her brothers and sisters.

I thank you for your dreading and fearing for my sake—I know well that there is some danger for me to grow altogether romantick

I have here too much opportunity to follow my inclination— But, my dear, if I am happy thereby, and if my romantick life has no evil influence over my disposition, if it does not spoil the few good qualities I think my self possessor of, what will be the harm of that? I think your uncle the Dean is wholly in the right when he says a complete happiness is not to be found on earth—but he said also one must *enjoy all the innocent little pleasures nature and fortune puts in our way*? Well, my dear, if I can render myself Joys by my solitary walks, if Werther and his exalted feelings carry me fancy to an imaginary World which pleases me more than the real one I do just what your uncle avises me to do, I enjoy these *innocent pleasures*?[10] Why if am happy should I trouble my head, and spoil my enjoymenets by thinking that it is not in that way that I ought to be happy.— As to what you say—Werther's love shall turn my head—is it not safer is it not better to love an imaginary object than an unworthy one? I had a mind to say a real one. Of our many afflictions is not *real* Love the cause from which imaginary Love is totally free? I have read somewhere, Love puts our happiness in the dependance of another.[11] Well, if the object exists only in our imagination, we shall ever be satisfied with it, we can do with it what we please—our Happiness remains in our own Hands—I had a mind, my dear, to speak to you of M.M. my second guardian—but it shall be for another time. my letter is already too long—The subject hailed me farther than I ought to have gone. I beg your pardon, my Emily Farewell.

Letter the Fifth

Emily to Harriet

Very well my dear. You first censure me, secondly you admire your self. In answer I shall only say: That the babies are not my brothers and sisters nor my Mother's own Children but those of Mr Peacock and the first Mrs Peacock the silliest woman on earth. Then I grumble against them and call them what they are troublesome babies but I tell and write stories to them I wash their dirty little faces, fingers &c. As to your Charlotte as she never existed her example is nothing at all to me. Those heroïnes whose virtues are but paper and ink may be what they please, There is no dificulty for them to live and die in the most extraordinary manner. Let Them have fifty children about them they will not suffer of the head ach. I laugh my dear at that part of your sermon. I told my Mother of your reproof on what I said of her. She smiled called me an impertinent girl, But

added: Stay but with me and say what you please. Now a word
on the apology of your romantick turn. I think it so strongly
argued that it might do for stark mad people. How happy is
the man that [ ] him self a king, a pope, a god! Adieu My dear.
Pray keep a sound little corner in your beautiful head.

Letter the Sixth

Harriet to Emily

How you treat me, my Emily! This time you are not kind at
all. Lest I should lost altogether your esteem, permit me to
intreat you not to judge of my true feelings by what I said in
my last letter. Think. Emily, how insipid our correspondence
would be, if I did answer to every thing you are pleased to say;
*Yes my dear; you are in the right; it is just also my way of
thinking—I will endeavour to change every thing you disapprove*, and the like. I am delighted with censuring and disput-
ing; it is one of my favourite enjoyments; when the person with
whom I dispute, is not below my own forces; then the little cor-
recting is fair, and must give no pain, no mortification to either
of the wresters. I will now very peacibly make you acquainted
with Mr M. my other guardian's disposition. I think he is no
more but fifty years; but he has already many infirmities of the
most advanced age—for instance he is almost bald, and more
than half blind—he has spent some years in his youth at Basil;
where he has got a knack of economy I think he was also a student there; he is a little more fashionable but Mr B. his heart is
incapable of tender feelings; still more of exalted *sentiments*.
So you must not fear for me in his society. he pretends to
understand horsmanship; to manage a horse; to teem a horse;
to cure a horse; it is the only strong inclination I have observed
in him. Though his twin is rather singular, his conversation by
its dryness grows soon tiresome. I should have said, his presence for as to a conversation, he can not be said to have any—
When both my guardians pay'd me a visit, Mr B was accompanied
by his only son, a youth of twenty, the most pretty I did ever

see. I could not help admiring him and as long as he remained silent, I looked upon him with a sort of pleasure. But when he spoke all was over; and I thought it a pity such beautiful eyes were lost on such an insignificant and silly creature. Now I no longer see or hear him; but still remember his fine features, his large black eyes, the good grace of his whole person, I doubt whether I did not mistake reserve for dullness, and a mind that does not chose to open itself, for an absence of any mind. If I see him another Time I may perhaps be able to judge. He looked sometimes like one occupied with the most profound thoughts. Was this chance, or was he taught so, or did he really think profoundly? His father is extremely fond of him; he has given him the best education he could; and now he looks with complaisance upon the fruits of his cares—Is all this folly, is it but blind fondness of a father, or is there something in the boy that deserves to make a father happy and proud? Adieu dearest Emily What does Mr Peacock do? What sort of a man is Mr Peacock?

Letter the Seventh

Emily to Harriet

Pray forgive me, my dear Harriet, my want of attention to that part of your letter you wrote before having received mine. I confess I did not at all think of your guardian till yesterday when I took your letter out of a drawer to read it over again. The man indeed deserves not any great notice should be taken of him but that he is your guardian and may perhaps have some son or Nephew that he will one day or other present to you as a sort of a lover I mean as a man offering to become a husband. I dare say you shall not even look at him except he has Werther's blue coat and yellow waistcoat. But the poor lad shall not be told of the merit of a blue coat and yellow waistcoat. Woe upon him if he does not in the least look like Werther, if he has never heard of Werther, if he never read Ossian and has no heroic no romantick no poetick turn![12] Enough of that for Mr B. has perhaps neither son nor Nephew, but what I say of this supposed young man would be true for any young man. Woe on any adorer of my Harriet that Should be wanting of all Werthership! When your guardian entered your house you was going to describe that house to me. Do describe it or trace a plan of it.

Tho' I am not over fond of those description, and use like Boileau to jump over a palace ånd run out a Royal garden I must needs know the house my friends lives in.[13] I must in a moment see where she sleeps and awakes, Where she eats her break fast and her diner; I must get acquainted with her library &c. Tell me wether your house stands on a hill, or on a flat ground; Wether you see or not from your windows your beautiful lake.

Tell me every thing that's agreable or disagreable to you and be ever sure of a simpatick feeling from your Emily.

Letter the Eight

Our last letters went off and arrived the same day. yours was extremely well come.

I am satisfied my dear. You are not perhaps so thoroughly Werthered, Romanticated, as one might imagine. A retograde step towards plain good sense could still be made by my amiable friend. So much the better and now in my turn I will fairly acknowledge that a romantick disposition is not half so desagreable to me as Vulgarity and narrowness of mind. The one I think can be call'd back little & than an elevated and generous way of thinking remains. That result of Nature duly tutored by experience and reflection is beautiful. But the other disposition grows worse and worse. Here Nature and experience have but one tendency, and the result of both is disgusting.

I hope young Mr B. is not a fool and then he may love you & become a proper husband. He is certainly handsome; that's something for it pleases the eye, he is also, by what you say, modest and well behaved; that's much. He would not make you blush by the foolish chat of talkative presomption nor by an unfashionable, ungenteel, countenance and manner. The attention you paid to a youth not drest like Werther, and the trouble you gave your self of telling me every thing in him that could admit of a favorable interpretation pleased me very much. Now for your reward you shall have the whole Peacock. in- and out side, origin, education and all.

His mother was the daughter of a man of some fashion and fortune of this country. She was educated by her grand mother a widow, whose husband had been many years curate at Court-lary. That man was learned and honest, his widow was sensible and good natured, and their grand child had beauty enlivened by quick parts. As she had many brothers and sisters and not quite your Charlotte's turn she wished to go abroad after the death of her grand mother and her father approving that scheme for his fortune devided between six or seven Children could afford but a very small portion to each, and besides he was him self neither old nor a strict economist. He then wrote to a friend in England who provided what they thought a proper place for the young girl. She went and lived happily for a year or two with a woman of quality whose only Child she was to take care of. But the Lady had a Nephew and the young governess was very pretty, more so than prudent. When she knew she was with child she turn'd almost mad of despair. The young man was a weak boy. Not daring to displease his parents, and unable tho' to bear his mistriss's tears, he shot himself to get rid of the conflict that tormented his brains. Six months after his father's death Mr Peacock was born. An annuyty has been left to his Mother who took the greatest care of his education and when he was about twenty placed him as a secretary with the king of Prussia's Envoy at London. At twenty five he married a limner's daughter who had neither wit nor prudence nor money. As the salary of a *Secretaire d'ambassade* was not sufficient to maintain in England a wife like his and their children he resolved to come to his mother's native country. She had given him every thing she could claim here which was not considerable tho' increased by the death of two of her father's children that were never married. His wife was brought to bed imediately after their arrival of a fourth Child, and the next year of a fifth; but she was hardly recovered when a rhumatick fever carried her off. an aunt of Mr Peacock has nursed the little of all his

Children; my Mother out of good nature took upon her self the care of the boy that was two years old, but after a month or two the poor Child dyed in her arms She and the father cried and mourned together Sighs of love soon mixed with sighs of grief and matrimony has ensued. There you have the man's story. Now look at the man. He is well made well bred, well dressed tall, handsome, polite, and has just sense enough not to be a fool, morals enough not to be a rake, knowledge enough not to blunder on any whatwhoever subject. I think I see in him a Mixture of his English father, his Tavane's Mother, and his German patron. A certain restraint hinders his politeness from looking altogether like that of a man of the first fashion but he has good grace and ease enough to charm those that see him here almost my half savage countrymen. The young girls admire & their admirers envy and imitate him. Their hair is drest, their cravate is tyed like his. an old honest german servant Which followed him here is consulted whenever a new coat is ordered, and as he understands cookery and lived once in a confisseur's shop Women as Well as Men ask for his aid and counsels in many occasions. His Master never opposes he should go where he can be useful . . . We have, My dear, *relief* and grace enough; a little More Money would not at all be amiss. I pay a pretty large stipend, and do in no way neither by ill manners. ill humeur, a slothful dress, disgrace the houlshold. But the word *dress* puts my in mind of some of our neighbours who come out of their woods, descend from their roks with such fine caps, such little shoes, such quantity of rubans that they make me laugh. Mr Peacock approbation is eagerly courted. Adieu My dear.

Letter the Eleventh

Emily to Harriet

I don't fear your anger Harriet. *You* are indeed *mild* an *sweet*. I am not. There is some generosity in me mixed with a great deal of impatience and rudeness. That's the caracter I would at all times gives of my self.

I thank you heartily for your proposal with regard to the little Peacocks, which I am far from rejecting but would not as yet mention to the father. Let it ripen a While, & let me study the disposition of the two girls that we may chuse her that most deserves your goodness & would be most likely to repay it. you were so far from surprising me with you proposal that I almost expected it. Hurry would spoil the merit of your generosity which ought to be free from all giddiness & false appreciations. There is an error in what you say of yourself; & your uselessness. At seventeen you need not, you must not do but Gather strength of body and mind, look about for the future, and actually live happy. Nothing else is required from you. Those busy bodies that imagine they are so necessary to the world act too much, think too little. doing no harm is wiser than endeavouring to do good. Be quiet then be satisfied, and we shall think of the little Peacocks by and by

I hope you have not been so cautious with respect of poor Mr B as I would have you in this affair. Here there is no haste, with a distemperd young man there may. His illness & your aunt Will prevent I daresay any misrepresentation of you complaisancy. The one makes it necessary the other hinders it from being improper. I have no leisure to day to say more. Only I'll tell you Mr Peacock cannot be called insignificant. His knowing much of the world, telling well, gracefully many a interesting anecdotes, saying agreably civil things all that diverts, pleases, makes him admired. He pays his *contingent* to society talk fully, largely. Besides he expresses him self with elegance in German, French, Italian as well as his native language. That's some thing too. We read together Hume's history of England, and we talk English when we happen to be alone or to have nobody except his children about us. This will make it still more easy for us to keep our correspondance in English. 'Twas indeed a very good scheme and agreement between us not to write but English to one another. God knows how many curious eyes we sent in that manner *about their business.* I don't think you have at all forgot Mr Groenwald's lessons. He had I daresay at Neuchatel at least no scholars like us. Adieu for this time (Mettez s'il vous plait dans la lettre de hier *which was thought* decent *for her grand Mother.* C'est le mot usité *She was decently provided for She lives decently &c* on dit comme cela.[14])

P.S. Pray tell me of young Mr B.

Letter the Twölfth

Harriet to Emily

Your letter, my dearest friend, was extremely welcome—It made an agreeable diversion to my thoughts and occupations—for, my dear, young Mr B. is arrived two days ago, He had no body but a servant with him. The poor boy is very much changed indeed; but no less agreeable, thought he has lost the lively colours of health. A languishing air spread over his whole person, still addes to his natural graces. He speaks but very little; he seems often absorbed in sad reflexions—I have observed in his fine black eyes the impression of the deepest grief. The sorrows of his mind have surely much contributed to his disease—The first time I saw him, I only admired his ele-gancies; now, he moves my heart—What can render unhappy a young man in so pleasant a situation, so tenderly loved by his father? It cannot be self reproach, for he is too young and looks too guiltless.—As to his disposition and talents, I have made very interesting discoveries—O Emily, how much I was in the wrong, when I thought he was a fool—his timidity, his reserve, his extreme modesty have betray'd me into that error—B. his not only a youth of parts, but he has very much instruction—He understands Italian and german as well, I think as Mr Peacok—he reads English th'o he does not talk it and he speaks french better than most people in this country do. Besides, he pofesses a charming talent, he draws well and paints in miniature.—My aunt is extremely fond of Mr B. she told me this Morning, the grandfather of this pretty youth had been, in her youth, the object of her love, and this love has been unhappy—I beseech you, dear Emily, to send me as soon as possibly, one of the little Peacok's—Your consent to my request gave me very much pleasure—The care of Mr B's health engrosses my mind too much.—I wish to find another object to think of.—I see him just now from my window,—he walks in the Linden trees Alley, leaning on his servant—his Doctor has already visited him twice—he has prescribed him Dietes and much exercise—I think he has communicated to me his pensive and sad humour—farewel, my dear—I shall soon write to you again—You desired me to tell you of young Mr B—Do you find I have obeyd?

Letters of Peter and William

(1796)[1]

Dear Peter. I am just arrived. What a busy world this world of London! What a bustle! What running! what riding!

The house of which I was shown a corner for my habitation is twice as large as our church. MyLord which I first met on the stair case appeard to be a small little man. He is tall though, he is above my size. I observed it when he stood speaking to me in his closet. MyLady is rather handsome but she paints as Kitty one of the maids told me when I commended her complexion; for its brightness had struck me. Lady Euphrasia is a pretty girl. Her sister MyLord's eldest daughter is at a boarding school. Farwell dear Peter I'll tell you more when I shall have seen more.

I carried yesterday your letter to your uncle, who received me very civilly, at first but when he saw by what you wrote to him that he was to pay me part of the money he owes to our family I thought he frowned. I would have thought the sum was but a trifle to a man so well drest and whose wife and daughters had so much gold about their ears, neck, fingers; His shop besides is filled up by what they call Mercery Ware but however 'twas not without reluctance he gave me five guineas, and he desired me not be in haste for the rest or rather he was sure, he protested, I could not be in haste. What occasion, said he, can a young lad just arriving at London possibly have for money. How can an elderly man, answered I, a man that lived in London long enough to get such wealth want so to keep all his money and that of other people besides. I am curious of plays You have already seen, I must see the Lions, Arlequin, and a thousand things besides. I'll perhaps want a Mistriss which I hope you do not . . . you're Merry I find, said Mr Ferris blushing as his wife shook her head. Well, you have five guineas now, and before they are spent I dare say MyLord will pay you a half years wages. Pray on what footing are you in his house. As a secretary I dare say, for your Cousin my Nephew tells me you write a fair hand and are not without some little college learning. Fy said I a secretary is shut up in his room or when he goes out keeps no company but with the sullen and fat marchand like your self or people of that sort, half gentlemen half slaves. I am and would be nothing but a nimble & running about footman. A Foot man cried the eldest Miss Ferris. And does Lady Sara who is at the same boarding school to which I'll be sent to within a few days Know you are our relation? I don't believe she does answered I laughing. But if it was worth my while to boast of such a relationship as this pray what misfortune or shame would it bring on you? Take care, Miss, I perhaps migth mention you not only as my cousin but as a proud and presuming little fool. Tears now of anger and spite filled her eyes, and I pity'd suffering pride tho' I despised it. We were all serious for a moment: I am sorry said Fanny, the younger daughter of Mr Ferris, Our cousin does not meet with a more chearful reception. Pray sir what is your name? William—Well now William let us shake hands and be friends. You're as welcome to me as if you were MyLord's secretary, nay a secretary of state. You look quik & sprightly, that's every thing to me. What did prompt you to leave your village.

I'll tell you plainly my dear pretty cousin, I'll tell you, tho' perhaps it may seem very odd and ridiculous to almost every body here. 'Twas Caleb Williams that made me wish to stroll about and look how things go on, what people of fashion, what people of wealth, what poor people are . . .[2] God bless me cried Mr Ferris. You dared to read Caleb Williams, a book of such bad tendency, a damned dangerous book, a book . . . Have you read it—interrupted I. God forbid. Exclaimed M. Ferris. I burst out in a fit of laughter Fanny smiled. Miss Ferris frowned Mrs Ferris said, meant, looked nothing.

Here a carriage stoping before the door, Mr Ferris had only time before he run from the back parlour to his shop to advise me never to Mention Caleb Williams before Mylord nor to any body of the house holding.

Adieu Peter. Fanny Ferris is a pretty girl. The rest of that family tho' they are belonging neither to the Falkland's and Tirels nor to the people oppressed by those sort of people, Tho' they are not very rich, and never were very poor seem to me not debased but base, not perverted but perverse.[3] I think Nature and society but that society to which nature must necessarily lead are here to blame. Fanny got safe I don't know how. Nature must have been milder to her than to her father mother and sister.

Letter the Third.

Indeed I could complain of nothing material and hitherto I would not give a guinea for the difference between MyLord's station and mine in his Lordship's house nay in the world. I am oftener tired but he is oftener weried. He stands at court and behind their majesties at the play houses, I stand behind him when he sups and dines. I see him yawn for want of thougt, as one could see me yawn from beeing sleepy if he happens to sit up longer than usual. I have been struck hitherto by no proofs of a hard nor haughty heart but only by what I would call a leasiness of judgment. People speak and reason and never go as far as I would have them. I created yesterday an odd sort of wonder amongst a numerous company of fashionable and elegant people that dined here. They spoke with admiration and feeling of the late Mr Howard who visited all the prisons in Europe and wished with so much ardour that the situation of the prisonners might be mended.[4]

That conversation put me in mind of Caleb Williams, and his prison was before my eyes. I felt as it were his chains, I eat the coarse and disgusting meat that was given him but not endowed with so much fortitude, I bedewed it with tears which actually fell on the back of MyLord's chair, over which

I leaned. William, William cried MyLord like one who had vainly ask'd several times for the same thing but with more surprise than impatience—What is the matter? William are you turned deaf—Lady Euphrasia who sat opposite to her father said. I think poor William weeps. What is the Matter ask'd MyLord mildly. Tell me William What made you weep. The conversation about M. Howard and the prisonner put me in mind.—Here I stopt remembering M. Ferris's caution—of what said MyLord. You never was in a prison. Never in my life MyLord. I would not go there out of mere curiosity. 'Tis a sad thing, to be sure said a gentleman. A Shokking Sigtht exclaimed another. That's the reason we admire so much M. Howard. May I ask one question MyLord? Said I. Do ask, replied MyLord. Pray ask cried Lady Euphrasia. Did any of your gentleman do any thing to make M. Howard's inquiries of use any thing I mean to mend the prisons. They all stared. No one even blushed. The question is not at all amiss said Lord George B***. William is a sensible Lad said my master. He was recommended to me by M. William Ferris his Godfather a man which I value for his sense and honesty. A brother perhaps of the mercery marchand said another Gentleman. Is he William Yes Sir.—I bought t'other day a fine pair of buccles at his shop said Lord George. Lady Euphrasia look'd impatient and rather out of humour. Euphrasia Have I heard said her Mother that the eldest Miss Ferris was here some days ago and desired from you to know at what school your sister was sent that she may board there too. Yes MyLady said her daughter. Her father said she wanted she should educated with young ladies of fashion. She is young and may weared off still the air one catches in a shop. replied the Mother and so saying she rose & went out of the room. Lady Euphrasia threw on me a look that spoke Poor William your feelings were inquired into but not gratified. I think Peter Fanny Ferris would not be an improper companion for Lady Euphrasia. Both families are almost alike.

Constance's Story

Translator's Note[1]

This extraordinary short story is the unpublished continuation of Charrière's novella, *Three Women*, which appeared in the collection *L'Abbé de la Tour* (1798).[2] It relates the story and background of the third woman, Constance, who originally crashed into the narrative when her carriage overturned one night in Altendorf, the small German village where the other two, Emilie and Josephine, had taken refuge, driven from their homeland by the French Revolution. For the whole of the published novella, we know nothing about Constance, other than that she is a rich widow whose husband acquired his money from unjust exploitation in the colonies, and who chooses to spend her money to promote various virtuous schemes for the relief of her friends, rather than attempt to return it. Her knowledge of the world and her wisdom set her apart from the other characters; she is rather on a par with the abbé himself, who in fact is so susceptible to her charms that he forces himself to leave the village where they had all been living so harmoniously together: this provides the framing narrative, as the abbé sets about telling the new set of friends among whom he finds himself about these three women, and when he finishes telling everyone about them, he is begged for new stories—hence the collection as a whole.

Constance is (again) a story within a story: Constance's own picaresque experiences of being treated as an object are set in counterpoint to the unfortunate story of her uncle's black mistress, ironically named Bianca. Unsurprisingly, given the fact that it was unpublished, it feels less finished than many of her other stories, and there are some abrupt switches in narrative perspective, which are rather disconcerting. It may help the reader to know that Constance's married name is Madame de Vaucourt, that her first husband was called Monsieur Le Muret, that her uncle's name is Victor, and his rich aunt Madame del Fonte. Victor and Bianca's daughter is called Blondina, and Mr. Kildary is Blondina's guardian. He is married to a cousin of Constance and Blondina's. Another female cousin is unnamed in the manuscript; we have called her Cousin Marie to avoid confusion. The maid who is forced on Constance is called Ducret, and the captain of the ship they travel to India on is called the Chevalier du Bouch ***, which is to say that his name is half withheld, in imitation of a real memoir; he is also called Monsieur du B***. The ship itself is called the *Pegasus*. One of the officers on the ship who plays a key role is called Monsieur de Mérival; his title is vicomte, or (in France, an aristocratic title did not prevent one from being called Monsieur, or Mister). Constance narrates the story to her newfound friends in Altendorf, who include Emilie and her fiancé, Theobald, as well as the vicomte, Monsieur de Mérival. At one point, Mérival takes on the narrative himself. The action takes place in Bordeaux (Constance's birthplace), Martinique (where Victor, Bianca, and Madame del Fonte's story unfolds), France, aboard the ship, in India (where Constance's father is making his fortune), and back in Paris in the early stages of the Revolution.

I was born in the famous Gironde; my father was from Bordeaux and my mother was Creole.³ In Bordeaux, my father served on one of the new law courts set up by Maupeou, which have been vilified by people who were vastly inferior to their creator.⁴ "We are falling but you will follow us," said my father to his opponents on the day the old courts were restored to power. "We may not be mature enough, but you are too mature, and we know what the consequences will be." When the Revolution came my father remembered what he called that "disastrous" measure, and said that "if we had not been destroyed the territorial tax would have been carried and France would have been saved."⁵ As one may imagine, he was not only critical about what had happened but also distressed, and it was never likely that a spirited and proud man such as he would easily submit to the scorn lavished by those eternally arrogant old authorities on those whom they cast into the wilderness. My father did not endure it for long; not only did he leave Bordeaux, but the desire to expunge his humiliation prompted him to look for a way of establishing himself outside Europe.

I was only a child at the time, and I stayed with my mother, an angelic woman who was devout without being fanatic, and as gentle as she was virtuous. She went to great pains to temper the flaws I had inherited from my father, and she did it not with long speeches but with the punishments and principally the rewards that were appropriate to my age. If I had some painful accident, "Sing, daughter; sing instead of crying," my mother would say to me. "I will give you a pretty gold necklace. That's how Henri IV's grandfather rewarded his daughter on a similar occasion; so, sing!" And I sang. If one of my friends had shamed me in some way, "Do not complain and do not seek revenge," my mother would say to me. "Tomorrow I'll give a ball for the little girls and you will have a lovely time." If only she had been able to eradicate my natural petulance. She weakened it, and that was something.

There was nothing remarkable about the rest of my education. My mother applied herself to moderating my passions and took care not to ignite the most dangerous of all, that of wishing to shine so brightly as to eclipse everyone else, to make people talk about us and prevent them from talking about anyone else. Talents seemed of little value to her in comparison with character and temperament. As for wit, she thought that we are born with as much of it as we'll ever have and that the most important thing is to avoid its errors and mad presumptuousness.

On receiving the news that my father had found in one of our colonies in the Indies what he had sought, that is, not only a very good establishment but also the hope of a brilliant fortune, my mother reacted almost with indifference.[6] She desired nothing beyond what she had. Do you want to see the picture of a tranquil soul? Here it is. Constance pulled a portrait out of her pocket that could have been her own in a slightly enhanced version had it only had a little more vivacity. I thought I could discern a slight tinge of melancholy. After we had considered it for a while, Constance looked at it herself, and her eyes reddened. Then she took up the thread of her tale. Without being animated, she was happy, or at least I think she was. All her hopes were in her daughter, and she barely missed a husband whose temperament was so at odds with her own. As for me, I was as happy as a child can be, and nothing in my character expressed any desire or need for great wealth. I combined the petulance of my father with a great deal of my mother's indolence, and it didn't take much to amuse and occupy me. I required no variety in my life and was hardly active, although I was subject to fits of impatience from time to time. If I ever emerged from my normal inactivity I would display great vivacity, but then I rarely did emerge. I can run and make great haste, as you have seen, my dear Emilie, but my preference has always been to stay in one place, and I have never exhausted my vivacity in endlessly chasing after new objects.

We were happy. A brother of my mother, Victor, arrived from Martinique and our fate was completely changed.[7] My mother, loving him tenderly, shared in his deep sadness, and the indolence that was natural to her developed into total inaction. I carried on being brought up and more or less educated by the things that surrounded me, by the discussions and sighs I heard, but I no longer was by my mother. I was about fourteen years old then. This is my uncle's story as I fitted it together from the different scraps he let fall, for he often talked without realizing that I was listening. What I have heard since convinces me that I have got nothing essential wrong, and that no one knew as much about the details of this terrible story as I did. This is one of the digressions that I warned you about, and it will be a long one. Please allow me not to curtail my memories, and to relate them in full.

When my grandfather and grandmother died they left one daughter of marriageable age and one son who was much younger. They were both in Europe for their education. The daughter married my father, while the son returned to Martinique after a few years, taking with him more personal graces than education. I believe that if he had never had more than the fortune that his parents left him, he would have been an amiable man of sense, as his character was as like my mother's as his features were, and the vestiges of the sweetest nature were still visible when I knew him. However, he became the object of the affection of an extremely rich aunt, Madame del Fonte, and she sought to divine his every wish so as to gratify it all the sooner. She would pay for his most costly fantasies, and rectify every indiscretion that could be rectified. His own mediocre inheritance was supplemented with all the misfortune of a young Croesus.[8] This woman rarely left her own plantation. Next to her own house, the prettiest in the whole island, she had a pavilion built for her nephew. He was free to invite whomsoever he wanted and to do whatever he pleased.

One can imagine how disposed he and his young friends were to take advantage of such liberty. Madame del Fonte, despite having been so thoughtless and so unreasonably indulgent in the rest of her conduct, took care to conceal young Bianca from them. Bianca was her favorite slave, the most beautiful and best proportioned of her compatriots that had ever been seen on Martinique. As black as ebony, she had been named Bianca for a joke and the name had stuck. After her nephew, Madame del Fonte loved nobody quite so much as her beautiful negress.

In her house was a closet of white marble with steps descending into a pool filled from taps placed all around the walls. The water drained away through numerous channels even quicker than it poured in, and as everything was made from marble, porcelain, and crystal, it all stayed dry, never suffering from its immersion. Bianca bathed there every day with her mistress and in fact never left it when my uncle and his young friends were on the plantation, which is to say that she entered it in the morning, only emerging in the evening once the young men had definitively withdrawn into their pavillion. I forgot to mention that the only light in the closet came from a sort of cupola and that the door was made to be indistinguishable from the rest of the walls when looked at from the outside. A key was needed to open it. One day, Madame del Fonte left her key in the lock after bathing, got dressed, and went off for a walk. Her nephew had arrived and, needing to consult her on some matter, was looking for her in every room he knew of. He came upon the key and the door of whose existence he had been entirely unaware. He opens it, and sees Bianca with water to her waist, arranging flowers in a vase. She starts laughing at the amazement of the young man, and quickly stripping the leaves from all the roses she is holding, she throws them around her. This pretty way of disturbing the water and concealing herself, this modest, ingenious, laughing, lovely gesture crowned my uncle's enchantment: from that moment he was lost in love. He sent his friends back to St. Pierre, where most of them came from, as soon as he could, and unbeknownst to them, returned alone to the pavillion. Madame del

Fonte bewailed her imprudence. It was too late to hide Bianca now, and so she let my uncle see her, flattering herself that living together at close quarters, his reason might return to him, for Bianca, although very adept at all feminine tasks, had no other talents, and her upright, naive mind had never been exercised. It seemed that a passion that was not fed by entertainment or any sympathy in taste or occupation could never become truly serious. But Bianca was moved by the love she inspired, and that added charm, along with her beauty, was enough. The young man left the plantation, returned, and plunging ever deeper into love, said to his aunt one day:

"Give me Bianca. I have to return to St. Pierre as I have been nominated to a position which requires my presence, and I will be unable to be here as much as I would like. Give me Bianca because I cannot live without her. She will serve me, but others will serve her. She will be the mistress in my house; she will be cherished; she will be happy."

"Yes, Victor, for a few weeks or a few months," said his aunt.

"No, forever," replied the young man. "I have no desire to get married."

"Does infidelity not come with marriage?" asked Madame del Fonte. "If being granted your desire is not enough, then some devious European woman will come and seduce you with those talents which seem so precious to you men when they adorn a new object. They will detach you from her; her only charm is her beauty, her only merit is her tenderness. Afterward you will tire of her, for nothing satisfies you for long."

The young man heard not a word of what had been said to him. He insisted, and his weak relative yielded, which is to say that she gave Bianca the freedom to follow Victor. He pressed her so hard that she surrendered, although not without some pain. Madame del Fonte's melancholy presentiments had passed into Bianca's soul, and moreover, she loved her. Even in her lover's embrace, she wept for her, and often wished to return. It was not until the birth of a child that she finally became reconciled to her lover and to her destiny.

"Now, master," she said to him, "I belong to you entirely, but how long will you belong to Bianca and her daughter?"

Two years and more passed without her having reason to complain of any cooling of his affection, and she reveled in her happiness and security without in any way relaxing her devotion to her duties. She it was who governed her master's household, made his clothes, kept his linens dazzling white, served him in his room and at table. The liqueurs, pastries, and preserves that he liked the most had all been prepared by her alone, and everyone envied my uncle a mistress who was as skillful and hardworking as she was beautiful and faithful.

This state might have lasted for a long time. My uncle had even written to Madame del Fonte that he was thinking of marrying Bianca and of legitimizing his daughter, who, mulatto though she was, showed signs of beauty. She was called Blondina. I have met her; the name Ebonina would have suited her very well, but despite this she was an unfailingly charming child. If Monsieur Le Muret had treated us with greater indulgence than he did, you would have met her, vicomte, aboard the *Pegasus*, and today she would be by my side.

Bianca's felicity therefore seemed assured and Madame del Fonte started to feel confident about her destiny, when a troupe of actors arrived in Saint-Domingue.[9] Two rather pretty and extremely brazen actresses separated from the rest of the troupe, having come to Saint-Domingue in the first place to exercise their every talent. I am unable to say whether they were distinguished exponents of the art they had publicly come to practice, but they excelled in the art of deception and never were coquetry, cunning, corruption, or unbridled audacity taken to such lengths. Their particular strength was in comic opera, and they had brought with them from Europe all that was newest in that genre.[10] Lacking professional actors, young people from the very best families lowered themselves to act with them, and my uncle, who was a very good musician and a passable actor, initially played in the orchestra, and then acted in a theater that he had had erected in his garden.[11] Bianca foresaw her misfortune, and so as not to have to witness an infidelity, which she felt she would be unable to endure, she begged my uncle to send her and Blondina to her old mistress. But he would not. In the bottom of his heart, he feared

Madame del Fonte's reproaches, but all he said to Bianca was that he couldn't do without her. Good God, what a situation! She had to work day and night to make a success of the shows in which her hateful rivals starred. She was in charge of lighting the theater, serving refreshments, looking after the costumes, and many other things. One day, serving drinks to her master, who had just finished singing a duet with Mlle Rosine, Bianca fell into a swoon. My uncle was very moved. "Poor Bianca! It's fatigue," he said when she came round. Bianca shook her head and said nothing. A few days later, obliged to go to a plantation that he had severely neglected, he sent a message to say that he would not be back until the evening of the following day. Bianca hesitated; she wondered whether she ought to take advantage of his absence to leave the house and seek refuge with her mistress. She was depressed and weak, and Madame del Fonte's plantation was far away; if she were met on the road, she might be brought back and treated as a runaway slave. "Bianca," she said to herself, "you no longer have a husband, and your daughter has lost her father. All that remains is a tyrant." She should have left during the night, but she spent it weeping. The second day came and was already well advanced when the two actresses arrived at my uncle's house, telling Bianca that he had told them to tell her to make them welcome, serve them, and do whatever they wanted. Bianca repeated this order to herself over and over.

"I am sorry," said Rosine, "to have left the letter I received from your master at home."

Her sister laughed at her. "Bianca has certainly no hesitation in believing us," she said.

"I did hesitate," said Bianca, "but I believe you. You have corrupted a man who was naturally good and honest to such an extent that I would believe anything."

Rosine and Marotte burst out laughing at this speech. Then they started inspecting everything around them with badly brought-up and vulgar curiosity.

"In this house there is a bath which I have heard is singularly agreeable; we wish to bathe in it."

It was a closet identical to the one Madame del Fonte had,

except that its marble was black. Bianca had asked for it to be
so. The two actresses started bathing and gave themselves up
to wild antics, ordering food, preserves, wine, and liqueurs to
be served to them there. It made Bianca choke with distress
and rage. Her master finally returned.

"It is true, is it not," said Rosine, "that you wrote to me to
come and do whatever I wanted here, and to command Bianca
to obey my sister and me as she would you?"

My uncle was stunned at such brazen behavior; he blushed
and stuttered. Bianca thought that he was blushing with shame,
and no longer harbored any doubts about the order having
been given. The two actresses continued to act the insolent
part that was more successful than they could possibly have
hoped, and seeing that they were dealing with such a weak
man, demanded jewels for each, announcing that they would
have supper with him, never slackening their insulting behavior toward Bianca or ceasing to exercise humiliatingly the
power they had usurped.

My uncle was in despair. Twenty times he was on the brink
of calling a halt to this vile scene; twenty times, as if under a
spell, he stayed mute and immobile.

Finally Bianca obtained leave to withdraw, but tormented by
the excruciating anxiety of jealousy, she was unable to sleep,
listening in spite of herself, so that she missed nothing that
could intensify her resentment and pain to their highest pitch.

It was an hour past midnight when the accursed actresses
took their leave. My uncle remained a victim to his shame and
remorse. He thought of going to find Bianca, but what could
he say to her? How could he admit he had been so weak; how
could he justify so much cruelty? He resolved to talk to her the
next day and swore to himself not only to break with the
actresses, but to have them banned from the island.

As he was getting into bed, Bianca came up to his door and
in a firm voice asked him if he would promise to send her back
to her mistress the next day. "Not tomorrow," my uncle
replied, and he wanted to add a few caressing words to console
her, but he heard that Bianca had already gone. He was not
inclined for sleep, and started to read by the light of a lamp he

had lit. In the end, fatigue brought sleep with it, and he wanted to put his book down, except that it slipped out of his hand and fell next to the table, out of reach of the bed. The lamp was still burning; a net curtain stretched over the low open window protected him from the flying insects that the light would have attracted.

Meanwhile, Bianca, furious and desperate, paces around the house and garden, the garden in which a theater has been erected. Reassured that everyone sleeps, that her master sleeps, she goes into his bedroom, not through the door but through the open window; she enters with a knife in her hand. The light is shining on her master's face. Watching him asleep, he no longer looks so guilty; motionless, she hesitates, sighs, and perhaps would have gone away if he hadn't made a slight movement. As he stirs, she recognizes in his features Rosine's lover and Bianca's tyrant, the man who refuses to end her woes and who aggravates them every day. All her fury returns. She rushes forward but her foot knocks against the fallen book, which she had not noticed. It makes a noise, and my uncle wakes up, and without clearly knowing whose hand is holding the steel he's pushing away, he shouts and calls for help. A dog barks; the whole household comes running. Bianca is surrounded.

"Let go of her, do not tie her up, do not hurt her!" shouted my uncle. "She is delirious, she is ill, she is mad."

"No," said Bianca, "I am entirely in command of my reason— take me away. I wanted to do something that is right, but I must still be punished for it, and ask only for a quick death."

My uncle tried every way of saving her he could think of; he told the judges she was with child.[12] Bianca denied it. . . . Pity, pity not Bianca but her lover. Oh what agony he suffered, how long it lasted! There was no interruption, no alleviation in a sentence of exceptional severity.[13] When he was brought to his aunt's house, he was barely recognizable, barely could he recognize her. Bianca, her sufferings, her crime, her death, were painted on their two faces; a silence of anguish sealed their lips. They did not dare speak for fear of saying or hearing things that would wrench their souls apart.

"Was it necessary to take her from me?" Madame del Fonte did say on one occasion.

"Did you teach me to restrain even the least of my desires?" replied her nephew.

After that they held back the bitter reproaches that filled their hearts, not so much out of pity for each other but so as to spare themselves.

Madame del Fonte fell into a decline and died. Whether out of negligence or because of some remaining affection for him, she had not altered the will, and left him the sole heir to her wealth. As soon as the will was read, my uncle ripped it up, and his relations, touched by his lack of self-interest, worked to secure for Bianca's daughter a niece's portion, promising to administer the money and to be guardians to the child if she ever lost her father. It was clear that the unhappy man could not live long.

He swiftly settled his affairs, and deluding himself perhaps that his remorse and regrets might in some way be decreased if he fled this island that was no longer anything other than a Tartarean pit to him, he took ship for Europe and arrived in my mother's house with Blondina. The sight of her caused him greater pain than pleasure, and yet he could not be parted from her even for a few hours without feeling excruciating conflict and torment.

This is the man that my mother and I lived with for nearly two years. He cost me my mother: first he took her attentions away from me, and then her life. He had not yet died when, overwhelmed with sorrow and fatigue, she caught an inflammatory fever, which also affected the nerves. She died a few hours after he. I was alone in the house with Blondina and the servants. I placed the child with a neighbor who loved her, and had the two corpses laid side by side. I kept vigil by them night and day until I was completely sure that they were no longer my mother or my mother's brother, but dead bodies that were beginning to rot.[14] Such courage displayed by a sixteen-year-old was greatly admired. Courage! What does that mean? I took little interest in the funeral and almost forgot to put on mourning; my insensibility was criticized. Will no one ever be reasonable? Oh, let us never abandon what we have loved if it may still breathe and feel outrage at our cowardly desertion! Emilie, if I die by your side, do not leave others to determine whether I am dead; do for me what I did for my mother and my uncle, but no urn, please; no inscription, no cypresses.[15] They would be useless to me, as I would never be able to see them, although if I did, perhaps I would take offense at being surrounded by such a number of safeguards against overhasty oblivion. I have not forgotten my lovely mother or my unhappy uncle in the slightest.

The following day Madame de Vaucourt said to us: "I do at least owe one piece of luck to the mournful story I told you— or perhaps I should call it bad luck—which is never to have fallen in love." Bianca! Victor! What cautionary tales! To desert the person who loves us, or be deserted by the one we love, what crime, what misery! And it seems to be inevitable. Eternal love and eternal charm seem not to be part of human nature, and if it does sometimes occur, does death not come to wrench such union asunder? But it was not this last consideration that frightened me; Bianca and Victor were my safeguard, and if ever anyone seemed agreeable to me, I immediately looked for his faults and reminded myself of my own. I said to myself, "This thing would be exasperating, that thing would be so boring. If it is I who starts to become detached, then perhaps I resemble my uncle and will finish up like him, and if it's the opposite . . ." and I shuddered to think of it. When I arrived in Altendorf I saw, Emilie, that you were already in love, and that you were passionately loved in return. Do not think that I would ever have tried to encourage these feelings, even though I approved of them; they had already been born, and I wished that they would make you happy. I now not only wish for that; I have hope. Sense like yours, allied to such a sweet, noble, and pure soul, will never allow itself to be abused or seduced. You will conduct your life in such a way as to create the best conditions for happiness and the fulfillment of duty. And your Theobald too; Theobald who has made your happiness his business, his glory, and his felicity will set aside everything that might distance him or even distract him from you. You will be faithful and happy, I venture to believe, and if death ever comes to take one of you away, the consciousness of having made that person happy will soften the other's pain. But why this digression? Why am I again telling you things that move you and that move me too? I should just pick up the thread of my tale and follow it.

Eight days after the deaths of my mother and uncle, I entered a convent with Blondina, and devoted myself to her alone. My father wrote to his relations instructing them to look after all my interests and to find me a reasonable husband of more or less mature age who would come with me to join him, and whose fortune he would make. To make the process quicker, he included all the necessary authorizations and letters of attorney. A search was set in motion, it was much discussed in public, and Monsieur Le Muret presented himself. He was looked upon as a kind and sensible man, he was relatively well brought up, his face was tolerably pleasant, he was thirty-six or thirty-eight years old, and claimed to be distantly related to my family. As no one cared much about me, my family were satisfied with believing in appearances and gleaning what could be learned from vague information. "No one can blame me for it; he is thoroughly eligible." That is what I heard a man responsible for "all my interests" say as he devoured a capon with truffles. I asked him to separate everything that had belonged to my mother from everything that had belonged to Blondina's father so that she could take possession of it; already, I had heard talk of how I ought to have a claim to it. "Your husband will sort it all out," said my epicurean. "I would be mad to give myself any trouble over something which is nothing to do with me," and he hastened my marriage so as to avoid having to hear anything else about business.

Do you know what this man of sense on whom I was being bestowed was like? He supplanted his older brother in the affections of the family, who had called the brother a numbskull for having married a very pretty but penniless girl with whom he was head over heels in love. My future husband had neglected his own father, a decent man and similarly dubbed a 'numbskull' for having lost all his money. Monsieur Le Muret was extremely attentive to uncles, aunts, and spinster cousins; he adopted their tastes and their fancies, was passionate about flower arranging with one, about hunting with another, was an out-and-out bigot with a third and always frugal and careful. He had never displayed what any of these people called a single vice and had been the saint and the wise man of both family and canton until the point when his older brother returned in a state of the most extreme indigence to implore the compassion of his relatives, his beautiful wife on the verge of death, and his charming children in rags. The relatives, more absurd and silly than wicked or hard-hearted, were extremely sorry to see him in such a state and hardened a little toward the inflexible sage, when it emerged that having acted every part, the single thing he could not feign was sensibility. He knew that a husband was being solicited for me and that apart from the wealth I inherited from my mother, I would also be offering the opportunity to acquire a great fortune. What a lure! Monsieur Le Muret did not waste a moment, and thanks to a reputation whose basis no one thought to inspect, he was rewarded with poor Constance.

The day after our wedding we went back to my home, and I requested him to arrange for Blondina to be given all her father's effects. He eluded my attempts, then delayed, and finally he refused point-blank. All the furnishings of the house were put up for sale, and no difference was made between the many things that belonged to my uncle and everything else. Mr. Le Muret went so far as to sell my uncle's clothes, his jewels, and even the pianoforte, which Blondina was just starting to play very charmingly. On that same day, one of her guardians, Mr. Kildary, arrived from Martinique, as much my relation as hers; that is to say, he was the husband of one of my mother's first cousins.

He found Blondina on my lap, and me in tears. Without any greater bond than the harmony of our sentiments, we told each other what we thought of what was happening. He nonetheless showed greater moderation than I did, and although he did not wish to contradict me for fear of embittering me further, he urged me to respect Monsieur Le Muret, not in himself, but because he was the master of my destiny. In addition, he put a stop to the looting by showing the will, which named him as my uncle's principal legatee and his executor. My uncle had taken this course in order to secure his wealth for his daughter.

I had never considered that I might be separated from Blondina, and I supposed that the only reason her guardian had come to Europe was to sort out her affairs. But after some days spent in continued delusion, I learned that he had come to take her back, and proposed to bring her up in her native country. Oh what anguish I felt when I found this out! I forgot my husband's ways of proceeding and implored him to help me get permission for her to go with us to join my father; he found a thousand difficulties preventing us from doing it.

"But think, I have only her that I know and that I love," I cried out, sobbing.

"You will have me, my dear wife," said Le Muret so phlegmatically and hypocritically that all of a sudden I hated him. Scourging him with a look that confounded him, I wiped my tears and, in a firmer voice, I said to my cousin:

"Sir, take Blondina. She would be very unhappy with a husband and a wife such as us."

"What is that? What does my dear wife mean?" said Le Muret, completely disconcerted.

I said nothing and left the room.

In the room I then entered was a young woman, another cousin, whose name was Marie and who had overheard the whole scene.

"How immature you are!" she said. "To ask, beg, or implore a man like that! To think you could melt a husband who is made of marble! I have one who is no equal to yours for selfishness, avarice, or callousness, but if I didn't lead him by the nose, he'd be pushing me about in an instant."

"Are you talking seriously?" I asked her.

"I am," she replied. "Come to supper at my house tomorrow and you will see. In your place I would have held on to Blondina and the pianoforte and everything else I wanted. Believe me. Laugh at Le Muret. Do not let the man who has acted the

slave to an entire aged family make a slave out of you. Treat
him as he deserves. Keep reminding him that he is expecting
his fortune from your father and that you can either help him
or ruin him. No childish scruples. Obey your head in every
instance and if by chance he expires out of vexation you can
consider the job well done."

I was barely older than sixteen and my mother had not
killed off the old man in me to such an extent that I was unable
to appreciate this lesson.[16] I became very close to this cousin,
and it was as if I was living in a new world whose existence my
mother, far from telling me about, had never even let me suspect. I enjoyed being amused and astonished by it, but when
the moment came to separate from Blondina, my heart cast it
all away and I thought that it would break in two. My cousin
let me cry for a few days before she said to me:

"Do you not see that that child would have been a great
embarrassment to you? At your age there are better things to
do than pamper a little Moorish girl.[17] Come about with me to
ballets and plays. You won't have the chance to do it again soon
unless you persuade Le Muret to leave without you, which
would perhaps be a good idea. His cunning features betray a
terrible man, or so it seems to me."

You will perhaps be surprised to hear that my cousin Mr.
Kildary, Blondina's guardian, had given me a similar warning.
He said he was in despair about not being able to delay his
departure and promised that if I and my cousin were able to
find some way of avoiding the voyage he would return to
Europe with his wife, children, and Blondina, and would consider himself to be my guardian as well as hers.

"This is no marriage," said he. "It is the monstrous combination of inexperience and candor with avarice and deceit."

But what could I do? My cousin Marie was too young and
too flighty to help me take such an extraordinary course, while
her father was much too heedless even to consider doing anything about it. Meanwhile, Monsieur Le Muret, who was desperate to go and whose time at least seemed to be fully taken
up with the business of preparing for our departure, suddenly
announced at the moment when I was least expecting it that

the rest of our furniture was to be delivered to the country house of one of his uncles, and that it was there that we would wait for the *Pegasus* to be ready to set sail. I was hardly given time to say good-bye to cousin Marie. After some days spent in indescribable misery and boredom, the wind blew favorably, and I left my native land with as much grief as if it had not in fact been a place of suffering for me. In the launch that transferred me to the ship I looked at Monsieur Le Muret and the deep sea in turn. There at least I have a resource, a haven, if things come to the worst, I said to myself. Do you remember, vicomte, my arrival on board?

"Oh yes," he said. "You amazed me. To begin with you were somber and pensive, and then you quickly became cheerful, dancing about everywhere. I didn't know what to make of you."

I decided to follow my cousin Marie's advice to the letter, and keep myself busy, entertained, and interested in anything rather than fall a victim to my grief or my enemy. I had learnt to consider Monsieur Le Muret as a man who would let me die of anguish rather than cede the slightest part of his empire or the least of his interests.

We brought with us anything that was likely to please my father, of whose tastes he had carefully informed himself. Anything affecting my own pleasure or convenience, he despicably economized on. For example, in his choice of a maid for me, he gave warning of his despotism. Instead of a lovely girl who had been precious to me for years, he forced me to take a woman called Ducret, a trollop and worse, a spy, as I was later to discover. In Bordeaux, whether because there was no opportunity or because Monsieur Le Muret was too busy with his own affairs, I had not noticed that he was a jealous man, but as a suspicious egotist, attentive at all times to his own interests, he was bound to be jealous, as in fact turned out to be the case.

After several days at sea everyone aboard the ship had found amusement except for him. He was often laughed at for his taciturnity, and I was more likely to mock him than anyone, without our ever obtaining anything more than an underhand smile in response. But gradually he began to be left out completely, and started throwing sinister glances at me, the Chevalier du Bouch***, who was our captain and a witty, educated, lovely man, and at the other officers, but no one riled him quite so much as the vicomte, Monsieur de Mérival, as we called him, who was the youngest, and doubtless in his eyes, the most handsome of them all. We played thousands of childish games. One day Monsieur de Mérival asked me what my first name was. I told him. "Oh what a pretty name!" he exclaimed.

"Well then, call me Constance, and for me it will be like hearing the voices of my uncle, my mother, Blondina, or my cousin Marie, all of whom I love a great deal. I have never been called anything but Constance by all the people I have loved. When I hear myself called Madame Le Muret I think I hear hatred or indifference speaking."

"But my dear wife, to be called Constance by a young man would not be decent."

"Oh it would be very decent; I know what I'm talking about," I said to him. "My cousin Mr. Kildary was handsome and still young, and he called me Constance." The vicomte was in a very difficult position. When he addressed me as madam, I did not reply, and when he called me Constance, Monsieur Le Muret twitched.

"Good!" I said to him one day, in the presence of the treacherous Ducret. "Just call me Constance; he'll get used to it."

The next day I saw that Monsieur Le Muret was looking paler and more serious, yellower, than he usually did. Monsieur de Mérival, on the other hand, was livelier than he ever had been. The word *custom* was uttered by chance.

"We do not become *accustomed*; we do not *get used* either to certain people or to certain things," said Monsieur Le Muret, throwing me a furious look. Monsieur de Mérival paid no attention to this speech. But I trembled and felt as if I'd been turned to ice by what he had said, without really knowing why. My sudden pallor was noticed.

"What is it?" asked the captain. "What is the matter? Are you seasick? Let's drink some punch; that will set you to rights."

We drank, and everyone became very cheery. Monsieur Le

Muret himself, who had doubtless noticed the impression he had made on me, seemed to cheer up a bit, and I was so well deceived that I showed him greater affection than I ever had before. And yet his rage had not abated; he left us for a moment, and I have since discovered that it was to sharpen his sword and load his pistols. He returned. Monsieur de Mérival and I were keeping ourselves amused with completing sorts of rhyming couplets that Monsieur du Bouch*** had given us. *Ocean* and *ark* were the two rhymes that were supposed to end the four lines. Let me have a look in the old notecase that I always keep about me. I think the four lines the vicomte and I wrote are still there.

> *When on the perfidious ocean*
> *With Bacchus love embarks*
> *We brave them all—sea, wind, e'en sharks,*
> *To ride the gales of emotion.*[18]

"Oh good God!" exclaimed the vicomte. "You remind me of the last happy moments I ever had."

"Here are mine," said Constance. "The aim is to tell the truth, not to boast."

> *If ever I perceive my ark*
> *Approaching stormy oceans*
> *Then as soon as I this remark*
> *I steer back to calmer motions*[19]

I spent a lot of time thinking up these bad verses. "This is very bad," I said to Monsieur Le Muret, "but I hope that you are still able to understand my thought and my intention."

I don't know whether he had the necessary sangfroid to read them nor if he heard what I said, but at the time I never doubted that he did. He smiled at me and looked at the vicomte's lines, which I had barely read. The next moment we were called to prayer. I put all these scraps in my notecase and then, without a glance behind me or any feeling of anxiety, believing that everything had been set to rights, and sternly stating my intention to myself never to cause Monsieur Le Muret such serious displeasure again, I stepped out of the cabin and went to the place where prayer was held. I was tranquilly listening and praying when suddenly I heard shouts and a horrible commotion. Monsieur de Mérival . . . but he will be able to tell you himself better than I can; I only heard about it secondhand.

"Oh heavens, what are you demanding of me?" exclaimed the vicomte.

"To conquer the feeling which should have been soothed by the story I just told," said Constance. "Do you think it has cost me nothing to recall all the excesses which led to this scene? Ultimately, it is I who is to blame for what happened and for the anguish you still feel. I am more truly to blame for Monsieur Le Muret's death than you, but I was so young, and I meant no wrong at all. Moreover, Monsieur Le Muret had displayed such an unpleasant side to me, that everything I knew about him then and everything I have since learnt leads me to conclude that he is so little to be regretted either by me or by society, that I have some trouble in knowing how to feel any reasonable remorse. If I had any, it would be for having caused you such bitter penitence. It is only since meeting you again, vicomte, that I have begun to feel that I was at fault, having long thought of myself as completely absolved. I felt with pain that no thoughtless behavior is pardonable and that our smallest faults may have the most dire consequences. My cousin Marie and her advice, me, my behavior, all these mad and reckless actions, today seem criminal to me, and for love of you, I wish I had never been advised by anyone other than my mother, and had spent my life as wisely and moderately as she herself did. But we cannot call back the past. Soften my regrets—overcome what I call your weakness and tell us about a scene whose well-known details will exonerate you from all blame and which would exonerate you in your own eyes too if you only had as much reason as feeling."

"Well," said the vicomte, "I will obey, but permit me to summarize as much as possible. Words spoken out loud have a force which our thoughts, however much anguish they cause, do not have. They are sharpened blades in a bloody wound.

This is why Victor and his aunt remained silent. Monsieur Le Muret stopped me as I was trying to leave the Captain's cabin."

"Go and fetch your sword or your pistols," he ordered me. "And choose your second as soon as you can. Here is mine," he said to a man he walked up to, and who tried to refuse him. "No," he said. "Be so indulgent as to prevent something worse than a duel, as I can no longer endure this young man staying alive. An accursed brother stole a fortune and a reputation which I spent thirty years working to secure; I abandoned a mistress whom I loved and betrayed a thousand promises to marry a child whom I do not know, while another child turns me into the toy of the child I am obliged to live with, to follow whom I am exiled from my country. I am a prey to my regrets as a lover and also to my jealousy as a husband. I can endure no more; go and fetch your weapons, I will bring mine and let us go to the place the furthest removed from where everyone else is assembled."

"I will come with you," said one of my friends.

We took our weapons to the designated place. Monsieur Le Muret and his second were waiting for us there.

He wanted to start fighting immediately.

"Let us start with the sword," he said. "And as we risk being heard and separated, if it goes on too long, we will curtail matters with pistols."

"For pity's sake, wait a moment," I said to him. "I would give anything in the world not to fight with you. I have never hated you, and you have just moved me to extreme pity. What! You had to abandon a mistress, and now risk being killed by me! Your death would grieve her even more than your infidelity, and your wife perhaps loves you, a wife of sixteen years of age—"

"Enough of this concern," said Monsieur Le Muret, drawing his sword. "En garde! Let us be done with this."

"But," said I, "I am not at all in love with Madame Le Muret, nor is she with me, and if you desire it I will give you my word of honor never to speak to her again in all my life."

Monsieur Le Muret ground his teeth.

"En garde!" he said again. I was going to reply again, but

my friend interrupted. "That's enough," he said. "It will look as if you are afraid."

"That's it, he is trembling," shouted Monsieur Le Muret. "His fear is a presentiment."

Simultaneously he rushed up to me in a fury, and struck a blow which I warded off, and in so doing, wounded him. The wound was not deep, and I had not struck hard, but I had aimed so accurately at the heart that he fell, convulsed, and died. I fainted and fell next to him; when I awoke I found myself in the hold, with irons on my feet and hands. Our two seconds were treated more or less as I was, until their testimony was heard in front of the tribunal, and backed up by the entire crew. We were unanimously acquitted and it was recognized that the fight had been forced on us. But I have never acquitted myself. My old gaiety and its mad games have not only disappeared forever, but even to think of them causes me pain. It was with that gaiety and those games that I tormented a man into forcing me to kill him.

Monsieur Le Muret ground his teeth.[20]

"En garde!" he said again. I might have replied, but my friend interrupted. "That's enough," he said. "It will look as if you are afraid."

"He's trembling," Monsieur Le Muret then shouted out, with a sort of fierce joy. "His fear is a presentiment."

"You are mistaken," I said, as I warded off a blow he was striking, and, having greater sangfroid than he, I strike a blow that stretches him out at my feet. We call and shout out for a surgeon. . . . I can still see the convulsions, which I then thought showed he was still alive. He was dead. I have seen death since, I have been surrounded by it, threatened with it, I have ordered it and perhaps even given it, but I have never felt a sensation similar to that moment. The impression it left will never be erased. By order of the captain I was put in irons and taken to the bottom of the hold. The two seconds were treated more or less as I was, and Monsieur du B*** forbade anyone to have any communication with us beyond what was strictly necessary, for fear, as he has since explained, that the testimony of our friends to the tribunal of the colony where we were to disembark would lose something of its force. This tribunal acquitted me but I have never acquitted myself. What I condemned in myself was not so much a fight and murder that had been thrust on me, but the mad gaiety and lack of consideration that had led to them. I renounced them forever, and even had I not renounced them, they had left me. I had not only the death of Monsieur Le Muret to contemplate but also everything he had told me about his life, and it was as if in my imagination a veil of black crepe had draped itself over society, our institutions, and the world.[21] That crepe is still there. I see everything in black. Nothing makes me feel sadder than when I look at myself, and so I have learned to look quickly elsewhere. I keep myself very busy and avoid thought as much as I can. And thus have I learned to make my existence bearable.

"Have I not succeeded in taking away some portion of your regret?" asked Constance, who was very moved.

"No," said the vicomte. "Not yet. On the contrary, you have brought my pain back to life. It had subsided a little. But it will pass. I will be as I was before, or better, perhaps."

"I barely breathed," said Constance, "until Monsieur de Mérival's acquittal. My eagerness to defend him encouraged people to believe that I was more interested in preserving him than I was, and the more I swore there was nothing between us apart from childish games, the less anyone was inclined to believe me. I know that Monsieur de Mérival was told that it was his duty to leave the instant he was freed so as to prevent my thoughtlessness from compromising us both. I did passionately desire to ask his forgiveness for the captivity, trouble, and in fact for all the disasters I had brought on him. My servant Ducret, to whom I confided this, offered to arrange for me to see him in secret. "In secret!" I exclaimed. "Why in secret?" But this word enlightened me as to how indecent it was for me to see him at all, and I abandoned the plan. Ducret's offer also enlightened me as to what her role and conduct on the *Pegasus* had been—until that point I had never thought about it. I sent her packing in disgrace, and I was wrong to do so. Wicked people have to be carefully managed, whatever class they come from. Hatred and circumstances can make the least among them strong enough to be harmful. To send her away more gently would have been enough, as I realized an hour or two too late, and with that thought, a crowd of others came jostling into my mind. Monsieur Le Muret's death had suddenly turned into a kind of abundant mine for all sorts of thoughts that propelled me out of childhood into a sort of maturity, although I still retained a certain amount of both my petulance and natural indolence. What petulance I still had has since been described, depending on the occasion, as amiable, praiseworthy, and precious liveliness, or as dangerous and blameworthy haste; the truth is somewhere in between."

As soon as I was able to begin to put off my mourning black, as soon as I was able to meet the inhabitants of the colony and those who passed through from so many different places, I received numerous marks of esteem and admiration. My story had not so much tarnished my reputation as added a certain fascination to my person. A seventeen-year-old Andromaque attracted the gaze of all, and even without my wealth I could have made a good marriage.[22] I was loved by people who did not and could not marry. I was sought by many men whose attentions were flattering to me, but I did not want another husband like Monsieur Le Muret, or a marriage for love, or love without marriage. I urged my father to let me breathe for a while, free of all chains, without any bond to anyone apart from him. As he was lovable, I loved him because I wanted to. He was indulgent and generous with me over my marriage as in every other way, and it was entirely of my own free will that fifteen or eighteen months after my arrival I married a man who had been consistently attentive but never insistent. I have never met another person who was so clever and had so little desire to show it. His manners were characteristic of no particular country or coterie, although they were pleasing to all. He knew all modern languages but only spoke his own unless absolutely forced to. In need, he could do whatever had to be done, although there was never any display or haste. On the contrary, he had to be pressed to do something that he knew someone else was capable of doing or saying. He gave the other person time, without even pointing out any unimportant error. Do not suppose, however, that this is because he was one of those people who are serious and reserved because they are indifferent to everything that is happening around them or because they have decided not to let themselves be measured or assessed so that they can seem immense, unassessable. No, it was nothing like that. His mind was at once so piercing and so calm that he always knew when it was the right moment to do something, and he would handle it with greater delicacy than urgency. This man had lived with my father for a long time and had the same easy morality as he. I have never met with anything so extreme elsewhere: they had it in either the most or the least damaging form. Their morality was so relaxed, and yet so unlike anything resembling depravity, that it almost passed unnoticed, did not degrade them, and was never shocking. They had no perverse maxims or ever did anything lacking in decency, and if their subalterns ever went beyond a certain level in vice they were severely reined back.

While they reigned, so to speak, over this colony, no one raised a voice against them, and yet I do not think that it was out of loyalty. My lack of penetration on this matter did not displease them. Whenever they saw me measure, weigh out, and pay merchants with the most rigorous exactitude for what they would have been only too happy to give me in return for a good word in the right quarter, my father would simply smile.

"She's doing very well," my husband would say, and he would help me to make sure that everything happened the way I wanted it to. I lived for a long while oblivious to the fact that we were paid to allow certain things that everybody was already allowed, as well as some others that should never have been allowed at all. Innocence had to pay for its security, vice for its impunity. Our protection was sufficient to safeguard the least adept, the most negligent, and the most iniquitous; it was necessary to the most capable and to the most scrupulous . . . to the most scrupulous! What am I saying? In these climes where people only endure the burning, suffocating heat so that they can earn money, which itself cannot be acquired without trickery and fraud, have I ever met a single person whose scrupulousness I would swear to? And even if that were the only price paid, and one that has to be earned back again so as to buy the freedom to do legitimate things, is that not already enough of a misdemeanor? It is true that you cannot corrupt corrupted honor, and yet if people have no choice but to follow perverse customs, out of greed they still embellish the perverted imaginings of those who preceded them. To begin with, as I said, I did not notice any of this. My father and my husband loved my innocence and concealed the truth so that I could retain it. Perhaps once they were sufficiently wealthy they would both have liked to return to the honesty that neither of them had lost the feeling for, but I think that they would have hardly dared to say it out loud, for fear of how it might be received. Neither knew if the other would become angry or consider it absurd. I believe that this was their situation. Perhaps they would never have been quite able to admit how wrong their previous conduct had been, and to have adopted a new one would have been tantamount to such an admission. And yet, unless I am much mistaken, it was their timidity toward one another that was the principal obstacle. And are we sure that a similar difficulty is not what has prevented many people from returning to the moderation, sense, and virtue that perhaps they missed? Perhaps there are many émigrés who thought of saying, "Let's go home while there's still time; if we love our King and our religion not with the fanaticism we lay claim to but as they deserve to be loved, then we must not desert the former and abandon the latter. Let us go home, let us make generous sacrifices and resist with courage so as to save our country and ourselves. Robespierre, Barère, Saint-Just were men, not tigers, much less hyenas; would they never have stopped to think: enough blood, enough horror, we must stop the executioners!"[23] If one of them had said it, perhaps the others would have eagerly voiced their own opinion, the hope of their heart that they had not previously dared to express. When surrounded by crooks and brigands, no one dares to express their revulsion at what is happening, for fear of being treated as a future informer, but in other sorts of groups I think shame produces the same effect as that direr fear. I believe that people who are half-decent would like, but do not dare, to say, "I am beginning to feel my conscience and to respect strict virtue"; I think that many kings would like, but don't dare, to say, "I am beginning to recognize the rights of the people"; many nobles, that "I am beginning to believe that our superiority over the common people is a fantasy"; many devout catholics, that "I am beginning to believe that it is possible to worship God without the aid of the Pope, and that to worship Him in a field is as good as worshipping him in a church."[24] Dare to speak, all you reasonable people, and if you, and you, are agitated by the shouting that you hear in place of applause, the shouting itself will identify you to your equals, and if you are rejected by your respective associates, you will unite among yourselves, and become the Areopagus of the world.[25]

Perhaps my husband loved me more than he wanted me to know. He used to say from time to time that nothing was so inconvenient for a wife as an amorous husband because there was no way of being sure that he wasn't jealous. He never discussed his feelings for me for longer than half of a quarter of an hour, but he took every opportunity to give me pleasure or spare me pain, and I no sooner wished for something than he gave it to me, or feared something than the object of my fear was removed. On once hearing my father tease me about the real or feigned passion of a man who was famous both for his wit and for his name, my husband said:

"I hope that your daughter will regard his passion with indifference. He can't be as clever as he seems, seeing as he sets so much store by it and goes to such lengths to display it. There is no need to display an inexhaustible treasure; one trusts in it, uses it, and that's all. Nor will that man stay here long. I would take pleasure in my wife's happiness whatever the cause, but were she to suffer, I would be the unhappiest of men. It is vital that for the love of herself, and of me, she avoid storing up regrets."

This was the only husbandly or loverly speech he ever made me, and it is clear that it was not what a jealous husband or demanding lover would say. Everything that he and my father did in respect to me was characterized by considerate, kind generosity. In my marriage contract, I had been given everything that is normally given in such cases, while in their wills these two men left their entire fortune to me, and they had also made certain acquisitions in my name whose ownership they wished to pass to me directly. Another time they made more acquisitions on my behalf under other names, and when they sent Mr. Kildary all the documents about my claims to their wealth, he was amazed by so much ingenious foresight. Was their thirst for gain and their indefatigable activity a mania; did they think that I'd be happier the richer I became; or had they become convinced that the rich would soon be almost reduced to poverty, that ruin would fall on the colonies, Holland and England, that Germany would be devastated, France overrun by thorns, its buildings in ruins, its fields lying fallow, neither land nor sea, industry or trade, agriculture or crafts capable of feeding mankind, and piles of gold needed to buy the smallest loaf? My husband and my father loved me, and amassed wealth for me that cost them their leisure and their life. I have paid them back with torrents of tears.

It was not until our return to Europe at the beginning of the Revolution that I came properly to understand this system of greed, its ways and excuses. I was no longer a child, and they knew that they had nothing to fear from my imprudence, believing that I had wisdom enough neither to aim at seraphic perfection nor to require it of others in the depths of a robbers' cave. This is without exaggeration the only label that can be given to almost every single legislator, minister, person who was denounced, and denouncer. The host of scoundrels was without number, and although many of them have been named, they will never all be named. To do that we would have to clear the whole of our poor nation. Yes, poor nation. Many people possessed only what they had stolen, and the great multitude of scoundrels was the justification for each individual scoundrel. It was only ever a thief who was being stolen from, only ever a cheat who was being caught. False witness, outrageous memories, and fraudulent deals were only ever made at the expense of someone who had previously done the same things, or would have done them, given half a chance, all day long. At that time I was still pining after some of my old refinements. "Why should I be allowed to do this?" I would ask myself of one thing or another that I now judged to be iniquitous. Why not? My father would only laugh: "Why should we let someone else get a good deal when we thought of it first? One hundred thousand *écus* are as good in my pocket as in my neighbor's."[26] At times I had aims that were more lofty than merely trying to prevent some lucrative fraud. Admiring the courage of the Queen and the geniality of the King, feeling sorry for their children, and respecting Princess Eli's virtues, I wanted to gain admittance to their court so that I could stop them from plotting and compromising each other, or weakly trying to attach themselves to some reed or another.[27] If simple resolute firmness was no longer of any use, I was mad enough to want to persuade them to leave, to abdicate, to abandon everything rather than abase themselves and be destroyed. But my one-sided struggle was not successful,[28] and every day their enemies gained ground and strength. At that time they were imprisoned in the Tuileries and must have had great need, or so I believed, of entertainment, conversation, and distraction. I flattered myself that I could give them all this and entertain them as I did the Baron d'Altendorf, or win their confidence as I did Emilie's.[29] I had pretty wicker baskets, laquer cabinets, ivory armchairs, precious gems, rare shells, birds of exquisite beauty, and a little monkey unlike any other in Europe. I flattered myself that I could amuse them with all this and with the tales I would tell; I thought that I would finally find a way of saying something reasonable to them. To secure the position of a lady-in-waiting would be enough for my purposes—the young princess would adore me, the queen would enjoy listening to me. Was I not perhaps just as clever as Madame Diane de Polignac, and as many others, none of whom had seen the ocean, the Indies, or crossed the line like I have?[30]

I did not dare confide my plans or my fervor and its romantic pride to anyone other than Mr. Kildary. I forgot to tell you that he had arrived in Paris at almost the same time as I. You can imagine how happy we were to see each other and what eternal conversations we had. He had a great deal of leisure time to spend listening to me. He had arrived from Martinique after having sent his wife, children, and Blondina to the Anglo-American islands, where he had friends and also compatriots, being English by birth. He had hoped to save his country, the blacks, the whites, the plantations, and the trade from decrees that were too hasty and seemed likely to be better only for killing.[31] Equally incapable, however, of intrigue or of receiving or making any payments for any purpose, for good or ill, he gave up trying to do the good he had hoped. If he did not leave France, it was because he did not know whether he'd be safe at home. He may also have foreseen the difficulties I might yet find myself in, and without telling me, and having feelings of strong friendship and love for me, he stayed. He sold some of his possessions in Martinique as well as everything Blondina owned. My husband bought them and gave them to me.

"We cannot know," he said, "whether you might not very much like to finish your days in your mother's and uncle's native country."

And thus I became the owner of Madame del Fonte's plantation. The pavilion and the white marble bath are my property, and are let at a measly price to a negro who has been a free man for many years, and in whom Mr. Kildary has complete confidence. He is generally supposed to be the owner of the estate and has preserved it until now from steel, fire, and from falling into complete neglect. People no longer work as they used to; they are indolent and demand payment.

But let me return to myself and to my virtuous and presumptuous intentions for the public good and for the salvation of the royal family. Anyone who has any sense and virtue will have wished to govern the state and the world at least once in his life. For some people this madness is active and is propelled and perpetuated by the movement it generates; for others it is only temporary and is limited to their thoughts. In my case, Mr. Kildary contained it and cured me of it. He represented to me that no one would ever believe that I was sacrificing part of my liberty uniquely for the benefit of others, and that people would not fail to ascribe my zeal to my desire to further the ambitions of my husband and father.

"What ambition?" I said. "Do they not do enough money transactions without me or the court, and how could my place as a lady-in-waiting possibly aid them?"

"Perhaps not at all," he replied. "But neither the public nor your father or husband would ever be convinced of it. They would think that you would be able to bring one or the other or perhaps both to prominence and that perhaps they would be chosen for the projects that so many people are already trying to obtain for themselves, despite knowing how difficult it is to keep them and how harmful to be associated with them. This is what would be said to the people whom you would most wish to persuade of your disinterested zeal, and they would be prejudiced against you, your father, and your husband. And in fact, however little you were seen to be in favor, your father and husband would ask more of you than you wanted or were able to do for them. . . ."

"But really," I said to Mr. Kildary, "are they thinking of posts in the ministry?"

"No doubt," he replied. "I have evidence of it, and why should they not? Many people are, and they are not half so able."

I was absolutely amazed. Neither of them had ever let me catch even a glimpse of such aims. Perhaps they hid them from each other, and did not tell me for fear of being betrayed to the other. Mr. Kildary suspected that this was the reason for their reserve, and did not doubt that after so many years of collaboration these two men had, once in Paris, become rivals in their ambitions. I could not believe it myself, and the explanation of their silence seemed rather to be owing to their long custom of never talking to me about things that were less than purely pleasant, or about anything that did not concern me personally. By this time they curbed themselves much less than before, as I have said, but although they saw that I would be less overwhelmed by the relaxed principles they held about anything concerning their interests than I might have been previously, and knew that I was in no mood to start behaving like a Don Quixote, forever armed and blade in hand, in defense of the sort of probity that no one believed in anymore, they also saw that I was neither favorable to nor even capable of any intrigue. What would have been the good of telling me about their plans? My father rarely talked, and my husband never merely for the pleasure of it. If his projects were known to those who undertook the same career, it is very straightforward to suppose that they dreaded him as much as I have been told they did, and I do not doubt that his recognizable superiority contributed a great deal to the hatred they bore him. He would have succeeded in doing what he had set out for himself, if not more scrupulously, then at least with more courage and truth than anyone. His zeal for the task at hand would not have been diverted or tainted, if I may venture to use such a term, by the hope of casting everyone else into shade or the pleasure of showing off. If we were able to read his memoirs today we would not see him justifying his own cleverness, which he never esteemed as anything other than an instrument and never thought of as a precious treasure that was worthy of admiration.[32] He would not even have explained his errors and faults. If he had been successful, he would have let his successes speak for themselves, and if he had failed, he would have kept silent. I am imagining memoirs, but it is absurd to do so; he would never have written any.

Saint Anne

(1799)[1]

"She doesn't know how to read! Can you believe it, she doesn't know how to read!" said Mademoiselle de Rhedon, Madame de Rieux, and Mademoiselle de Kerber all at once to St. Anne, as Mademoiselle d'Estival left the avenue in front of the château de Missillac, taking a path across a meadow on her way back to the small holding where she lived.

At his mother's urging, St. Anne had fled France during Robespierre's reign. He had sought refuge in a neutral country, and therefore had no difficulty being allowed to come back. He returned on July 2, 1797, at nine o'clock in the morning.[2]

He was eagerly awaited. His mother had assembled his female relations to welcome him. Their fathers, husbands, and sons had all perished, or were still, like other members of the French nobility, living in that sad exile that they had brought upon themselves, initially freely chosen, but later enforced, and whose imprudence has since been so thoroughly deplored.[3]

All these ladies wept on seeing St. Anne again, and he felt a great deal himself—he had just traveled across the Vendée![4] His mother introduced him to his cousin Mademoiselle de Rhedon, who lived with her. She was an orphan. The nation had just returned her father's possessions to her, and during the desperate times, she had been left the sole surviving heir of two uncles.

To begin with, St. Anne was regaled with such grim tales that he wished he had never returned. The ladies telling them seemed to enjoy it, and as he barely responded, and not once exclaimed in horror, they thought he lacked feeling, and prolonged what they did not realize was torture. At midday, just

as he was about to beg them for mercy, he saw Mademoiselle
d'Estival walk in. Almost without noticing what he was doing,
he went up to her and relieved her of a basket of rosy cherries
that she was bringing Madame de St. Anne. She was extremely
hot. She removed her hat, and he took that too. "Oh, cousin,"
she said, "You are here! I am truly very pleased to see you."

It makes no difference at all to the reader whether Mademoiselle d'Estival had blue or black eyes, whether her face was
round or oval, whether she was short or tall, beautiful or
merely passable. St. Anne himself barely noticed, but what he
felt when he met her was something that he had never felt
before. He abandoned the task of listening to his lady cousins
and conversing with them to various other people, and followed Mademoiselle d'Estival to the stables, for she wanted to
visit a dog that had just had puppies. On her way back she
noticed a chicken that was dragging its foot. She picked it up
and saw that its leg was broken. With St. Anne's help, she set
the leg. One of the cooks had burnt her arm, so together they
bandaged it. Despite doing all these things with great dexter-
ity, she had a number of rather bizarre ways. She found out
when the healing herbs had been gathered, and then, counting
on her fingers, she worked out how far from full moon it was,
and then told the cook that she predicted a rapid recovery.
St. Anne smiled. Mademoiselle d'Estival spoke badly, and her
inelegant language was all the more striking for the occasional
exact and accurate technical word or glittering poetic expression neatly placed in the middle of a vulgar and incorrect
phrase. At eight o'clock in the evening, she wanted to go home,
and all the young ladies, along with their newly returned cousin,
accompanied her to the end of the avenue. St. Anne would
have gone farther with her, but it had just been raining a little,
and his companions were apprehensive about what the damp
grass they would have to walk through would do to their trail-
ing skirts.

"She can't read," they said, once she had disappeared. And
once he had returned to the château, the first thing he heard
his mother say was: "She can't read!"

"What does that matter?" said St. Anne rather impatiently.

Everyone cried out. Initially he did not want to say anything further, but on being pressed, he said to his lady cousins:

"I have already glanced at the smattering of books that there are here, and I think that it would have been just as good not to know how to read them. I would even doubt that in your entire lives you have ever read a single line that was worth reading."

These ladies found this way of thinking so extremely strange that some of them assumed that he was angry with them, and others that he was ill tempered in general. Not one of them asked themselves in what way reading was useful to them. Madame de St. Anne, who had a great deal of natural penetration, saw that her son was in love with Mademoiselle d'Estival, while Mademoiselle de Rhedon was distressed that anyone had ever given that young lady anything to read.

By the morning of the following day, St. Anne saw that the inhabitants of the château had already cast off that general tendency, that almost uniform characteristic that they had all displayed on his arrival. Regrets about the past and attentiveness to the present vary according to temperament. Madame de St. Anne, resolute, cold, ambitious, spent her time silently restoring her fortune, and as she had not lost a great deal, this task was made relatively easy. Madame de Rieux grieved for a husband, and also dreamt of restoring her losses, or at least she did while St. Anne was being expected, and for the first few hours after his return. But this hope was already almost destroyed, and a little bitterness was discernible in the attentions she paid him. Mademoiselle de Kerber, naturally lively and acerbic, poked fun at St. Anne, and mordantly ridiculed those who had overturned his fortune and prospects. General characteristics exist only in the eyes of bad observers.

"You will be extremely bored here," said Mademoiselle de Kerber to St. Anne as they ate breakfast together. "You have already informed us that you find us rather poor company."

"Did I say that?"

"Almost," said Mademoiselle de Kerber. "And as you dislike reading, what will you do?"

"Me, dislike reading?" exclaimed St. Anne. "Madam," he

instantly said to his mother, "will you be so kind as to give me the key to the library? I remember that it is particularly well constituted."

"Would you read aloud to us?" asked Madame de Rieux. "It would be so extremely obliging of you."

"My intention," said St. Anne, "is to reread my Latin classics, but if you wish it, I will read you Rollin's Roman history when we are all together.⁵ I would like to reread that too."

"That is rather old," said one of the ladies.

"Very well, Rapin's *History of England*."⁶

"That is rather long," said someone else.

At that point a parcel of new stories arrived; it was eagerly opened and examined. The names of the authors were decisive for all the ladies. There were some stories that they swore to devour, others that they wanted to send back to the bookseller on the spot, with a very pointed reminder not to send similar productions again. Madame St. Anne took no part in this business, and her son went up to her and asked her why it was that Mademoiselle d'Estival had not learned to read.

"You are unaware of her history, perhaps?" replied Madame St. Anne.

"Yes, and when I left France, I did not know that Monsieur d'Estival had a daughter; I did not even know that he was married."

"Well, he wasn't. He had this child with the gardener's daughter, who had become his housekeeper. She was a clever woman, or at least a canny one, and when war broke out in the region, she spoke to him about the danger he would be in, and how difficult his daughter's situation would be, were he to be killed. The marquis was moved by what she said, and immediately married the mother to legitimize the child. He was one of the first to be killed, and his château was burnt down. Madame d'Estival initially sought refuge in Nantes with a relation of hers, a calico manufacturer. She then went to Vannes to live with a doctor, and afterward fled to Brest to a shipbuilder. Since peace has returned to the region, she has been living in a farm very near here. It was the only thing that could be salvaged from Monsieur d'Estival's possessions."

"I understand," said St. Anne. "The mother did not know how to read, and couldn't teach her daughter, who has therefore taken greater care to pick up everything that she saw and heard around her. Yesterday when discussing the colors used in the manufacturing of calico and medicinal herbs, she stunned me with her knowledge."

"Did she not tell you stories about sorcerers? Her head is full of them," said Mademoiselle de Kerber.

At this point, Mademoiselle d'Estival came in. Madame de St. Anne went to attend to her duties, Madame de Rieux to get dressed; Mademoiselle de Kerber picked up one of the new stories and went to read in the garden. Mademoiselle de Rhedon was the last to stay, and if she had not felt half-proud and half-discreet, she would not have left Mademoiselle d'Estival and St. Anne. These two went off to inspect the cook's dressings, find out how the chicken was doing, and play with the puppies. After that they went for a rather long walk round the surrounding fields and meadows. Mademoiselle d'Estival showed the young man plants that were excellent for healing eye ailments, but "you must never pick them until sundown," she said. Throughout their conversation St. Anne was struck by her strange mixture of precise knowledge and simplicity.

When it was time for dinner, they returned.

"I do not think Mademoiselle d'Estival wishes to dine with us," said Mademoiselle de Kerber, "for we would be thirteen around the table." Mademoiselle d'Estival carefully counted.

"No," she said, "there will only be eleven of us." And she sat down.

A second later Madame de Rieux saw a spider on her shawl and let out a piercing scream. Madamoiselle de Kerber, her neighbor, leapt up and ran away. Mademoiselle d'Estival, seated at the other end of the table, also got up, picked up the spider, and took it away.

"Well, that tells you about different educations," said Mademoiselle de Kerber. "One learns to handle a toad as if it had been the prettiest canary."

Mademoiselle de Rhedon looked at St. Anne and saw that he looked flushed.

"What you said is very out of place," she said in a low voice
to Mademoiselle de Kerber. Mademoiselle d'Estival discussed
certain animals that are supposed to be poisonous but are not,
and moved on to the stings of bees and wasps, and snake bites,
as well as the remedies that can be used to cure them. After
dinner she asked Mademoiselle de Rhedon to play the tune on
her harp that she played so well, and after having done what
was asked of her, Mademoiselle de Rhedon asked her in her
turn to sing, accompanying her as skillfully and obligingly as it
is possible to do. She had to give her a little help as she accompanied her, Mademoiselle d'Estival not having any training in
music, and making mistakes or losing her place, despite having a very good ear and, more important, the most beautiful
voice in the world—it was full, sweet, and flexible, and she
could easily retain the tunes that she heard. Mademoiselle de
Rhedon was rather delicate, and it did not suit her to sing, but
she could play many instruments and also dance extremely
well. Mademoiselle d'Estival had only ever danced the jig and
gavotte, and all the other dances that peasant women dance.

This is how St. Anne spent the first two days after his return,
and many more after them, the only difference being that he
would often spend a couple of hours alone in his room, either
reading or writing to an intimate friend of his. In the evenings
he sometimes played backgammon with his mother and sometimes went to visit his neighbors, but conversation with them
was restricted to so narrow a range of subjects, the party spirit
limiting any other sort of spirit, that if politeness had compelled him out of his own home, boredom rapidly propelled
him back again.[7]

The ladies with whom he lived were not very happy with
him. They found him argumentative. He avoided disagreeing
with them about things but allowed himself to attack their
words or phrases, finding the former incorrect and the latter
unsuitable.

"Is it by chance, mister purist," Mademoiselle de Kerber
said one day, "that you never criticize Mademoiselle d'Estival's
language?"

"There would be too much to do," replied the person in

question. "If one can neither read nor write, how can one speak properly? Did you know, cousin, that in me you have a relation who can't read or write?"

"I have been told so," casually replied St. Anne.

Tears came to the eyes of Mademoiselle de Rhedon. "I cannot understand why we make such a point of it," she said, weeping. "I have blamed myself for doing it a thousand times. I think about it all the time, and it gives me so much pain and makes me feel so ashamed that I am very pleased to have the chance of admitting it today. It gives me great relief to do so, and I hope that my heart will be less tormented by it in the future."

"Why pain and shame?" said Mademoiselle d'Estival, tenderly embracing her in her distress. "It was a very good way of describing the way in which I have lived until now to St. Anne. I was more or less ignored by my father, and then persecuted by his enemies. I am convinced that the interest he shows in me comes in part from this. Had you already heard my history," she asked St. Anne, "when you came with me to see the puppies?"

"No," said St. Anne.

"I am very glad to hear that," said Mademoiselle d'Estival. "Your attentions date from that moment, and I am very glad that they are not only owing to pity, but to a certain . . . what shall I call it? Sympathy is the word, I think, which I felt when I first met you, and which must be reciprocal if it is true sympathy. But again, I think that your friendship for me has been increased by what you were told about my having been taught nothing, not even to read. Next winter, would you teach me to read?"

"Willingly," said St. Anne.

"I will come for my lesson every day whatever the weather," she said. "But until winter I would rather not read; I prefer to walk around during the beautiful season, and spend my time in autumn harvesting the fruit, and this year I hope it will be abundant."

These words, said so unself-consciously, made a profound impression on St. Anne. His mother shook her head, and

Mademoiselle de Rhedon, even more moved than before, had to leave the drawing room.

A few days later, Mademoiselle d'Estival having not come to the château all day, St. Anne proposed that they take an evening walk, and it may be imagined in which direction he led the party. It was the first time he'd been to the farm. He walked in front. A big guard dog suddenly burst out of the house, ran up to him, and bit him on the arm so hard that it drew blood. The screams of his companions brought Madame d'Estival and her daughter running out. The mother said everything it was natural to say. The daughter, having helped St. Anne to take his coat off, laid the wound bare, washed it, bandaged it, and tranquilly observed that it would cause no trouble at all. She said the problem was that St. Anne had too fine an air, and that the same thing had happened a few weeks before to another man dressed as well as him.

"What a prodigious democrat the dog is!" said St. Anne, laughing.

"What do you expect?" asked the young person. "The only people that he sees here are a few artisans and some poor people we give soup to. No gentleman from the neighborhood has ever come to see us; it is true that the war has left us very few."

"I think," said Mademoiselle de Kerber, "that you should have that dog killed immediately."

"No," said Mademoiselle d'Estival. "Everyone would think that he had shown signs of rabies, and it would cause anxiety on St. Anne's behalf. He is a faithful guard dog, and we need him here. Without him my mother and I would be too vulnerable. We have no one but Castor to defend us. Come here, Castor. Come, you wretched dog; ask my forgiveness."

Castor prostrated himself in front of his mistress.

"Mother," she said, "would you be so kind as to get some bread for Castor? These ladies will see that he can behave himself very well, and that this accident, which I am very vexed about, is nonetheless not serious."

Although Castor ate bread and drank the water spilling from the well around which the ladies were seated, they still looked so frightened that Mademoiselle d'Estival was puzzled.

"He won't bite you," she said. "He is used to your dresses, because I wear them too."

"But he was in a frenzy."

"Not anymore. He is eating and drinking. Look, he's going up to St. Anne. Cousin, please be so kind as to give him this lump of bread."

"Good God, how unwise!" exclaimed Mademoiselle de Kerber.

"Unwise, mademoiselle?" Madame d'Estival tartly remarked. "I will become vexed on my daughter's behalf. If she were not sure of what she is doing, would she do it? Who do you take her for? Because she does not scream and wail like you do you think she has no soul and no good sense? Would she endanger her cousin, the first of his entire family ever to have honored us with a visit? Believe that there is nothing to fear, because she does not fear anything, and keep your exclamations to yourselves."

"If the thing were even in doubt," said Mademoiselle d'Estival to St. Anne, "I would willingly accompany you on a pilgrimage to St. Hubert, but in truth there is nothing to fear.[8] Only I do wish Castor hadn't bitten you and that your mother's dog had bitten me very hard when I went to visit her little puppies."

St. Anne concealed his emotion as best he could, with the aid of a few bad jokes about St. Hubert's tomb, the omelet to be had there, and the rings that one brings away, and then, having put his jacket back on, he went into the house and asked for milk, cherries, and bread, which he shared with Castor.

"If ever you have some perilous errand to run, we will lend him to you," said Mademoiselle d'Estival, "and you will see that he will be your friend and protector."

"How lucky Mademoiselle d'Estival is!" said Mademoiselle de Rhedon to St. Anne as he gave her his arm for the return journey. "Not knowing how to read, having a dog that bites— everything turns to her advantage."

He found nothing to say in reply, and she was amazed to have said so much.

The next day over lunch Mademoiselle de Kerber asked St. Anne what great advantage he saw in not knowing how to read, "For," said she, "it is clear that that is Mademoiselle

d'Estival's great merit, and that you have a much greater preference for her than you do for us."

"You are saying too many things at once," said St. Anne. "Let
us simplify your question if you want me to give you a reply."

"Very well, monsieur. Let us simplify it. Would you prefer
us not to read?"

"It makes no difference to me."

"Do you think it would be better if we were unable to read?"

"I think it's really quite immaterial; reading is one of your
amusements and is neither better nor worse than any other."

"Would you like to be unable to read?"

"No, I am very happy that I can read."

"Would you like to be the only man in France who could
read?"

"No, I am very happy that some people can read, and I
would prefer them be more educated than they are, not less."

"Would you prefer the people not to know how to read?"

"I dislike generalizing labels, as I have already said a thousand times."

"Well then, would you prefer your cartwright, your miller,
and your gardener not to know how to read?"

"I don't think I would be vexed if they couldn't."

"Or the children of peasants and villagers not to read?"

"I would be very happy if that were the case. It would avoid
the disadvantages of having freedom of the press."

"You will be satisfied, then," said Madame d'Estival. "Our
village schools already closed five or six years ago."

"Let's not talk about this anymore," said Mademoiselle de
Rhedon. "I can see Mademoiselle d'Estival coming."

In effect, she had come to find out how St. Anne's wound
was, and asked his permission to come and look at it. He said
that when he had got up, he had taken the bandage off and
that there was nothing there to see.

"Castor's extremely well, and when you next visit he will
give you the best welcome."

With that, she made ready to return home directly. She said
that her mother was expecting her to come and help with some
household tasks.

"Let's walk with mademoiselle as far as the avenue gate," said Mademoiselle de Rhedon.

St. Anne asked for nothing better, and everyone would have gone even farther if they hadn't met Madame de Rieux's mother-in-law and her sister, who was Mademoiselle de Kerber's mother. They had been at Missillac for St. Anne's return, but had not stayed. They had now come to fetch their daughter-in-law and daughter, respectively. The only person to remain in the château with its owners was Mademoiselle de Rhedon, who had lived there permanently since the tragic death of her parents. Mademoiselle d'Estival came almost every day; often, Mademoiselle de Rhedon went to fetch her, and the constant encounters of these two rivals made for a very affecting spectacle. One of them brought a total lack of self-consciousness to their meetings, the other immense generosity. Madame de St. Anne watched and worried—her son loved Mademoiselle d'Estival. He perceived neither his mother's designs nor the other young person's inclination, but he could see perfectly well that Mademoiselle d'Estival loved him.

One evening the topic of conversation had been ghosts. St. Anne, who did not normally intervene on unimportant matters, had this time spoken up against harmful terrors. It was late; the evening was very beautiful; the moon seemed to be playing at creating ghosts in the gardens where they sat.

"I will walk you home," said St. Anne to Mademoiselle d'Estival. "You would be frightened if you went alone."

Once they had left the gardens and the avenue they were just about to follow the usual path, when St. Anne said, "Let's go a longer way. It is too beautiful to be shut inside. Let's go round by the village."

"Yes, but," said his companion, "we will have to pass by the graveyard. Will you not be afraid if you only have me? I will have you, so I hope I won't be afraid."

"All protection is equally good against ghosts," said St. Anne, "and if I am able to reassure you, it will be that much easier for you to reassure me, as I probably won't be afraid in the first place."

They reached the graveyard and were welcomed and followed

by little bluish flames coming from under the earth. Mademoiselle d'Estival pressed closer to St. Anne.

"I have often seen these will-o'-the-wisps," he said. "I will explain what causes them to you whenever you want. Let us sit down a moment on this old wall. I love this place; I came many times when I was little, and it was here that I saw my beloved old tutor buried. Can you hear the barn owls? I love their mournful call."

"I don't," said Mademoiselle d'Estival. "But yes, let's sit down."

Although she wasn't heavy, the wall crumbled beneath her and she fell.

"Now I really am near the resting place of the dead," she said. St. Anne picked her up and looked for a more robust section of the wall. She sat very close to him, her shoulder resting against him.

"Your beloved tutor buried here!" she resumed. "Tell me all about it. How old were you, and what did he die of?"

St. Anne told her, and as he did so, was much moved.

"This is what it is to be reasonable," said Mademoiselle d'Estival. "I would be completely unable to come here if you were under the earth, and yet you loved your tutor a great deal."

St. Anne embraced his cousin, and it wouldn't have taken much for him to forget himself even further.

"Your heart is beating beneath my shoulder," she said. "Are you frightened?"

"Perhaps," he said, and in effect, the august presence of the dead had made itself felt, and their voice had made itself heard, saying to him: *Desecrator! Stop.*

Once he had calmed down and regained his poise after feeling such opposing emotions, St. Anne remembered that in olden times tombs were respected as much as altars, and after a moment of silence, he recited out loud:

> Not far from Troezen's gates, among these tombs,
> My princely forebears' ancient burial place [. . .]⁹

"What are you saying?" exclaimed Mademoiselle d'Estival. "Are they prayers? I hope that fear hasn't made you delirious."

"No," said St. Anne.

"Me, I am perfectly content, and if put to it, I would be able to quiet your fears. These dead people wouldn't want to do us any harm, even if they could; what would be the point? You said so yourself before, and now I think the same."

"You put it much better than I," said St. Anne. Mademoiselle d'Estival was starting to talk again, but St. Anne was not listening to her.

"Would you like to be my wife?" said St. Anne.

"My mother," said Mademoiselle d'Estival, "has already asked me if I wanted to marry you, and I told her that I didn't. But on the subject of my mother, I think she might be getting worried; it's getting late, and I have to go home. We won't walk fast, and as we go along, I'll tell you what made me give her that reply."

"There is something about marriage," she continued, "that I do not understand at all. In Estival I knew a peasant family whose oldest daughter was disagreeable and ill tempered, who abused her husband, beat her children, and treated her father and mother without any respect, and yet was tolerated and even highly regarded. She was always pregnant, and was only treated even better. Her younger sister was good, sweet, lovely, and active. She had been forbidden from marrying a young laborer who lived nearby, and was suspected of seeing him in secret. She was immediately turned out of doors. She may now be begging for her bread. There is something very mysterious about marriage, therefore. It has advantages and privileges that I cannot divine. I saw my mother get married not long since. People never stopped telling me how lucky I was. Before, they called her Marie, and I was known as Babet, and afterward we were called Madame and Mademoiselle d'Estival, but far from having gained from it, we were only more hated and persecuted, for the name of Estival was reviled by almost everyone, or at least it was where we were concerned. I heard my mother being told that she could have saved the château d'Estival if she had still been called Marie and me Babet. And yet she had desired the marriage ceremony, and she had urged my father to go through with it. But I never saw them together once after they were married, because we had to run away, and he went to fight and was killed. For a long time, we fled from one place to another, and it was always dangerous and exhausting. Since we have finally found refuge on our little farm, we haven't been treated very much better. Your mother, and I am not blaming her for it, has always been very cold with us. Nonetheless, my mother wanted me to come to the château every day, hoping that I would win her good graces, but it has only been a pleasure for me since you were there. And I still hear people whispering to each other that my father did my mother a great honor to marry her, and that it is a lucky thing for me that he did. I cannot see any advantage, apart from meeting you. Perhaps without that marriage you would not have wanted to recognize me as a relation, although I still would have been. You will tell me that none of this has much bearing on the question, and in effect I do not know why I can't get beyond it. I will still have, I hope, enough time to tell you the essential things, but you can see that the marriage that I have been so much congratulated upon has brought me great unhappiness, and you can understand that for me the word and the ceremony look like the bringers of bad luck.

"After it took place, I lived in Nantes with a husband and wife who said nothing to each other at all; marriage did them neither any good nor any harm, or so it seemed to me. In Vannes I lived with a man whose wife ceaselessly said to him, 'Before we were married you were gentle and obliging, you gave me everything I wanted; there were no jewels too beautiful for me, no shawls too fine, no hats too elegant. And now it's completely the opposite, and you hardly give me enough money to keep house.' 'That is because,' the husband would say, 'you spend it on adorning yourself so that you are more attractive to all comers. You have changed a lot, or else I was a complete idiot before, and marriage has opened my eyes.' In the house where I lived in Brest, there was a wedding. I never saw anything so eager as the groom before the celebration, and nothing so cold once it was over. From the following day he was a changed man. You see, cousin, why it is that I am so frightened, particularly where you are concerned. It would be no good telling me that you have also done me great honor, given that my grandfather, who is still living, was a gardener at Estival. I would consider myself very much to be pitied, and all the more so as I would probably still love you when you no longer loved me, for that is what happened to the woman I was telling you about. Unfortunately she loves her husband. She apologized for him to us, saying, 'My God! He is still the same as he was, except toward me; how, having liked him, could I now dislike him?' But she had changed no more than he had, except that she cried a good deal because he gave her reason to, whereas before he had given her a reason to be happy, which makes one more attractive than grief does. By the time we left, her beauty was already withering away; she was like a flower on whom the sun no longer smiles. But here we are. Do not be afraid of Castor now that you are with me. Castor, Castor! Come, Castor. Lie down at my cousin's heels. Give him your paw—the other paw. Very good, well done!"

St. Anne, although hardly in a fit state to take any pleasure in these childish tricks, stroked the dog as much as he was able, after which Mademoiselle d'Estival took the key out of her pocket, opened the front door, held out her hand to St. Anne, and shook his, wishing him a good night.

He was awaited at the château with much impatience.

"Where have you been for so long?" Madame de St. Anne said to him curtly enough.

"At the village graveyard," replied the young man.

"Alone, or with Mademoiselle d'Estival?"

St. Anne pretended not to have heard, and as if he had forgotten something, left the room, returned, and sat down at table, affecting to be completely at ease and entirely unpreoccupied. Half an hour later, he was handed a letter. He recognized Mademoiselle de Kerber's handwriting, broke the seal, and after having glanced over the whole letter, read aloud what follows:

You will triumph, cousin, and I am vexed to say so. But the story is too good not to give myself the pleasure of telling it. This morning we were reading a sublime novel. The heroine was enduring unheard-of trials with angelic patience. At the death of her beloved husband, she cuts off her beautiful hair, and places it in his coffin. Madame de Rieux and I wept. My good aunt had taken off her glasses and put her work down so that she could hear better, and my mother had put aside her spinning wheel, which was making too much noise despite having been greased only yesterday. We had to stop for a moment, and Madame de Rieux and I both said to each other, "How wrong St. Anne is! How such reading exalts and refines the soul! What woman would not become more gentle, tender, and faithful to her duties!" We resumed our reading, still weeping, still admiring, for the widow sentences herself to a perpetual retreat, and lives in tears and good works. But one of our neighbors is just being announced, a squire in previous times, but now an administrator, who, except for his fortune, which is decent in every sense, is one of the greatest nonentities in the world. What does Madame de Rieux do? She runs off to the mirror to check the arrangement of her hair and shawl, having forgotten our Artemisia so thoroughly that we might never have been speaking of her at all.[10] My mother ordered something to refresh our man, who was very heated. The footman, who was carrying a glass filled with wine from Bordeaux, tripped, and the glass fell and shattered. The wine spilled right across my skirts, which happened to be white. My mother was incensed and started scolding the footman, and I would have done the same if shame hadn't held me back, for I was very put out, and my mood did not improve until I thought of you and what I would tell you. I warned Madame de Rieux that I would reveal how she had behaved, but to my intense amazement, she had not even been much struck by the difference between the impressions the book had made on us and the way we had behaved. "Well? What is strange about that?" she asked me. "We admire such-and-such a character in a book, and then we do what suits us. Did you want me to receive him with my hair all over the place?" Of course that is going too far, but if the conclusions that I drew from my reading were not as ill-thought-through as hers, I didn't benefit from them any more than she did, nor did my mother. In short, you may well have been right that it might have been just as well for us not to know how to read.

"I do not think," said Mademoiselle de Rhedon, "that little accidents would make me forget the advice that a book had just given me; they are like a friend's advice. But there are troubles which would make anything more reasonable that I might have read or heard useless to me." Her eyes filled with tears as she said this.

"Your childhood was beset with misfortune," said St. Anne. "Woe betide anyone who would henceforth distress you voluntarily!"

"Voluntarily! That is not what I fear," said Mademoiselle de Rhedon. But she was speaking to a man who could not hear her.

Madame de St. Anne had left them when Mademoiselle de Kerber's letter was read out, and Mademoiselle de Rhedon felt that she also ought to retire. Twenty times before she left St. Anne she was on the point of repeating his mother's question: "Were you at the graveyard alone or with Mademoiselle d'Estival?" It seemed to her that if he had been able to keep such a fearful girl in that mournful place, then the fate of both of them must be decided. "Let us know," she said to herself. "He refused to tell his mother, fearing that he was becoming the subject of inquisitive and importunate observation, but he will tell me. If my fate is decided, let me know it. I can bear anything better than not knowing." Twenty times she opened her mouth, but the words that needed to be said died away on her lips.

Once more in his room, St. Anne, after much reflection and reverie, and realizing that he would not be able to sleep, decided to write. He started a letter to his friend Tonquedec, to whom he had given very regular accounts of himself and everything around him since his return to Missillac. This time, however, he felt awkward about writing, and would have much preferred to see and talk to him.

A man of sense and feeling only ever reluctantly admits to himself that he is in love, that is to say, subjugated and deprived of a part of his reason. It is even harder to make this confession to anyone else, especially a respected friend whose esteem we need before we can respect ourselves. We feel that this confession will not raise us higher in his estimation, but we cannot tell exactly how far it may make us fall. Moreover, friendship can feel jealous of love. So what could he do? St. Anne determined to reply to Mademoiselle de Kerber, flattering himself that if he managed to focus his mind on a truly interesting question, he would succeed in distracting himself and in calming the agitation he had brought back from the graveyard and the farm. This is what he wrote:

Where do you get your candor and your excellent mind from, my dearest cousin? If you owe even the slightest part to your books, then I am reconciled to them, and even humbly offer them my respects. It is only a question of being the best that we can be both for ourselves and for others. No matter where it comes from, and whether it's about reading or thinking, reading or seeing and hearing. If it is permissible for someone of my age to have an opinion, then I would say that novels and plays in prose and verse, which are the commonest reading matter of decent young people of both sexes, must be useless, unless it is by chance that a word that we read there makes us think about things that concern us and which the author never even considered. And yet the worst newspaper, poster, or book catalogue can sometimes do us the same service, without our losing any time over hunting out happy coincidences which, in my view, we should simply wait for. Conversation, the sight of society, and nature will bring them to us if we are disposed to grasp them. It seems to me that what Rousseau says about the theater, in his admirable letter to d'Alembert, should be extended to reading any play, and in general to almost all the reading that women and young people undertake.[11] Read this letter, cousin, seeing as you have been taught to read, and let it finally convince you that what happened yesterday at your house happens everywhere and to everyone.

As for books of knowledge, I do not find them any more useful than novels for people who are only undertaking superficial study of the subject or who do not limit themselves to the forms of knowledge which are connected to their own profession. For example, if I see a lawyer learning about the fine arts or a sculptor about politics or a doctor about war, and they then start discussing their new area of study, I simply shrug my shoulders if they talk nonsense, and want them to change profession if they show talent.

Cousin, I am not sorry to see the old schools destroyed and the new ones still not set up. Let knowledge be difficult to acquire. Let talent steal it, so to speak. Let it be the fire of the sky courageously stolen by some Prometheus.[12] Let it be the golden fleece, object of the wishes and efforts of the valiant Argonauts, and let labor, danger, and indefatigable perseverance be required before it can ever be won.[13] The mind is strengthened by work. Each obstacle to overcome offers the opportunity of acquiring a new faculty. Have we ever seen the children of the great, surrounded by tutors who smooth their path to knowledge, learn anything at all? Henceforth, I would like talent alone, which half intuits its knowledge, to want to learn what cannot be intuited. It will learn without primary schools, national institutes, universities, or academies.[14] I would like man, already enlightened by nature in some way, to strive alone for that illumination which the lights of knowledge bring. He will pay dearly for his knowledge, because the prolonged study and constant, deep meditation which transform the thoughts and experience of others into our judgment, wisdom, prudence, and courage exhaust both mind and health.[15] It is not the sort of work which is suited to human nature, and the man who devotes himself to it will have, I fear, neither a soft nor a long existence, but he will have followed an almost irresistible inclination, and will have had the joy of fulfilling it. Let this man be rewarded for his work and his successes by being honored by his nation; let it consult him; let him govern it. Let us entrust ourselves to him, and, being called neither by nature nor by fate to this beautiful if arduous career, let us work the fields; let our women spin, let the weaver transform our linen, our hemp as well as the fleeces of our ewes, into clothes. I know that our ignorance will be accompanied by the errors of yore, but superficial knowledge is so often harmful, and in place of the handful of prejudices which it removes, we have a sort of pride which I fear much more. Cousin, you will suppose that this whole system is the work of Mademoiselle d'Estival, or rather that it is inspired by her, but the groundwork was laid long ago. Many is the time, on seeing the tears of a schoolboy and the rod of the master, that I have asked myself: what is it all for? Many times, when other people asked: why allow this to be printed? I have said: why teach people to read? I loved Mademoiselle d'Estival before knowing that she had not been taught to read. But when I found out, I was surprised that I had not guessed, and I was very glad. It seemed to me that she saw and heard better, that her mind was clearer and her memory more accurate. It seemed to me that by not knowing anything about many things, she was better able to know the things that were actually useful to her. My bias does not go so far as to admire the popular errors that her mother has filled her mind with, but they do not vex me very much, and I prefer her to believe in ghosts than not to believe in the immortality of the soul. I would prefer her to worship the sun than not to worship anything. I know everything that is normally trotted out about this well-worn subject, but that doesn't change it, in my view. Man is destined to make mistakes and to bear the sometimes disastrous and cruel consequences of those mistakes; he is destined to make mistakes and for this reason he is destined never to have anything other than imperfect and limited knowledge. Errors will always occupy the void left by knowledge. The skeptic varies his errors rather than avoid them, since man is unable to remain in perpetual doubt. He can easily keep returning to it in his mind, but the objects that surround him all incessantly force him away from it, and if you could see inside the head of a Pyrrhonian philosopher, you would see him being superstitious twenty times per day.[16] Mademoiselle d'Estival, despite her childish terrors, allowed herself to be taken this evening to the village graveyard, and there, with the respected shade of my old mentor for witness, I wanted to swear eternal faith to her, but she told me that she didn't want to become my wife, and explained her reasons extremely clearly. I do not think I will be unable to refute them, and I am much more afraid of my mother's arguments. She has said nothing yet, but her looks spoke very clearly when I returned from the graveyard. This is why I am writing to you rather than going to bed. I would be unable to sleep. Come back here, I beg you, in a few days. I think that you might be able to speak to my mother on my behalf. She will listen to you; she likes your mind. I feared it, myself; I felt that you had a spite which sometimes overcame your natural generosity, but your letter reassures me. The person who is able to write to me expressly to tell me that I have won in an argument we were having is capable of all sorts of good things; in any case, who better could I ask? Tonquedec is not here; Mademoiselle de Rhedon is too young. I have honest people as neighbors—but if I do not need them to know anything, I do need them to have sense and wit—more than anything I am afraid of stupidity. So please come, for you have a great deal of sense and wit, and if you put your mind to helping me, you will succeed.

Once dawn had broken, St. Anne went to pace across the fields. He returned to rest in the gardens, remaining there until a bell summoned him to breakfast.

His mother noticed that he had not changed his clothes since the previous night, and put several questions to him that left him embarrassed for an answer. Authorities generally are in the habit of questioning. If they are not told the truth, they normally find that eyes will tell them everything they want to know. After breakfast Madame de St. Anne told her son to follow her to a part of the garden where she was sure that their conversation would not be interrupted.

"Do not suppose," said she, "that anything which has been going on in your mind has escaped me. I had hoped that your initial error of judgment would not have had such long-lasting consequences. I had hoped that constantly finding yourself between a raw mind and a cultivated one, between a crude and vulgar nature and talents which have been refined by study and taste, would help you to chose as you ought; I believed that the more you saw Mademoiselle d'Estival and Mademoiselle de Rhedon, the less you would be attracted to one, and the more you would become attached to the other. It has happened differently, and it is for me, in the absence of your own judgment, to direct you in the appropriate way. Know then that I will never consent to an alliance which, giving you Marie Blanchet for your mother-in-law, would mean my grandchildren had Monsieur d'Estival's gardener for their grandfather. He surrendered his daughter to his master, and she must have been happy with this shameful deal, as she lived with him for a long time, content with being a concubine, and known to be so by everyone. Yet the father and daughter were the best of their race, and some of their close relatives have been seen at the head of the gang which burnt our châteaus and laid waste to our land. Marie Blanchet's uncle, enraged that his niece had wanted to become a lady, would have slit her lord's throat if he could have, and it was he who set light to the château d'Estival. If I allowed you to follow such an insane and bizarre inclination, it would not be long, given the censure you would incur, before you came to hate your disastrous passion and its object, as well as the mother who had been too weak to prevent your unhappiness. But I declare that I will prevent it, and that you are in no danger. I declare that I do not want to hear another word about any such marriage. I declare that if you do not promise never to think of it anymore, I will not allow Mademoiselle d'Estival to come to the château ever again. I could even compel her and her mother to leave the farm where they are living, as your grandfather had a claim to it which I could enforce the instant I wanted to. As they have no money to pay for a court case, they would find that they were lucky to be in a position to surrender the farm for an equivalent one that I would offer them."

"Heaven preserve me," said St. Anne, "from bringing such a disaster on them and on yourself."

"On me? What can you possibly mean, sir?"

"It is a great disaster to be unjust, madam, and it is a disaster which very often brings others with it, which one has no right to complain about in the circumstances."

"Drop your casuistical reasoning this instant," said Madame de St. Anne. "I will hear my son's learned lessons another time. For now, let him listen to a mother who has never, since the moment he was born, wasted a thought on anything other than him, his fortune, and his happiness."

St. Anne bowed, but was unable to utter a single word of gratitude.

"I have said enough about Mademoiselle d'Estival," continued Madame de St. Anne. "Let us discuss Mademoiselle de Rhedon. She has long been intended for you. Her father, soon before his death, commended her to my protection, and expressed the wish that she should become my daughter. How could I fail to fulfill such a sacred vow?"*

St. Anne said nothing, although his mother, having made her tone both imposing and full of pathos, expected a response. The silence that he kept said: "If you could fulfill this vow without me, you could view it as entirely obligatory, but currently powerless to do anything other than exhort me, your obligations go no further, and from this moment you can consider yourself absolved." Madame de St. Anne started to speak again.

"I have sent away various extremely eligible suitors for this precious girl that her father in some ways bequeathed to me. In accepting a certain authority over her, did I not also contract certain commitments?"

St. Anne continued to say nothing at all, and after a moment of silence, he made a movement as if to leave, but his mother obliged him to stay.

"I have been a widow since I was twenty-one," she said. "Monsieur de Rhedon was barely any older. He had wit, talent, and ambition, as well as grace and merit, but he did not then have, far from it, the wealth that he since acquired. I sacrificed to you everything which might have encouraged me to listen to him. Monsieur de Rhedon was desolated, and took

* Author's footnote: How often this noble pathos has been used to conceal the most ignoble passions and intentions! How often it has replaced goodness and reason! We respect, we adore the memory of a friend or a father, and are deaf to the living voice of a wife or a son. For the last thirty years in particular everyone has adopted the tone of drama and romance, speaking in its insipid and hypocritical language, and our humanity is limited to funerary urns, elegies, and epitaphs.

the feelings which I had rejected elsewhere, and his disappointment led him to make a hasty choice which did not find favor,
and never would have done. He could have married much
better. Another of his relations would have brought many
advantageous aspects with her, but he chose the first person to
present herself, and his daughter, whose prospects during her
childhood were much less glittering than they should have
been, has always seemed to me to have a claim on me for compensation, because it was in some way my fault that fortune
had favored her so little, for, I repeat, her father could have
married much better than he did."

"Oh Good God!" exclaimed St Anne. "If that had been the
case, she would never have been born. She is the fruit of that
hasty union; she is the daughter of her mother as much as of
her father."

"That's enough of your logic, sir," said Madame de St. Anne
haughtily. "Mademoiselle de Rhedon has always inspired me
with a very fond interest, and your marriage has long been the
object of my every wish. She is beautiful, well born, well
brought-up, and very rich. I like her and she suits me. You will
marry her, if you do not wish to make me repent of all the care
and sacrifices I have lavished on you, and see my affection
change into coldness and disgust."

As she pronounced these last words, Madame de St. Anne
stood up and looked away from him. She walked off, leaving
him in a state of mind that is almost impossible to describe.
"Enough of your logic—drop your casuistical reasoning," he
repeated to himself aloud. Although what had been said left
him with a sickening impression and feelings of bitter unhappiness, he was grateful for what had been done for him, and
felt that he owed his mother respect, if not obedience. Feeling
emotions of a hundred different sorts, sometimes he was distressed that Mademoiselle d'Estival had not responded the
previous evening, such that he now saw himself as incontro-
vertibly promised to her and unable to withdraw, while sometimes he was glad still to be free, so as to be able to avoid
disobliging and grieving his mother. He remembered having
seen Monsieur de Rhedon eagerly intent on paying attentions

to a once adored object. At thirty-eight he was handsome and agreeable; what must he have been at the age of twenty-five? The sacrifice that Madame de St. Anne had made to maternal love was no doubt very meritorious, but, said St. Anne to himself after a moment of tenderness, it was not to love so much as to maternal or even personal ambition that the sacrifice had been made. "And, moreover, did I ask for this sacrifice to be made? Mother, why did you not marry Monsieur de Rhedon, and why don't you let me marry Mademoiselle d'Estival? But you probably did not love your suitor very much, and perhaps you hardly even loved your son."

Dinner was almost over by the time St. Anne sat down at table. Fortunately, they had guests. The excuses he made were accepted and he did not have to endure the piercing gaze of his mother. But Mademoiselle de Rhedon changed color when she saw him and asked him why he was so pale, and whether he was ill. He assured her that he was entirely well, but that he felt tired, having spent part of the night writing.

"I replied to Mademoiselle de Kerber," he said.

"The cause that you are defending to her," said Mademoiselle de Rhedon, "is very important to you, and you will have been very glad to confirm your disciple in her new belief. God knows the extent to which women who read will have been ill treated in your letter!"

"If it hadn't already gone, I would have shown it to you," said St. Anne. "So you can see that there can have been nothing offensive in it about well brought-up, educated people. I look at the effects and not at the causes, and where a woman is judicious, generous, and amiable, it is unimportant to me whether she is or isn't able to read."

These last words had become so important to Mademoiselle de Rhedon and to St. Anne, they contained so many ideas and recalled so many memories of such vivid interest, that one blushed as he said them, and the other as she heard them. Madame de St. Anne saw that they were having an animated conversation, and flattered herself that she had not spoken in vain.

Toward evening, St. Anne resolved to go to Tonquedec to visit his friend.

The faithful Herfrey, Gaul or not, a western Breton of the very best sort, who had various orders to carry out, would be staying in Missillac until the following morning, and then leave for St. Anne, where his master would be.*

For it was the birthplace of his family that St. Anne was going to visit.

In one of the outbuildings of a dilapidated and tumbledown old château lived a farmer with his wife and son. The moon and the glittering stars lit the traveler's way, and sun was just beginning to make them disappear, when he arrived at their lodging. He knocked. No one was yet up, and as in these unhappy times people are quick to distrust, the inhabitants were afraid, but St. Anne said his name and they opened up. The people were relations of Herfrey. They made up a bad bed for him, and yet its white sheets were spotless, and St. Anne, exhausted by two nights without sleep and a long walk, got into it and slept as if he had been free of love and distress.

When he woke up, his first thought was for his mistress— but let us retrace our steps, that is to say, go back to Missillac and to the moment of St. Anne's departure.

Mademoiselle de Rhedon saw him leave. He might only have been going for a stroll. Perhaps he was going to visit Mademoiselle d'Estival, but there was something more serious in his gait: his steps were more regular and his bearing more composed than normal; in short, there was something completely indefinable about him that conveyed to Mademoiselle de Rhedon that he was going on a journey. If she wasn't sure that this was the case, she feared that it might be. He came down the avenue and went quite close to her without seeing

---

*   Author's footnote: It is claimed that the inhabitants of Armorica, or Lower Brittany, are descended from the ancient Gauls. (The editors of the OC explain that Charrière probably got this from La Tour d'Auvergne's *Origines Gauloises, Celles des Plus Anciens Peuples de l'Europe, puisées dans Leur Vraie Source, ou Recherches sur la langue, l'origine, et les antiquités des Celto-Bretons de l'Armorique, pour servir à l'histoire ancienne et moderne de ce peuple, et à celle des Français* (Paris: Quillau, 1796), which her letters show she was reading in May 1797, just before starting *Saint Anne*).

her. She made a little noise, but he didn't hear it; he was too preoccupied. When he did not appear at supper, Madame de St. Anne showed some surprise, but her servants told her that Herfrey had not left the château, and she was reassured. Mademoiselle de Rhedon was even more anxious about it, thinking of him traveling alone at night. She pretended that she had a dreadful headache, and said she was going to bed. Herfrey was waiting for her in the corridor, and deftly, without her maid seeing, handed her a letter.

Mademoiselle de Rhedon ordered that she be left alone, and opening the letter with a trembling hand, read as follows:

> I am leaving, my beautiful cousin; I am leaving, because I have to—my mother has plans for me to which at the moment I am unable to subscribe. If only I could be sure that you have remained in ignorance of them, or that you have viewed them with indifference! Your disdain and scorn, although I might perhaps not merit such severity, would distress me less than any flattering regrets. I commend Mademoiselle d'Estival to your care; please be so kind as to tell her not to worry about me, that I have gone to see a friend, and have been unable to bid her good-bye. Even if she could read a letter, I wouldn't write her one. She will only have news of me from you. I picked up my pen twenty times to write to Madame de St. Anne, but my hand was unable to trace a single word. Good-bye, my beautiful, amiable, my generous cousin; good-bye.

Herfrey had no sooner handed over the letter than he left the château and went to the gardener's house, such that when Madame de St. Anne sent for him, he could not be found, and thereby avoided all the questions she intended to put to him. The following day at dawn, he left, after having charged the gardener to tell Madame de St. Anne that her son had gone to see a friend and would be away for a few days.

Madame de St. Anne was so angry that she very nearly forbade Mademoiselle d'Estival from ever setting foot in the château again, and she would have done it, without regard for either misery or innocence, if she had not feared that

Mademoiselle de Rhedon would see and understand both her own vexation and her son's passion. She knew, moreover, that any humiliations inflicted on a loved one only intensify love until it will no longer submit to any restraining authority, seeing it as its duty to rebel. She therefore limited her vengeance to treating her extremely coldly, hoping that, without going so far as to banish Mademoiselle d'Estival from her house, she would make it so unpleasant for her that she would stop coming. But the latter came to see Mademoiselle de Rhedon, who, apart from feeling attached to her because of her misfortunes, her merit, and her charms, also endlessly repeated to herself, "St. Anne commended Mademoiselle d'Estival to my care—I have no way of making myself agreeable to him other than to treat the person that he perhaps prefers to me with kindness." "*Perhaps*," she would say, for she could tell from St. Anne's note that there was an obstacle preventing him from asking for her hand, and yet she did not clearly see that this obstacle was Mademoiselle d'Estival herself. Mademoiselle de Rhedon, without being vain, was aware of her own advantages, and knew very well that Madame de St. Anne did not want Mademoiselle d'Estival for a daughter-in-law. It is also true that while love does suffer from ill-founded fears, it is even more fertile in sweet errors.

St. Anne, far from Missillac, continued to see everything that was happening as clearly as if he had been there himself. He remembered the threats his mother had made about Madame and Mademoiselle d'Estival, and he also remembered the cold reception that had made, for a time, the young person's visits to the château so painful.

"If my mother was cold and haughty before resentment had the chance of penetrating her heart, what will she be like today?" wondered St. Anne. "I can see her vexed and infuriated, affecting disdain for an object who she nonetheless knows is fully able to thwart her views, and halt the execution of her designs. Perhaps she is considering how to keep her at a distance and out of my way. She is still powerful enough to succeed against two isolated women without support or advice. Furthermore, even if she doesn't banish them from their sanctuary, she is capable of making it so unpleasant for them that even banishment would be preferable. I have to provide another one for them. I can and I must. It is up to me to compensate them for the persecution which I will no doubt bring on them. Here I am the master. These ruins belong to me. Thanks be to my grandfather, who wanted me to have the use of them before age bestowed other rights on me! I can rebuild this dwelling. And who knows whether I won't live here myself with the person I love? Who knows whether it won't be as much for me as for her that I will have had it rebuilt?"

This hope, although distant, vague, and uncertain, invigorated the young man's soul and gave him courage. He went over to the old manor.

"This is where my ancestors lived; that is where Mademoiselle d'Estival will live," he said to himself. Past and future, merging and pressing on his soul, suffocated the sense of the present. Pride took no part in his differing sensations. Seeing old towers, now the home of sinister birds, he was amazed that these warlike defenses had been allowed to continue to exist when they were now so impotent to resist anything, be it the authorities armed in the name of the law or a great crowd made strong by its sheer audacity. "I am sorry, antique families of barn owls and tawny owls," said St. Anne. "I am sorry to have to destroy your homes, but you really cannot stay; your cries would terrify the person to whom I wish to offer a smiling and pleasant home."

Herfrey not yet having arrived, St. Anne rushed to Auray, where he found a professional man to whom he gave the job of inspecting his château and seeing what could be preserved after having knocked down the old towers and all the outdated vestiges of eradicated feudalism. After having made a careful inspection, he was then to draw up a plan and an estimate, which St. Anne would consider on his return from Tonquedec, and after which he would be able to give the necessary orders. On the way back from Auray he made a detour to visit a monument of the ancient Druid religion. He saw what is claimed to be one of their altars, and recalled a tradition according to which they used to sacrifice people there.[17]

"This sort of religion must be horrible," said St. Anne to himself, "but it's all the same to me whether acts of cruelty are committed by error or passion. What difference does it make if one sacrifices one's equals to an ill-conceived god, to oneself, to one's resentments, or to one's greed? Paganism had its victims. Christianity had its own, and philosophy does not spare those whom it regards as its enemies."

So as to meditate in more comfort, St. Anne had sat down on the trunk of a cut-down tree at the edge of a wood. Two men were walking near him, in the shade of several old oaks, and as if the place had inspired them all with similar thoughts, he heard one of the men say to the other:

"Our priests had nieces, but we should look to see whether our solons do not have their own sweethearts![18] Our priests did not get married, and were accused of disorder and bad morals, but let us go and look in the countries where priests do marry, so we can see whether their households are always properly edifying, and whether their flocks are never neglected or scandalized! I miss the time when our most distinguished writers were polite and chaste, and when even our theater was a school of purity, decency, and of all the combined virtues."

"A fine school!" said the other, as he walked, laughing. "Yes, a fine school whose precepts have no effect whatsoever on the people who deliver them. Ask our actresses whether their lovers found them shier than usual after performing Virginie or the rose-girl of Salency.[19] You would have had to be walking around with your eyes shut not to have seen the evidence that our theaters, poetry, prose, and all our books have had no effect whatsoever on our morals, and have stayed, so to speak, outside our souls. And so I would see all known books burnt without throwing a single drop of water on the flames which consumed them."

And so saying, this enemy of books sat down near St. Anne, whom he saw sighing.

"I am too old to do without books myself," said his companion, "and even less would I be able to do without a friend molded by books, to whom books have taught everything, and whom they have taught to speak against them with such force and grace. What an ungrateful person you are! You are beating your nurse!"

"You disarm me very skillfully," said his friend.

"I have just heard," said the other, "that young St. Anne is in the neighborhood, and that he is hoping to restore the château of his fathers. If he comes to live here, I hope that he loves books, that he has books, that he lends them to us, and that he speaks and acts like an educated man."

St. Anne, who was already standing and ready to go, stopped and looked at them, unsure whether to say anything. Some inexpressible modesty in the young man sealed his lips. He satisfied himself with giving them a polite and affectionate greeting, particularly the one who was hoping so much from his stay in the area.

"That's him," said the other one. "I had half-recognized him because of his resemblance to his father, but the air with which he greeted you convinces me of it."

"So much the better," said his friend. "He has an excellent physiognomy and it made me like him directly."

Herfrey arrived in St. Anne at the same time that his master returned. He related what he had done at Missillac, and said that Mademoiselle de Rhedon had turned pale and that her hand had trembled when she took the letter he had handed her. As for the rest, he had no idea.

That same evening the two travelers set off for Tonquedec, where they arrived without accident. Night had fallen, and an old servant was doing the rounds of the château with a dog and a lantern before raising the drawbridge.

"Who goes there?" he shouted to the travelers.

"St. Anne and Herfrey," came the reply in a familiar voice.

"Good God! Welcome," cried out old Duval. "But how vexed I am! What bad luck!"

"What's the matter?" asked St. Anne.

"My master left for Missillac yesterday," continued Duval. "He hesitated a long while over which way to go, and in the end took the wrong one, as it turns out, seeing as you came the other way, and therefore didn't meet each other. But either way, we need supper and beds. Marie-Rose! Marie-Ursule!

Where are you? Fetch some spit-roast meat, a salad, and eggs. Then sheets, but first give the late Madame de Tonquedec's room, which is the prettiest, a good sweep before you make up the bed for my master's friend." Honest, simple, old-fashioned hospitality, how much I respect you!

A good deal of dew had fallen that evening, and the travelers' clothes were rather damp. Duval lit a bright, crackling fire and made them stand close to it, and, brushing the sparks that were leaping out back into the fireplace all the while, he told them local stories, and how his master, returning after his long absence, had been welcomed by his servants and old vassals, who had never stopped missing him. It was well known that he hadn't left the country of his own free will but that he had been forced to by his uncle and mother, "and therefore," said Duval, "we made sure that he was never put on any of those miserable lists that people are tortured with.[20] His return was celebrated with a fine party, and he would have been very happy himself, had his mother not died in his absence. Her death had spoiled everything, and despite being rich and perfectly the master of his own fortunes, he is bored here. So we are all pressing him to get married, and may he find a woman who resembles his mother!" Duval said no more for a while, and went to hasten the preparations for supper, which, in his view, were not coming along fast enough.

The next day, after a night of sleep such as can only be had after a long journey on foot, St. Anne went to visit all the places that were dear to his memory. His father had been Monsieur de Tonquedec's best friend, and Monsieur de Tonquedec had loved him as much as his own son, and had often invited him and his tutor to stay. The child had been much happier there than in Missillac, his mother having always been more imposing than fond. She had always taken greater care of her son's fortune than of his pleasure.

Once St. Anne had had a good walk around the château and bathed in the little river that flowed nearby, he came back and settled himself down in his friend's room to write him a letter. His motive in coming to his house had been twofold: he wanted to see him, and he wanted to get away from Missillac.

To go back there to meet him did not seem reasonable. To oblige him to return home immediately might annoy him. St. Anne thought that the best thing might be to give him a rendezvous in Auray. Apart from being able to complete his arrangements with the architect, he had also liked the place. He wanted to go back to see the Druid altar with Tonquedec, he wanted to sit on the edge of the wood with him, on the same tree trunk, and he felt that perhaps he might also be able to continue with the same meditations and see again the two friends whose conversation he had found so intriguing. There are moments in life that it would be wonderful to relive, but generally we have to be content with just remembering them. Let us get them used to coming to visit us very often. They would cheer our existence, and keep at bay other memories that haunt us like mournful specters, latching on, the better to torment us.

St. Anne had not yet finished his letter when Duval came to tell him that dinner awaited him.

St. Anne was unable to get Duval to sit down with him, but nothing was easier than to make him talk. Herfrey was waiting on his master, and sometimes smiled at the loquaciousness of this Nestor of footmen.[21]

"I was saying last night that we are all hoping that our master will get married," said Duval. "As long as he finds a woman worthy of his late mother, an excellent lady! Pious, charitable, of simple morals, an enemy to pride, forgiving of the faults of others, despite her own life being exemplary and irreproachable! You know, sir, that my master allows me to speak to him as I did when he was only a child and I was his tutor—not, it is true, in book learning, being barely able to read and write myself, but in the ways of behaving in the world, and how best to avoid blame and repentence. So I speak to him as I used to, without him ever becoming vexed at the little liberties I take; on the contrary, he encourages me, and he only really has me to talk to here, his godson Franck, who serves him very affectionately, being no more than a child, which means that generally he tells me whatever is on his mind, more as if he were with an old friend than an old servant. So, sir, one time when

I was on the subject of marriage, he said a word which made me hope that my wishes would be granted. If that happens, sir, I will invite you to the wedding, and you will have more right to be there than anyone else, because you will have supplied the dish without which there would have been no supper."

"Me?" said St. Anne. "I don't understand you, my friend; you must be clearer if you want me to understand you."

"Well, have you not written pages in your letters to him about a young cousin of yours, a certain Mademoiselle d'Estival?"

When he heard this name, St. Anne turned as pale as death. Duval was almost behind him, his hand resting on the chair, and saw nothing, but Herfrey saw it so clearly that he quickly gave his master a glass of wine. "Drink, sir, drink," he said in a tone that startled St. Anne. He looked at Herfrey, blushed, and smiled.

"It was a name," continued Duval, "which my master threw into the conversation and which gave me the idea that I have just told you. I turned it over in my mind by myself until the following day, and then I said to him: 'But sir, perhaps your friend will take this young lady for himself.' 'Well!' said my master, 'his mother is not the sort of woman who will allow him to marry a ruined orphan. In her house there is a very rich young lady who bears a name which used to be a very fine one; she is very pretty and very amiable, according to what St. Anne says about her. She is the one he is destined to marry. Madame de St. Anne is young and has a large personal fortune. One has to be one's own master, and already enjoy the use of one's parents' entire fortune, as is unhappily the case for me, to marry Mademoiselle d'Estival without contradiction or difficulty, and despite the fact that her mother is a peasant with nothing to recommend her and that her father's château was burnt and everything inside it looted.' 'Well,' said I to myself, 'that is in truth not a very good alliance,' but I said nothing to my master, and to begin with I thought, 'never mind! So long as the girl is worthy of my late mistress, that's the main thing.' My master is rich enough for both of them, and it would be better to have a single iota more of merit and goodness than another hundred thousand *écus*. These things should not even be set or measured against each other. My late mistress had a sister who was also good and worthy, although not as much as she, and that difference was very important, because while we were in paradise here, in the other lady's house people were only mediocrely satisfied. There they enjoyed neither the respect nor the affection that we had here. But, sir, will you allow me to be so bold as to ask whether your cousin is pretty?"

St. Anne did not reply, and so Duval went up to Herfrey, and whispered to him: "Your master is distracted, or he doesn't quite know what he ought to say, for these fine, clever people with their great education sometimes make such subtle distinctions that over the tiniest thing they will say neither yes nor no; so you tell me: is she pretty? You're hesitating too; is it that she is ugly, then, and you are too decent to say so?"

"No, it's certainly not that," said Herfrey. "Mademoiselle d'Estival is far from being ugly."

"So she's pretty, or beautiful?"

"She's better than beautiful or pretty," said Herfrey, still speaking low. "She has such a truthful, good, straightforward air, and nonetheless seems to have so much sense and cleverness that you would be inclined to ask her advice as if she were a doctor, or play with her as if she were a child. What she looks like depends on the occasion. She can look serious or cheerful according to what is required, but she always looks," said Herfrey, raising his voice bit by bit, "honest, amiable, angelic. When you see her, you think you will never tire of looking at her, and that you love her more than anything you have ever seen or ever will see. Those who depend on her will be happy forever, and her husband will be the happiest of men; but if it is your master who is to win her, if she is taken away from us, only to be brought here, I will never be able to come back here so long as I live."

Herfrey had forgotten himself so completely and become so completely transported during his poetic harangue that he did not think that he was talking in front of his master, but once he had finished speaking, he looked at him, and saw him lying back in his chair, his handkerchief over his eyes, weeping unrestrainedly. Herfrey's sudden silence making him remember where he was, he abruptly stood up and ran outside to get some air, his hand over his forehead to hide his distress. Duval brought him coffee in the garden, and never suspecting that he had made him feel mortal pain, advised him to go and rest in a shady spot, which he led him to, until his headache should pass.

On returning to the château, St. Anne tore his letter up. Twenty different projects suggested themselves to him. He rejected everything that was not worthy of a firm and generous soul, and he who wished he could have been carried to Missillac on the wings of the wind, resolved to return there by foot, and to go, as he had on his way, by St. Anne and Auray. "I must not," said he to himself, "break my word to the architect to whom I promised to give the job of rebuilding my house. He will have drawn up a plan and an estimate that I need to see. One is lost the instant one sacrifices one's word and convenience, that is to say, duty and honor, to one's desires."

And so he went to St. Anne and to Auray. He saw the plans, corrected them, agreed and signed the conditions, and gave guarantees for the payment of materials and labor; in a word, he did everything he should have, but he did it without pleasure. The spell had burst, and he already saw Mademoiselle d'Estival married to Tonquedec. Her mother would never allow her to refuse such an honorable and advantageous suit, and in any case, Tonquedec could never be displeasing; he was better than St. Anne; he might be a little colder, but he was more reasonable. Mademoiselle d'Estival would never come to live in St. Anne, but he would, and he'd be happier there than in Missillac, once she was no longer there.

The architect had just left, and he was walking to and fro in front of the château, ready to leave as soon as Herfrey appeared. He dreaded returning home, and yet he wanted to hasten it.

"Perhaps I'll be home," he thought to himself, "before Tonquedec has made his decision." And so he was just about to set off, when the two men whose conversation he had followed in the wood suddenly arrived, introduced themselves, and said that they had come to pay him a visit. St. Anne controlled himself, and made them very welcome. "It was not more than three days ago," he thought, "that I was hoping to see them again, and that I was writing to tell Tonquedec about them, and asking him to come and meet me here. Is it their fault that all my desires have since changed into melancholic indifference?" St. Anne asked his farmer to bring wine and cider, and told Herfrey that he wouldn't be leaving that evening yet. Reminding the two friends of the discussion they had been having, he encouraged them to talk, and their talk was clever and candid. The one who had been against books said:

"Well, what put the finishing touch to my distaste for all writers and writerly productions is the fact that nothing that they say is true; to my mind that means it can never be interesting. People trot out the same commonplaces every day on the most tired subjects, and without the party spirit which prides itself on reading everything which the party spirit writes, the leaves of a thousand tedious volumes would never even be opened. I know that many of our writers, the most creative and the most repetitive alike, could tell us many curious things, and yet refrain from doing so, and that their party would bring them down if ever they saw fit to reply to any of the questions that a man outside their parties might wish to pose them. The party reader wishes to be blind, and so much so that he will accept boredom in exchange for being kept in the dark. Without mentioning the arguments that one is obliged to limit oneself to, there are only certain facts which one is allowed to rehearse; those can be repeated a thousand times. The rest is supposed never to have happened. Certain days and hours never happened; they have been erased from the registers of time, and therefore such-and-such an event had no cause, and such-and-such another one had no effect. Ask any questions about these delicate points, and you are an enemy; your sacrilegious voice will be drowned out. It's like Clodius creeping into a place where important mysteries are celebrated, bringing terror with him.[22] It is not enough to veil the good goddess, it is not enough to dissimulate and keep quiet; things are invented.[23] Those who would hesitate to slander their enemies nonetheless see it as their duty to decorate their heroes with virtues which they never had. Unable to attribute public actions to them which the public knows nothing about, they bestow private conversations on them, and make them speak a language they never had. If, while caging reason and corrupting history, they still allowed fiction to range freely, truth might have been able to find shelter there, and fables could have told the truth. But the pages of an impartial novel are torn up the same as a history which goes too close to the truth. Aesop and La Fontaine would never dare, in some cases, to make the king of beasts magnanimous; in others, they would never dare accuse him of tyranny.[24] But enough of books!" exclaimed the man who had been speaking. "It makes us all bad tempered." He then brought the conversation back to the reason for their visit, and both men expressed their happiness at the idea that St. Anne would return to live among them. They then informed him of their current occupations and each offered their services; one said he could inspect the building, and the other that he could suggest better ways of cultivating the land. St. Anne accepted promptly and civilly; he knew that circumspection gives no pleasure to a man in good faith who wishes to be useful.

"Bring us," said one of the men as they left, "a woman who is like you, whose bearing and conduct inspire as much respect as affection, and who is, so to speak, from no specific century, so as to suit all of them better, from the golden age to the current time."

"Alas!" said St. Anne. "I had almost hoped to bring you such a person."

Feeling his face change and his eyes fill with tears, he apologized for his weakness.

"Why apologize? Why?" exclaimed the two men. "Your charming lack of reserve makes us feel even fonder of you, and in these times of egotism and distrust, individual attachments are precious; they are the comfort and consolation of life."

St. Anne said good-bye to the farmer and his family, the old manor house and its owls sentenced to a sad exile; he left them eleven days after his departure from Missillac.

His friend had been there for five. Traveling on horseback, along with Franck, his godson and pupil, who had already accompanied him on longer journeys, Tonquedec had needed no more than two days to cross the peninsula from one end to the other. On his way he had discovered that St. Anne would not be there, but this setback was not so bad as to prevent him from feeling any pleasure on arriving at Missillac.

He saw the two young ladies walking in the avenue that his friend had told him about, and he had no difficulty recognizing them both. Mademoiselle d'Estival's charm was in her bloom and physiognomy; Mademoiselle de Rhedon's was in the delicate regularity of her features. Mademoiselle d'Estival was taller, Mademoiselle de Rhedon more elegant. In one, a happy naturalness devoid of rusticity shone forth, characterizing her movements and form; there was greater art in the other, but there was nothing mannered about her—she was simply a little more self-conscious.

"You must be the friend whom St. Anne went to see," said Mademoiselle d'Estival to Tonquedec as soon as he had reached them. "I think there are resemblances between you and him. How unfortunate it is that he is not here."

"It is worse that he will not find me at home," said Tonquedec. "He will not find the consolation that I do here."

Mademoiselle de Rhedon replied politely and modestly to this compliment. They accompanied Mademoiselle d'Estival back to the farm, and then Mademoiselle de Rhedon returned to the château with Tonquedec. They spent their journey praising Mademoiselle d'Estival.

After the initial courtesies had been exchanged between Tonquedec and Madame de St. Anne, Tonquedec spoke of Mademoiselle d'Estival, and Madame de St. Anne, whether she espied the reason that had brought him or whether she suddenly realized how she could turn his journey to her advantage, praised Mademoiselle d'Estival even more than Mademoiselle de Rhedon had done. The latter was surprised, having always thought that Madame de St. Anne did not do Mademoiselle d'Estival justice. Mademoiselle de Rhedon did not realize that one can purposely abstain from praise, and similarly that one can praise on purpose *so as* to bring about a certain result and not *because* one approves or admires. She had praised without design, and never guessed Madame de St. Anne's purpose, but like her, she hoped that Tonquedec would find Mademoiselle d'Estival pleasing.

The following day, on the pretext of discussing with Mademoiselle d'Estival a visit on which she was to accompany Mademoiselle de Rhedon to some relations of hers, Madame de St. Anne invited her to the château for luncheon, which was something she had never done before. Madame d'Estival immediately devined Madame de St. Anne's intentions, and for once she was pleased about them. These two women differed only in the way they had been brought up, and there was something common to both that made them understand each other.

"My mother must be very pleased" said Mademoiselle d'Estival to Madame de St. Anne, "with the favor you are conferring on me, as she has made me dress with more care than usual today, and told me to do everything I could to deserve your generosity."

Madame de St. Anne smiled as she looked at Mademoiselle d'Estival, who was in fact very well dressed. She saw that the mother understood and approved her design, and from that moment she thought the thing was done. Mademoiselle d'Estival, receiving more encouragement than usual, was lovelier than usual, and soon felt so much at ease that she nearly spoiled everything: she talked about her cousin with such fire and such true affection and eloquence that Tonquedec nearly saw how much she felt for him.

"You are courting my son's friend," said Madame de St. Anne, "for he is as favorably disposed toward him as you are, and he loves him as much as you do."

"That would be difficult," said Mademoiselle d'Estival.

Madame de St. Anne steered the conversation into other channels, and in a private moment she had engineered with Tonquedec, said to him:

"I am sure you can see which young woman is intended for my son; I would like it if a decent man were able to consider my other young relation."

"That cannot fail to happen," said Tonquedec.

"It is true," continued Madame de St. Anne, "that everything conspires in her favor. In my eyes, her misfortunes only add to her attraction. Her mother, as you know, is a peasant from the Estival estate."

"What does that matter?" said Tonquedec.

"I admit," replied Madame de St. Anne, "that she is a woman of sense, and that she was never attached to anyone other than Monsieur d'Estival, and to his and their daughter's interests."

Madame de St. Anne said many other things, adapting herself to what Tonquedec said, praising what he praised, and foreseeing his objections, the better to overturn them. By the end, there was not a panegyric that she had not made or a piece of advice she had not given; she went along with the conversation and gently encouraged the decision that was quite ready to be made.

The following day, in the absence of the two young ladies whom Madame de St. Anne had sent off very early in the morning to visit Madame de Kerber, Tonquedec became a little bored. He was particularly irked by Mademoiselle d'Estival's not being there.

"Can you already be in love?" asked Madame de St. Anne with a smile.

"No," he said. "But it suits me to get married. I might have hesitated between your two relatives, if one of them had not already been intended for your son. He has praised both to me in his letters, but particularly Mademoiselle d'Estival. He spoke about her *con amore*" ("I believe it," thought Madame de St. Anne), "and perhaps he has disposed me more favorably toward her than to Mademoiselle de Rhedon. Moreover, the pleasure of providing a happy and stable fate for someone who lacks those things attracts me; after all, what sort of support is a mother like hers; what sort of a fortune is a smallholding, an orchard, and a garden?"

"Not much, it is true," said Madame de St. Anne.

"Moreover," continued Tonquedec, "without being exactly in love, I do find her charming."

"Do we want to go to the farm?" said Madame de St. Anne.

"You will be able to see that it is really not very much for two women to live off."

They went. Tonquedec said to Madame de St. Anne, "Do you think, madam, that it is my mother-in-law that I am going to meet?"

"I do not know," replied Madame de St. Anne, "but I would not be much surprised if you were to decide to ask the mother for her daughter's hand directly."

"That would be rather prompt," said Tonquedec.

"Mademoiselle d'Estival does not conceal anything," said Madame de St. Anne. "As you have seen her, so she is; you also know her perfectly from my son."

Madame d'Estival did not display her surprise when they arrived, and she made sure not to say anything about it being the first time that she had ever seen her proud cousin close up. Like her daughter, Madame d'Estival was clever, shrewd, and even tactful, but these qualities, differently employed, had developed in other directions. The more people knew the daughter, the more they loved her, but to be satisfied with the mother, it was necessary to avoid seeing her for very long and also to avoid being with her when she put off constraint, particularly when she was either very pleased or very angry, because then the thin coat of varnish that covered the extreme vulgarity of her soul and ways would fall away entirely.

The conversation was initially rather cold but gradually it gained interest. Madame d'Estival spoke about her misfortunes with moderation and courage. She was sorry for her daughter, but felt that she herself deserved nothing better, and moreover that her life was far advanced, and that what she had undergone would quite naturally hasten its end. But her daughter! She was not yet seventeen years old! Tonquedec was moved all the more because it seemed as if no one was trying to move him. Madame de St. Anne took so little part in the conversation that one might have thought she wasn't listening. Various characteristics that her son had written about in his letters, various judgments about Mademoiselle d'Estival returned to trace themselves in Tonquedec's mind, telling him, "The emotion you feel is not only inspiring you with a noble aim, but it is also disposing you to perform a wise action. Obey this impulse, for it is a good guide."

"Would you like me to become responsible for the object of your solicitude?" he said to Madame d'Estival. "Would you like to give me your daughter?"

"From everything which I have heard about you, sir," replied Madame d'Estival, who was concealing her joy with an air of thoughtfulness, "and not only what I have heard about you, but what I can see for myself, my daughter could not fall into better hands, and nothing could make me happier nor give me greater peace of mind."

Tonquedec glanced at Madame de St. Anne and saw no surprise in her eyes, only faint approbation.

"Perhaps you may consider that I am going rather fast," Tonquedec said to her, "but Mademoiselle d'Estival's fate touches me deeply. Moreover, having read what your son wrote to me about her, I feel as if I know her, and as if I am guaranteeing my own happiness by pledging to do everything I can to ensure her own."

"I commend your decision," said Madame de St. Anne. "People have concluded the important business of marriage thousands of times on the basis of much less knowledge, after nothing greater than a quarter of an hour's conversation, an inspection of rental income, and some ancient parchment."

"My daughter is yours," said Madame d'Estival.

"Providing she consents," interrupted Tonquedec.

"I beg you to have a good enough opinion of her not to doubt it. Mother and daughter are happy to have you, one as husband, the other as son-in-law."

This was enough for Madame de St. Anne, and these words having been said in a tone that was beginning to get a little too eager, she decided that it would be best not to allow Madame d'Estival to say any more. She therefore took her leave very politely, and she and Tonquedec climbed into the barouche that had arrived for her. On the pretext of its being a beautiful evening on which to show him the neighborhood around Missillac, she made the journey last until she was sure that Mademoiselle d'Estival would have returned to her own home. She thought it very important that her mother should mention the marriage to her first, rather than Tonquedec, to whom she might give an answer that would spoil everything.

Mademoiselle de Rhedon was therefore alone in the château when Madame de St. Anne and Tonquedec returned. She talked about the day she'd had with pleasure and interest, saying that Mademoiselle d'Estival had lent it its charm with the extremely subtle and penetrating questions she had asked and observations she had made about everything that was new to her.

"At Madame de Kerber's house, we met the man whom her daughter told us about in that letter, and for whose sake Madame de Rieux set her hair to rights. He is much better than Mademoiselle de Kerber told us he was, and therefore Madame de Rieux does not judge him to be unworthy of coquetry. Well, he only paid attention to Mademoiselle d'Estival, whom he had already met once, and I truly would not be surprised if he came to ask for her hand in marriage at the earliest opportunity. He told her that he would have the honor of seeing her again soon."

No skill, not even Madame de St. Anne's, could ever have conceived of saying anything better. Tonquedec, who had been looking rather thoughtful during the drive, cheered up on hearing Mademoiselle de Rhedon's account, and when she finished on the words we have just heard, he felt thoroughly joyful and said, laughing;

"He may come *soon*, but it will still be too late for this suitor, or so I presume." The joy that he felt was not childish, nor was it triumphant. Tonquedec was happy with the decision he had made and happy with his choice, but it was tinged with some of that fear and anxiety that any man must feel in a similar postion. He must have been and indeed was very glad not to feel any particular attachment to Madame d'Estival, who would have been as delighted with any son-in-law as with him.

Madame d'Estival, seeing that her daughter was tired after her outing and the sight of so many new things, waited for the following day before mentioning the great affair that she had just concluded without consulting her, the person who was most concerned by it.

"Thank me," she said. "I made a match for you yesterday, and a very good one too."

"But St. Anne hasn't come back," said the young person. "You are joking, no doubt."

"No," said her mother, "I am not joking in the slightest," and she went on to tell her what you have just read.

"What!" exclaimed Mademoiselle d'Estival. "To marry me off without asking the opinion of my cousin, the first and only man who has ever shown any interest in me, and for whom I feel strong affection? He thought of me; he told me so."

"Why did he not speak to me like this man did?" said her mother. "I asked you whether you wanted him to be your husband, and you told me you didn't."

"But I was frightened of marriage," said Mademoiselle d'Estival, in tears. "Oh God, if I had been able to foresee all this, I would have replied differently to him and to you."

Her mother let her weep for some time, and eventually said to her, "You must be mad."

"Dear God, I am not," said the young person. "I am not mad, but I was when I imagined that St. Anne would be like the other husbands I have seen, the one in Nantes who never spoke, and the one in Vannes who was so hard, and the one in Brest who had no thought for his wife from the day after their wedding. Why did I go and clutter up my mind with all those people? Why did I remember them and not simply consent to spend my life with a man whom I love as I love myself?"

"Hold your tongue," her mother said curtly. "I want to hear no more of this wildness. It is a sin for a young woman to speak of a man in this way, particularly if she is promised to another. I am ashamed of having brought you up so badly, for you not even to realize how wrong what you are saying is."

Thus scolded, Mademoiselle d'Estival said no more and simply wept. Her mother soon stopped hiding her extreme impatience with these tears.

"Is it also a sin to weep?" the daughter asked bitterly. "Do I have to run off and sing my thanks to Madame de St. Anne for the husband she is giving me so that I don't get her son? Now I see how clever she has been, and what the purpose of her recent kindness, the day before yesterday's invitation, and yesterday's visit was—"

"Be quiet, little girl," interrupted Madame d'Estival. "Do not judge the conduct of those who are wiser than you; soon you'll be accusing your own mother."

Then, calming herself a little, and taking care not to allow her daughter to catch hold of the slightest possibility of refusing a marriage she disliked, she said to her:

"You will live with a man who is very gentle, very good, and very kind in a house which is very well situated—"

"Oh my God! That's precisely not what I was hoping for, and precisely the worst part of my unhappiness," said Mademoiselle d'Estival. "I will have to leave this place where I have been happy for the first time in my life. A few weeks ago, I did not know what happiness was; recently I have been happy, and already it has to end, or rather, it is already over." And her tears flowed more copiously than before.

"You are an ungrateful wretch," said her mother. "Yes, an ungrateful wretch. You love no one but yourself; you spare no thought for a mother who has sacrificed herself to your happiness. What do you think it was like for me to have to press your father to marry me? What did I personally stand to gain? My own family's hatred was very clearly displayed, as has been the disdain of my husband's, of which I receive new evidence every day. I do not think that proud Madame de St. Anne would ever have allowed her son to become my son-in-law, but if he had married you in spite of her, how do you suppose she would have treated us, and me especially, and what would there have been to compensate me for those humiliations which, being as I now see you are, you would hardly have bothered with? This is the only place I have to live. I would have been abandoned here alone, while you would have gone off to scintillate nearby, forgetting me as if it hadn't been I who brought you into the world."

"My God, what are you saying?" exclaimed Mademoiselle

d'Estival, kissing her mothers' hands. "Me, forget you! Me, wanting to scintillate! I barely understand what you are saying, it is so far from my thoughts."

"Listen," her mother said, "I know the world a little better than you. What is far from your thoughts today may be something which suggests itself tomorrow. If your husband and his mother were to treat you well, you wouldn't trouble about your own mother any longer; although if you were scorned at the château, you would be running back to the farm in tears."

"But," said Mademoiselle d'Estival, "was it so urgent to make a match for me? You saw from what I said to St. Anne that I did not think it was urgent in the slightest."

"What a child you are!" said her mother. "Do you not think that it costs money to dress you as you are and to live as we do, however frugally that may be? I wanted you to be dressed as a young lady should be, and I knew why I wanted it too. A parade of poverty tempts nobody; for it to touch people, it needs to be suspected but not seen. You might very well say to those fine ladies, as you did on the day the dog bit your cousin, that 'he is used to your dresses; I wear them too,' and I was very pleased you did. But never suppose that the pears and the apples in our orchard are what allow you to say *I wear ones like you.* It is by means of some old savings that I am able to keep you on the footing that you have always been seen on; I hoped to attract the good luck that finally arrived yesterday, and I will take good care that it doesn't escape me."

Mademoiselle d'Estival, more humiliated than grateful, was distressfully gazing at her clothes when her mother added, "But it's not all dresses and decent shawls, bonnets and hats that allows one to appear in society; more than anything else one needs enough to eat and drink, and one or two bad hay and fruit harvests would have deprived us of our basic needs. What would we have done then? Would you want your mother, who is no longer young, to get herself employment as poultry maid for one of your proud relations?"

"No, Mother, no!" cried out Mademoiselle d'Estival in anguish. "And yet if I were brave enough . . ."

"Don't be brave; I forbid you to be brave and command you

to obey," said her mother, curtly. "A marriage such as you are presented with has always been the object of my wishes. My peace of mind requires that our keep be ensured. It would suit me to leave a neighborhood where I am despised, and get away from a woman and a family who treat me with disdain. Consider this well, and show the man who wants you that you are marrying him joyfully if you do not wish to lose your mother's affection and provoke his hostility."

And thus Madame d'Estival's speech, which had followed Madame de St. Anne's in almost all respects, ended in the same way, and almost with the same words. The two mothers had done a great deal, one for her son and the other for her daughter, and now desired a great reward, each employing the object of her tender care as a tool to obtain it, in such a way as to make one doubt whether their tenderness had ever been equal to their egotism. At the very least they had only ever loved after their own fashion, consulting nothing but their own tastes and moods when molding the destinies of those they loved best. The faculty of feeling for others, of being able to put oneself in someone else's place, is much spoken of, but do we really possess that faculty? Where do we find the model for a sensation that we have never felt? To love as we find it agreeable to be loved, we need organs that are almost the same, modified by habits that are almost the same. Two brothers or twins must feel this sweet and happy love for one another, and divorced from its individual curse, the tale of Oedipus's children would be badly imagined, whereas the story about Castor and Pollux is exactly right.*[25] Let us say that of the two mothers, the more reasonable was Madame d'Estival, and that her motives were of a different, more powerful order than Madame de St. Anne's; they consequently had greater impact. Moreover, the young girl, younger than her suitor, did not know as he did that a mother's authority has limits.

---

* Author's footnote: A man who has not only subtle organs but also sagacity, thoughtfulness, varied experience, and a good memory would not be able to be a party man—he feels for everything that suffers; he weeps for all sorts of suffering.[26]

This conversation between Madame and Mademoiselle d'Estival took place in the morning. After dinner, Tonquedec came to the farm, accompanied by Mademoiselle de Rhedon.

"Have you spoken to your daughter?" he asked the mother on first approaching her.

"I have not failed to," she replied. "You will find her a little pensive. It is a big thing for a girl to change her state, and chance has willed that she has only ever encountered ill-assorted couples in all the places we sought refuge in, one after the other; husbands and wives were either cold to each other, or fought like cats and dogs. She became horribly afraid of marriage. Is that not true, daughter?" she continued, addressing Mademoiselle d'Estival as they moved toward her, and who, as Tonquedec saw, had a sad air about her, and eyes that were still red from all the tears she had so abundantly shed.

"Do I have the bad luck to look like one of those cold or angry husbands that you have seen?" he asked her, as he took her hand.

"No indeed," she replied.

"Do you fear," he resumed, "that I will behave in the same way that caused you pain on behalf of those other wives?"

"I have," said she, "no reason for such fears."

"Your fears would distress me immensely," said Tonquedec, kissing her hand.

Mademoiselle d'Estival was moved. She smiled and wept.

"Let us discuss nothing that is not cheerful," said her mother. "We wept enough when there was reason to do so; now we have every cause to be happy, so I hope that we know how to celebrate."

Tonquedec then looked around him and praised the property and the arrangement of everything he could see.

"Your residence," said he, "is pretty, your meadows fine, and your trees laden with fruit."

"This house is dear to me," said Mademoiselle d'Estival.

"We shall come here whenever you want," said Tonquedec. "I much prefer these sorts of houses to larger residences. We rely more on ourselves for enjoyment here. We are much closer to everything around, to everything and everyone whom we hope will contribute to the happiness and amusement of our lives. We can hear the wife we have chosen breathe, we can see her move; servants, if we have any, work under the eye of their master and are encouraged by him. A dog that we are fond of is right there; we can stroke him whenever we want. The husband has his book to hand, the wife her work."

Mademoiselle d'Estival listened to Tonquedec with pleasure.

"I would be very glad," said she, "to return here sometimes"; she was thinking about the cousin that she would be able to see there.

"We will come back," said Tonquedec. "I promise you, and all you will need to do is to express the wish, and we will come. If you want to repair something here, to carry out some improvement, that will be our first care; you cannot imagine how much I desire to please you and to make you happy."

Madame d'Estival was extremely pleased with the turn the conversation had taken, except when Mademoiselle de Rhedon conveyed Madame de St. Anne's invitation to be so kind as to allow her daughter to spend the rest of the evening at the château, she showed some unwillingness.

"Oh," said Tonquedec, "you can entrust her to us; she is not safer with her mother than she is with a lover like me."

He did not guess what Madame d'Estival feared.

"Be careful," she whispered to her daughter as she pretended to set her hair to rights, "and be sure not to say a word about your cousin."

Madame de St. Anne, who had precisely the same fears as Madame d'Estival, had summoned musicians from Nantes, and gave Mademoiselle d'Estival the first concert she had ever heard. During the supper that followed, Madame de St. Anne made sure the giddy distractions never ceased, so as to silence memories and prevent conversation. It was known that Mademoiselle d'Estival had never seen fireworks, and several rockets that had been procured greatly amazed her. Finally, Madame de St. Anne herself accompanied her back to the farm with Mademoiselle de Rhedon and Tonquedec. The following day she was fetched, and found a great number of people at the château. People were whispering the news of her marriage to each other. Madame de St. Anne received congratulations with feigned modesty.

"It is not I," she said to someone who was heartily congratulating her. "I have played no part in this affair. Tonquedec saw her, and did justice to her."

Mademoiselle d'Estival heard her, and particularly saw her talking; she saw that her eyes gave the lie to her words, and felt such aversion to her that she applauded her mother's dislike. Her aversion was so strong that the good luck of not having her as a mother-in-law almost consoled her for not being married to the son. "Not only is she proud; she is also false," she said. "She was kind to me so as to be rid of me; to depend on her would have been a misery. She would have hated me, and to take revenge, would perhaps have set me and her son against each other. She is now telling everyone that she has had nothing to do with this marriage, which in fact she is deeply involved in, so that he isn't angry with her. Yes indeed, deeply involved. I can see in her eyes how pleased she is to have removed me from her son by giving me to someone else." A few tears of resentment rather than grief fell down her cheeks. Tonquedec was watching her and saw her weep. He felt alarmed, and going up to her, he asked her what was causing her tears.

"Indignation," she said.

"Against whom?" said Tonquedec.

Mademoiselle d'Estival would not tell him, but when he looked around, he saw that only Madame de St. Anne could have occupied her attention at that moment. As a result of a turn in her thoughts, she spoke to Tonquedec with greater confidence and pleasure than she had ever done. For the first time their conversation was free and lively. Tonquedec considered himself to be happy and, attentive to everything that could please the person who was making him feel such an agreeable sentiment and who was giving him such sweet hopes for the future, he admired the vivacity of her eyes, the bloom of her complexion, the beauty of her hair; he even noticed that she had small feet and that her hands were extremely beautiful.

At that moment, a letter was brought to him. Madame de St. Anne, paying attention to everything that was happening, saw the letter, and thought she could see that it was from her son. However, she did not dare ask to see it, and he went out of the room to read it.

As he came back in, Madame de St. Anne went to meet him.

"By the greatest chance in the world, I have a notary in the house," she told him. "After he's finished with the papers he came for, would you like him to draw up your marriage contract? It would be speedily done. You no doubt know what benefits you wish to bestow on your future bride; she brings only her charms as her dowry." And seeing that Tonquedec was hesitating, she added, "And then you could go and sign the contract at the farm, or request Madame d'Estival to come here."

"No," said Tonquedec, "it is not as urgent as that. Your son writes to tell me he is coming back immediately; I would prefer to wait for him, and the celebration I would like to hold after signing the contract will be more pleasant if he is there."

"As you wish," said Madame de St. Anne, blushing. "But this feast, you could wait until the wedding to hold it; there's no hurry once the contract is signed."

"No," said Tonquedec. "I would rather do as I have just said; I will wait for St. Anne. It is his close relation that I am marrying; he will sign the contract."

At that instant it occurred to Tonquedec that Madame de St. Anne had pushed things forward very quickly, and he had some suspicion of what her interest in it might have been. He was amazed not to have thought of it earlier, and not to have been surprised that a woman of a character such as he knew hers to be could be so kind to Mademoiselle d'Estival and her mother. He remembered what he had said to Duval in that conversation that the latter had related to St. Anne. The most acute man does not notice the trap that a clever woman holds out for him until he is already half-caught.

Troubled by these reflections, and wanting distraction,

Tonquedec proposed to Mesdemoiselles de Rhedon and d'Estival that they go for a walk. They ended up at the farm, and Tonquedec and Mademoiselle de Rhedon did not depart until nightfall. The other guests had not yet left the château. They were playing cards in a drawing room overlooking the avenue, but as the room was brightly lit, they could not see what was happening outside, and the avenue looked completely dark.

The two travelers, St. Anne and Herfrey, were therefore able to enter the château entirely unseen. This is what St. Anne had hoped, and he had arranged for them to arrive as late as possible. How his heart beat as he climbed the stairs! His eyes, tricked by love and fear, made him think that two men talking politics on the balcony were Tonquedec and his cousin deep in conversation. He told Herfrey, who successfully convinced him that this was not the case, but he could not be dissuaded from the belief that even if the future couple were not on the balcony, they were sitting next to each other in the room, and that Madame de St. Anne, delighted with the marriage, was celebrating it with a glittering gathering. Although these were still only conjectures and fantastical imaginings, they were vivid and agonizing, and hardly of a sort to soothe the pain of hearing young Franck, who saw him going into his room, cry out as he ran to welcome him:

"Oh what a good time you have chosen to return! We are getting married, sir; your good friend is getting married, and you will be at the wedding. We even thought we might sign the contract this evening."

Fortunately St. Anne was close to a chair, and he fainted, dropping into it.

"Your master is ill," said Franck to Herfrey as he came in.

"It's only travel fatigue," said Herfrey, and ran off to fetch what he thought most appropriate for the condition of his master, whom he left in Franck's care. The swoon did not last long, and his return to consciousness was extremely painful. And yet he had to find a way to control himself; he had to show that he was a man. St. Anne thought he could be allowed a few hours to consider the air and tone that he should adopt, and requested Franck to tell his master that he would not see him until the following day.

"I can hear him coming back from his walk with Mademoiselle de Rhedon," said Franck. "He would be very sorry not to be allowed to come and greet you directly."

"Let him come in, then," said St. Anne, slightly relieved by the thought that at least he was not with Mademoiselle d'Estival.

Tonquedec, informed by his young servant, came in, but he found St. Anne with such a changed voice and burning skin that he judged it better to leave him to rest. He conferred with Herfrey and Franck, and they agreed that they would not tell anyone, not even Madame de St. Anne, that her son was back.

The night was a painful one for the two friends, but both thought what friends must think. "I will not disturb Tonquedec's felicity," St. Anne said to himself. "If St. Anne loves his cousin, I will give her up," thought Tonquedec.

In the morning, Tonquedec quietly visited St. Anne. He was sleeping. Tonquedec was a little reassured, and sat by his bedside, waiting for him to awake. It was a pleasure for St. Anne to open his eyes and see his friend. In a good heart, jealousy is neither bitter nor unjust; love does not stifle friendship. St. Anne asked Tonquedec to inform his mother and Mademoiselle de Rhedon of his return, and to ask them not to visit him until the afternoon.

"As for you," he said, squeezing Tonquedec's hand, "if you haven't anything better to do . . . if you can do it without putting yourself to any inconvenience—"

"Anything better to do!" interrupted Tonquedec.

"Come back and spend the morning with me, then," said St. Anne.

While St. Anne had slept and for the duration of this short conversation, the curtains had been drawn, and the bed placed so that Tonquedec was unable to see his friend's face. On his return, he was struck by how pale and drawn he looked, but he made no comment, and St. Anne did not complain of any illness or sorrow. Their conversation was not very animated, but it was reasonable and gentle. St. Anne told him about the short journey he had just undertaken, not omitting the two

friends or their conversation and in particular the bad opinion
one had held of the writers and readers of the day, and of
books in general.

"It is entirely true," said Tonquedec, "that a century and a
half of the richest literature that any nation has ever been able
to boast of has not enlightened us very much or given us better
morals or greater humanity."

This subject led to political quarrels. Both were firmly
resolved never to become involved, and to let their country
adopt the ideas of the greatest number, which would sooner or
later, in their opinion, gain the upper hand. In this they may
have been mistaken: there are so many people who, taken
together or separately, do not provide the spectator with anything better to look at than a machine incapable of will or reason! St. Anne can hardly have understood this when he
persisted in rejecting collective terms and, worried that people
would have an inadequate sensation of the happiness or misery of their fellow men, insisted that one should say, "The soldiers are suffering from hunger," rather than "The army is
badly provisioned," or "The peasants work too hard," "Artisans are not paid enough," and "Honest merchants are being
ruined," rather than "Agriculture is short of labor," "Gold is
being saved, not spent," or "Business is being disrupted."
Tonquedec and St. Anne shared the same feelings. Both found
it completely absurd to consider placing one century back in
another one, as a clever man recently put it, not least given
that some countries are still subject to the authority of ecclesiastical and secular princes of all denominations, to chapters,
orders, and bodies with special privileges—one century cannot be contemporaneous with another century, particularly
in countries whose borders meet.[27] Tonquedec and St. Anne
each said, "I will not attack any new men or new opinions. If
I am attacked or if you are attacked, I will defend both you
and me."

After an hour or two of such discussions, and a further
quarter of an hour of silence, Tonquedec said to his friend:
"Have you not been told that I am getting married? Why is it
that you do not mention it?"

"Franck told me," replied St. Anne, lowering his gaze and keeping it fixed on the plans his architect had drawn up, which he had shown his friend, "and I was not sure whether his authority was such that I should believe it. If it is true, I wish you joy. No one will be so happy for you as I."

"I believe it," said Tonquedec. "Your mother praised your young relation to me a great deal."

"I am grateful that she did her justice," said St. Anne.

"The situation this young person finds herself in touched me even more than her charms and her merit," resumed Tonquedec.

"Such a sentiment is worthy of you," said St. Anne. "Be happy and make her happy." St. Anne had succeeded in controlling himself so well that the few words he spoke did not betray his feelings. He spoke of other things, and Tonquedec left him still unsure of what he felt, and yet he resolved not to allow the day to end without discovering the sentiments of St. Anne and the young woman. "If she prefers him and if he loves her, then there is no more to be said," he thought.

To begin with, after dinner, he went to fetch Mademoiselle d'Estival, who did not give in easily, such was her aversion to the château and Madame de St. Anne. However, her manifest aversion so reassured her mother that she would not commit any imprudence, that Madame d'Estival compelled her to accompany Tonquedec. Madame d'Estival was even more pleased with him that day, and even more willing to oblige him than she had been on the preceding days.

At the château they met Mademoiselle de Kerber, who had just arrived and who had not yet been told that St. Anne had returned. Madame de St. Anne and Mademoiselle de Rhedon had not yet seen him, and were not entirely free from anxiety on his account, and although they felt the same anxiety, neither admitted it to the other. They both noticed that Tonquedec had not yet mentioned St. Anne to Mademoiselle d'Estival, and this intensified the vague fear they both felt, and which in Madame de St. Anne's case dated from the night before, when Tonquedec, having read his friend's letter, had insisted that they wait for him before signing the contract. From the moment his suspicions had first been aroused, none of this had escaped Tonquedec, and he felt even more suspicious.

Everyone was therefore rather silent, Mademoiselle de Kerber the same as the others. She had heard about Tonquedec's marriage, and knew from the letter that St. Anne had written her the night before he left how distressing it would be for him; she felt this so strongly that for his sake she dreaded his return, which she supposed was imminent. Mademoiselle d'Estival was the least embarrassed of anyone present, as the direct orders of her mother, Madame de St. Anne's artfulness, and Tonquedec's own merit had combined to reduce her to a state of such submission that she was resigned to her fate. She broke the general constraint.

"My mother is very happy today," she said, "and today has been an eventful day at our house. Firstly—but that's not what has made my mother so happy; on the contrary—firstly, a letter was delivered to us, and I think it must have been immensely delayed, as we have never had a letter delivered to the farm before, and the people in the post office at Vannes or wherever it was did not know our name, nor where 'the farm near the château de Missillac' was; in sum, I think the letter was very delayed and passed through many hands before landing in mine. Look!" she said to Mademoiselle de Rhedon. "Doesn't it look a mess? But although we could read our own name despite it being very badly written—look, *Mademoiselle d'Estival*—it's definitely addressed to me, and what it contains has remained a secret, as no one can read in our house, as you know. I laughed when I saw my mother open it after having paid the postage; it must have been for appearances and because other people were watching. I have every confidence in you," added Mademoiselle d'Estival, still addressing Mademoiselle de Rhedon. "Would you be so kind as to take the letter and to read it once you've put your gloves on?"

"Give it to me," said Mademoiselle de Rhedon. "I am not so refined as you suppose."

So she took the letter, which she saw had been written by Herfrey and sent from Tonquedec, and this is what it said:

Dear Mademoiselle,

I do not know whether my master has told you that he loves you, but in any case I am making so bold as to tell you myself. I have been suspecting it for some time and now I am sure of it. He was so distressed on learning that his friend had gone to Missillac with the intention of courting you that I thought he would die from the pain. I warn you that if you marry either Monsieur de Tonquedec or anyone else apart from my master, he will be a dead man, and you would be very distressed, I am sure, and as for me, I would not long survive such a calamity. I am, mademoiselle, but only on condition that you marry no one other than my good master, your very humble servant, Pierre Herfrey.

P.S. I know my master. He may say nothing at all. He loves his friend tenderly, and also considers that a man should stand firm and be courageous in the face of calamity. But don't believe him.

Mademoiselle de Rhedon was exceedingly upset by this letter, but she concealed her distress. Mademoiselle d'Estival asked her to tell her what she'd read. "Not now," her friend said in a voice that was much changed, "for the love I bear you, do not demand it of me."

Madame de St. Anne gestured to take the letter that was causing such distress, but Mademoiselle de Rhedon gestured her refusal. After a few moments of thought, she made a sign to Tonquedec, ushered him out of the room, and gave him the letter.

She then returned to her place, and Tonquedec came not long after. Madame de St. Anne looked extremely displeased.

"I see," said she, "that no one in my house has less authority than I. A man who has been known for no more than three days is given preference over me by someone for whom there is nothing I do not do, and on whose behalf I expose myself to a thousand unpleasantnesses."

Mademoiselle de Rhedon said with some pride, "I do not know what obliges you to, madam. I have done what I must do."

Mademoiselle d'Estival, startled by what she was seeing and

hearing, said nothing, and the silence had again become general, when Mademoiselle de Kerber asked what the other great event was that had happened that day at the farm.

"Oh! That," said Mademoiselle d'Estival. "There was nothing mortifying about it. That man whom Castor bit two or three months ago, and that I told you about after he bit St. Anne, the same person that I met in this house three days ago, came to tell us that he owed sixty-five thousand francs to my father, including two years' interest, that the documents that proved the debt may well have been burnt along with the rest of the château but that he recognized it nonetheless, and that he was ready to pay us in whatever currency we preferred. Then he asked if he could talk privately to my mother; I went out and sat on the wall around the well to wait for their discussion to come to an end. It didn't last long. 'I give my word,' said my mother, as she saw him out, 'a few days sooner and we could have discussed business, for your offers are very generous and your conduct extremely honest.' 'To whom shall I make out the money, madam?' asked the man as he left. 'I will let you know,' said my mother. He left, and I went in. 'I would like it,' I said to my mother, 'if we used this money to buy a good house in Estival, which I think you prefer to any other place in the world,' and it is true that my mother still misses it. When she is happy, she speaks the Estival dialect, and tells stories about Estival; when she is in a bad mood, there is nowhere good apart from Estival and she doesn't like anything in Nantes, Vannes, Brest, or at the farm, which I on the contrary have found very good and very agreeable . . . particularly during a certain time."

Madame de St. Anne said to Tonquedec, "You are to be congratulated on such an arrangement," adding in a lower voice, "it would relieve you of a burden."

"Perhaps it is you, madam, who should be congratulated," interrupted Tonquedec.

"Me!" said Madame de St. Anne.

"You," repeated Tonquedec. Madame de St. Anne did not understand him, but this mysterious word, added to the other mysteries, put the finishing touches to her dismay.

A moment later Mademoiselle d'Estival, turning by chance toward the window, saw Herfrey come out of the château.

"Herfrey!" she exclaimed. "Herfrey is here!"

"Did you not know that my son has come back?" said Madame de St. Anne.

"I did not know either," said Mademoiselle de Kerber. "Why did you not tell us?'

"He is indisposed," said Tonquedec. "We did not wish to distress you. I am the only person to have seen him. I think, however, that it is nothing worse than travel fatigue that has caused the discomfort he is currently suffering from."

"God grant that that's all it is," said Mademoiselle d'Estival.

Mademoiselle de Kerber shook her head.

"What do you mean?" asked Madame de St. Anne.

"Are you seriously asking?"

"Certainly, and I would be glad if people would place a little more confidence in me than they have been doing of late."

"Read this, then," Mademoiselle de Kerber told her, giving her the letter that St. Anne had written the night before he left, and pointing at the last sentence.

Mademoiselle d'Estival was visibly suffering. "St. Anne is ill," she said to Tonquedec with a sigh. "I am no longer surprised at how dejected you look today. The instant you arrived at the farm I noticed it, and I mentioned it to my mother, but she only told me that I was mistaken, and a foolish creature who gets worried at nothing."

"*Who gets worried*," repeated Tonquedec. "Would you be upset to see me seriously ill?" he asked with emotion.

"What a question!" exclaimed Mademoiselle d'Estival.

"Are you at all attached to me?"

"How could I not be attached," she replied, "to a man who is my cousin's best friend, who is as just, honest, and kind as he is, and who has shown me nothing but generosity as well as the desire to see me happy?"

"You are not reading," said Mademoiselle de Kerber to Madame de St. Anne.

"But," Tonquedec continued, "if you had to choose . . . ?"

"Good God!" exclaimed Madame de St. Anne, who was in

effect listening more than she was reading. "What does all this mean? What is the point of encouraging the babble of a child?"

"A child?" Tonquedec said haughtily. "You wanted this child to become my wife. It is apparently my business to know her feelings, and it is permissible, I think, for me to try to discover them. Tell me, my beautiful, my little sweetheart, tell me without being embarrassed which of us you love best—me or your cousin?"

"Oh, my cousin," said Mademoiselle d'Estival. "I met him first, he is . . . he is . . . that is, I love him."

Simultaneously, Tonquedec, who thought he could hear St. Anne pacing from a side room to the hall and back again, realized the truth, which was that St. Anne could not quite bring himself to come into the drawing room. He went to fetch him, and taking him by the hand, and feeling him tremble, said, "Don't worry. Everything has been cleared up; you will be pleased. Come."

St. Anne came in. Mademoiselle d'Estival cried out, for he was as pale as death, and could barely walk.

"I surrender her to you," said Tonquedec. "She is yours; her heart belongs to you."

Then everyone went to the assistance of them both. Mademoiselle de Rhedon wept freely, and what she felt for herself looked like great sensibility for the feelings of others. Things gradually calmed down, and everyone learned to understand each other. St. Anne saw that everyone was to be praised; such friendship and generosity had never been seen before. Tonquedec was the best of friends, Mademoiselle de Rhedon the most generous of rivals. Mademoiselle de Kerber, enlightening Madame de St. Anne, had compelled her to accept with good grace what she could not prevent. Having concealed the first force of her emotion from spectators, she returned to her son's side and embraced her future daughter-in-law.

"I offer," she said, "to accompany you to your mother's house and explain to her the changes that have been made, and ask her if she will grant your hand in marriage to my son."

"What goodness!" exclaimed St. Anne, and he kneeled down in front of his mother, who raised him up and embraced him. But the shock of what he had undergone was so violent that he asked if the visit could be delayed for an hour. During that time, Herfrey's letter was read to Mademoiselle d'Estival, and St. Anne went to find Herfrey to embrace him and give him the news of his marriage. When he returned he felt well enough to go to the farm. His mother had had the horses harnessed to the barouche, which took them along very gently.

What was said at the farm is easy to imagine, as well as how persuasive Madame d'Estival found the offer that Madame de St. Anne hastened to make to buy or build her a house in the village where she had been born. The idea had come from Mademoiselle d'Estival, and it suited everyone. Madame d'Estival was so delighted, describing the house that she would like the most and that just happened to be for sale, that she hardly saw anything in her daughter's establishment beyond her own establishment and reintegration into her village.

"I won't call you an *ungrateful wretch* anymore," she said to Babet as she embraced her. "Your thought for me was an excellent one." She turned round to St. Anne.

"I give you my Babet; she is the best daughter in France. Her great friendship for you, which I had thought would be at my expense and also rather misplaced, brought her some rather harsh words from me, but now I find it very good that she should love you. Love her with all your heart." And she placed her daughter's hand in St. Anne's.

"Babet," he said, "I will love you with all my heart."

Madame de St. Anne, who was almost as keen as Madame d'Estival that her son's future mother-in-law should go and live somewhere else, suggested that her son immediately write a letter at Madame d'Estival's dictation and send it to a person she knew who would arrange for the proposed purchase to take place directly. This letter took some time, as they had to send to the château for writing materials, but it was too dear to Madame de St. Anne's heart for her to show any impatience. Mademoiselle d'Estival, whose idea it had first been, now discovered that she found it more distressing than gratifying. The imminent prospect of being separated from her mother affected her deeply. St. Anne did nothing in all this other than what he was told; so long as he had Babet, it didn't make any difference to him whether her mother came or not. What everyone else wanted was what suited him the best.

They were therefore kept busy at the farm for a very long time, and the three people left in the château had all the time in the world to talk to one another.

Initially there was almost no conversation at all, then some constrained remarks were exchanged, and finally discussion became animated.

Mademoiselle de Kerber, reading what was in Mademoiselle de Rhedon's heart, suddenly said to her, "There is nothing so boring as attending a wedding, unless you're getting married too. Choose: either come home with me to my mother's house, or allow me to write to poor Ville-Dieu."

"Who is Ville-Dieu?" asked Tonquedec.

"A humble and loving admirer of Mademoiselle de Rhedon, whom Madame de St. Anne peremptorily banished, and who occasionally writes to me to preserve the shadow of a relationship with the lady of his thoughts."

"Or with you," said Mademoiselle de Rhedon. "I thought that he meant to marry me, but that you were more to his taste. He talked to me endlessly about the charming vivacity of your mind, and found that when everyone else was dejected, you were the only one who still retained life and character."

"You said nothing to him at all," said Mademoiselle de Kerber, "while Madame de St. Anne treated him as one treats a man whom one wishes to keep at a distance, and without me he would have been very miserable; that's all he meant. My age was also closer to his than yours was, and that brought a little more ease and life into our conversations."

"From everything I hear," said Tonquedec, "I do not really see that Mademoiselle de Rhedon has any reason to ask you to write to Ville-Dieu."

"It's all very well her remonstrating," said Mademoiselle de Kerber. "He really was very attached to her. It was not yet clear while he was courting her what her fortune would be, and it was only Madame de St. Anne, who was using friends to act on her behalf, who had distinct expectations, yet Ville-Dieu wished with all his heart that he would be accepted."

"If all that is needed to have a claim to Mademoiselle de Rhedon is to feel her worth thoroughly, to find her infinitely amiable, good, and generous, to admire her face, her graces, and talents, then I am second to no man," said Tonquedec. "My purpose in coming here was to find a companion. St. Anne had spoken to me about his two cousins with equal praise, but I was in no doubt that his mother intended him to marry the one who was rich and well connected, and the first word Madame de St. Anne addressed to me showed that I was not mistaken. If my choice was uncertain at that point, my conduct could not be. Everything has changed, or rather, that which was not known has now been revealed. Mademoiselle de Rhedon herself informed me by giving me the letter that St. Anne was in love, and Mademoiselle d'Estival, who had not, so far as I know, communicated her feelings to anyone, or anyone apart from her mother, suddenly expressed them. May I now be permitted to pay my addresses to the person who might perhaps have received them first, had I not been laboring under a misapprehension?"

Mademoiselle de Rhedon blushed, and Mademoiselle de Kerber promised not to write to Ville-Dieu. Madame de Rieux, however, was also in correspondence with him, and she wrote to him the day after St. Anne's marriage to Mademoiselle d'Estival, and Ville-Dieu soon appeared at Missillac. He would have renewed those attentions that had previously been rejected, had Tonquedec's gallantries not already made enough of an impression on Mademoiselle de Rhedon for everyone to foresee that one day they would be accepted. Ville-Dieu, as Mademoiselle de Rhedon had said, loved the vivacity of Mademoiselle de Kerber's spirit, a vivacity that did not prevent her from being extremely good-hearted. Indeed, she had just given proof of the daring and active form her kindness took, and Tonquedec, St. Anne, and even Mademoiselle de Rhedon herself told Ville-Dieu about it. And so he made his decision, offered her his hand in marriage, and was readily accepted. Their marriage will be taking place soon. And that is not all. The character of the man whom Mademoiselle de Kerber had rather disparagingly mentioned, on the occasion of Madame de Rieux forgetting the heroism of the widow in the novel in her eagerness to make herself presentable, has been shown in a new light: he has been courting his creditor's daughter. Madame de Rieux considers that this shows her coquettishness to have been justified, and it will no doubt be rewarded with greater success when she finds a more honest and less shrewd man to use it on. St. Anne has already sent her his praise and congratulations.

"I do assure you," he said, "that I did not at all share Mademoiselle de Kerber's sentiments." (It is quite good enough for reading to be merely useless; it would actually be harmful if, after various novelistic follies that cost the author nothing, one were to sacrifice one's truest, most natural and honest feelings because of a book. Let a few of Werther's admirers kill themselves, and some madwomen spend their lives weeping for something that perhaps they should never have loved in the first place.[28] In real life, it is most important to avoid imitating an implausible novel.)

It was the evening before his wedding that St. Anne made this speech to Madame de Rieux. He had not dared to speak this freely to Mademoiselle de Rhedon. Nonetheless, he now said to her, "If tomorrow you were to promise my friend that you would replace the wealth he ceded to me, my happiness would be complete."

"Must I," said Mademoiselle de Rhedon, blushing deeply, "do everything that you want? You did not want me to give you what I would have wished to."

"You have already given me," said St. Anne, kissing her hand, "proofs of the most generous attachment. Complete them." And he brought Tonquedec to her.

"You wanted it to be tomorrow," said Mademoiselle de Rhedon.

"Why should it not be this evening?" said St. Anne, "if, as I see, you are already decided?"

He then turned to his friend and said to him, "I owe my happiness to you. Allow me to boast of having hastened yours."

What he said gave such pleasure to Tonquedec that Mademoiselle de Rhedon did not wish to contradict it.

Madame de St. Anne was visibly the person who was the least content of everyone gathered in her house. And yet Madame d'Estival was leaving, which was something; the house had already been bought, and on his mother's advice, St. Anne had arranged for his future mother-in-law to have quite a considerable pension, which would be paid so long as she remained unmarried. Such a clause would never have crossed St. Anne's mind, but he had to give some satisfaction to a mother deprived by her son of her dearest wishes. When St. Anne took the papers that guaranteed her pension to Madame d'Estival, she laughed, and said, "The gift is yours, the condition is your mother's, but she is quite wrong to make it. I am every bit as proud as she is, and even less likely to marry again, for if some king or elector were to present himself, she would take him, and I want neither a prince from former times nor a representative of the people or even of the executive power."[29] St. Anne assured her that it was all his mother's idea. "You have such a natural right to any fortune I and your daughter possess that I would never have thought of giving you anything in the form of a special contract."

Mademoiselle d'Estival picked up the deeds, and then, giving them back to St. Anne, said with some indignation, "Read it aloud again, please; I was not listening the first time." He read it.

"Is it not rather sad," she continued, "not to know how to read? Although, no, it was a good thing that I could not read Herfrey's letter. I would never have dared to give it to Tonquedec as Mademoiselle de Rhedon did. However, in the future, I think it would be more agreeable for me to be able to read, and you will teach me as you promised; I hope you will also teach me to write."

"I wouldn't advise it," said Madame d'Estival. "Ignorant as she is, she loves you, and you find her charming—don't turn her into a learned woman; everything which changes something we love spoils it, and I can still remember the only lines

of verse I ever knew. My uncle the schoolmaster repeated them
to me so many times that I will remember them all my life. But
he would never teach me my ABC's, however much I begged
him. A woman, he would say, who knows her letters would
want to learn to read, and once she knew how to read, she
could teach herself to write without assistance. Now, I have it
from a wise man that:

> She has no need, whatever she may think,
> Of writing table, paper, pen, or ink.
> In a proper house, the husband is the one
> To do whatever writing's to be done.[30]

St. Anne found it entertaining that Molière had been inter-
preted in this way by the teacher.

"It really does not matter to me," said he to his future wife,
"whether you can read and write or not; what does matter to
me is that you should shake off all your fanciful fears. The day
after tomorrow on our way to or from the church, you might
come across some object which you think is bad luck. Would it
not be dreadful to see my joy, and I venture to say yours too,
poisoned by this random encounter? Perhaps it may make a
lasting impression, or might return whenever you have some
slight reason to be anxious. The sinister omen would not have
brought about our bad luck, but it would then produce it. You
and I will make each other's happiness; the rest is merely
superstition."

"I will only believe," said Mademoiselle d'Estival, "what
you believe, and if you do not believe in overturned salt cel-
lars, broken mirrors, the number of people seated round a
table, then it's over; I have already stopped believing in them."

"This is truly a good omen for me," said St. Anne, and he
allowed himself to embrace her.

"Softly, softly," said her mother. "The day after tomorrow
is very near, and you can wait."

Mademoiselle d'Estival remembered the graveyard, looked
at St. Anne, and smiled.

The great day came, that day for which Madame d'Estival had wished to save up all the privileges of marriage and the delights of love. She led her daughter to the altar, and straight after the ceremony, embraced her, and walked away without a word. Then she turned round and called out, "Adieu, Babet!" A carriage was waiting for her outside the church; she climbed into it and was immediately driven to Estival.

That evening the farm saw happy Babet return once more, now in the company of her happy husband, who, a few days later, took her to Auray, to introduce her to the two friends, and to hurry along the repairs to the old manor house of his forefathers.

Notes

INTRODUCTION

1. Isabelle de Charrière, *Œuvres complètes*, vol. 1, ed. Jean-Daniel Candaux et al. (Amsterdam, Netherlands: G. A. van Oorschot, 1979–1981), p. 342 (letter of 3–6 November, 1764). Translated in Janet Whatley and Malcolm Whatley, *There Are No Letters Like Yours: The Correspondence of Isabelle de Charrière and Constant d'Hermenches* (Lincoln, NE, and London: University of Nebraska Press, 2000), p. 210.
2. Jean Starobinski, "Les Lettres écrites de Lausanne de Madame de Charrière: inhibition psychique et interdit social," in *Roman et Lumières au XVIIIe Siècle*, ed. Werner Krauss (Paris: Éditions Sociales, 1970), pp. 130–152 (p. 131).
3. *Œuvres complètes*, vol. 1, p. 273 (letters of 21 and 23 August); *There Are No Letters Like Yours*, p. 148 (translation slightly adapted).
4. *Œuvres complètes*, vol. 8, p. 24; see p. 8.
5. Gillian Dow, "Contemporary Reviews of Charrière's Writing," p. 1. We would like to record our gratitude to Gillian Dow for her immense generosity in making her as-yet unpublished work available to us.
6. Dow, "Contemporary Reviews of Charrière's Writing," p. 11.
7. Dow, "Contemporary Reviews of Charrière's Writing," p. 3.
8. Dow, "Contemporary Reviews of Charrière's Writing," p. 5.
9. See p. 394, n.3.
10. Dow, "Contemporary Reviews of Charrière's Writing," p. 7.
11. Dow, "Contemporary Reviews of Charrière's Writing," p. 9.
12. *Œuvres complètes*, vol. 8, p. 251; C. P. Courtney, *Isabelle de Charrière (Belle de Zuylen)* (Oxford, England: Voltaire Foundation, 1993), pp. 416–417.
13. *Œuvres complètes*, vol. 8, p. 412; Courtney, *Isabelle de Charrière*, p. 602.
14. *Œuvres complètes*, vol. 9, pp. 258–259; Courtney, *Isabelle de Charrière*, pp. 675–676.
15. Courtney, *Isabelle de Charrière*, p. 676.

THE NOBLEMAN

1. "Le Noble, conte moral" (1763), *Œuvres complètes*, vol. 8, pp. 11–43.
2. La Fontaine, *Fables* (1669–1693), vol. 8, no. 24, "L'Education," or in Norman R. Shapiro's free translation, "Breeding," *The Complete Fables of Jean de La Fontaine* (Urbana and Chicago: University of Illinois Press, 2000), p. 222. He translates this line as "We follow not our forebears' path."
3. "Le Noble, conte moral," *Journal étranger, combiné avec l'année littéraire* 8 (August 1762); Amsterdam, Netherlands: van Harrevelt (1763), pp. 540–74. In fact the August 1762 issue did not appear until 1763. The story was published separately in Amsterdam later the same year, and most copies were bought up and removed from the market by Charrière's scandalized family. Kees van Strien suggests that Evert van Harrevelt, the most likely publisher, may have agreed to sell them all to Charrière's father, but that he withheld some copies, which he sold to Jean Herman Schneider, with the proviso that he must allow a decent time to elapse before marketing them; this, in van Strien's view, accounts for the fact that there is no record of the reprint having been sold before April 1764. See Kees van Strien, "The Publication History of *Le Noble*," *Cahiers Isabelle de Charrière/Belle de Zuylen Papers* 5 (2010), pp. 27–34.
4. These are Ancien Régime feudal rights that allow the seigneur or lord to arbitrate on all cases of law on his land. There were three levels: high, middle, and low. Charrière gives the extremes, that is, the highest and the lowest; the highest conferred the right to impose the death sentence, while the lowest involved minor misdemeanors as well as rents, taxes, or fines payable to the lord (the middle level involved crimes nonpunishable by death, including brawls, theft, and so on; it also arbitrated in questions of inheritance and legal guardianship).
5. Compare with the celebrated opening paragraph of Jane Austen's *Persuasion* (1818): "Sir Walter Elliot, of Kellynch-hall, in Somersetshire, was a man who, for his own amusement, never took up any book but the Baronetage; there he found occupation for an idle hour, and consolation in a distressed one; there his faculties were roused into admiration and respect, by contemplating the limited remnant of the earliest patents; there any unwelcome sensations, arising from domestic affairs, changed

naturally into pity and contempt. As he turned over the almost endless creations of the last century—and there, if every other leaf were powerless, he could read his own history with an interest which never failed—this was the page at which the favourite volume always opened: ELLIOT OF KELLYNCH-HALL." *Persuasion*, vol. 1 (CUP 2006), ed. Janet Todd and Antje Blank, ch. 1, p. 3.

6. It seems unlikely that a story whose heroine carries the name Julie, and was written in 1762, would not be referencing Jean-Jacques Rousseau's best seller *Julie, ou la nouvelle Héloïse*, which had been published in 1761.

7. "Work" in relation to women designates sewing and embroidery; Julie is therefore a skilled needlewoman.

8. Fénelon's immensely influential and much reprinted *Aventures de Télémaque* (1699) follows the wanderings of Telemachus, son of Ulysses, accompanied by Mentor, who sets up an ideal city-state, Salente, which was taken to be a criticism of Louis XIV's rule; Lesage's *Histoire de Gil Blas de Santillane* (1715–1735) is a knockabout picaresque novel and fictional autobiography that follows the ups and downs of its everyman hero in an unfair world; he eventually rises to become the favorite of the Spanish prime minister.

9. This reminds us of the anxieties to do with precedence that *Persuasion* records. Elizabeth Elliot, Sir Walter's eldest daughter, is described as "doing the honours, and laying down the domestic law at home, and leading the way to the chaise and four, and walking immediately after Lady Russell out of all the drawing-rooms and dining-rooms in the country" (*Persuasion*, vol. 1, ch. 1, p. 7). His youngest daughter, Mary, married to Charles Musgrove, is offended and causes offense by questions of precedence: "Again; it was Mary's complaint, that Mrs. Musgrove was very apt not to give her the precedence that was her due, when they dined at the Great House with other families. . . ." Her sister-in-law observes to the middle sister, Anne (the heroine of the book), "how nonsensical some persons are about their place, because all the world knows how easy and indifferent you are about it: but I wish anybody could give Mary a hint that it would be a great deal better if she were not so very tenacious; especially, if she would not be always putting herself forward to take place of mamma. Nobody doubts her right to have precedence of mamma, but it would be more becoming in her not to be always insisting on it" (*Persuasion*, vol. 1, ch. 6, p. 49).

10. "We wish primarily to please the person who pleases us" echoes Aristotle's statement about friendship: "A man becomes a friend whenever, being loved, he loves in return" (*Eudemian Ethics*, VII.ii.1236). For a discussion of friendship in the eighteenth century, as well as suggestions for further reading on the subject, see Adam Sutcliffe, "Friendship and Materialism in the French Enlightenment," *Representing Private Lives of the Enlightenment*, ed. Andrew Kahn, SVEC 2010:11, pp. 251–268.

11. Valaincourt is a typically mellifluous noble name; it is also the name of the hero of Ann Radcliffe's *Mysteries of Udolpho* (1796).

12. Julie's "work" is her sewing. See note 7.

13. Clovis (c. 481–511) was king of the Franks, whose territory he greatly extended; he died in Paris and exists in national cultural myth as the founder of France.

14. King Ninus, in Greek mythology, was the king of Assyria, conqueror of all of western Asia, and founder of the biblical city Nineveh.

15. A catechism is a summary of the articles of the Catholic faith from the New Testament to the present day; Jean-Regnault de Segrais (1624–1701) was a poet, translator, and writer, most famous now for having been Madame de Lafayette's secretary while she was composing *La Princesse de Clèves* (1678), which was in fact published under his name to protect her; he had held a similar supporting role with respect to *Madame de Montpensier*. Charrière is probably referring to a miscellany of different pieces by him, such as his *Œuvres diverses* (Amsterdam, Netherlands: François Changuion, 1723), containing anecdotes of court life and some poems, including his imitation of Latin poets, *Eglogues*. He was held by Voltaire to be a true man of letters. Jean Racine (1629–1699) was a tragedian, most of whose tragedies are still regularly acted today—we might single out *Andromaque* (1667) or *Phèdre* (1677); *Gil Blas*—see note 8.

16. Renaud de Montauban, also known as Rinaldo di Montalbano, was a fictional character supposedly from the court of Charlemagne, complete with magical horse and special named sword. He first appeared in a twelfth-century poem titled *Les Quatre Fils Aymon*, and thereafter became a stock character in heroic epics, most famously reappearing in Ariosto's *Orlando furioso* as one of the knights besotted with love. For Julie to say Valaincourt is descended from Renaud de Montauban is equivalent to saying he's descended from one of the Knights of the Round Table—Lancelot or Galahad, for instance.

17. Extraordinarily, it was a feudal right to have a dovecote, and forbidden to the common people.

18. The Sovereign Military Hospitaller Order of St. John of Jerusalem of Rhodes and of Malta was founded c. 1048 as an order of monks particularly devoted to the care of the sick. It was granted independence from the Church in 1113; the Knights Hospitaller became famous as warrior priests during the crusades, and governed Malta in 1530–1798, hence their name, the Knights of Malta. Only the nobility were allowed to join the order, and so as a title it was synonymous with aristocracy. This is still the case today, and they still fund hospitals.

19. The Hail Mary is a traditional Roman Catholic prayer calling on the Virgin Mary.

LETTERS FROM NEUCHÂTEL

1. *Lettres neuchâteloises* (1784), *Œuvres complètes*, vol. 8, pp. 35–89.

2. Publisher's note, second edition, 1784. Cecil Courtney tells us that *Lettres neuchâteloises* was "first published anonymously in Lausanne (with imprint 'Amsterdam') in January, February or March 1784; [the] second edition, also anonymous, [was] published shortly afterwards in Geneva (likewise with imprint 'Amsterdam') with corrections and the poem 'Peuple aimable de Neuchâtel,'" (*Isabelle de Charrière*, p. 745). This translation uses the text of the second edition.

3. We never learn more about what exact trade Henri is engaged in, although the repeated references to letters needing to be sent out tell us that he is a clerk of some sort.

4. Does Henri also earn a wage from his work? It is not clear. His uncle may have arranged for him to be paid in kind in this way, seeing as his job is the result of a prior relationship between his father (presumably now deceased) and his employer, and Henri has a certain level of preferential treatment. The "spending money" he receives will not cover his clothes or lessons, and his uncle will pay for those. One louis (in French currency) was worth 168 Batz in the local currency (http://www.boudry -historique.net/page99.html), so Henri's 10 louis spending money equates to about 420 Batz every four months, or 1,260 annually. According to Norbert Furrer's study of living costs in Lausanne in 1798, a well-paid priest would earn 8,922 Batz

annually; the burgomaster (chief magistrate, or mayor), 6,276 Batz; the director of the hospital, 5,202; while a day porter (as in some who has concierge-type duties of managing a building) would earn 2,190. The (female) teacher of the hospital school would earn 1,490 Batz per year, while the person responsible for maintaining and winding up the town's clocks would have 1,000 Batz per year. The daily expenses of a well-off household with five family members was 36 Batz, and the expenses of an identically constituted household at subsistence level was 12 Batz. Henri has 3.45 Batz spending money per day, with rent, food, and washing already taken care of. Half a pot of wine (a seemingly common in-kind payment for a day's laboring) would cost 2 Batz, but as we find out that Henri doesn't seem to drink much or even approve of drinking (see his remarks in Letters III and IX), he clearly does have some spending power. We will find out later what he spends it on. We cannot be sure that the figures given here provide an absolutely reliable comparator, as prices and wages may have changed to some extent between c. 1784 and postrevolutionary 1798, but assuming that these figures are as close as we can get, they seem to tell us that Henri can indeed consider himself relatively well off. See Norbert Furrer, "Le coût de la vie à Lausanne en 1798" in De l'ours à la cocarde; régime bernois et révolution en pays de Vaud (1536–1798), ed. François Flouck et al. (Lausanne, Switzerland: Editions Payot, 1998), pp. 79–96, table 5 (p. 92), and "Estimation des dépenses journalières d'un ménage 'aisé' et d'un ménage 'modeste' à partir du prix de pain, à Lausanne en 1798," p. 96.

5. In the late eighteenth century it was still contentious for women to act, and certainly for respectable women to do so, as anything that involved women performing in public was seen as tantamount to prostitution. Readers familiar with Jane Austen's *Mansfield Park* (1814) will remember Fanny Price's virtuous horror at the acting escapades of her cousins. The acting profession as a whole was seen as morally dubious, and in the city-state of Geneva no public performances of plays were allowed at all. Jean-Jacques Rousseau had strongly supported this policy in his *Letter to d'Alembert on the Theatre* (1758). Henri is German, and in fact female actors had already started appearing in Germany— Caroline Neuber (1697–1760) was one of the earliest and most illustrious of them, although women had already been on the stage in France and England since the mid- to late-seventeenth

century. Related issues of female performance and immorality feature elsewhere in Charrière's work: see *Letters from Mistress Henley*, note 10, and *Constance's Story*, note 11. See Eric A. Nicholson, "Women as Actresses and Playwrights" in *A History of Women: Renaissance and Enlightenment Paradoxes*, ed. Natalie Zemon Davis and Arlette Farge (Cambridge, MA: Belknap Press, 1993), pp. 309–318.

6. To be able to put "de" in front of one's name is taken as a sign of social rank and pedigree. Voltaire's actual name was François Marie Arouet; he renamed himself François Marie Arouet de Voltaire. Balzac did the same thing, and became Honoré de Balzac. Charrière's maiden and married names proliferated in the aristocratic "de" (or "van"). The right to use the "de" could be conferred, normally indicating the ownership of a property and thus a certain level of wealth.

7. This parade, which still takes place toward the end of November and which inaugurates the yearly fair, started off life in medieval times as an armorers' parade, subsequently becoming associated with the anniversary of the dedication of the church, and finally mutating into a feast day to celebrate the town of Neuchâtel and its citizens. Twenty-four citizens, or "bourgeois," of Neuchâtel parade from the town hall to the castle and back again, accompanied by drums and pipes. They wear traditional armor, and two boys carry flaming torches in front of each man.

8. It is a *petit écu*: See the following note.

9. The coin is *un gros écu*, which according to the *Œuvres complètes* edition was worth two *petits écus*. A *petit écu* was worth 21 Batz in the Neuchâtel currency of the time, so Henri had given Julianne 42 Batz (http://www.boudry-historique.net/page99.html). According to Norbert Furrer, 32 Batz would have been enough to buy a pair of shoes, the price of sewing a shirt was only 2 Batz, and a washerwoman would earn about 8 Batz per day, while a woman paid on a daily rate to do cleaning would earn just over 6 Batz. Julianne is probably in this low bracket, so 42 Batz is indeed a large sum. Furrer also tells us that a household of means might have three times as much income as a subsistence household. The former would spend about half of its entire income on expenses such as rent, heating, and clothing, while a subsistence household would spend one quarter of its income on such things, the remaining three quarters going to food. See Furrer, "Le coût de la vie à Lausanne en 1798," pp. 79–96.

10. "Meaning" is in English in the original, with an authorial note explaining that it is an English expression that has no equivalent in French. As "meaning" can be translated both as *sens* and *signification*, it is not precisely clear what *meaning* Charrière is investing "meaning" with here (no doubt it gains in weight and suggestiveness by being in a foreign language). "To mean," however, could be translated as *vouloir dire*, that is, "to want to say," which has overtones of intentionality that *signifier* (to signify) does not, and *vouloir dire*, moreover, has no corresponding noun. I am grateful to Kate Tunstall for suggesting this particular reason. Susan van Dijk further points out that the Dutch term "mening" may also be resonating for Charrière here, and that it means precisely the same thing.

11. This alludes to political quarrels in Geneva, an independent city-state whose political structure was extremely rigid and increasingly resented over the course of the eighteenth century. There were four different categories of inhabitant: the citizens (*citoyens*), the burghers (*bourgeois*), the residents (*habitants*), and their children (*natifs*). Power was invested only in the top rank, the citizens, and taxation fell most heavily on the disempowered and poor. This situation simmered away with occasional attempts to redress the balance in 1707, 1734, and 1737. Rousseau's *Social Contract* (1762) and follow-up, *Letters Written from the Mountain* (1764), further stirred debate (Rousseau was himself a citizen of Geneva), and there was more social unrest in 1766 and 1782. There were two broad factions, whose names Charrière gives here: the *Représentants* (representatives), who supported a partial democratization of the system, and the *Négatifs* (negatives), who opposed them. In 1782 a revolution brought the Representatives briefly to the fore, but an army composed of French, Bernese, and Piedmontese soldiers reimposed the old system. The French Revolution had an immediate impact on Geneva, and democracy was introduced in the constitution of 1794. Switzerland as we know it came into existence in 1798, complete with constitution, as the Conféderation helvétique, although not all separate states, or cantons, joined straightaway. One sympathizes with Henri here: the history of Switzerland and its cantons is extremely complicated, and the conversation the lady is trying to have with him is not clearly datable, although one assumes a certain contemporaneity between the uprising of 1782 and the publication of *Letters from Neuchâtel* in 1784. The

clearest and most satisfactorily detailed explanation of the events is to be found on the French-language educational site Atrium: http://www.yrub.com/histoire/hd4.htm (Histoire de la Suisse, "La mouvementée République génévoise"). See also E. Bonjour, H. S. Offler, and G. R. Potter, *A Short History of Switzerland* (Oxford, England: Clarendon Press, 1952), pp. 202–203. John Wood's *General View of the History of Switzerland, with a Particular Account of the Origin and Accomplishment of the Late Swiss Revolution* (Edinburgh, Scotland: Peter Hill and G. Cawthorne, 1799) is also helpful and has a certain immediacy (see especially p. 302).

12. This supposed convention is also satirically invoked by Jane Austen when describing Catherine Morland's feelings for Henry Tilney: "Whether she thought of him so much, while she drank her warm wine and water, and prepared herself for bed, as to dream of him when there, cannot be ascertained; but I hope it was no more than in a slight slumber, or a morning doze at most; for if it be true, as a celebrated writer has maintained, that no young lady can be justified in falling in love before the gentleman's love is declared, it must be very improper that a young lady should dream of a gentleman before the gentleman is first known to have dreamt of her." *Northanger Abbey*, ch. 3. With thanks to Gillian Dow for suggesting this parallel.

13. The Val-de-Ruz is a small rural district in the hinterland of Neuchâtel.

14. The Huron is the main character in Voltaire's philosophical fiction, *L'Ingénu* (1767). The initials are Mademoiselle de Kerkabon's, but in the story, the person who changes is in fact her niece, Mademoiselle de Saint-Yves: in love with the Huron, and desperate to save him from the Bastille, where he is imprisoned, she obtains his freedom by sleeping with a powerful official. The struggle between love and conscience kills her (Voltaire, *L'Ingénu*, ch.18).

15. Philibert de Chalon (1502–1530), Prince of Orange, Count of Burgundy, and successful general.

16. See note 4 for information about what this sum might represent.

17. Z*** is thought to be a not very covert reference by the author to herself: one of Charrière's most recognizable names was (and still is) Zuylen. This seems plausible, not only because Z is a relatively rare letter in names, but also because of the rather distanced perspective the "caustic commentator" adopts.

18. This poem was included in the second edition of *Lettres neuchâ-teloises* as a response to its hostile reception by the people of Neuchâtel. See Courtney, *Isabelle de Charrière*, pp. 350–354.

LETTERS FROM MISTRESS HENLEY PUBLISHED BY HER FRIEND

1. *Lettres de Mistress Henley publiées par son amie* (1784), *Œuvres complètes*, vol. 8, pp. 91–122.

2. "*J'ai vu beaucoup d'Hymens*, &c" comes from La Fontaine's fable "Le Mal Marié" (book VII, number 2), or, in Norman R. Shapiro's free translation, "The Man Who Married a Shrew," *The Complete Fables of Jean de La Fontaine* (Urbana and Chicago: University of Illinois Press, 2000), pp. 158–159; the full line is "*J'ai vu beaucoup d'Hymens, aucuns d'eux ne me ten-tent*," which we translate as "Many are the marriages I have seen, and not one do I find tempting." Charrière had cited this same line in a letter to Constant d'Hermenches on January 21, 1768: "*J'ai vu beaucoup d'Hymens, mais pas un ne me tente.*"

3. The book in question is a novel written by one of Constant d'Hermenches' younger brothers, Samuel Constant, not inciden-tally, Benjamin's father (his name was Juste). *Le mari sentimen-tal*, published in 1783, was an epistolary novel in which a husband writes to his friend about his increasing disenchant-ment with his marriage. At the age of 46, Monsieur Bompré had married a younger woman, and it turned out badly; he consoled himself with his previous objects of affection—his house, his animals, his servants, his neighbors. But Madame Bompré cru-elly removes all these sources of comfort one by one—she takes down the portrait of his father, moves the furniture, has his dog killed and his horse sold, dismisses an old retainer, and ends up accusing him of seducing a young peasant girl whom he'd been helping. He shoots himself.

4. Nanon and Antoine are Monsieur Bompré's beloved servants, and Hector, the dog's name (see previous note).

5. In Jean-Jacques Rousseau's immensely influential educational novel-cum-treatise, *Emile* (1762), the narrator meets a young Englishman, Lord John, on his grand tour in Venice. A letter arrives from England, and Lord John's tutor reads it out loud. Lord John reacts to the letter, which is all about how the girl

promised to him has been devoting herself to embroidering some ruffles for his cuffs, by tearing off the ruffles he is wearing and throwing them into the fire. It emerges that he was given the now burnt ruffles by a Venetian lady not long before (there is no mention of any Marquise). This is therefore a picture of fidelity holding out against temptation. See Rousseau, *Emile*, book V (Rousseau, *Emile*, *Œuvres complètes*, vol. IV, ed. Bernard Gagnebin and Marcel Raymond [Paris: Gallimard, 1969], pp. 853–854).

6. For a comparative contextualizing explanation of sums, see *Cécile*, note 4.

7. "Nabob"—initially "Nawab," the name of a high-ranking official in Muslim India—generalized into English use as "nabob," meaning "a wealthy, influential, or powerful landowner or other person, esp. one with an extravagantly luxurious lifestyle; a British person who acquired a large fortune in India during the period of British rule" (OED).

8. The name of the house, Hollow Park, is in English in the original.

9. La Fontaine, *Fables*, book 1, no. 22; translated Shapiro, *The Complete Fables of La Fontaine*, pp. 25–26. This is the old story of the oak that boasts to the reed of its strength, and is then uprooted by a violent wind, while the reed simply bends and returns to its previous shape. Charrière mentions it again in her fairy story, *Eaglonette and Suggestina, or On Pliancy*, see this volume, p. 177.

10. Rousseau had eloquently put the case against teaching La Fontaine's fables to children in his discussion of "The Crow and the Fox" in *Emile* (1762; also mentioned in note 4: *Emile*, pp. 351–357). His opposition was threefold: first, children had no idea what the fables actually meant; second, if they were told what they meant, they learned some bad lessons, such as that some people lie and swear; and third, the fables don't tell the truth about the reality of things; for example, they suggest that crows speak, and so forth. His heroine, Julie, also rejects La Fontaine for the education of children (*Julie, ou la nouvelle Héloïse, Œuvres complètes*, vol. II, p. 581). Madame de Genlis's tragic novella, *Mademoiselle de Clermont* (1802), stages a key seduction scene around the (feigned) rejection of fiction in favor of history (*Mademoiselle de Clermont*, ed. Raymond Trousson, in *Romans de femmes du XVIIIe siècle* [Paris: Laffont, 1996], p. 787). Interestingly, whether the recital of La Fontaine's fables should or should not play a part in the education of a young child reappears in Charlotte Brontë's

Jane Eyre: the young Adèle Varens treats her new governess to a display of her accomplishments, showing off in turn her singing, her speaking, and her dancing. Jane Eyre finds it all in very bad taste, and by the end of the novel is pleased to see that "a sound, English education [had] corrected in a great measure her French defects" (*Jane Eyre*, ed. Jane Jack and Margaret Smith [Oxford, England: The Clarendon Press, 1969], p. 124 [vol. 1, ch. XI], p. 576 [vol. 3, ch. XII]).

11. "Foster sister" was the term then used to indicate the relationship between two children who had both been breast-fed by the same woman, i.e., the first Mrs. Henley's wet nurse was the mother of the housekeeper. Until Rousseau's *Emile* (book 1) changed opinions, it was rare for high-ranking women to breast-feed their own child. See note 17.

12. Persian cats were new to Europe, and much in fashion. The important salonnière, Mme Helvétius, apparently had a "vast troop of Angora cats" (Simon Schama, *Citizens: A Chronicle of the French Revolution* [New York: Knopf, 1989], p. 76). Nicole Castan tells us that "the vogue for house pets reveals a new attitude toward nature and animals, which were no longer regarded as 'wild'" (*A History of Private Life*, vol. 3, ed. Philippe Ariès and Georges Duby [Cambridge, MA, and London: Belknap Press, 1989], p. 424). See also Theresa Braunschneider, "The Lady and the Lapdog: Mixed Ethnicity in Constantinople, Fashionable Pets in Britain," in *Humans and Other Animals in Eighteenth-Century British Culture: Representation, Hybridity, Ethics*, ed. Frank Palmeri (Aldershot and Burlington, VT: Ashgate, 2006), pp. 31–48. Charrière in fact consistently misspells "Angora," writing "Angola" instead. We have silently corrected this, but despite the fact that this was a common eighteenth-century mistake, it is of some interest, in that it shows Charrière having a strong sense of the colonial exotic, of colonial trade, which is nonetheless somewhat confused geographically; similarly, we see her later confuse India with the Indies (i.e., the Caribbean), and in *Constance*, she mixes Martinique with Saint-Domingue (see note 9). See note 14.

13. Guildford is in the county of Surrey, not far from London, and was in the late eighteenth century a small market town.

14. Governor Bridgewater was the suitor Mistress Henley had rejected, choosing virtue over wealth. Charrière means India, not the Indies (the Caribbean islands were known as the Indies). See comments above, note 12.

15. None of these crossings-out are in fact recorded; the resulting letter is of great simplicity and eloquence, and the initial modest denial perhaps serves to enhance this effect.

16. Mistress Henley's contemplation and exaltation of nature allow us to trace her philosophical-religious influences. The physico-theologian, Abbé Pluche (1686–1761) influenced many eighteenth-century readers with his *Spectacle de la nature*, 9 vols. (1732–1750), which describes the extraordinary intricacy and activity of creation, inferring from it God's goodness and wisdom. Mistress Henley owes something to him as she contemplates nature, but unlike him, she does "not know its ends" and therefore refuses to see creation as a proof of God's existence. (See *Cécile* note 48 for a statement that is closer to Pluche's position.) She also echoes Rousseau's "Profession de foi du vicaire savoyard," in which the vicar professes his amazement and even fear at the complexity of the universe (Rousseau, *Emile*, in *Œuvres complètes*, vol. 4, ed. Bernard Gagnebin and Marcel Raymond [Paris: Gallimard Pléiade], p. 573, 580; in translation, *Emile, or On Education* [electronic resource], translated by Barbara Foxley; revised by Grace Roosevelt [New York, 2003], http://www.grtbooks .com/rousseau.asp?idx=2&yr=1850&aa=A&at=MI&lst=7&sel= 1, book IV, paragraphs 975, 990–991 [among others]). The spider is an old free-thinking metaphor for the soul of the world, to be found perhaps most famously in Diderot's *Le Rêve de d'Alembert* (see Isabelle Moreau, "L'araignée dans sa Toile: Mise en Images de l'âme du monde de François Bernier et Pierre Bayle à l'*Encyclopédie*," in *Les Lumières en mouvement: La circulation des idées au XVIIIe siècle*, ed. Isabelle Moreau, [Lyon, France: ENS Editions, 2009], pp. 199–228). With grateful thanks to Neil Younger for his physico-theological erudition.

17. The issue is whether to breast-feed or not; the custom of women who could afford not to, was to pay a wet-nurse to do it for them. Rousseau's *Emile* began the immense shift of attitude that changed this practice (*Emile*, p. 255). See note 11.

18. The term "vanity" was *amour-propre* in French; *amour-propre* is a term with dire overtones for Rousseau, and he analyzes it as being at the root of the damage society does to the individual, teaching people to assess themselves uniquely in comparison with others—this leads to envy and vanity. See Rousseau, *Discours sur l'origine et les fondements de l'inégalité*, *Œuvres complètes*, p. 219 (note XVI); *Discourse on Inequality*, trans. Franklin Philip (Oxford, England: Oxford World's

Classics, 1994), p. 115 (note O), and *Emile*, *OC*, vol. IV, p. 493.
Rousseau contrasts it with the more natural *amour de soi* or
"self-love"/ "self-respect."

19. William Murray, First Earl of Mansfield (1705–1793), was a
Scottish-born barrister who served as Lord Chief Justice (1756–
1765), reforming English law. He is famed, among other things,
for his 1772 ruling that slavery was unlawful in England.

20. Marian Hobson explains the medical theory behind this idea of
a physiological shutdown in response to equal and opposite pres-
sures in her article "Pantomime, Spasm, and Parataxis: *Le
Neveu de Rameau*," in *Diderot and Rousseau: Networks of
Enlightenment*, ed. Kate E. Tunstall and Caroline Warman,
SVEC 2011:04 (Oxford, England: Voltaire Foundation, 2011),
pp. 93–113.

LETTERS WRITTEN FROM
LAUSANNE: CÉCILE

1. *Lettres écrites de Lausanne, première partie* (1786), *Œuvres
complètes*, vol. 8, pp. 123–180. We have adapted the title to
make clear to the reader that the tale we are giving is Cécile's;
that is to say, all of part one, the first few letters from part two,
and two short, unpublished "sequels."

2. The editors of *Œuvres complètes* confess they have no idea who
this "Marquise de S***" might be, saying that Charrière's letters
tell us nothing on the subject (*Œuvres complètes*, vol. 8, p. 133).
Is it possible that she might be referring to the well-known writer
Mme de Genlis, one of whose titles was the Marquise de Sillery?
Her *Adèle et Théodore* is mentioned in note 21.

3. Cécile's mother is alluding to religious differences. The wealthy
part of her family has returned to the Catholic faith, whereas her
grandfather refused and had to leave France. This presumably
dates back to Louis XIV's revocation of the Edict of Nantes in
1685 (although the dates seem a little stretched), a point at which
France's many Huguenots (Protestants) fled the country.

4. It is not easy to make these figures meaningful. Colin Jones tells
us that in 1789 a pound stirling exchanged for about 22.5 French
pounds. Assuming that the exchange rate had not changed
unrecognizably between 1784, when this novel is set, 1788,
when it was published, and 1789, Cécile and her mother's income
of 1,500 French francs (the franc at this point is an interchangeable

term for a "livre" or pound, decimalization not being introduced until 1795) can be converted into 66 English pounds, and can be set into some sort of English context by comparing it with Jane Austen's figures: Bingley, we know, is rich and has an income of "four or five thousand pounds a year." Cécile's income looks very low, especially when we consider that Mr. Bennet agrees to give Lydia a yearly sum of £100, and considers it perfectly affordable and probably slightly less than he would have been paying for her hats and so forth were she still to be living at home. However, when we compare the dowries, the picture looks a little different. Miss King has a dowry of £10,000, and thus attracts Wickham's attention away from Elizabeth. Cécile will have 38,000 French pounds when her mother dies, which equates to £1,688, and is thus considerably more than the few hundred pounds Elizabeth can expect to inherit. Cécile and her mother's £66 may not look like much to live on, but the cost of living in Lausanne would not have been as high as in England, and clearly it must have been enough to keep one servant (Fanchon, whom we will meet later); their income is equivalent to 4 percent of the total. If we convert these sums into the contemporaneous Lausanne currency of Batz, we find that a French franc was worth 7 Batz, and that their income of 1,500 French francs is worth 10,500 Batz, or 28.77 Batz a day. This puts their income above the midpoint between the income of a household of means (36 Batz a day) and one at subsistence level (12 Batz a day), but given that there are only two of them, as opposed to the five who are supposed to make up the expenses of this putative household, Cécile and her mother seem to have a certain amount of disposable income. However, we see how difficult it is to make these figures mean anything reliable when we reconsider what Cécile's mother says—that with income and expectations as low as this, Cécile will find it very difficult to find a husband. See Colin Jones, "Currency," *The Longman Guide to the French Revolution* (Harlow, Essex, England: Longman, 1988), p. 236; and Norbert Furrer, "Estimation des Dépenses Journalières d'un Ménage 'Aisé' et d'un Ménage 'Modeste' à Partir du Prix de Pain, à Lausanne en 1798," in *De l'ours à la cocarde; régime bernois et révolution en pays de Vaud (1536–1798)*, ed. François Flouck et al. (Lausanne, Switzerland: Éditions Payot, 1998), p.96. I am indebted to the Swiss Web site http://www.boudry-historique .net/page99.html for the equivalents of French and Swiss currencies in 1788.

5. Goiters are now known to be caused by a lack of iodine. Iodine was unknown until 1811, when it was first isolated by Bernard Courtois; it was not until 1850 that Gaspard Adolphe Chatin demonstrated that "iodine can prevent the development of endemic goiter and cretinism" ("Goiter, Endemic, Prevention of, by Iodine," J. E. Schmidt, *Medical Discoveries: Who and When* [Springfield, IL: Charles C. Thomas, 1959], p. 194).

6. For the medical context of this view about the curative and/or preventive properties of certain sorts of water, see Roy Porter, ed., *The Medical History of Waters and Spas, Medical History*, supplement no. 10 (1990).

7. Cretinism was related to thyroid deficiency, as Thomas B. Curling demonstrated in 1850, the same year that Gaspard Chatin demonstrated the use of iodine in preventing both goiter and cretinism (see the entries related to cretinism in Schmidt, *Medical Discoveries*, p. 115). Scrofula in fact designated a cluster of conditions and is no longer recognized as a disease. It seems to have included ulcers, swellings, a specific form of tuberculosis that affected the lymph nodes, and various skin conditions, including eczema. Since medieval times, it had been believed that the kings of France and England could cure it by touching the sufferer, and it was therefore known as the King's Evil (this practice was discontinued in the late seventeenth and early eighteenth centuries, as the belief in the divine right of kings diminished). See Roger K. French, "Scrofula," *The Cambridge Historical Dictionary of Disease*, ed. Kenneth F. Kiple (Cambridge, England: Cambridge University Press, 2003), pp. 292–294; and the informative Wikipedia entry http://en.wikipedia.org/wiki/Tuberculous_cervical_lymphadenitis#Signs_and_symptoms (accessed 11/26/2010).

8. Charrière replaces the notion that the King might cure the disease himself with the enlightenment proposal that a prize should be offered for medical progress relating to it. Indeed, *le gros cou* or "fat neck" (goiters, see note 5) was felt to be a particularly serious problem in Switzerland: In the early 1900s it was estimated that more than 50 percent of Swiss 15-year-olds suffered from it. It was not until 1922 that iodine was regularly put in table salt, and the problem eradicated. See P. Bischof, "Le gros cou," *Forum Médical Suisse* 41 (10 October 2001): 1025–1031, available at http://www.medicalforum.ch/pdf/pdf_f/2001/2001-41/2001-41-485.PDF (accessed 11/26/2010).

9. See note 4 for information about currencies and value. It was common practice for the eldest son to inherit the largest portion of the inheritance.

10. The five sons cannot go into trade because if they do so they will forfeit their status as nobles.

11. A reference to Molière's play *Ecole des femmes*, or "school for wives" (1662): *"Je ne sais ce que c'est, Monsieur, mais il me semble/Qu'Agnès et le corps mort s'en sont allés ensemble"* (It's very strange, but Agnès has vanished, Sir/I think that corpse has run away with her" (V.v, lines 1612–1613; *The School for Wives*, translated by Richard Wilbur, in *Five Plays*, introduced by Donald Roy [London: Methuen Drama, 2000], p.106). These lines refer to Agnès and her lover, who, after a fall, had been supposed dead by Agnès, although he had only been pretending.

12. The Vallée de Joux is a secluded high-altitude valley with several lakes, including the 6-mile-long Lac de Joux, about 30 miles north of Geneva and Lausanne.

13. A canon is a functionary of a church or ecclesiastical order, and a canonicate could be inherited along with some hereditary titles, therefore inversely indicating aristocracy. The King of France, for example, was hereditary canon of the churches in St. Hilaire de Poitiers, St. Julien du Mans, St. Martin de Tours, Angers, Lyon, and Châlons. See "Chanoines héréditaires," *Encyclopédie, ou dictionnaire raisonné des sciences, des arts et des métiers*, ed. Denis Diderot and Jean le Rond D'Alembert (1751–1772), University of Chicago: ARTFL Encyclopédie Projet (Spring 2010 Edition), Robert Morrissey (ed.), http://encyclopedie.uchicago.edu/. Knights of Malta or Knights Templar are a Christian order that requires proof of nobility to join it. See *The Nobleman*, note 18.

14. These pensions were indeed granted to those known as "necessitous lords" or more commonly "poor lords," but they were made not in recognition of some more general claim based on their noble pedigree but rather specifically in order to enable those members of the House of Lords "whose needs were so great that they required financial assistance to perform their political functions" (Clyve Jones, "The Scheme Lords, the Necessitous Lords, and the Scots Lords": The Earl of Oxford's management and the 'Party of the Crown' in the House of Lords, 1711–1714," in *Party and management in Parliament, 1660–1784*, ed. Clyve Jones [Leicester, UK, and New York: Leicester University Press,

and St. Martin's Press 1984], pp. 124–167). With grateful thanks to Perry Gauci for this reference.

15. These towns were all famous for their spas and mineral water.

16. Samuel Auguste Tissot (1728–1797), also known as Simon-André, was a famous and influential doctor who published, among other reprinted works, L'Onanisme (1760, on the inevitable physical degeneration brought about by repeated masturbation—his most lurid examples are of the female gender) and De valetudine litteratorum (1766), which was published in French the year after as Avis aux gens de lettres (and which discussed the disastrous ill health brought about by excessive study). He visited Charrière at Colombier at least once (see Philippe Godet, Madame de Charrière et ses amis, vol. 1, [Geneva, 1906], p. 179).

17. A tax farmer, under the Ancien régime system, was a person who had bought the right to collect taxes on behalf of the king. Such men often became very rich, and were a key target of hatred during the French Revolution.

18. The River Scheldt had been closed to shipping from 1585, when the Dutch rebelled against their Hapsburg masters. The Northern Netherlands created a republic, and separated from the Southern Netherlands, or Spanish Netherlands, whose ports, Antwerp and Ghent, were henceforth closed to trade ships. This had the beneficial effect (for the Northern Netherlands) of channeling great wealth to Amsterdam. The Spanish Netherlands passed to Austria in 1714, after the War of the Spanish Succession. The Austrian Holy Roman Emperor, Joseph II, decided to attempt to reestablish trade rights and routes, and in 1784 declared war (a conflict known as the "Kettle" or "Cooking-Pot" war, after the only shot apparently fired supposedly hit a kettle); as a result the Treaty of Fontainebleau (1785) determined that the Scheldt would remain closed, but that the Dutch Republic would compensate the Southern Netherlands for their loss of trade. See Michael Hochedlinger, Austria's Wars of Emergence, 1683–1797 (Harlow, Essex, England: Longman, 2003), pp. 373–374.

19. By the eighteenth century, smallpox was responsible "for 10–15 percent of all deaths in some European countries, 80 percent of the victims being under 10 years of age" (Alfred W. Crosby, "Smallpox," Cambridge Historical Dictionary of Disease, p. 301). It became a target for Enlightenment reform once variolation techniques (artificial infection of healthy people) had been popularized in England by the traveler Lady Mary Wortley

Montagu, and in France by Voltaire in his *Lettres philosophiques* (1734). For more on the history of inoculation, see Catriona Seth's magisterial work, *Les Rois aussi en mouraient: les Lumières en lutte contre la petite vérole* (Paris: Desjonquères, 2008).

20. Jean Terrasson (1670–1750) was the author of the didactic novel *Séthos, histoire ou vie tirée des monumens anecdotes de l'ancienne Egypte, traduite d'un manuscrit grec* (1731), immediately translated into English as *The Life of Sethos: Taken from Private Memoirs of the Ancient Egyptians* (1732).

21. Allusion to Madame de Genlis's immensely popular novel *Adèle et Théodore* (1782), translated as *Adelaide and Theodore, or Letters on Education* (1783). Gillian Dow points out that *Adèle et Théodore* consistently outsold Laclos's *Liaisons dangereuses*, also published in 1782, in both France and England until 1830 (Stéphanie-Félicité de Genlis, *Adelaide and Theodore* [London: Pickering and Chatto, 2007], p. XVII). The novel also features in Jane Austen's *Emma* (1815), when Emma likens herself to one of its characters (vol. 3, ch. 17). This, combined with the familiar reference in Charrière, tells us the extent to which *Adèle et Théodore* penetrated European reading consciousness, and transcended national boundaries.

22. Whenever either Cécile or her mother is mentioned as engaged doing "work," they are busy sewing.

23. Lausanne was situated in the French-speaking Pays de Vaud, which was governed by the German-speaking oligarchy in Bern; Lausanne in particular was ruled by a bailiff from Bern who was sent every three years from the senate. For a more detailed account, see Charles Burnier, *La Vie vaudoise et la Révolution: De la servitude à la liberté* (Lausanne, Switzerland, 1902).

24. Bern was governed by the Conseil des Deux-Cents (council of two hundred), and only members of certain families were eligible to join it. A councillor would be a member of this "council" or "senate" and thus a powerful aristocrat of rank.

25. As Cécile's mother divines, her ideas here are not new. In the French context, they had been articulated powerfully by Michel de Montaigne (1533–1592). See, for example, his comparison of the nobility and honor of the Conquistadores and Incan rulers in his essay "Of Coaches," in Montaigne, *The Complete Works*, translated by Donald M. Frame (New York, Toronto, and London: Everyman's Library, 2003), pp. 831–849.

26. This is somewhat of an exaggeration. But it is true that women had some access to scientific education, although it was by no

means systematic and probably only as much as aristocratic women or the daughters of learned men had ever had. Emilie du Châtelet, the mathematician and translator of Newton's *Principia*, was one of these special cases. Diderot famously had his daughter instructed in anatomy by Marie Marguerite Biheron (1719–1795). Yet Rousseau's influential educational treatise, *Emile* (1762), by no means recommended opening up intellectual pursuits of any sort to women. Charrière herself had had lessons with the professor of physics and medicine of the University of Utrecht, but in fact preferred mathematics, which she adored (Courtney, *Isabelle de Charrière*, p. 45; *There Are No Letters Like Yours*, pp. 57–58 [letter to Constant d'Hermenches, February 25–March 5, 1764]). On Châtelet, see Judith Zinsser and Julie Candler Hayes, eds., *Emilie du Châtelet: Rewriting Enlightenment Philosophy and Science* (Oxford, England: Voltaire Foundation, 2006); on Diderot, see Shane Agin, "Sex Education in the Enlightened Nation," *Studies in Eighteenth Century Culture*, vol. 37, 2008, pp. 67–87; on the education and status of women in France and in Europe more widely, see Roland Bonnel and Catherine Rubinger, eds., *Femmes savantes et femmes d'esprit: Women Intellectuals of the French Eighteenth Century* (New York: Peter Lang, 1994); Margaret Hunt, *Women in Eighteenth Century Europe* (Harlow, Essex, England: Longman, 2010); Peter Petschauer, *The Education of Women in Eighteenth-Century Germany: New Directions from the German Female Perspective: Bending the Ivy* (Lewiston, NY: Lampeter, Mellen, 1989).

27. Charrière here indicates her position as a vitalist in the vitalist-mechanist debate, which animated medical circles throughout the long eighteenth century; by the end of the century, it was felt that the "mechanical" investigation of the body via anatomy was utterly inadequate for the understanding of the living body. Some aspects of the vitalist-mechanist argument mapped onto atheistic/religious debates about the existence of the soul, which is what Charrière seems not far from evoking here with her allusion to love. See Roselyne Rey, *Naissance et développement du vitalisme en France de la deuxième moitié du 18e siècle à la fin du Premier Empire* (Oxford, England: Voltaire Foundation, 2000); Caroline Warman, "What's Behind a Face? Lavater and the Anatomists," in *Physiognomy in Profile: Lavater's Impact on European Culture*, ed. Melissa Percival and Graeme Tytler (Newark, DE: University of Delaware Press, 2005), pp. 94–108.

28. Michiel Adriaenzoon de Ruyter (1607–1676), a Dutch admiral much admired for his heroism; Maarten Harpertzoon Tromp (1597–1653) and his son Cornelis Maartenszoon Tromp (1629–1691), both also Dutch admirals, famed for their victories over Spanish and English; and Abraham de Fabert (1599–1662), marshal of France. All four men were celebrated examples of modesty and courage.

29. A cadogan is either the bow that ties the hair back or the hair itself; that is, what is now known as a ponytail. It was often accompanied by elaborately curled bouffant hair framing the face. This hairstyle was very popular before the Revolution but went out of fashion soon after. The portraits by Thomas Gainsborough or the paintings of Marie Antoinette in the 1780s contain many examples of the style.

30. Allemande: "a kind of dance" (Boyer, 1797); "a name given to various German dances" (OED).

31. Don Quixote is the eponymous hero of the novel by Cervantes (1615), and became synonymous with outmoded notions of chivalry and honor.

32. The American War of Independence (1775–1781).

33. Reversis is a card game, the ancestor of the current game Hearts. See David Parlett, A History of Card Games (Oxford, England: Oxford University Press, 1991).

34. One wonders what is being referred to here, other than pornography in general. Sade's work, whose heroes would fit the description of "men of determined vice" rather well, did not start publishing until the 1790s. Valmont, the libertine antihero of Laclos's Dangerous Liaisons (1782), is sufficiently determined in his vice, but "ill-imagined" is hardly the way Dangerous Liaisons strikes us now. Cécile's mother may be guilty, as Charrière's own reviewers were, of putting moral considerations above all others (see the Introduction, p. xxiii).

35. The word in French here was des Lucrèces; that is to say "Lucretias." The story of Lucretia is a founding myth of the Republic of Rome and is recounted by Livy and Dionysius of Halicarnassus. She was supposedly raped by the king's son, Tarquin, and committed suicide rather than live with her shame. She is famously the heroine of Shakespeare's poem The Rape of Lucrece (1594), and her name became synonymous in French with an ideal of incorruptible virginity. Interestingly, however, des Lucrèces could also be supposed to refer to the Roman poet Lucretius (c. 99 BC–c. 55 BC), whose name in French is also Lucrèce: he

was the author of the materialist poem *De Rerum Natura*, which transmitted much of Epicurus's philosophy to posterity and was tarred with the same brush as Epicurus, becoming incorrectly synonymous with debauched sensuality. The word in Charrière's sentence unambiguously means "prudes," but it is nonetheless significant that the term contains its direct opposite, not least because the type that Cécile's mother is describing *appears* extremely virtuous but *in fact* is depraved.

36. Adrienne Lecouvreur (1692–1730), now better known as the heroine of Francesco Cilea's opera *Adriana Lecouvreur* (1902), was a French tragic actress. She was much championed by Voltaire, who mounted an outraged and ultimately successful campaign to have her buried in sacred ground (she, as all actors were, had been denied a Christian burial). Maurice de Saxe (1696–1750) was a German aristocrat who entered the French service and became a brilliant general and eventually marshal general of France. When he was given the title Duke de Courlande, Adrienne pawned her diamonds to finance him. (Their relationship provides the plot of the opera, albeit unrecognizably altered.) A later liaison of Maurice's produced an illegitimate child, Marie Aurore, who was the grandmother of Amandine Aurore Lucile Dupin, better known as the writer George Sand, whose fictional accounts of women trying to improve society, not least via less constrained marriages and better organized societies, Charrière anticipates in many ways.

37. Agnès Sorel (c. 1422–1450) was the mistress of King Charles VII (1403–1461, reigned 1422–1461). She supposedly galvanized his patriotic feelings during the Hundred Years' War (1337–1453) with England, and therefore contributed to France's ultimate victory (which involved the English being driven out of France and obliged to renounce their claim to the French throne).

38. Cornelia (c. 180–110 BC) was the mother of Gaius Sempronius Gracchus and Tiberius Sempronius Gracchus; she brought them up to venerate the public good above all other things, and they tried to introduce democratic reforms before being assassinated. Cornelia is therefore an example of courageous patriotic motherhood. Octavia (c. 70–11 BC) was the sister of Augustus; her second husband was Anthony, whom she married in an attempt to bring the two together (Anthony divorced her to marry Cleopatra). Cato the Younger's daughter Portia was the second wife of Brutus, one of Julius Caesar's assassins. She was reputed to have been a devoted wife, and legends surround her: she was supposed

to have cut her own thigh to test her endurance and ability to resist torture (she decided she was unable to, but although Brutus accepted her conclusion that she only had a weak female body, he was impressed with her spirit); she is also supposed to have committed suicide when he died.

39. We have been unable to determine who these characters are; Cécile's mother may simply be indicating personal acquaintances.

40. This is a reference to François-André Danican Philidor (1725–1796), whose *Analyse du jeu des Échecs* (Analysis of the game of chess, 1749) was extremely popular; it went through 70 editions between publication and 1871. Philidor features in the opening paragraph of Diderot's curious dialogue *Rameau's Nephew* (probably composed around 1760, first published in Goethe's German translation of 1804), much of which takes place in a chess players' café.

41. The Penates are the Roman household gods.

42. Denis Diderot (1713–1784) was an Enlightenment philosopher, best known during his lifetime for being the editor, with d'Alembert, of the multivolume *Encyclopédie, ou Dictionnaire Raisonné des sciences, des arts et des métiers* (1751–1772), which is arguably the most important publication of the Enlightenment. He was thought by many at the time to be an inflexible atheist, and therefore possibly dangerously immoral. His own writings were very little known by his contemporaries, mostly because they remained unpublished until long after his death, although his famous *Letter on the Blind* (1749) was thought to deny the existence of God and was banned (although these two aspects are not necessarily causally linked). It now seems to be an overstatement of the case to suppose that *Letter* was atheist in any straightforward way, and it was certainly very concerned with moral questions. See Kate E. Tunstall, *Blindness and Enlightenment: An Essay, with New Translations of Diderot's* Letter on the Blind *and La Mothe Le Vayer's "Of a Man Born Blind"* (New York and London: Continuum, 2011).

43. *"Des chaudières bouillantes/ Où l'on plonge à jamais les femmes mal-vivantes."* Molière, *Ecole des femmes* (School for Wives), Act III, scene 2, lines 727–728 (*The School for Wives*, translated by Richard Wilbur, in *Five Plays*, introduced by Donald Roy [London: Methuen Drama, 2000], p. 67). Arnolphe is speaking, hoping to terrify Agnes.

44. *"O Eucharis, si Mentor me quitte, je n'ai plus que vous"* (Oh Eucharis, if Mentor leaves me, I will have no one but you), from

Fénelon's *Aventures de Télémaque*, book VI. Fénelon's immensely influential and much reprinted *Aventures de Télémaque* (1699) follows the wanderings of Telemachus, son of Ulysses, accompanied by Mentor (whose name gave us the word and the concept). Julie, the heroine in *The Nobleman*, also had a copy.

45. Catriona Seth points out that for the eighteenth-century reader, the name Fanchon, being a diminutive, can only refer to a servant.

46. *The History of Scotland* (1759) by the Scottish historian William Robertson (1721–1793), which contains a moving account of Mary Queen of Scots (who is mentioned in the following sentence).

47. Philidor's style was noted for its insistence on the importance of pawns. Might this be symbolic?

48. Alexander the Great (356 BC–323 BC), the Greek king of Macedon, pupil of Aristotle, and conqueror of immense stretches of territory, from the Adriatic to India. Presumably Alexander's virtue refers to courage.

49. A materialist view of change and movement seems to be intercut here with ideas of equilibrium, which owe more to medieval and renaissance models of the great chain of being: the materialist perspective is given by the dreaming philosopher d'Alembert in Diderot's *Le Rêve de d'Alembert* (1769): "*Changez le tout, vous me changez nécessairement; mais le tout change sans cesse*" ("Change the whole, and you will necessarily change me; but the whole is constantly changing"), *Le Rêve de d'Alembert*, ed. Jean Varloot and Georges Dulac, in Diderot, *Œuvres complètes*, vol. 17 (Paris: Hermann, 1987), pp. 137–138; *D'Alembert's Dream*, translated by L. W. Tancock (Harmondsworth, England: Penguin Classics, 1966), pp. 180–181 (translation modified). For more on the great chain of being, see Arthur O. Lovejoy's classic work, *The Great Chain of Being: A Study of the History of an Idea* (Cambridge, MA: Harvard University Press, 1964, first published in 1936).

50. Cécile's mother is quoting Corneille's tragedy *Rodogune* (1644): "*Il est des nœuds secrets, il est des sympathies,*" Act I, scene V, line 359.

51. Cécile's mother is close to a religious position articulated by the physico-theologian Abbé Pluche (1686–1761), whose *Spectacle de la nature*, 9 vols. (1732–1750) describes the extraordinary intricacy and activity of creation, inferring from it God's goodness. See also *Letters from Mistress Henley*, note 16.

52. *Lettres écrites de Lausanne, seconde partie* (1787), *Œuvres complètes*, vol. 8, pp. 181–189.

53. The full title of this second part is "Caliste, or the Continuation (etc.)." We have not replicated the full title as we are not offering *Caliste* (as explained in the introduction), but only the first three letters, as they continue Cécile's story.

54. A league was a pre-decimalization measure of about 4 kilometers; three quarters of a league is therefore 3 km, or just under 2 miles.

55. Antoine Galland's translation of *The Arabian Nights*, first published as *Les mille et une nuits* in 1704–1717, was the first European version of this immensely influential set of stories; *Gil Blas* refers to Lesage's *Histoire de Gil Blas de Santillane* (1715–1735), also owned by Julie in *The Nobleman* (see note 8); Anthony Hamilton (1645–1720) was a Jacobite exile in the French court, and famous for pastiche fairy tales such as *Le Bélier* (the ram), *Fleur d'Epine* (the mayflower), and *Les Quatre Facardins* (the four Facardins), which were published in 1730; *Zadig* (1747) is a philosophical tale by Voltaire. Galland, Hamilton, and Voltaire are all writing fairy stories, the latter two heavily influenced by Galland, whom they pastiche.

56. Bern and the Two Hundred: Charrière explains what this means in the next sentences. See note 23 for further elucidation.

57. The burgomasters were the magistrates who governed Amsterdam.

58. Fanchon is their servant (we met her in letter XIV), Philax is the dog (we have not met him before), and Renens is their destination, 3 or so miles from Lausanne (it is now a suburb).

59. Guinea was the old name for a vast stretch of territory in West Africa, now covering such countries as Benin, the Ivory Coast, Equatorial Guinea, Liberia, Sierra Leone, Togo, and parts of Nigeria and Cameroon. It used to be crudely divided into the products it traded, that is, the Slave Coast (Benin and Nigeria), the Gold Coast (Ghana), the Ivory Coast (which still bears this name), and the Pepper Coast or Grain Coast (Liberia and Sierra Leone).

60. Cécile's attendance at the bedside of the dead man foreshadows Constance's even more explicit wake, when she sits day and night by her dead uncle and mother to be sure that they have actually expired, and that their corpses are decomposing (see p. 294). W. R. Albury tells us that there was considerable anxiety about being able to prove death until the advent of anaesthetics in the mid-nineteenth century. See W. R. Albury, "Ideas of Life and Death," in *The Companion Encyclopedia of the History of*

Medicine, vol 1, ed. W. F. Bynum and Roy Porter, 2 vols. (London and New York: Routledge, 2003), pp. 249–280.

61. Mary Magdalene, one of Jesus's disciples, has traditionally been identified as a repentant prostitute. Indulgences were the infamous pre-Reformation system whereby the Catholic church allowed the faithful to pay fines for committing sins and thereby be forgiven. It is not clear what, apart from these very general references, Charrière is specifically alluding to here, although she may be paving the way for the story of Caliste (see note 64), who started her career as an actress and then was a kept mistress before meeting Milord's cousin; she therefore plays the role of a penitent Madgalene. Caliste, or "Calista," was the heroine in Nicholas Rowe's *The Fair Penitent* (first performed in 1702 and immensely popular throughout the century), and in playing that role, Caliste first made her name, and is ever after known by it.

62. This letter is addressed by Cécile's mother to the English lord's cousin.

63. This is his reply.

64. Letter XXI commences the story of Caliste; in fact it is a sustained first-person narrative of some 40 pages in which William, whom we have hitherto known only as the English lord's cousin and tutor, relates his ill-fated love for the eponymous heroine, and more ominously for the *Cécile* part of the story, his inability to break with convention and marry her. He had had insufficient resolution and vigor. Letters XXII–XXV then bring the story up to date: William learns of her death, and is plunged into grief.

65. *Lettres écrites de Lausanne, suite II* (unpublished and undated fragment), *Œuvres complètes*, vol. 8, pp. 241–243. Sequel 1 is a response to *Caliste*; we therefore omit it. We refer the reader to the introduction for our reasons for not including *Caliste* here. None of the three sequels were published.

66. Methodism is a protestant Christian movement with its own distinctive church founded by John Wesley (1703–1791), which gathered many supporters in England in the eighteenth century. It was initially a field church (that is, preaching was done in the open air, as no Anglican church would allow it inside and it had no churches of its own), and was strongly linked to supporting the rights and spirituality of the common people as well as being pro-democratic and anti-hierarchical. It was already an important force by the end of the eighteenth century and became

linked with prison reform, the birth of the trade union movement, and nineteenth-century temperance drives.

67. We omit the last sentence, which rather abruptly introduces the
death of Caliste and therefore both confuses and disrupts the
narrative.

68. *Lettres écrites de Lausanne, suite III* (unpublished and undated
fragment), *Œuvres complètes*, vol. 8, pp. 245–247.

69. Note the date, that is, 10 years later than the first publication.

EAGLONETTE AND SUGGESTINA, OR, ON PLIANCY

1. *Aiglonette et Insinuante, ou la Souplesse*. Conte (1791), *Œuvres
complètes*, vol. 8, pp. 249–260.

2. This "Bien-né" or "well-born" prince was Louis XVI (1754–
1793), and the sketch Charrière alludes to was her short story of
the same title, published as part of her *Observations et conjectures politiques* (1788), containing observations on Dutch and
French politics and also an "Apologie de la flaterie" (*Œuvres complètes*, vol. 10, pp. 57–110; "Bien-né" is pp. 82–84, 87–89).
"Bien-né" is only a couple of pages long, and depicts a good-
hearted king, given over to hunting and eating, and oblivious to
the government of his kingdom. One day, he asks for wisdom, and
a fairy of the same name appears to him. She advises him to eat
and drink less, to stop hunting, and to pay attention to the well-
being of his subjects, which he does, with excellent results all
around. He ends as happy "as a King can be" ("Bien-né," *OC*,
vol. 10, p. 89).

3. *The Observations et conjectures politiques* were published in
Neuchâtel; "Bien-né" and the observations about French affairs
were published in two Paris editions in 1788. Cecil Courtney
tells us that the 1791 Paris reprint of *Aiglonette et Insinuante*
gives the names of those imprisoned as being the printers Désau-
ges, father and son, and the Palais-royal bookseller, Philippe
Denné. Courtney suggests that the woman "who took pity on
him" may well have been Charrière herself, as she knew Breteuil,
"whose signature is on the order to imprison Denné" (Courtney,
Isabelle de Charrière, p. 417).

4. Maria-Teresa (1717–1780), daughter of the Holy Roman
Emperor, Charles VI, married Francis (1708–1765), the eldest

surviving son of the Duke of Lorraine, in 1736. Although Francis was technically the Holy Roman Emperor, and Maria-Teresa his consort, in effect Maria-Teresa reigned from 1740 until her death in 1780. Their fifteenth child was Marie-Antoinette (1755–1793), who married the future Louis XVI in 1770.

5. Louis the Magnificent is Louis XIV (1638–1715, ruled 1643–1715), builder of Versailles, self-styled "Sun King."

6. La Fontaine, "The Oak and the Reed," *Fables*, book 1, no. 22; translated by Shapiro, *The Complete Fables of La Fontaine*, pp. 25–26. This was the fable that Mistress Henley teaches her stepdaughter to recite; see *Letters of Mistress Henley*, p. 80.

7. This might be a reference to the suspected flight of the king; there had been rumors about this since January 1791, and when the king wanted to travel to Saint-Cloud on April 18, he was prevented by angry crowds. Ironically, this then did cause a frustrated king, feeling imprisoned, to attempt to escape; this is the famous flight to Varennes on June 21; the family was captured, brought back, and thereafter represented by their enemies as traitors and cowards. See "Fuite du roi" in Jean Tulard, Jean-François Fayard, and Alfred Fierro, *Histoire et dictionnaire de la Révolution française, 1789–1799* (Paris: Laffont, 1987), pp. 837–838. In fact, Isabelle de Charrière tells a friend that she has already sent her story to Marie-Antoinette in a letter dated June 10, and it had already been on sale for a week on May 25 (Courtney, *Isabelle de Charrière*, p. 586). So she might well be referring to the rumors, but cannot be referring to the actual flight.

8. See Diderot's similar analysis of this issue in LUI's famous pantomime of the servant mentality that according to him afflicts the entire nation apart from the king, and reduces everyone to servile positions (*Le Neveu de Rameau*, *Œuvres complètes*, vol. XII, ed. H. Dieckmann and J. Varloot [Paris, Hermann, 1989], p. 190, and in English, *Rameau's Nephew and First Satire*, translated by Margaret Mauldon, introduction and notes by Nicholas Cronk [Oxford: Oxford World Classics, 2006], p. 85). There are certain references and images that are common to Diderot and Charrière— see *Cécile*, p. 96 (the spider), p. 142 (Philidor), p. 156 (change)— note 39, but as we also see in *Cécile* (p. 143), Charrière had no real knowledge of Diderot's works, most of which were indeed completely unknown at the time, and she dismissed him as an atheist and potentially therefore immoral person. She had met him a number of times in 1774 at the Russian Embassy in the Hague,

and reports having (rather aggressively) questioned him about his relationship with Rousseau (see Courtney, *Isabelle de Charrière*, p. 303).

9. Joseph II, Holy Roman Emperor, reigned 1765–1790, although (see note 4), his mother retained the power until her death in 1780. He was an enlightened, reforming, dogmatic, and paternalistic emperor who believed in the power of the state; his reforms were resented and resisted.

10. Dionysius II, son of Dionysius I, Tyrant of Syracuse, was forced to surrender his rule and retire to Corinth in 344 BC: Cicero, in his *Tusculan Disputations* (c. 45 BC), states that Dionysius was unable to give up the exercise of authority, and thus exchanged the sceptre for the ferule, or schoolmaster's rod (book 3, section 12); this story seems without foundation, and had already been discredited in Louis Moreri's *Grand dictionnaire historique, ou le mélange curieux de l'histoire sacrée et profane* (first edition, one volume only, 1674; twentieth edition, ten volumes, 1759; see the article "Denys II"). However, it seems to have remained in circulation, and references can be found in numerous French and English writers of the eighteenth and even nineteenth century, as a Google Books search will show: the historical novelist, Walter Scott (1771–1832; see *Kenilworth*) refers to it, as does the essayist Charles Lamb (1775–1834, *Elia*), among others.

11. Zenobia, the famous queen of the Syrian city-state Palmyra; she conducted wars of expansion in Asia Minor and in AD 271 declared her son Augustus; the Emperor Aurelian defeated her and brought her to Rome. Charrière is probably referring to Edward Gibbon's *Decline and Fall of the Roman Empire (1776–1788)*, vol. 2, ch. 11: "the Syrian queen insensibly sunk into a Roman matron."

12. Cornelia (c. 180–110 BC) was the mother of the Gaius Sempronius Gracchus and Tiberius Sempronius Gracchus, who were bywords of civic virtue and self-sacrifice; they are also mentioned in *Cécile*, as is Cato's daughter, see note 37.

13. Cato the Younger's daughter Portia was the second wife of Brutus, and a model of devoted wifeliness; see previous note. *** designates the Dauphin (title of the heir to the throne), Louis-Charles de France (1785–1795), and "Mad." (the usual eighteenth-century abbreviation for "Madame") refers to "Madame Royale," that is Louis XVI's and Marie-Antoinette's eldest child, Marie Thérèse Charlotte de France (1778–1851).

ÉMIGRÉ LETTERS

1. *Lettres trouvées dans des portefeuilles d'émigrés* (August 1793), *Œuvres complètes*, vol. 8, pp. 411–472.
2. The letters are sent between April 19, 1793, and July 2, 1793; the letters in the sequel are dated July 3–16, 1793. This was the year in which the Revolution became what is now known as the Terror. The following information is drawn from Colin Jones's *Longman Companion to the French Revolution* (Harlow, Essex, England: Longman, 1988), ch. 1. On January 21, 1793, Louis XVI was guillotined, on February 1 France declared war on Britain and Holland, and on February 24 a general levy for the armies was announced; this provoked serious unrest in the Vendée. Regular troops were sent against the rebels in the Vendée in May; rebel resistance was strong and, grouped into the Royal Catholic army, also known as the Christian army, they seized Thouars (May 5), Parthenay (May 9), and Fontenay (May 25). The Vendeans had further victories but were defeated at Luçon on August 13 and then decisively crushed at Savenay on December 23. The revolutionary armies began to be successful on all fronts in this latter part of 1793, and continued to be so. The early months of 1794 would be marked by mass executions of rebels. Meanwhile, Robespierre was voted onto the Committee of Public Safety on July 27, 1793, and terror was officially instated as "the order of the day" on September 5. Marie Antoinette was executed on October 16. Robespierre would fall on July 27, 1794.
3. Germaine's father, the Marquis de ***, is with Condé's army, which the Prince of Condé had set up in 1791 in Worms, on the Rhine. Other émigré forces, led by Louis XVI's brothers, the Comtes of Provence and Artois, and known as "the Princes' army," were stationed in Coblenz. Initially supported by the Austrians and part of the Austrian army, they participated in the invasion of France in April 1792. The forces led by Provence and Artois were disbanded by the Prussians in January 1793, after having been blamed for the defeat at Valmy (September 20, 1792); only Condé's army remained under arms. It stayed on the banks of the Rhine until 1795, and was successively under the orders and in the pay of the British, the Austrians, and the Russians. Condé disbanded it in 1801. At the beginning of 1793, Claude Louis de La Châtre (1745–1824) formed a regiment subsidized by the British called the Régiment Loyal-Emigrant. The

reference to Maastricht during the siege is probably to the Battle of Neerwinden (March 18, 1793), at which the Austrian forces under Coburg inflicted a crushing defeat on the French revolutionary army, who, under General Dumouriez, had led an ambitious offensive into Holland in February and captured Breda. The French were temporarily driven out of Belgium. Dumouriez himself emigrated in April 1793.

4. Covent Garden Street does not exist, but the area of Covent Garden did and does; it is in the center of London, and in the eighteenth century was shifting from being an area of aristocratic habitation to a red light district.

5. See note 2.

6. *Émigrés* was a term coined during the Revolution to designate those who left France because of the events. The first wave of emigration started in July–August 1789 but intensified after the attempted flight of the King in June 1791 (see *Eaglonette*, note 7); from October 31, 1791, emigration was made punishable by death. The "Jacobins" was the popular name for a club of deputies from the northwestern province of Brittany and their supporters, derived from the Couvent des Jacobins that it met next door to. Its real name was the "Société des amis de la constitution," and it became the most powerful and most radical of the parties. Robespierre was its leader.

7. "Let us be friends, Cinna, it is me who is urging you" (Pierre Corneille, *Cinna* [1639], Act V, scene III, line 1701). The emperor Augustus, having discovered a love-motivated plot on the part of his closest friends to assassinate him, offers clemency to all involved.

8. The editors of the *Œuvres complètes* suggest that Truguet may be Admiral Laurent Jean François Truguet (1752–1839), and that the insults he had to endure would have dated from his yearlong stay in England, and would have been inflicted by émigrés. However, the letter seems to be invoking the distant past, and Laurent's "brave Truguet" cannot be aristocratic, given that he is patronized by these "gentlemen," whereas Admiral Truguet was an aristocrat.

9. "Girondins" is a label that grew up around supporters of deputies from the Gironde, a department in southwest France created during the Revolution and whose capital is Bordeaux. Broadly, they were anti-centrist moderates, arguing that Paris, being only one of 83 departments, should have only an 83rd of the influence. The Girondins' power was greatest between 1791–1793;

their leaders, including Madame Roland, were executed on November 9, 1793. Jacobins: see note 6. The Legislation was a subcommittee of the Convention that considered matters relating to the reform of law and administration. The Convention was named after the American constitutive assembly and was set up in August 1792 after the monarchy had been overthrown; it operated until October 1795, and had executive and legislative powers. The editors of *Œuvres complètes* consider that Charrière has a particular person in mind here for Laurent's brother: They hypothesize that she has confused Armand Gensonné (1758–1793), who presided over the Convention March 7–20, 1793 (presidents held post for two weeks only), and was from Bordeaux, as Laurent seems to be (see letter XIX), with Charles Jean Marie Barbaroux (1767–1794), who was a Girondin from Marseille faithful to Madame Roland. They explain Laurent's signature, L. B. Fonbrune, as being Laurent Barbaroux Fonbrune. These models may well be resonating in the background for Charrière and her readers without their needing to be supposed to be close portraits.

10. "Burnt by more fires than I lit" (Jean Racine, *Andromaque* (1667), Act 1, scene IV, line 320). Pyrrhus is declaring his passion to Andromaque, saying that he suffers more pain from the anguish of his repulsed love than any he has inflicted in war.

11. Catriona Seth suggests that this is likely to be an allusion to the famous line "Full many a flower is born to blush unseen," from Thomas Gray's *Elegy Written in a Country Church-Yard* (1751), which was much quoted in the period, in French as in English.

12. Laurent is being rude about Condé's army. The reference to the mistress is not clear, although it may be that he has confused Condé's army with the more chaotic Prince's army, led by the unimpressive Comte de Provence (1755–1824), brother of Louis XVI and future Louis XVIII, whose favorite, the Comtesse de Balbi (1753–1832), had helped organize his escape and who was with him in Coblenz. See note 3 for information about these armies.

13. Sailors are mythically famous for their free and colorful language (viz. the old jokes about foul-mouthed parrots previously owned by sailors). In this context, the ships of the French Royal Navy, replicating their highly stratified society in an extremely compressed space, became test cases of revolutionary feeling, and repeated mutinies (in Brest, Rochefort, and Toulon) forced out many in the officer ranks of the navy, many of whom became émigrés. The "sans-culottes" were famously pro-democracy, pro-

equality, and therefore pro-revolutionary. They were a mainly Parisian, mainly artisan movement, and their name means "without breeches," describing their rejection of the previous custom of wearing tight breeches to just below the knee, along with stockings, etc. They adopted the more practical and cheaper trouser, which is still the dominant fashion for men. Presumably these rather specific references simply mean here "disrespectfully."

14. The Irish lord's French is supposed to be rather faulty. What he actually says is *"Madame la Duchesse est extrêmement bien, j'espére!"* which is a literal rendering of the English idiom "to be very well." We have therefore rendered this as a literal translation of the French idiom *aller bien* (to go well), which means "to be well."

15. Boulle or boule tables, heavily inlaid with brass and marquetry and named after their principal proponent, André Charles Boulle (1642–1732, also spelled Boule and Buhl), were indicators of extreme luxury.

16. The Rue du Roule is in the 1st arrondissement in Paris, very near the Louvre, and the point may be to expose the French émigré comte's extreme provincialism, as he laughs merrily at the idea that anyone could mistake the Rue du Roule for the Rue du Rouleau. *Roule* does not mean anything as a noun; its related verb is *rouler*, "to roll"; *rouleau* means "scroll." It may also be that the difference in pronunciation between *rue* and *roue* was then as now a common feature of teaching French to foreigners. A horrible tongue twister that uses these sounds is *"la roue sur la rue roule; la rue sous la roue reste"* ("the wheel on the road rolls; the road under the wheel stays"), which is not only hard to say, but makes all kinds of nonsense if you get it wrong.

17. Assuming that the duchess is thinking in French livres and not English pounds (the word in French is *livre* for both), the sum of 45,000 French livres is worth about 2,000 English pounds, which is a considerable yearly income, although not as much as the heroes of *Pride and Prejudice* enjoy: Mr. Bingley has an income of between 4,000 and 5,000 pounds, while Mr. Darcy has 10,000.

18. Émigré property was sequestrated to the nation on February 9, 1792; on July 17, 1792, it was decreed that it could be sold.

19. Sans-culottes: see note 13.

20. See *Cécile*, note 55.

21. *Un fossé* is the French term for moat or ditch. His name is therefore slightly jokey, meaning Viscount of the Moats (or Ditches).

22. "Chevalier" is a title indicating aristocratic pedigree, and is often conferred on younger sons, etc. It means "cavalier," i.e., "knight."

23. Brelan, or three of a kind, is related to modern poker.

24. Germaine is quoting a song that runs "Guillot, Guillot," etc.; the parody is based on General Gillot, who was at that point in charge of the defense of Landau and besieged by the Prussians.

25. Louis XVI had been executed on January 21, 1793; Marie Antoinette would be guillotined later the same year, on October 16, 1793.

26. "Anarchist" was a very common term in the political pamphlets of 1793; it retained its etymological sense of "enemy of all power."

27. Louis-Philippe-Joseph, Duc d'Orléans, known as Philippe-Egalité or Philip-Equality for his support of the Revolution (1747–1793); he voted in favor of the execution of the King, who was his cousin. He was himself arrested on April 6, 1793, for his links with Dumouriez (see note 3) and executed on November 6, 1793. Maximilien Robespierre (1758–1794), a lawyer, who became the foremost Jacobin during the Revolution and was leader in all but name between July 1793 and his downfall in 1794; he spearheaded the Terror, instigating a number of purges, and was hostile to dechristianization, instituting the Cult of the Supreme Being.

28. The Gauls besieged Rome in 390 BC, as the Roman historian Livy recounts in his *History of Rome*, book V, chapters 39–41.

29. Montesquieu (1689–1755) wrote one of the key Enlightenment texts, investigating the relative and cultural nature of political systems and laws, *De l'esprit des lois* (1748). Thomas à Kempis (1380–1471) was a medieval monk, the author of *The Imitation of Christ*. Louis-Pierre Anquetil (1723–1808) wrote *L'Esprit de la Ligue* (1767), a history of the French religious wars of the sixteenth century. Jean-Jacques Rousseau (1712–1778) was the immensely influential philosopher, much read writer, and official hero of the Revolution (his remains were transferred to the Pantheon on October 11, 1794); Laurent might have been reading almost anything he wrote, including the *Social Contract* of 1762. Charles Rollin (1661–1741) was a historian and the author of the *Traité des études* (1726–1728), a modernizing treatise on education, which argued that it would be a good idea to have school books in the vernacular and also that national history as well as

ancient history should be studied. Charrière was very interested in theories of education, as *Cécile* shows perhaps most clearly. Rollin is mentioned again in *Saint Anne* (see *Saint Anne*, note 5).

30. These were the rallying calls of Girondins and Jacobins respectively (see notes 6 and 9). For more on the *république une et indivisible* see note 61. The republic was proclaimed "one and indivisible" on September 25, 1792.

31. The structure of government as ratified in the 1791 constitution (September 3, 1791) was split into two parts: the executive, led by the King, who appointed ministers (it had no initiative in legislation and was unable to block it, and in effect the monarchy was abolished September 21–22, 1793); and the legislature, which was unicameral, stayed in office for 2 years, and had 745 members, elected by the departments (the number of deputies any given department could send depended on its size and population). The constitution of 1793 or Year 1 (June 24, 1793) decreed that the form of government involve one unicameral legislature, named the "Convention" after the American model, with yearly elections and one executive council, composed of 24 members chosen by the legislature.

32. The Revolution had suppressed the monopoly official theaters had previously enjoyed, and theaters sprang up everywhere in the new era of deregulation. However, Laurent was not the only commentator to feel that this might be having an immoral effect, and censorship of theaters would be introduced on August 2, 1793, with the instruction that any plays that "deprave public spirit or reawaken royalist sentiment [are] to be closed down."

33. "Ci-devant" was a revolutionary neologism. It became widespread in 1792, even before aristocratic titles had been de facto abolished with the proclamation of the Republic on September 25, 1792, thereafter being indicated by the use of "ci-devant." It means "heretofore," "previously," or more simply, "ex," as in "ex-princes," but the term was so current that it seems jarring to translate it. Charles Dickens, for instance, in his *Tale of Two Cities* (1859), uses it widely (in the mouths of the vulgar revolutionaries, of course).

34. "Young Capet" is Louis XVII; Capet was the surname given the French royal family to reduce them to the level of ordinary mortals. Marie Antoinette was consistently addressed as Veuve Capet (Widow Capet) during her trial. In fact, Capet had been the name of the French royal dynasty that reigned 987–1328.

Louis XVI was a Bourbon, a name that possibly had too much regal resonance for contemporaries; calling him Capet also infers, it is suggested, that the Bourbons were impostors.

35. Cressier, a small town near Neuchâtel.

36. Alphonse, as the previous disappeared letter intimates, is in Neuchâtel. The marquis is in Worms, Germaine in London, Pauline and Laurent in the Vendée, Alphonse in Neuchâtel, and the abbé nearby.

37. On November 29, 1791, it was demanded that all priests take the civic oath contained in the Constitution of 1791 within one week ("I swear to be faithful to the nation, the law and the king, and to support in every way I can the constitution of the kingdom decreed by the National Assembly as constituted in the years 1789, 1790 and 1791," Constitution of 1791, Title II, article 5). A further oath "to defend liberty and equality" was imposed on all state functionaries, including priests, on August 14, 1792. Official penalties included arrest and deportation.

38. *Constitutionnel* (constitutional) designates the "constitutional clergy," that is, those who adhered to the Civil Constitution of the Clergy of July 12, 1790, which rationalized (the exact term!) the church in France, introducing a new ecclesiastical organization, a new system of appointment, a new system of ecclesiastical self-government, and a new career structure (see Colin Jones, *The Longman Companion to the French Revolution*, pp. 240–241). *Monarchien* (translated as "monarchic" to avoid confusion with monarchianism, the early church heresy) designates not monarchists in general (i.e., people who support a government organized around a monarch) but much more specifically "those Anglophile deputies of the Constituant Assembly who in the Summer and Autumn of 1789 advocated a British-style bicameral legislature" (Jones, p. 417).

39. "Amphibian" in pre-Revolutionary parlance had been a rather specific insult, designating those common people who claimed to be noble. Here it seems to have a more general and figurative weight.

40. Cato the Younger, also known as Cato of Utica (95–46 BC), was a stalwart and incorruptible defender of the Roman republic and a famed orator; he committed suicide when it became clear to him that Julius Caesar was going to terminate the republic. Charrière uses the life of his daughter Portia as an exemplum in *Eaglonette* (note 13) and *Cécile* (note 38).

41. Roche sur Lay in the Vendée

42. Louis XIV

43. Primary assemblies were "meetings of active citizens under the two-tier electoral systems established by the Constitutions of 1791, Year III and Year VIII; their main political function was to choose electors of the deputies to the National Assembly" (Colin Jones, *The Longman Companion to the French Revolution*, p. 403). What the Assemblée constituante actually consisted of was initially representatives of the three estates (i.e., nobles, clergy, and "third estate," which included everyone else); they met on May 5, 1789, declared themselves the Assemblée nationale on June 17 and Assemblée nationale constituante on July 7, arrogating to the assembly legislative power, and the right to draw up the constitution, which it duly did, with the Declaration of the Rights of Man issued on August 27, 1789, and a constitution in 1791. It was a one-chamber system. They dissolved themselves on September 30, 1791; the Legislative Assembly took its place, to be replaced on September 20 by the National Convention.

44. Cicisbeo: "The name formerly given in Italy to the recognized gallant or *cavalier servente* of a married woman" (OED).

45. Catriona Seth points out that in literature of all sorts, La Flèche, meaning literally "arrow," was a very common name for a domestic servant. Presumably it plays on the idea of the servant being (hopefully) "speedy" in the execution of his tasks. Is it ironic that this hierarchizing cliché has found its way into a novel debating the Revolution—or does it explicitly label Des Fossés as an unenlightened émigré?

46. An ell is the old English equivalent of the old French *aune*— despite local variation, it would be slightly more than a yard or meter. The point being, his cravats were very long, and therefore expensive to buy and requiring a valet to maintain.

47. On November 9, 1791, a law was passed against the émigrés, stating that if they did not return by January 1, 1792, they would be accounted conspirators against France and their lands sequestrated (see note 18).

48. The Battle of Valmy, September 20, 1792. See note 3.

49. Aristeides (530–468 BC) was an Athenian statesman known as "the Just"; Cincinnatus (519–438 BC) is a hero of early Roman history who is supposed to have been called from the plow to serve the city and defend it against a warring tribe, which he did, resigning his function after sixteen days and returning to the farm. Both were exempla of modesty and rectitude.

50. That is, the affairs of Condé's army.

51. La Fontaine, "L'Aigle et l'Escarbot," *Fables*, book 2, number 8. The literal translation is ours. For a fluent version of the entire poem, see "The Eagle and the Dung Beetle," *The Complete Fables of Jean de la Fontaine*, translated by Norman R. Shapiro (Urbana and Chicago: University of Chicago Press, 2007), pp. 36–37, line 9.

52. Maratism after Jean-Paul Marat (1744–1793), a physician by training, and in the Revolution the incendiary editor of the gazette *L'Ami du Peuple*—by extension it means incendiary republicanism. He was supposed to have been heavily involved in the September Massacres (September 2–6, 1792), in which many prisoners across France were slaughtered, and which revolted the Girondins (see note 9). He was famously assassinated in his bath on July 13, 1793, just over one month after the date of this letter, by Charlotte Corday, a woman whose émigré brothers had Girondin sympathies.

53. Alphonse has adapted the following line from Racine's *Bérénice* (1760): "*Dans l'Orient désert quel devint mon ennui*" (Act 1, scene IV, line 234).

54. Mistress C*** is Susette Moula, daugher of Frédéric Moula, who had taught mathematics in Berlin and St. Petersburg and retired to Colombier, where Charrière and her husband lived. Susette took up a post at Windsor in 1777, and married a captain in the British navy, Allen Cooper, in 1786. Her sister, Marianne, remained an intimate of Charrière's—she was a fine musician and had a talent, Courtney tells us, for "cutting out silhouettes in paper." Her silhouette of Charrière is exquisite. See Courtney, *Isabelle de Charrière*, p. 324 and 600 (silhouette reproduced on p. 523).

55. In English in the original. The translator has not amended it, despite its oddity!

56. This appears to be a pen portrait (see her letter of 5/17/1793) of the novelist and political thinker Benjamin Constant (1767–1830), whom Charrière had met in Paris in 1787, and with whom she struck up an ardent friendship, which endured in its most intense form until September 1794, when she sent him to pay a visit on her behalf to Germaine de Staël, who lived near her, but whom she did not personally wish to become intimate with despite Staël's repeated advances. Constant and Staël became inseparable, and the relationship with Charrière soured. However, the last letter she ever wrote, on December 10, 1805, was addressed to him. She died on December 27. His famous novel,

Adolphe (1816), is recognizably influenced by her *Caliste* (1787, part 2 of the *Lettres écrites de Lausanne*; see *Cécile*, notes 52 and 61). He was, as it happens, the nephew of Constant d'Hermenches, with whom she had enjoyed a passionate epistolary relationship, which endured from 1760 to 1776; see Isabelle de Charrière, *There Are no Letters Like Yours: The Correspondence of Isabelle de Charrière and Constant d'Hermenches*, translated with an introduction and annotations by Janet Whatley and Malcolm Whatley (Lincoln, NE, and London: University of Nebraska Press, 2000).

57. Courtney tells us that this is a portrait of Charrière herself (*Isabelle de Charrière*, p. 601).

58. This may refer to the establishment of the Commission des douze (Commission of Twelve), set up on May 18 to investigate subversion in the Paris commune and its sections. Its members were principally Girondins and their supporters.

59. Divorce was legalized on September 20, 1792, and would remain on the books until Napoleon's Code Civil of 1804; it was thereafter technically possible, but in effect difficult to obtain, and fell into disuse. Napoleon himself divorced his first wife, Josephine de Beauharnais, in 1810, so as to marry Marie-Louise of Austria. The Ancien Régime law of primogeniture, which meant that the eldest or only son typically inherited any family wealth to the detriment of other children, male or female, was abolished on 17 Nivôse, year II (January 6, 1794), and children henceforth all inherited equal portions of a parent's fortune; this included, as from the law of 12 Brumaire, year II (November 2, 1793), both legitimate and illegitimate offspring. For more on inheritance law during the Revolution, see Jean-Louis Halpérin, "Le Droit Privé de la Révolution: Héritage Législatif et Héritage Idéologique," *Annales historiques de la Révolution française* 328 (April–June 2002), paragraph 9, accessed January 6, 2011, http://ahrf.revues.org/628.

60. The editors of the *Œuvres complètes* explain this reference as follows: Edward Russell (1653–1727) was an English admiral who won a great victory over the French at La Hougue (Jersey) in 1692. In 1688 William of Orange and Mary deposed her father, James II, who had been seeking to reimpose Catholicism in Britain as the established religion. James sought exile in France, and war was declared between the two countries. Admiral Russell had maintained a correspondence with the deposed king. This quotation is probably a paraphrase from Sir John

Dalrymple's *Memoirs of Great Britain and Ireland* (Edinburgh and London: 1771–1788, 3 vols): "But in all his correspondence, he entreated James to prevent the two fleets from meeting, and gave warning that, as he was an officer and an Englishman, it behoved him to fire upon the first French ship that he met, although he saw James upon the quarter-deck" (vol. 1, p. 498).

61. The Republic had been proclaimed *"une et indivisible"* (one and indivisible) on September 25, 1792. "Liberty" was a key word of the Declaration of the Rights of Man of 1789, but "equality" didn't make it into the Declaration until the revised version of 1793, and "fraternity" as a concept was not included until the Constitution of 1795; there was no clear moment when the republican motto suddenly erupted onto the scene. See Mona Ozouf, "Liberty, Equality, Fraternity," in *Realms of Memory: Rethinking the French Past*, vol. 3, ed. Pierre Nora (New York: Columbia University Press, 1996–1998).

62. See note 33 on the abolition of aristocratic titles; as an extension of this emphasis on equality, elaborate forms of address and the polite form *vous* were all dropped. The address *citoyen* or *citoyenne* replaced all titles and honorifics. On November 8, 1793, the Convention decreed that *tutoiement* (the use of the informal address) would be henceforth obligatory in all government institutions.

63. *La Jeunesse* (Youth) is Bartholo's doddery old servant in Beaumarchais's farce, *The Barber of Seville* (1775). La Jeunesse doesn't actually have any lines like these in the play; his main appearance is in Act II, scenes VI–VII.

64. Battle of Lens (1648), the concluding battle in the Thirty Years' War (between most powers in Europe, but focusing in the end on France and Austria). The siege of Barcelona, one of the concluding events in the War of the Spanish Succession (1701–1714); Barcelona fell on September 12, 1714, to French and Spanish troops after heroic resistance. The Battle of Krefeld (1758) was part of the Seven Years' War (1756–1763), which involved many countries; this particular battle was between French and Prussian troops, the latter party prevailing and pushing the French back across the Rhine. The Comte de Gisors was a popular leader, the only child of the French minister of war, the Comte de Belle-Isle.

65. The first Brutus (as opposed to the second Brutus, Caesar's assassin and Portia's husband, who has been mentioned before) is Lucius Junius Brutus, who, according to Roman tradition, became

consul in 509 BC after overthrowing the rule of the Etruscan kings; he counts as one of the founders of the Republic. Jérôme Pétion de Villeneuve (1756–1794) was a politician and lawyer, appointed mayor of Paris in November 1791 and president of the Convention (September 20, 1793). He supported slave emancipation and was known as "Pétion the virtuous." He fled arrest in June 1793, and is thought to have committed suicide. Antoine Joseph Santerre (1752–1809) was a wealthy brewer from the Faubourg St-Antoine, an area of Paris to the east of the Bastille, and one of the places in which revolutionary unrest first sparked. He participated in the storming of the Bastille, and was made a commander of the national guard in August 1792; promoted to the rank of general, he was sent to the Vendée in May 1793, and was victorious at Doué-la-Fontaine, but defeated at Coron, and then imprisoned. He was released after the terror. Pierre-Gaspard Chaumette (1763–1794) rose from a humble background (his father was a cobbler) to become a medical student in Paris in 1789. He embraced revolutionary politics and, as a *procureur-syndic*, that is, a local official, was an important voice in the capital in 1793–1794, and was one of the founders of the *culte de la raison* (worship of reason). Robespierre, who halted the dechristianization process, had him executed on April 13, 1794.

66. Divorce was legalized on September 20, 1792 (see note 59).

67. See note 2. The Vendeans captured the town of Saumur on June 9, 1793.

68. Roche sur Lay.

69. "Wh" for "whore"; Laïs of Corinth, a famous courtesan of Ancient Greece; Aspasia, mistress of the Athenian statesman Pericles, reputedly a clever woman who enjoyed the conversation of Socrates.

70. "It should all be burnt": this remark is made about libertine novels (authors unspecified), and resonates interestingly with Simone de Beauvoir's famous tract about the most extreme of all libertine writers, Sade (1740–1814): *"Faut-il brûler Sade?"* ("Must we burn Sade?"), 1955.

71. "Clélie," heroine of Madeleine de Scudéry's 13,000-page novel, *Clélie, Histoire Romaine* (1654–1661), a picaresque love story intercalated with theoretical discussions developed in Scudéry's salon, the best seller of its century, and according to Joan De Jean, the novel that "inaugurates the French novel's close association with psychological realism" ("Clélie, Histoire Romaine," *New Oxford Companion to Literature in French*, ed. Peter

France, [Oxford, England: Clarendon Press, 1995], p. 178). Cyrus was the hero of Scudéry's *Artamène, ou le grand Cyrus* (1649–1653), while Faramond was the hero of La Calprenède's *Faramond ou l'histoire de France* (1661–1670, unfinished), which projected a "heroic mythification of contemporary courtly ideals" back in time (Jonathan Mallinson, "La Calprenède," *New Oxford Companion to Literature in French*, p. 428). For an excellent and contextualizing introduction to these novels, see Gillian Dow, "Criss-Crossing the Channel: French Influences on the Eighteenth-Century Novel, 1660–1832," in *The Oxford Handbook to the Eighteenth-Century Novel*, ed. J. A. Downie (Oxford, England: Oxford University Press, forthcoming).

72. Moloch was a divinity worshipped by the ancient Israelites; children were apparently sacrificed to it. In common parlance, it has come to be understood as meaning excessive sacrifice.

73. In Greek mythology, the Minotaur was a monster, son of Zeus and therefore half brother of Minos, King of Crete. He was imprisoned in a maze specially built for him and known as the labyrinth, and each year was fed seven young men and seven young women from Athens. One year, Theseus offered himself as a victim, and with the help of Minos's daughter, Ariadne, he killed the Minotaur and escaped from the labyrinth.

74. The editors of the *Œuvres complètes* point out that this is an important differentiation, and that it introduces a notion that had no specific word at that time, that word being "subjectivity." It is first recorded in English in 1812, used by poets, first Southey, then Coleridge (1821) (OED).

75. Of course, to the marquis's eyes, the "rebels" of the Vendée are not rebels at all, but loyalists. The editors of the *Œuvres complètes* point out that these places are not plucked out of the air, but that the marquis has good reason to mention them. After the purge of the Girondins on June 2, 1793, many Girondin deputies fled to the provinces and appealed for support. Normandy, Brittany, Bordeaux, and Provence had all responded, but the unrest that had overtaken Lyons from the end of May quickly mutated into a Royalist revolt, and in Provence also counterrevolutionary elements spearheaded the rebellion.

76. *Suite des lettres trouvées dans des portefeuilles d'émigrés* (August 1793), *Œuvres complètes*, vol. 8, pp. 473–482, first published in the OC. Possibly written, according to the editors of the OC, in August 1793, that is, as the first part was being published. Charrière mentions them in a letter to Therese Huber (May 15, 1794).

77. See note 3 for information about Condé's army, which was indeed not a free agent, being subsumed into the Austrian army, and under its orders during this period.

78. "Laughers," the direct translation of Charrière's neologism, *rieurs*.

79. Germaine is referring to the anecdote Alphonse related at the end of letter XVIII.

80. Louis Alexandre, Duc de la Rochefoulcauld d'Enville (1743–1792), a nobleman with liberal ideas and friend of Benjamin Franklin; he translated the *Thirteen Constitutions of the United States*, which appeared in French in 1778. He was a deputy at the meeting of the Estates General in 1789, and one of the 47 noble deputies who rallied to the cause of the Third Estate on June 25, 1789. He became a member of the Constituent Assembly (see note 43), and when that disbanded, he joined local politics and became *président* of the newly created Département de la Seine (an area that included Paris and the Seine basin); he opposed Pétion (see note 65), and suspended him from his post as mayor of Paris, which gained him the enmity of the Jacobin faction; he resigned after the events of August 10, 1792 (when the monarchy was overthrown), and left Paris. He was attacked and killed on September 4, 1792, a victim of the September Massacres (see note 52).

81. The promissory note or *assignat* was a system of paper money that was issued by the French revolutionary government between April 17, 1790, and February 19, 1796. We have chosen to translate this as "promissory note" so as to keep its unfamiliarity—the "bank note" is too familiar to us, and we are unable to see the novelty or more properly speaking, the "revolutionary" nature of this scheme.

82. Exactly as in published transcript. The story is broken off here.

A CORRESPONDENCE

1. There are fragments from *two* novels here, *A Correspondence* and *Letters of Peter and William*. Both seem to have been composed in 1796. The *Œuvres complètes* published them for the first time (see OC, vol. 8, pp. 485–504).

2. Letters 1 to 5 (pp. 259–265) are entitled "Fair Copy." It is incomplete: the original letters follow, but they are also incomplete. *A Correspondence* arises from an exercise Charrière devised in 1796

to teach English to her friend Isabelle de Gélieu (1779–1834); see her letter of October 24, 1796 (*Œuvres complètes*, p. 485): "She is writing from the Vaud area [in Switzerland] and is the age she actually is. I write from Tavanes and am a young lady a little older than the other one. Thirty letters are written, and there is material for more than one hundred." Charrière's character is Emily; Gélieu's Harriet. Gélieu would have been 17 at the time; Charrière, 56. Charrière corrected and revised everything as they went along. The other letters have unfortunately been lost. We transcribe them, and have not altered anything, from spelling and grammar to syntax and repetition, the point being to allow the reader to savor her original English.

3. *The Tales of Mother Goose*, from Charles Perrault's *Histoires ou contes du temps passé, avec des moralitez* (1697), first translated as *Mother Goose Tales* by Robert Samber in 1729 (they include the now embedded favorites Tom Thumb, Cinderella, Little Red Riding Hood, etc.). Marie Leprince de Beaumont brought out her fairy stories, including her immensely popular version of *The Beauty and the Beast*, under the title *Magasin des enfants* (London, 1756, 4 vols). An English translation of the first volume, titled *Magazin des enfans: Or, the Young Misses' Magazine*, came out as early as 1757; as *The Monthly Review, or Literary Journal* 17 (London, printed for Ralph Griffiths), p. 604, article 45, explains that they tried to make education enjoyable, and were immensely popular. Madame d'Epinay's *Les conversations d'Emilie* (Leipzig, 1774), dedicated to her 6-year-old granddaughter, Emilie, and translated into English as *The Conversations of Emily: Translated from the French of Madame la Comtesse d'Epigny* in 1787, and popular in both languages.

4. Allusion to Goethe's *Sorrows of Young Werther* (1774), one of the founding texts of Romanticism, in which the eponymous hero, a young man of exquisite sensibility, falls in love with Charlotte, who is engaged to someone else, and does not love Werther, who commits suicide.

5. *Soi-disant*: in French in the original, meaning "so-called."

6. The word *rêverie*, translatable either as "reverie" or "daydream," became widespread in response to the other founding text of Romanticism, Rousseau's *Rêveries du Promeneur Solitaire*, or "Reveries of the Solitary Walker" (1782), in which the author looks back over his life and meditates on injustice and morality in a series of ten walks. "Solitary walks" replace *rêveries* in the

rewritten second version of the letters, which confirms that it is a reference to Rousseau. See note 9.

7. See note 3 for information.

8. See note 4 for information.

9. This last sentence is in fact directed from Isabelle de Gélieu to Isabelle de Charrière.

10. See note 6.

11. We cannot trace this reference.

12. James Macpherson's poem about the Celtic hero Fingal, supposedly written by a newly discovered Celtic Homer, Ossian, was first published in 1761.

13. Nicolas Boileau-Despréaux, known as Boileau (1636–1711), poet, satirist, and critic. We have not been able to locate the source for this anecdote.

14. Charrière's instruction to Gélieu: "Please put in yesterday's letter *which was thought* decent *for her grand Mother*. This is the word used. *She was decently provided for She lives decently &c* that's what one says."

LETTERS OF PETER AND WILLIAM

1. *Letters of Peter and William* seems to be by Charrière alone, and not to form part of any pedagogical language exercise. There are only these three letters, and the editors of the *Œuvres complètes* surmise that Charrière wrote them in direct response to William Godwin's novel, *Caleb Williams*, which she was reading in spring 1796. For more on *Caleb Williams*, see the following note.

2. William Godwin, *Things as They Are; or, The Adventures of Caleb Williams* (London, 1794): "This work is remarkable as an early example of the propagandist novel, as a novel of pursuit, crime, and detection, and as a psychological study. It was designed to show 'the tyranny and perfidiousness exercised by the powerful members of the community against those who are less privileged than themselves,'" *The Oxford Companion to English Literature*, ed. Margaret Drabble, 6th ed. (Oxford, England: Oxford University Press, 2000).

3. Falkland and Tyrrel are characters from *Caleb Williams*: Falkland is an idealistic and benevolent country squire; Tyrrel an arrogant and tyrannical one, who is murdered. Falkland is

initially suspected, but Hawkins, a peasant whom Tyrrel had persecuted, and his son, are arrested and executed. Caleb Williams is Falkland's secretary, and becomes convinced that his master was indeed the murderer. He spends some time in prison under a false charge. Godwin included footnotes in his text to support his political points, referring his readers to John Howard's *State of the Prisons in England and Wales* (1777), among other works.

4. John Howard (1726–1790), English prison reformer, author of *State of the Prisons* (see previous note). He was a congregationalist, that is, a member of a dissenting Protestant church with close ties to Calvinism, the religion of most Swiss Protestants; it was also not far from Methodism, which Charrière mentions in passing in an unpublished addition to her *Letters Written from Lausanne* (see *Cécile*, note 66).

CONSTANCE'S STORY

1. *Histoire de Constance, Œuvres complètes,* vol. 9, pp. 145–168 (perhaps written in June-July 1795, after *Trois femmes* had been finished, although before its publication in 1798; see *Œuvres complètes,* vol. 9, p. 34).

2. Isabelle de Charrière, *Three Women, a Novel by the Abbé de la Tour,* trans. Emma Rooksby (New York: Modern Languages Association of America Texts and Translations, 2007).

3. "Famous" Gironde presumably because of the Girondins (see *Émigré Letters,* note 9). "Creole" meant "European in origin but born in America," from Boyer's *Dictionnaire François-Anglois, Anglois-François,* 1792 edition. The OED expands: "In the West Indies and other parts of America, Mauritius, etc.: *orig.* A person born and naturalized in the country, but of European (usually Spanish or French) or of black African descent: the name having no connotation of colour, and in its reference to origin being distinguished on the one hand from born in Europe (or Africa), and on the other hand from aboriginal." Often, though, it had racist overtones, implying degeneration of one sort or another. In *Jane Eyre* (1847), Bertha Mason, Mr. Rochester's first wife, provides an extreme example of this depiction of the creole as degenerate.

4. René-Nicolas de Maupeou (1714–1792), Chancelor of France, tried to reform and systematize the French judiciary, removing

the old *parlements* (parliaments) in 1770, which had traditionally dispensed justice, and replacing them with a single centralized law system and magistrates who could not be removed from their posts. These reforms were greatly disliked, and one of the first things that Louis XVI did on coming to the throne in 1774 was reinstate the old system, which he came to regret (see the following note).

5. An existing tax, called the *corvée royale* (royal burden), was levied for the upkeep of roads. Aristocrats, clergy, and various other groups were exempt from paying it. The finance minister Turgot issued an edict in January 1776 abolishing it and replacing it with a "territorial tax," which all landowners would pay. After immense opposition, it was revoked on August 11, 1776.

6. He is in fact in India, not in the Indies. French India included Pondichéry (now Puducherry), Karikal, and Yanaon (now Yañam), on the Coromandel Coast; Mahé, on the Malabar coast; and Chandannagar, in Bengal. The French East India Company was liquidated in 1769, and all its possessions passed into the ownership of the French crown. Several ports, including Pondichéry and Chandannagar, remained in French ownership until 1954. Brycchan Carey points out that in the eighteenth century, the "Indies" could refer to anywhere that was not Europe or Africa, especially in French usage.

7. Martinique was colonized by the French in 1635, and is still a "département d'outre-mer" of the French state. In the eighteenth century it was extremely valuable because of the sugar trade.

8. Croesus (c. 560–546 BC), last King of Lydia in Asia Minor, proverbial for his great wealth.

9. Saint-Domingue was a French colony between 1659 and 1804, when, after thirteen years of revolutionary resistance, it finally won independence and was renamed Haiti. This story would have been written while the violent revolution was still under way. But Madame del Fonte and her nephew Victor are supposed to live in Martinique, a different French colonial island of the Caribbean. Charrière has slipped from one to the other, and it is not clear whether the slip is a conscious attempt to bring the Haitian revolution to mind. See *Letters from Mistress Henley*, note 12, for further examples of colonial confusion. With thanks to Brycchan Carey for pointing out the revolutionary context.

10. *Opéra-comique*: "Term for a French stage work of the 18th, 19th, or 20th centuries with vocal and instrumental music and spoken dialogue (though it may also include recitative). Its origins are found in the 18th-century Parisian Fair Theatres (known from about 1715 as the Opéra-Comique) and also the Comédie-Italienne. The essentially popular appeal of these repertories formed the antithesis of the stately *tragédie mise en musique* and allied works at the Académie Royale de Musique (the Opéra). Soon, however, a broad range of subjects and styles was developed: *drame* and other literary and dramatic models became important." Grove Music Online.

11. We encounter similar impulsive puttings-on of plays, construed around the moral degeneracy of the gentility, and similarly associated in various ways with the Caribbean sugar plantations, in Jane Austen's *Mansfield Park* (1814) and Charlotte Brontë's *Jane Eyre* (1848). Bianca, Fanny, and Jane are all revolted observers and unwilling assistants in the masquerades of others.

12. Execution of death sentences was suspended if a woman was pregnant.

13. The *code noir* of 1685, slightly modified in 1724, states that "*L'esclave qui aura frappé son maître, sa maîtresse ou le mari de sa maîtresse ou leurs enfants avec contusion ou effusion de sang, ou au visage, sera puni de mort*" (Article 33, Code Noir of 1685; article 27 of the Code Noir of 1724), i.e., that any slave who hits his master, mistress, or their children, causing bruising or bleeding, or who has hit them in the face, will be punished with death. Article 42 of the 1685 version states that torture and dismemberment are forbidden, and that only the master is authorized to whip a slave; the corresponding article 38 of the 1724 version states this same prohibition in slightly stronger terms. Constance's fate, the author implies, must be worse than mere execution.

14. See *Cécile*, note 60.

15. Emilie is Constance's friend: with Joséphine, Emilie's maid, they are the "three women" of which this story is the unpublished continuation (see notes 1 and 2).

16. The editors of the *Œuvres complètes* point out that this is an allusion to St. Paul's Letter to the Ephesians, Chapter 4, verses 22–24: "That ye put off concerning the former conversation the old man, which is corrupt according to the deceitful lusts; And be renewed in the spirit of your mind; And that ye put on the new man, which after God is created in righteousness and true

holiness," *The Bible, Authorized King James Version with Apocrypha*, ed. Robert Carroll and Stephen Prickett (Oxford, England: Oxford World's Classics, 1997).

17. "Moor" was a current term for an African and/or black person.

18. Isabelle de Charrière wrote a letter to her friend César d'Ivernois in June–July 1795, asking for his judgment of a different version of these lines.

19. Finn Fordham considerately helped with the translation of these verses, and not only the translator but the reader also should be very grateful that they weren't left in their previous appalling state. That they are still quite embarrassing is not his fault.

20. The following lines give a different version of the duel between Le Muret and the vicomte. They are clearly a rewriting of that first draft, and they amplify the horror of the event, giving extra or slightly different details that contribute to the picture of the vicomte's guilt and distress. They also move the tribunal to the colony itself.

21. It was the convention that relatives of someone who had just died would wear black for a period of up to a year; crepe was often the material specified.

22. Andromaque (Andromache) is the heroine of Racine's play of the same name (1667); she was Hector's widow.

23. Maximilien Robespierre (1758–1794), see *Émigré Letters*, note 27; Bertrand de Barère de Vieuzac, a lawyer, initially a moderate but later an associate of Robespierre and a member, like him, of the infamous Committee of Public Safety, which was at the height of its power from the summer of 1793 until Thermidor (July 1794, when Robespierre fell); Louis-Antoine-Léon de Saint-Just (1767–1794), an extraordinary orator and close political associate of Robespierre, guillotined with him.

24. Methodism was in its early days a field church; see *Cécile*, note 66. (B. Carey adds that John Wesley, its leader, was a notable opponent of slavery.)

25. The Areopagus was, in antiquity, the ruling council of Athens, constituted of elders of the city who had all previously held high public office. It is therefore synonymous with an oligarchy of wise men.

26. An *écu* was worth three livres or francs. For various attempts to contextualize sums in pre-Revolution France, see *Cécile*, note 4.

27. Princess Eli was Louis XVI's sister, Elisabeth de France (1764–1794); she was guillotined, like her brother.

28. This reminds us of Charrière's own attempt to influence Marie Antoinette by sending her *Eaglonette and Suggestina* (1791). See elsewhere in this volume.

29. See Emilie and Constance's growing intimacy (*Three Women*, trans. Emma Rooksby, pp. 44–49), and the baron's discovery that "time dragged dreadfully on the days when they did not visit," p. 46.

30. To "cross the line" means to cross the equator. Diane de Polignac (1749–1793) was an intimate friend of Marie Antoinette's; she was given the position of governess to the royal children in 1782. She fled into exile after the storming of the Bastille, and died in Switzerland in December 1793, probably from cancer, but also much affected by the execution of the queen.

31. Is this a reference to the Haitian revolution? Charrière has already mapped Martinique onto Saint-Domingue (Haiti) before, see note 9.

32. In the wake of the Revolution, there was quite a spate of self-justificatory memoirs, of which Garat's, minister at the time of the September Massacres (see *Émigré Letters*, note 52), are a good example.

SAINT ANNE

1. *Sainte Anne* (1799), *Œuvres complètes*, vol. 9, pp. 263–310.

2. Maximilien Robespierre (1758–1794); see *Émigré Letters*, note 27. His "reign" was from mid-1793 to mid-1794. The only countries that had neutral relations with France during the entire period (1793–July 1797) of St. Anne's absence were Denmark, the Republic of Genoa, and Switzerland until it lost part of its territory to the Cisalpine Republic in October 1797 (in its later reincarnation as the Helvetian Republic, in 1798, it became an ally of France, the U.S., and Venice). The rest of Europe was at war with France. St. Anne returns on July 2; on June 27, the laws of October 25, 1795 (known as 3 Brumaire, year IV in the Revolutionary calendar), and December 4, 1796 (14 Frimaire, year V), relating to émigrés were repealed. These laws had denied public office to émigrés and their relatives and confined their wives to their domicile in 1792, where they would be under municipal surveillance. St. Anne returns as quickly as he possibly can, given the time it would have taken for the news of the repeal to reach him, and for him to cross France and get to

Brittany. Considering the distances, he must have been in exile in Switzerland.

3. The bone of contention was that to the French revolutionary government, being an émigré was tantamount to being a traitor, not least because so many were soldiers in armies fighting against France (see *Émigré Letters*, note 3). There were various principal waves of emigration, first after the fall of the Bastille, in July 1789, second after the thwarted flight of the King, in June 1791, and third after the September Massacres, in 1792. Laws against them became increasingly harsh: on October 23, 1792, all émigrés were banished in perpetuity, and stood to be executed as outlaws if they were caught in France; bounties were put on their heads. From March 28, 1793, émigrés were regarded as legally deceased; anti-émigré legislation was codified on November 15, 1794. See the previous note, and *Émigré Letters*, note 47.

4. The Vendée had been a center for anti-revolutionary resistance, and had temporarily met with some success (see *Émigré Letters*, note 2).

5. Charles Rollin (1661–1741), *Histoire Romaine Depuis la Fondation de Rome Jusqu'à la Bataille d'Actium*, 16 vols. (Paris: Chez la Veuve Estienne, 1738–1748.). With respect to St. Anne's preference for history over fiction, see a similar discussion in *Letters from Mistress Henley*, note 10. The reader will note that this work that St. Anne proposes to read out loud has 16 volumes; the *Histoire d'Angleterre* has 10. Rollin also features in the *Émigré Letters* as one of the authors whom Pauline recommends to Laurent (see *Émigré Letters*, note 29).

6. Paul Rapin de Thoyras (1661–1725), *Histoire d'Angleterre*, 10 vols. (The Hague, Netherlands: Alexandre de Rogissart, 1724–1727).

7. "Party spirit" in the sense of belonging to the same ideological party, which in the French revolutionary context equates to Jacobins, Girondins, émigrés, etc., and therefore to life-or-death allegiances.

8. St. Hubert was a French saint from Toulouse (c. 658–727), the "apostle of the Ardennes," popularly invoked in the cure of rabies; it used to be the practice that a metal key, known as St. Hubert's key, would be heated and pressed on the area where a person had been bitten, and the effect of the heat would be to cauterize the wound and kill the virus. More generally, however, dogs were branded in advance so as to protect them.

Saint-Hubert (in modern-day Belgium) is also the name given to the place where his relics were brought, and it became a center of pilgrimage.

9. From Racine's tragedy *Phèdre* (1677), Act 5, scene 1, lines 1392–1393. Hippolyte is addressing his lover, Aricie, proposing that they meet to swear eternal love and then escape. In these lines, he is suggesting that he and Aricie take their vows at his ancestral burial ground and thereafter consider themselves married. The translation is John Cairncross's, from his *Iphigenia, Phaedra, Athaliah*, translated and introduced by John Cairncross, (London and New York: Penguin Classics, 2004), p. 205.

10. Artemisia II was the sister and wife of Mausolos of Caria, in whose memory she built the Mausoleum of Halicarnassus c. 353 BC (*The Oxford Companion to Classical Literature* [Oxford, England: Oxford University Press, 1989]).

11. Jean-Jacques Rousseau, *Lettre à d'Alembert sur les spectacles* (1758). In this letter, Rousseau responds publicly to d'Alembert's article on Geneva in the *Encyclopédie*, in which d'Alembert criticized Geneva for its prohibition of theaters and suggested that the taste of the town in general would improve were it to have one. Rousseau, born in Geneva, was outraged, and so were the Genevans. His counterattack followed broadly moral lines. Rousseau is an important interlocutor for Charrière; see *Letters from Mistress Henley*, notes 5, 10, 16, and 17.

12. Prometheus, the Titan in Greek myth (that is, from an older generation of divinities than the Olympian gods, of whom Zeus was the chief), who supposedly stole fire from the heavens to give it to humankind.

13. In Greek myth, Jason and the Argonauts set sail to find the stolen Golden Fleece and return it to Jason's half-uncle Pelias, usurper of Jason's rightful throne, who had promised to give the throne back if he were brought the Golden Fleece. King Aeetes of Colchis, where the fleece was kept, agreed to surrender it if Jason performed many seemingly impossible tasks, which he did, with the help of the king's daughter, the witch Medea, whom he later married. New disasters then ensued. Jason is a model epic hero.

14. The editors of the *OC* explain as follows: the debate regarding primary schools was very current at the time. The Convention (see *Émigré Letters*, note 9) had decreed that there should be one primary school per commune of 400 inhabitants (October 21, 1793) and that school would be compulsory and free (Loi

Bouquier, 19 December 1793). The Convention had to give up on
this idealistic project, abandoning the idea of compulsory attendance and accepting that it would be impossible to set up so
many schools (Loi Daunou, 25 October, 1795). The *Institut
national*, or National Institute, was set up in October 1795, and
replaced the abolished Académie française, Académie des sciences, and other academies that had been closed down in 1793;
it was renamed the Institut de France in 1806, and in 1816 the
academies were given their old names back, although retaining
the Institut de France umbrella.

15. An opinion given medical currency by Samuel Auguste Tissot
(1728–1797), whose *De Valetudine Litteratorum* (1766), published in French the year after as *Avis aux gens de lettres*, discussed the disastrous ill health brought about by excessive study.
He features in *Cécile*, note 15.

16. Pyrrhonism is a school of skeptical philosophy: skeptics resolved
to doubt anything that was not firmly proven, and therefore sig-
nified extreme rationalism.

17. The editors of the *Oeuvres complètes* consider that Charrière
obtained this information either from d'Auvergne's *Origines
gauloises* or from Caesar's commentaries on the Gallic Wars,
which he fought in 58–52 BC.

18. Solon (640–561 BC), Athenian statesman and poet, and as
archon (holder of the highest office), moderate reformer.

19. Virginie is the heroine of Bernardin de St. Paul's immensely popular tragic novel, *Paul et Virginie* (1788), in which the children
of two French women who have moved to Madagascar grow up
and fall in love. Virginie is sent by her mother to France to learn
to read and to gain an education; thereafter they are separated
by more than just space, as Paul is unable to read her letters.
When Virginie returns to Mauritius, her ship is wrecked in the
bay, and she drowns, dragged down by her clothes after refusing to do the natural thing and take them off; she chooses virtue over life. It is an allegory of the disastrous self-alienation
brought about by society and education, and was much influenced by Rousseau. It was adapted for the stage (*Comédie ital-
ienne*) in 1791, with music by Kreutzer. The Rose-Girl of
Salency was the annually crowned "Queen of Virtue" in the
rose festival of Salency, a local festival that had become famous
after a newly married Madame de Genlis discovered it in 1766.
The "rose girl" became a much-written-about character, and
there are a number of theatrical adaptations, any one of which

Charrière's gentlemen could be discussing, including Charles
Favart's *La Rosière de Salency* (Paris: Veuve Duchesne, 1770)
and Edmé-Louis Billardon de Sauvigny's *La rose ou la fête de
Salency* (Paris: Gaugeury, 1768). See Sara Maza, "The Rose-Girl
of Salency: Representations of Virtue in Prerevolutionary
France," *Eighteenth-Century Studies* 22, no. 3, (Spring 1989):
395–412.

20. This refers to the list of known émigrés, inclusion on which
entailed confiscation of property and rights, being outlawed,
and subject to the death sentence. See *Emigré Letters*, note 3.

21. According to the *Oxford Companion to Classical Literature*,
Nestor, in Greek myth, was the son of Neleus and the King of
Pylos. He features in the *Iliad*, and is supposed to have lived to a
great age, fulfilling the role of an elder statesman, full of long-
winded advice and inclined to be anecdotal.

22. Publius Clodius Pulcher (93–52 BC), Roman patrician, notorious
for his violence and profligacy. He profaned the (female) mysteries
of Bona Dea, or "good goddess," in 62 BC by dressing up as a
woman, and was prosecuted. Cicero proved that his alibi was
false, and earned Clodius's enmity.

23. The "good goddess" (see previous note) was another name for
Cybele, primarily a goddess of fertility. Festivals were instituted
in her honor, and during the (closed) rites, men and male animals were veiled.

24. Aesop, supposed author of what have come to be known as Aesop's fables, which are short tales with a moral at the end, in
which the characters are often animals. Aesop was supposed to
have been a slave in the sixth century BC. Jean de La Fontaine
(1621–1695) wrote verse fables, which came out between 1668
and 1694; Charrière often quotes him (*The Nobleman* and *Letters from Mistress Henley* both carry epigraphs from La Fontaine).

25. In Greek myth, Oedipus and Jocasta's sons, Eteocles and Poly-
neices, killed each other fighting over the kingdom of Thebes.
Castor and Pollux appear in different stories, sometimes as twin
brothers and sometimes as friends. The story alluded to here
relates that when the mortal Castor died, the immortal Pollux
agreed to share his immortality with him, so they would spend
half the time in the Underworld and half with the gods on Mount
Olympus. They are identified with the Gemini constellation.

26. The definition of "organ" changes radically over the course of the century, and is a perfect case study for the advances of medicine. In 1740, the official dictionary published by the Académie Française stated *organe* meant "the instrument serving the senses and operations of the animal"; by 1762 it was no longer the "instrument" but "the part of the body," although in polite speech it was a synonym for "faculty." Charrière's usage draws on the earlier, more general definitions, rather than anything more specifically medical. See Caroline Warman, "La vie et l'âme de l'organe dans la Pensée Vitaliste de Bordeu, Diderot, et Bichat," in *Repenser le vitalisme: histoire et philosophie du vitalisme*, ed. Pascal Nouvel (Paris: Presses Universitaires de France, 2011), pp. 157–165.

27. We have been unable to trace the source of this comment.

28. Reference to Goethe's *Sorrows of Young Werther* (1774; see *Fragments*, note 4). A wave of suicides followed its publication.

29. An "elector" was originally a hereditary title relating to the ability of this person to "elect" the Holy Roman Emperor, but as the latter became simply the hereditary monarchy of the Hapsburg empire, "elector" became synonymous with "duke," "prince," etc., being inferior to the rank of king.

30. Molière, *The School for Wives*, translated by Richard Wilbur, in *Five Plays*, introduced by Donald Roy (London: Methuen Drama, 2000), Act 3, scene 2, seventh maxim. Molière's *Ecole des femmes* (1662) is a comedy in which the deluded antihero, Arnolphe, supposes that he is educating the perfect wife for himself; in this scene, he has his intended, Agnès, read out a number of maxims about how to be an excellent wife. In fact, Agnès is in love with Horace, whom she marries. It is therefore ironic that Mme. d'Estival's uncle, a schoolmaster, cites these maxims as good advice about proper wifeliness.

THE STORY OF PENGUIN CLASSICS

Before 1946 . . . "Classics" are mainly the domain of academics and students; readable editions for everyone else are almost unheard of. This all changes when a little-known classicist, E. V. Rieu, presents Penguin founder Allen Lane with the translation of Homer's *Odyssey* that he has been working on in his spare time.

1946 Penguin Classics debuts with *The Odyssey,* which promptly sells three million copies. Suddenly, classics are no longer for the privileged few.

1950s Rieu, now series editor, turns to professional writers for the best modern, readable translations, including Dorothy L. Sayers's *Inferno* and Robert Graves's unexpurgated *Twelve Caesars.*

1960s The Classics are given the distinctive black covers that have remained a constant throughout the life of the series. Rieu retires in 1964, hailing the Penguin Classics list as "the greatest educative force of the twentieth century."

1970s A new generation of translators swells the Penguin Classics ranks, introducing readers of English to classics of world literature from more than twenty languages. The list grows to encompass more history, philosophy, science, religion, and politics.

1980s The Penguin American Library launches with titles such as *Uncle Tom's Cabin* and joins forces with Penguin Classics to provide the most comprehensive library of world literature available from any paperback publisher.

1990s The launch of Penguin Audiobooks brings the classics to a listening audience for the first time, and in 1999 the worldwide launch of the Penguin Classics Web site extends their reach to the global online community.

The 21st Century Penguin Classics are completely redesigned for the first time in nearly twenty years. This world-famous series now consists of more than 1,300 titles, making the widest range of the best books ever written available to millions—and constantly redefining what makes a "classic."

The Odyssey continues . . .

The best books ever written

PENGUIN CLASSICS

SINCE 1946

Find out more at www.penguinclassics.com

Visit www.vpbookclub.com

CLICK ON A CLASSIC
www.penguinclassics.com

The world's greatest literature at your fingertips

Constantly updated information on more than a thousand titles,
from Icelandic sagas to ancient Indian epics, Russian drama to
Italian romance, American greats to African masterpieces

•

The latest news on recent additions to the list, updated
editions, and specially commissioned translations

•

Original essays by leading writers

•

A wealth of background material, including biographies
of every classic author from Aristotle to Zamyatin, plot
synopses, readers' and teachers' guides, useful Web links

•

Online desk and examination copy assistance for academics

•

Trivia quizzes, competitions, giveaways, news on
forthcoming screen adaptations